"Who did you say we are today?" Duke asked as the bus pulled away from the station.

"Lee and Amanda Barkley."

"Oh yeah. If someone calls my name, would you please punch me? It was much easier when I didn't have any identity; now I have too many," Duke grumbled as he turned to look out the window.

"After Grand Junction, where are we going?" Skylar asked in hushed tones.

"Oh, I don't know. Just on west I suppose." Duke stretched his legs out as best he could. "I sure wish God would reveal a little more to me. Then maybe we could just go home."

"He will in His own time," Skylar said as she picked up her overnight bag. "He's never late in doing things. Remember that."

Duke turned in his seat and looked into Skylar's eyes. "He's never late by whose clock?"

"His clock. You just have to learn patience." Skylar reached into her carry-on bag and pulled out her Bible. "Here do some reading."

First, I'm Nobody

by

Kasandra Elaine

God Bless You,

Elaine

Psalm 56:3&4

This is a work of fiction. Names, characters, places, and incidents are either the product of the author's imagination or are used fictitiously, and any resemblance to actual persons living or dead, business establishments, events, or locales, is entirely coincidental.

First, I'm Nobody

COPYRIGHT © 2008 by Elaine Bonner Powell and Kasandra M. Paris

All rights reserved. No part of this book may be used or reproduced in any manner whatsoever without written permission of the author or The Wild Rose Press except in the case of brief quotations embodied in critical articles or reviews.

Contact Information: info@thewildrosepress.com

Cover Art by *Kim Mendoza*

The Wild Rose Press
PO Box 708
Adams Basin, NY 14410-0706
Visit us at www.thewildrosepress.com

Publishing History
First White Rose Edition, 2008
Print ISBN 1-60154-262-3

Published in the United States of America

Dedication

From Elaine:

To my only sister, Martha, who, as we have gotten older, has become a cherished friend. You and my favorite brother-in-law, Kenneth, have supported me through a lot of rough times.

Curtis, you and Myra are very special to me. You're the best Bubba.

Bud, what can I say, you're pushy and bossy, but I love you. You never let me, or Elisa down, and we put you through a lot. You and Vernell stepped up to the plate, and I love you.

Terry, I hope, even in heaven, God lets you know I'm published again. I love you and miss you.

From Kassy:

To my sisters: Krissy, the one with a tough exterior and a marshmallow heart; Karolyn, the independent one who likes to hide the hard things in her life from me; and Katrina, the baby who always had a mind of her own. My apologies to you all for having to follow me through school. I know it was hard living up to the "perfect student". If I had it all to do again, I'd work harder at letting myself get into a little trouble.

Prologue

Their lone car traveled toward Oklahoma on a remote strip of a two-lane North Texas highway in the dim light of dusk. Joe and his companion were oblivious to their surroundings, consumed by the blaring rock music coming from the car's radio.

Their loud conversation was interrupted only by a pause to take another drink from the beer bottles clutched in their hands. As Joe took a deep draw of the amber liquid in his long-necked bottle, the car swerved off the edge of the road, throwing gravel and dirt into the air. He jerked the steering wheel and pulled the Mustang back onto the pavement.

"Hey man, you're driving in the ditch as much as you're driving on the road," slurred the teenage passenger.

"You insultin' my driving?" Laughter filled the vehicle. "I guess we're gonna have to sober up before we get to Oklahoma. Roll down the window and let some fresh air in here." The dry North Texas wind rushed in as they finished off their bottles of beer.

"Hey, Tom, watch this." The driver threw his bottle over the top of the car and hit a road sign as they passed by. The car swerved again and there was a jolt as the red Mustang hit something.

Joe twisted the steering wheel hard and pulled the car back into the right lane. Then he stomped on the brake, bringing the car to a squealing halt. For several long seconds, silence drifted through the twilight around the sports car as clouds of dust swirled around them.

Tom finally broke the eerie silence. "Man, what'd you hit?"

"I don't know. I didn't see anything. Did you?"

"Naw. Whatever you hit musta been big." Tom got out of the vehicle and staggered to the front. "Joe, you got a huge dent in this fender. Must've been a deer or somethin'. I'm gonna check back down the road and maybe see what it was."

Joe opened the door of the 1969 sports car with a shaking hand. "I gotta check this out. My dad's gonna kill me if his car gets messed up." He teetered his way around the car and dropped to his knees, moaning as he saw the damage.

The headlight was busted, and the fender had a big dent. Luckily, it wasn't rubbing the tire so he could drive the car on home to Broken Bow without having to call his father or a wrecker. The car was his dad's favorite, and he knew he was in serious trouble. His hand shook as he rubbed the deep dent.

A curse flew from his mouth. He wiped his forehead with the back of his hand. "Dad's gonna kill me." Reaching up, he tried to pull the fender a bit straighter.

"Hey, Joe...you better come here."

Joe stood up, and the world tilted. He steadied himself for a moment with a hand on the car before weaving the few yards down the highway to where Tom stood staring into the ditch.

"What? Don't tell me I hit somebody's prize bull." Then he noticed the sick look on his friend's face.

Tom pointed to the ditch. The crumpled form of a man lay in the weeds. The boys stood and stared at the lifeless figure.

"Oh man! Is he dead?" Joe finally choked out; his whole body trembling.

"I can't see him breathing! What're we gonna do? We've got to get help."

Tom pulled out his cell phone and flipped it open.

Joe grabbed it away from him. "Man, we can't call the cops. I'll be charged with drunk driving, maybe even murder." He slumped to the ground beside the lifeless body in the grassy ditch. Damaging his father's classic car was bad enough. This could be the end of his life.

"We've got to do something," Tom said. "We can't just leave him here."

"He's already dead, so it won't matter to him if we call for help tonight or if someone finds him tomorrow. He can't be any more dead."

With shaking hands, Joe began to search through the stranger's pockets. All he found was a wallet containing a couple hundred dollars and some credit cards. He slipped the money out of the wallet.

"What are you doing?"

"Well, this won't do him any good, and it will go a long way to fixing my dad's car. Now let's get out of here." Joe shoved the money into one of his pockets and the wallet in another.

"Aren't you gonna leave his wallet?"

"Nope." He rose to his feet, suddenly feeling sober. Panic and a need to get away filled him.

The boys ran back to the car and started for home. A couple of miles away, Joe pulled the wallet from his pocket and tossed it out the window as they crossed a bridge over a large creek.

Tom looked at him for a long moment. "Doesn't any of this bother you?"

Joe didn't answer right away. Instead he pulled the car off onto the side of the road and opened the door. Leaning over, he threw up. When he finished, he pressed his back against the seat and wiped the bitter bile from his lips. He found himself longing for one more mouthful of the beer that had gotten him into this mess so he could get rid of the nasty taste.

"I don't want to go to jail, and I don't want my dad to ever find out what happened tonight." Tears pooled in his eyes. His stomach clinched, and for a moment, he thought he might be sick again.

Tom reached over and patted him on the shoulder. "It'll be okay. We'll just come up with a good story, and no one will know any different. Besides, that guy shouldn't have been walking this late anyway."

Joe put the car into gear. The young men agreed to tell their folks that a deer had run out in front of them. It was believable and would keep them both out of trouble. At least that's what they told each other.

****

"He's coming around."

The words sounded distant. He opened his eyes only to be blinded by a colored swirl of flashing lights. Keeping his eyes closed was easier, so he quit struggling, and his eyelids fluttered shut again. Disembodied voices filled the darkness but made no sense as pain surged through his body. With pain like this, he couldn't be dead and in heaven. He guessed hell was a possibility, but it seemed those voices he could hear in the distance wanted to help him. Hopefully that meant he was still alive.

"Hey, mister, can you tell us your name?"

He forced his eyes to open and tried to say something, anything, but nothing would come out. His head throbbed as though someone were driving nails through his skull. The swirling lights tormented his brain. He closed his eyes to block them out. It might be better if he had died. He stopped fighting and slid back into the darkness.

Chapter One

Skylar McCrea drove toward her north Texas ranch in her dad's 1959 pickup. She sang along with an old tune on the radio, and her truck seemed to hum along with her. She had just mailed the entry fee to register her prize stallion for the upcoming horse show in Fort Worth. She prayed Skylark's Son would be as good a horse as his sire had been. Skylark had won a room full of trophies in his career.

Her singing halted when she spotted what appeared to be a leather jacket lying beside the road. As she drove by, it crossed her mind how often she had noticed various articles of clothing on or alongside the roadways of America. She wondered what people did as they drove along, just decide that one shoe wasn't needed anymore. In this case, it was a jacket someone had flung out the car window. Her curiosity got the better of her, so she turned the truck around and drove back to the spot where she had spied the jacket.

"Surely no one would have disposed of this on purpose," she mumbled as she examined the expensive-looking leather garment. She checked for identification but found nothing except three initials monogrammed on the inside breast pocket, JBC. She threw the jacket onto the seat of her truck and drove toward home.

A smile crossed Skylar's face as she drove through the gate of her ranch. She couldn't help but read the sign with great pleasure—Lazy M Ranch, Home of Skylark, Champion Thoroughbred. Pulling up to the house, she spotted her foreman, Redigo, walking toward the barn. She jumped out of the truck and ran to catch him.

"Redigo, what did Doc Peters say about Skylark's Son?"

The older man had been foreman of the Lazy M since she was a little girl and she loved him like an uncle. She looked at him objectively as she waited for his answer. Even in his early fifties, he was still a handsome man. His black hair was beginning to gray at the temples, but that only made him look more distinguished.

He pulled his cowboy hat from his head and wiped the sweat from his brow with a red bandana as he answered, "He gave him a perfect bill of health."

She smiled and placed her truck keys in the pocket of her khaki colored Capri pants. "Great. He's all set to show in Fort Worth. I put the final papers in the mail this morning."

She fell into step beside him, and the two continued into the barn, where Billy, one of the ranch hands, was grooming their hope for a future champion.

"I got a call from Wilmington in Virginia." Redigo cast her a sidelong glance before he continued. "He's offered a ridiculous stud fee for Skylark. He begged me to get you to change your mind." He stepped over to the stall and propped both arms on the top rail. "Really, Skylar, what's your problem with him?"

She stuck her right foot on the bottom rail of the stall and gazed at Skylark's Son. "I saw one of his handlers mistreating a horse last year at the Atlanta show. I just think he needs to keep a closer eye on his investments."

"Did you mention the incident to Wilmington?" He opened the stall door and began to rub the horse's long nose.

"Yeah, the first time he called. When he made light of the whole thing, I told him to find stud service elsewhere." She watched in admiration as the foreman spoke soft, soothing words to the horse.

"Well, when I talk to him again, I'll make it very clear the Lazy M isn't interested in his business." He looked at Billy and said, "Good job, son. You're gonna make a horse handler yet." He patted the young man on the shoulder as he left the stall and closed the gate.

Skylar heard the intercom beep and walked to the speaker, "Yes, Addie, do you need something?"

"The flour you were supposed to pick up for me in town."

"Oh, I'm sorry. It's in the truck; I'll bring it right in."

As she left the barn, Redigo fell into step beside her.

Just before they reached the pickup, Addie called out the door for Skylar to come to the phone.

"You go on in; I'll get the flour," the foreman said.

****

Redigo walked into the kitchen and placed the bag of flour on the counter as Skylar hung up the phone. Holding the brown jacket out toward her, he asked, "Who does this belong to?"

"I saw it on the side of the road, several hundred feet from the ranch entrance. I was curious and stopped to pick it up. It looks expensive. There's no identification in it, so I can't get it back to its owner."

"I heard there was an accident last night along the stretch of road where you picked this up." Redigo tossed the jacket over the back of a chair and then poured himself a cup of coffee.

"Yeah, I heard that, too," Addie said. "Madge called this mornin' and told me some fellow got hit by a car."

"Hmm, maybe the jacket belongs to the victim," Skylar said. "There're some initials monogrammed on the inside. Was the man badly hurt?"

"Madge said they carried him into Denton to the hospital," Addie said.

"Well, I'll give Dan Tate a call later at the sheriff's office and see if he knows anything." Skylar reached over and pinched a piece of crust from the fried chicken Addie had dished up on a platter. A light rap on her knuckles from Addie's wooden spoon warned her away before she had the chance to snatch another bite. She grinned. Her beloved housekeeper had eyes in the back of her head.

"You two get out of my kitchen. I'll call you when lunch is ready."

Skylar laughed and strode toward the door. Redigo settled his hat on his head and pushed the door open ahead of her. He obviously knew better than to question Addie's authority in the kitchen. Skylar followed him out the door and back to the barn.

****

"That was a great practice run," Skylar commented as Billy walked Skylark's Son over to where she and Redigo were standing.

Redigo snorted his disagreement. "It was okay, but

Son's still not clearin' those triple jumps as well as I'd like to see him do." The foreman took the horse's reins from Billy as he dismounted and led the thoroughbred toward the barn.

Skylar followed close behind him. "How much daylight do you want to see between the horse and the rails? Son just went that round ten seconds faster than Skylark ever did. You're just partial. In your eyes no horse will ever be as good as Skylark."

Redigo stopped and turned to face her, his dark brown eyes twinkling. "Listen here, you spoiled brat, don't you go accusin' me of being partial. I'm just tryin' to get you another winner. If you think you can do better, be my guest."

She stomped her foot in the dirt and looked him in the eyes. Her mouth twitched as she struggled to keep from smiling at her friend. "Why you old coot, you're not just trying to get *me* another winner; training two world champions would be quite a feather in your hat."

"Hey, would you two quit arguing? Skylark's Son deserves some extra special treatment tonight, and you're upsettin' his delicate digestive system." Billy took the reins from Redigo and shook his head as he started to walk away.

"You'd just better see to it that he gets an extra measure of those sweet oats, Billy. Else you'll be lookin' for a new place to laze away your time pretendin' to be workin'." Redigo smiled at Skylar as he teased the young man.

"Yeah, yeah, I'm quakin' in my boots. Who do you think you'd get to take my place? Nobody wants to work for a grouchy old man like you. Besides, I've already dumped that extra measure in his bucket." Billy laughed as he led Skylark's Son into the barn.

"Young whippersnapper ain't got no respect for his elders. I oughta fire him. Serve him right."

Skylar walked up behind her foreman and pushed his battered Stetson forward on his head. "Yeah? Like Billy said, nobody's rushing the front door to work for you, grouch."

Redigo readjusted his hat as Skylar ran toward the front of the barn. "Git on up to the house, young lady, before I take a willow switch to you."

She laughed at her foreman's joking threat while she made her way to the main house.

Later that evening she noticed the leather jacket hanging on the coat rack. Glancing at her watch, she realized it was too late to call her friend, Deputy Sheriff Dan Tate. She would call him first thing in the morning to see if the jacket belonged to the accident victim.

****

Dr. Green finished examining his patient, made a couple of notes and handed the chart to the nurse. "Has he regained consciousness at all?"

"He's drifted in and out most of the day."

"Has anyone been able to find out his name?"

The nurse shook her head. "No. He's awake long enough to ask for something for pain, but that's about all."

"Well, I'm not surprised. He has a bad concussion, plus going through surgery. Maybe tomorrow we can find out something about him. He probably has family somewhere who are worried. From the boots he was wearing, he wasn't a normal hitchhiker. A down-on-his-luck fellow doesn't wear full-quill ostrich Ropers."

"Yeah, I'm sure he'll be thrilled when he wakes up to learn he has only one boot."

"Well, he'll probably be happier to know he has only one boot than he would be to wake up and find out he has only one leg." The doctor turned to exit the room.

****

The man lying in the bed could hear voices and knew they were talking about him. He kept asking, "What's happened to me?" But the strangers seemed to be ignoring him as they continued with their conversation. *Why don't they answer me?*

He kept listening to them talk and wondered why he would have a concussion and what did they mean when they said he could have lost a leg? *Do I have both my legs?* He felt pain in his lower extremities but he felt pain all over so he just wasn't sure if his legs were all right. He tried with all his might to open his eyes, but the eyelids just wouldn't cooperate.

I have to find out what's happening to me. Maybe I can lift my arm and get their attention. He tried but his arms felt as though they weighed a hundred pounds each. Nothing about his body was cooperating with him. His brain was sending out commands but to no avail.

Help me, please help me. The harder he tried the more frustrated he became. His thoughts became a mass of confusion as the pounding in his head beat a rhythm like a frenzied drummer. He prayed this would all be over soon.

I've got to have some relief. That was the last thought that passed through his mind before he drifted into a restless sleep.

****

Skylar picked up the telephone receiver, dialed the number to the Denton County Sheriff's Office and asked for Dan Tate. The call was transferred, and she heard a couple of rings before the click of the call being answered came over the wire.

"Deputy Tate. Can I help you?"

"I sure hope you can," Skylar said when she heard her friend's voice.

"Skylar McCrea. To what do I owe the privilege of a phone call from you?"

"I heard a guy was hit by a car out close to my place Sunday night."

"Yeah. It appears to be a hit and run. Did you do it? Is that why you're calling?"

Skylar laughed at the teasing question from the deputy. "No. I didn't even know about it until late Monday morning, but I found a leather jacket lying beside the road and thought it might belong to the fellow."

"Could be, but right now, I can't tell you. We haven't been able to question him. He was pretty messed up from what I understand. Hopefully, today he'll feel up to talking, and we can get a lead on what happened. He didn't have any identification on him. Was there anything in the jacket?"

"No. Just the initials JBC inside the jacket."

"That's too bad. A driver's license would have really helped."

Skylar heard Dan sigh. "Well, if you find out he's missing a leather jacket, let me know. I'll bring it by the station the next time I'm in town, unless you want to see it sooner."

"No. That'll be fine. We don't even know if the jacket and the man match."

"Okay, talk to you later, Dan. Give Trina my love."

****

The Wednesday after the accident, Dr. Green entered his patient's room to find the mystery man staring at the TV on the wall. "It's good to see you awake. I'm Dr. Russell Green, the fellow who put those casts on you."

The patient turned his face toward him, his skin pale beneath the bruises. The man had a blank look on his face, but Dr. Green could see panic in his patient's eyes. "Is something wrong?" He placed a chair beside the hospital bed and seated himself so he would be on eye-level with his patient.

"I don't know my name." The man's breathing began to increase. "I've got to have a name. I've got to have a past. Who am I?" The man was frantic and his breathing was increasing by the second.

"Now try to calm down. Take some slow, deep breaths for me." Dr. Green spoke softly and kept a watchful eye on his patient. "After an experience like you've had, it's not uncommon to block things from your memory. I'm sure this is only temporary."

His breathing was still a little ragged, and the panic remained in his eyes, but the man looked as though he was becoming somewhat calmer. "Is it common to block *everything* out? I don't remember anything before flashing lights and terrible pain. Did I have any identification?"

"Not that we found. We were hoping you could give us that information. What do you remember?"

The patient rubbed his free hand through his hair. "I remember waking up in excruciating pain and seeing a lot of colored, flashing lights and hearing a lot of people yelling."

"As I said, it's normal to block out a traumatic experience. It'll all come back to you." Dr. Green tried to sound encouraging. "The police searched the immediate area where you were found, but, as I understand it, they came up empty. There were no abandoned cars in the area either, so they figure you must have been hitchhiking somewhere."

"So, there's nothing to give me a clue to my identity?"

"Nothing that we can lay our hands on right now. We'll run a few more tests, but I'm sure you'll have your memory back in a day or so. Just try to rest. The police want to question you, but I'll hold them off for a couple more days. You need to get your strength back."

The man turned toward him, fear still evident in his eyes. "Are you sure I'll get my memory back? Are you sure this is only temporary?"

Dr. Green sighed heavily. "I can't give you a guarantee, but like I said, you've suffered a terrible trauma. It's not uncommon for this to happen. We'll pray it's temporary."

****

The man watched the doctor leave the room and then looked around his unfamiliar surroundings. Who was he? The question kept running through his mind. He had to have a past. He didn't just suddenly appear out of nowhere. His head began to throb again. He didn't know if the pain was from his injuries or from the frustration he was feeling.

Do I have a wife and children? What did I do to earn a living? He looked down at his hands. They were soft and smooth. *I guess whatever I did it wasn't manual labor.* He shook his head as if trying to jar something loose that would help him remember but all it did was make his head throb even more. Placing his hands on either side of his head, he attempted to stop the pounding but it didn't help. He might not know much else at the moment, but he did know enough to push the red button to get a nurse to bring him something to take the pain away. He knew when the medicine began to work that at least for a time he would free his mind of all thoughts.

Chapter Two

Friday morning Skylar drove into Denton to do some errands and took the jacket by the Sheriff's office. Her friend, Dan, told her the mystery man was still a mystery. Apparently he had amnesia and remembered nothing about his past life. The jacket held no clues for now. Dan decided he would hold on to it in case the accident victim recovered his memory and recognized it.

"What's going to happen to the fellow if his memory doesn't return?" Skylar asked as she was leaving Dan's office.

"I don't know. I guess you'd have to ask Russell Green that question."

"Russell's his doctor?"

"Yeah," he grabbed a file from his desk and started out the door. "Skylar, I have to be in court in thirty minutes. I'll see you later." Grinning, he called back over his shoulder, "Hey, should I bother to go see your nag next week at the Fort Worth horse show?"

"If you want some good entertainment, you'd better," she followed him down the hallway.

****

Jake shoved the posthole digger into the hard ground. Sweat drenched his short, black hair beneath his Texas Rangers cap. Tugging it off, he wiped the moisture from his forehead with the tail of his western-cut work shirt. Settling the cap back on his head, he decided to take a breather.

Stretching, he listened to the country music blaring from the radio in his pickup. Redigo had sent him out earlier to replace some of the old, wooden fence posts with new, metal t-posts along the front property line. It was a backbreaking job, but the beat of the music helped him establish a rhythm. He strode to the old pickup.

Once at the truck, he reached into the cooler and

drew out a cold bottle of water. With a quick twist, he snapped the seal and removed the cap. He guzzled the icy liquid as he rested on the ground in the shade of his truck.

Cooled off by the water and rest, he stood and grabbed the digger once again. Moving down to the last section of the fence, he raised the long tool and dropped it with a thud. Pulling the handles apart he lifted and hauled out a chunk of black, Texas soil and dumped it off to the side. As he did, he noticed the sun glinting off something shiny a couple of feet away.

Jake thrust the posthole digger back into the same hole and left it to check out the shining object. "Probably somebody's soft drink can," he muttered to himself as he crossed the grassy ground.

"Huh, what's this?" Jake picked up a leather briefcase. "Now, how did you get here?" He scratched the side of his head and looked up and down the road in front of him. Turning it over in his hands, he noticed the initials JBC engraved in the brass plate beneath the handle. He pressed the buttons next to the latches—nothing happened.

"Well, I guess somebody else'll have to figure out who you belong to." He chuckled; his habit of talking to himself had brought many teasing jabs from his friends over the years. Good thing none of them were around now. He took the case back to his truck and flipped the back seat forward before dropping the briefcase into the narrow space behind it. He'd give it to Redigo when he got finished.

After setting all the posts and stringing the barbwire, Jake drove to the feed store to pick up some grain for the horses. Back at the ranch, he unloaded the feed and stacked it in the barn and then got caught up in the chores he needed to do around the Lazy M ranch.

****

"Look, I'm tired of this designer gown you people furnish. Do I have any clothes here?" the patient asked the nurse as she came to check his vital signs again.

The nurse finished listening to his heart and lungs before she answered his question. "Well, you were dressed when they found you on the road, but your clothing suffered as much as you did, if not more."

"And just what does that mean?" The look on his face must have been comical because Jan Ingram laughed at him.

"The paramedics cut your shirt and pants off you. Then, when you got to the hospital, someone in ER had to cut your right boot off." Jan shrugged. "About all that's left untouched is your left boot and a sock." She paused and took a deep breath. "I'm sorry, but it was save your life or your clothes." She lifted her right eyebrow and looked directly at him. "Most of the nurses agree they made the right decision when they chose to save you. Wouldn't you agree?"

He grinned at her teasing. "Yeah, I guess so." Then with a heavy sigh he replied, "Well, that's great. Since I have no clothes, no money and no earthly idea who I am, I guess I am destined to spend the rest of my life in one of these lovely gowns."

Jan gave him a big smile as she looked up from the clipboard where she had been making some notes. "I must say you do look better in it than most people. At least that faded green does bring out the color of your eyes."

He rolled his eyes and smiled back. "Thanks a lot."

Placing the pen in her uniform pocket, she sat down in the chair beside the bed. "I have some good news for you."

"That'll be a change."

"We nurses decided we couldn't refer to you as 'the patient in room 244' forever, so we decided to call you Duke Green."

For the first time, he laughed. He did it without thinking about the mess he was in, and it would have felt really good if it hadn't hurt his head so much. After catching his breath, he asked, "Just where did you come up with a name like that? I thought most unidentified patients were referred to as John or Jane Doe."

Nurse Jan Ingram nodded her head. "That's true, but you're different. You need an identity of your own. So we took a very scientific approach to finding you one."

His smile widened. "So now I'm a science experiment?"

Jan laughed. "No. We just thought long and hard

about a name for you. Since you came in with one boot, we deduced that you might be a cowboy. We voted and decided our favorite cowboy of all time was John Wayne, also known as the Duke. The Green we got from your eyes, plus the fact you are Dr. Green's patient." He couldn't contain the laughter, although it caused his head to throb with pain. It touched him to know the nursing staff cared enough to worry about a name for him.

"I guess I can live with that for now. I have to admit I like it better than John Doe." He took a deep breath and repositioned himself for a little more comfort before he spoke again. "All of the nurses have been really great to me. I hope when my true identity comes out we don't learn I'm wanted for murder in fourteen states."

Jan stood to her feet. "Me, too. But we can all testify that, while you were in our care, you behaved like a perfect gentleman." She gave him a warm smile. "Do you need anything before I go, Mr. Green?"

Mr. Green sounded too formal, but for some reason the name 'Duke' felt comfortable. "Please, just call me Duke. I think I can remember to answer to that." He gave Jan a crooked grin which she returned.

A nurse tech entered the room at that moment with his dinner tray and set it on the over-the-bed table. Duke lifted the cover to check out his food. "I would appreciate it if someone would cut up my meat for me. It's a little difficult to do one-handed."

"Tammie can do that for you. Let me know when you need something for pain." The nurse left the room.

The tech smiled as she picked up the knife and fork. She started a casual conversation with him while she cut the meat into bite-sized pieces.

****

Duke jerked awake from the dream he had been struggling through. Sweat beaded on his forehead, and his heart thudded hard enough to cause his hospital gown to vibrate. He panted as though he had been running for miles. His uninjured hand ached, and he looked down to see he had wadded up a large portion of the bedding during his dream. He forced his hand to relax and turn the blanket and sheet loose.

His dream continued to haunt him even as he lay

awake. Duke sought to make sense of the lingering bits and pieces. Someone had been chasing him. In the dream, he had been desperate to get away from the danger of being caught.

Duke wiped the sweat away with the back of his good hand. Reaching over, he picked up the Styrofoam cup filled with ice water. He drank until only ice remained in the cup. His hand trembled as he put the cup on the table. Light streaming in from the streetlamps outside filtered between the blinds and lit up the face of the wall clock. Three o'clock. Still a few hours before daylight and shift change.

He groaned. The unease lingering from the eerie nightmare might keep him awake for the remainder of the night. He wanted sleep, but he didn't want to dream again. Duke found the remote and turned on the TV. Maybe the silly sitcom reruns would lull him to sleep and keep the nightmares at bay.

****

The next afternoon Duke looked up from the magazine he was reading to see Dr. Green entering the door.

"I understand we may be related," the doctor said with humor in his voice.

"Have you found out something I need to know?"

The doctor walked to the side of the bed. "No, nothing like that. The nurse just told me they had named you Duke Green."

Duke chuckled. "Yeah. I guess it's better than a lot of things they might have come up with."

The doctor looked back down at the chart in his hand. "I've gone over all your test results. There doesn't appear to be any physical reason for your amnesia. I believe it must be caused from the shock you received, so I'm confident that, in time, you will get your memory back." Dr. Green took out a small light and flashed it in and out of one eye and then the other.

"How much time, Doc? It's terrible not knowing if you have a family waiting for you and wondering what happened." Duke swallowed hard.

Dr. Green shook his head. "I don't know how long it will take. You'll probably start getting bits and pieces back a little at a time. Then one day everything may just fall into place." He jotted a note on Duke's chart. "By the way, the police would like to talk to you. Do you feel up to it?"

The mere word 'police' sent a stab of fear snaking through his Swiss cheese consciousness. Duke felt as though his heart stopped beating for a few seconds. His reaction made him think his dream might have been the truth trying to crowd its way back into his conscience mind.

What if my dream is a reenactment of something that really happened in my life?

If the police got involved, his nightmare might turn into reality. But, in weighing his options of living a life with no memory against possibly finding out who he was, the scales tipped to the side of wanting to know. Drawing in a deep breath and swallowing hard he gave the go ahead Dr. Green sought.

"Tell them to come ahead."

****

"You don't remember *anything*?" the deputy asked again.

Duke shook his head. "I remember waking up to dead silence all around me, and then realizing I must still be alive because I hurt too bad to be dead. The next thing I remember is of a lot of flashing colored lights and people shouting. That's it." He balled his fist in order to keep his hand from shaking. His heart began to race again. What would they find out?

Deputy Tate made a few notes on a small pad. "Well, we don't have much to go on. The driver may have pulled to the side of the road a few feet ahead of where you were found. A leather jacket was picked up across the road. It has the initials JBC monogrammed on the inside. Do those initials ring any bells?"

Duke's mouth was so dry he couldn't speak. He shook his head.

"We can run your fingerprints and see what happens. If you have any kind of criminal record, or if you've ever been given any security clearance, we'll turn that up. Otherwise..." Deputy Tate shrugged.

Duke gave a laugh that seemed nervous even to him.

"I don't know whether to hope you find out something or not. I might find out who I am and wind up in jail."

The deputy's face looked like stone.

"There is that possibility," Deputy Tate said. His tone said as much or more than the simple words he spoke.

Duke sighed deeply. "Anything has got to be better than not knowing a single detail about my life so go ahead, Deputy Tate."

The deputy nodded. "I'll send someone over to take your prints." He flipped his notebook closed and left the room.

Duke shuddered as the door clicked shut. *What have I let myself in for?*

Chapter Three

"By the way, Dan, any news on the mystery man?" Skylar asked. Dan and Trina Tate had come over for dinner when Skylar had gotten back from the three-day event in Fort Worth. They had wandered down to the barn to check on Skylark's Son.

"No, we ran his prints through the computer but came up empty." The deputy stroked the horse's nose as the animal nudged him for another treat.

"What's going to happen to him?"

"I don't know. We checked for any missing person reports, but nothing showed there either. If he has a family, they haven't put out anything on him, at least not that we've seen. So it's really not a police matter at this point."

Skylar couldn't seem to get the mystery man out of her mind. Dan's words didn't help. What would happen to someone who didn't know anything about his past?

****

Almost a week had passed since Skylar had found the jacket that might belong to the injured man. Her conversation with Dan last night over dinner had left her more curious than ever—to the point she had taken an unnecessary trip into Denton to get a firsthand look. Skylar stepped out of the elevator on the second floor of Newcomb Memorial Hospital and walked over to the nurses' desk. A woman about her own age dressed in navy blue scrubs looked up at her.

"May I help you?"

"I hope so. I'm looking for a patient."

"The patient's name?"

The woman looked back at her computer screen. Skylar paused and tried to figure out what to say, shifting the small vase of red carnations she had picked up in the gift shop from her right hand to her left. She hadn't thought it would be this tough to get in to see the man who had been injured across from her ranch. When she didn't answer, the woman looked up over the computer monitor at her. The woman's eyes narrowed and her brows drew closer together.

"Uh, well, I don't know his name, but he was hit by a car just outside of my ranch. I'd like to talk with him."

"Ma'am, I'm sorry, but I can't give out information about patients to just anyone. The person you're looking for might not want to see you."

Skylar tried to think of something to say that would change the woman's mind. "I understand that. I, uh, just thought…"

"Skylar McCrea, what are you doing up here?" Jan Ingram asked as she walked around a corner.

Skylar's relief at seeing her friend came out as a deep sigh. "Jan, I'm so happy to see you."

"Are you up here to visit someone?"

"Well, sort of." She explained to Jan about the accident near her home.

Jan patted Skylar's hand when she finished her story. "Hmm. It's a bit unusual, but give me a minute."

Skylar watched Jan disappear around the corner again. A couple of minutes passed before Jan reappeared and motioned for Skylar to join her.

"The patient said to tell you to come on in." Jan pointed to the door beside them.

"Thanks, Jan. I owe you for this."

"No problem. I'll see you at church."

Skylar hesitated a moment to gather her wits before she knocked on the door of room 244. A deep male voice invited her in. Pushing the door open, her gaze locked with a young man who had the most amazing green eyes she had ever seen. Eyes like these seemed out of place on a man with dark blonde hair. He should have had red hair.

"Can I help you?" he asked.

Stammering a little, she finally managed to introduce herself. "I'm Skylar McCrea. Thanks for seeing me. Your accident happened on the edge of my property. I found a leather jacket close to where they found you. After hearing about the accident, I thought it might belong to you. So I took it to a friend at the Sheriff's office. I've sort-of been keeping up with your progress. I hope you don't mind."

She felt herself blushing as she rambled. Her stomach seemed to be filled with a thousand butterflies, an abnormal feeling for her. She was known for her ability to stay calm. Maybe she was just a little out of practice meeting good-looking men her own age.

A smile covered the man's face. "Not at all. What man in his right mind would object to a beautiful woman's interest in him? What have you got there?"

She blushed once more at his compliment. "Uh...oh, I brought you some flowers. I know how impersonal a hospital room can be. I thought they might cheer you up a little." Thankful to have something to break the flow of conversation, she moved closer to the bed and set the small vase of flowers on the table next to it.

"The flowers are beautiful, too. Thanks."

Skylar still felt uneasy. *Where is my composure? I'm never this nervous.* She had nerves of steel and dealt with tough situations all the time. An awkward silence filled the room before Duke finally spoke.

"So Skylar, you said I was found on the edge of your property. Is that property a house, business, what?"

Ah, a safe topic. She could talk forever about her ranch and the horses she loved so much. She seated herself in the chair at his bedside. "I have a small horse ranch. I train and show horses in equestrian events."

She watched as Duke scratched around the top edge of the cast on his right leg with a drinking straw.

"Ever have any that won a big title?"

She smiled at the question. She began to answer, and then hesitated. She loved talking about her horses, but for some reason she felt uneasy sharing her life with someone who couldn't remember his own.

"Well, did you?"

He began to scratch more vigorously easing the straw further down the cast. If he wasn't careful, he was going to lose the straw.

"Are you supposed to be doing that?"

"My leg itches like crazy. I've got to do something. Talk to me, please; maybe that will take my mind off my discomfort."

"I had one world champion eventer. That's a horse that is entered in competitions that last three days. The first day the horse is put through a series of dressage movements. That's kind-of its proper, elite ritzy show-off day. The next day the horse has to participate in a cross-country race that is filled with a series of jumps and obstacles over a long distance. That's its gritty day. Then finally the horse has to demonstrate its ability in show jumping. That's the tough day because the horse had to expend so much energy the day before. It's hard to have the energy to go over all those jumps in the ring after running and jumping pretty much at full speed for miles the day before."

Duke gave her an easy smile. "What's your horse's name?"

"Skylark."

"Skylark? That sounds kind-of familiar."

"Do you think you remember him?"

"Yeah. Well, maybe. But didn't there used to be a car called a Skylark?"

"Yes."

"Then maybe I'm confusing your horse with the car. Who knows?"

Skylar felt nervous again and began to fidget with the bottom button on her navy blue shirt. He must have sensed her discomfort because he smiled at her and changed the direction of the conversation.

"Say, I know, let me tell you about myself. I'm Duke Green."

She interrupted him, "I thought you didn't know who you are."

"Oh, I don't really. You see I was born a few days ago in this very room. The nursing staff named me. I have several wonderful friends already and by coincidence most of them happen to be in the medical profession. Can you imagine that?"

Skylar began to laugh at his easy manner. "At least you are well taken care of." She didn't think she could be as flip about her missing memory if she were in his place.

He now absentmindedly used the straw to scratch under the cast on his left arm. "That's true. I have a lot of time to think lying here in this bed and have developed several scenarios for myself."

She figured that not having any memory must be a terrible thing, but she admired the manner in which he was dealing with his situation. "Really. What are they?"

"Well, one is that I was snatched by aliens and was dropped out of the spaceship with my memory erased."

She laughed as he continued.

"Another possibility is I could be the result of some weird scientific experiment and was born full-grown with no past. Then, again, I could have done something really terrible and be on the run from the cops."

"You have a rather interesting imagination." The corners of her mouth turned up into another smile.

"Yes, I guess I do. I've also invented pasts for myself. Like I'm the son of the wealthiest man in the world. Or maybe I have a wife and five kids somewhere worried that something's happened to me. Perhaps I'm a famous movie star. But since no one seems to recognize me, I guess I couldn't be too famous could I?"

His look was so deep she thought he might actually be peering into her soul. She blushed again and shifted her gaze away from his for a brief second. Then she joined him in his game of make-believe. "You could be the man under the Ronald McDonald suit or the Jack-In-The-Box man. That way you would be famous, but no one would know your face. Once all those bruises clear up on your face, we may all realize you're Harrison Ford."

"Hey, you're good at this, too, but I don't think I'd like to be the redheaded clown. Now that Jack character is pretty clever on all those commercials." He made eye contact with her again. "Do you think Harrison Ford is handsome?"

Skylar could feel the heat rising in her face. She hadn't blushed this much since she was sixteen. "Yes, he's cute in a rugged sort of way."

"Oh, so you think I'm cute."

How did she get trapped into this conversation? She stood and walked to the window. An older section of the hospital stretched out in front of his room. "You have quite a view if you like looking at air conditioning units," Skylar chuckled. "I understand they charge more for a room with a view."

Her effort to distract him didn't appear to be working. She could see his reflection in the window. His grin told her he was enjoying her discomfort way too much. Then he let her off the hook.

"Of course, my situation could be like one of the soap operas I've been watching. Maybe some evil man erased my memory and had plastic surgery done on my face. I could be your long-lost brother, and you wouldn't even recognize me."

She turned to face him again. "I can say this about you; you have a sense of humor. I didn't have any brothers, so you don't belong to my family."

"Are you sure about that? There are a lot of secrets revealed on the soaps. Maybe your father had a life you didn't know about."

He laughed as he teased her, and suddenly she noticed what a captivating smile he had. His face showed lines indicating his humor, but she could see that sadness still remained in those dark green eyes. They talked for a while longer before Skylar left.

****

Duke watched as the door closed behind his visitor. Skylar McCrea was a beautiful woman. Her blonde hair had threads of red running through it. *Strawberry blonde is the name for hair like that. But what do I know? I can't even remember my own name.*

He groaned as he shifted his leg to a more comfortable position. Her eyes captivated him. Large, blue ones. A deep sky blue like the color of the sky in northwestern Wyoming.

That stopped his thoughts. How did he know what the sky looked like in Wyoming? Had he ever been there? He pressed his memory. But all that happened was a sharp, shooting pain running from his right eye through to his right temple. He closed his eyes and leaned his head back against the pillows. Breathing deeply, he worked on relaxing.

He still wondered why Skylar had come to visit him. She appeared sincere. But who knew? His judgment couldn't be counted on with his memory missing. What might she really want? Unless she knew something he didn't, she couldn't think she'd get any money out of him. He didn't have any. She had looked nervous at the beginning, but when she talked about her ranch and horses she had relaxed. He'd almost guarantee that had been the truth coming from her then.

She said the accident happened near her ranch. Maybe she feared he'd try to sue her or something. Wait...maybe she had hit him. Could that be why she'd dropped by, to see if he recognized her? He pondered the idea for a minute and then shook his head. No. She wasn't that kind.

He couldn't figure out why she'd come to see him, but she sure brightened up his day. Her smile would light up any man's life. Her husband was a lucky man.

****

She couldn't get Duke out of her mind as she left his room. Turning her steps away from the parking lot, she walked across the street to try to get the answers to her questions as to Duke's fate. Russell Green might be a doctor but he was also her cousin. He would understand her wanting to help.

"The doctor's with a patient right now," the receptionist informed her. Skylar had not met this woman so she must not have been working for Russell for very long.

"I just need a minute of his time. Could you tell his nurse that Skylar McCrea is here?"

The receptionist slammed her pen down on the desk. "I don't think it will do any good, but I'll tell her. You can have a seat over there. I'll be right back."

The receptionist went into the back of the office while Skylar paced the floor. Moments later the doctor's nurse appeared at the door. "Skylar, what brings you by the office?" Nurse Jackson asked.

"I need to talk to Russ. Can he spare a few minutes for me?"

"Come on back. I'll see what I can do."

She followed the nurse into Russell's office. "Wait here. I'll tell the doctor you need to see him as soon as he comes out of exam room four."

Skylar made herself comfortable on the couch and thumbed through a magazine while waiting for her cousin to appear.

The tall, lanky doctor walked into his office. "Hey, cousin, what brings you in to see me? Has there been a death in the family or something?"

She laughed at his comment. "Now, Russ, occasionally I come to see you for no reason."

"Not really. You only seem to come if you want something, or you need to inform me about something tragic," he teased. He kissed her forehead and then sat down beside her on the couch.

She nibbled on the inside of her lower lip, knowing his comment was close to the truth. Neither of them had much family and they really didn't spend enough time together. She'd have to do something about that. "Well, I do need something from you this time. I need some information."

"See, I told you. Information about what?"

She stood and began to pace around the small office. "It's not a what; it's a who. Duke Green." She watched his face lose its smile as he returned to his professional demeanor.

"Now, Skylar, with the HIPPA laws, I can't discuss a patient with you, as you well know."

She sat back down beside her cousin and tried a different tactic. "Well, I can talk to you about him, can't I? I'm not a medical person."

"How do you know about this patient anyway?"

"The car hit him just outside my main gate."

"Oh...I didn't realize that." He paused. "You don't know him, do you? He's not a new hand you've hired, is he?"

"No; I just met him."

He interrupted her, "How?"

"Never mind about that. I just want to know what's going happen to him when he's discharged, *if* he still doesn't have his memory back. That's not confidential; that's being a good Christian and showing concern for my fellow man." She laughed.

"That's pushing the issue a bit. Why have you formed such an interest in a man you don't know?"

"Since his accident happened not far from my place, I'm just curious. He seems like a nice guy. So what's going happen to him? Will he stay in the hospital until he's recovered, since he has no place else to go?"

"With no memory, no money, and needing care for an extended period of time, what do you think might be a good alternative for him?"

Her chest tightened as a terrible thought crossed her mind. "Since he has no family or friends to care for him, I guess a nursing home would be his only choice."

Russ shrugged. "That's a possibility."

"How about a rehab facility?"

"Hypothetically, if you don't have money or insurance, it's difficult to get someone into a lot of places these days, especially rehab facilities."

Again she stood and began to pace the office. "That just stinks. I sure hate to see someone like him have to go to a nursing home, but could he even get into a place like that without money or insurance?"

"When someone is down on their luck, social services works to get them some help. However, that is almost impossible when a person has no identity."

"So someone like Duke Green winds up on the street?" She sank back down on the couch.

"Or at the Salvation Army, if we can get him a space there, or one of the other local shelters. The problem is a patient with injuries like his has to have care. He can't make it alone. The homeless shelters don't usually accept people with major medical needs. They're not equipped for it."

"Then where will he go?" she asked.

Her cousin shrugged. "That's the problem. If you come up with any suggestions, let me know."

"What about the churches in town? Any of them able to help?"

"Social services has spoken with the larger ones. They have no facilities to help with long-term care. Some of them help with medications or medical supplies, but that's about it." Russ reached over and patted her on the arm. "Sorry, Skylar, I've got to cut this short. I do have paying customers in the waiting room. Let's get together sometime to just visit."

She hugged her cousin. "I'd like that. Since we're the only family one another has in the area, besides Aunt

Tess. We really should spend a little more time together. I'll give you a call. Maybe you and Evelyn can come out to the ranch for a barbecue before long."

"Sounds good. Give her a call and set something up. I'll see you later."

Her cousin grabbed a chart and opened the door to go see his next patient. She followed him out and waved goodbye just as he opened the door to exam room three.

****

Skylar looked at her watch as she settled into her SUV. The visit to Duke Green's room and then to Russell's office had taken about an hour. She had some time before she needed to be back at the ranch, so she decided to stop by to visit her Aunt Tess. Since Aunt Tess suffered from Alzheimer's, her aunt never knew whether anyone visited her in the nursing home or not, but Skylar made sure she saw her at least once a week.

As she walked down the hallway toward her aunt's room, the strong aroma of ammonia filled her nose and her eyes watered. Feeble cries of "Help me" rang over and over as patients begged for attention. The people seemed so all alone. A deep, sharp pain in the middle of her stomach stabbed at her. That was the thing she disliked the most about coming to visit her aunt. The nurses and techs did their best, but there were too many residents and too few staff members. She said a prayer for all those in pain, whether physical or emotional, as she made her way down the corridor to her aunt's room.

Her aunt was seated in a geri-chair when she entered the room. "Good morning, Aunt Tess. You look good today." She walked across the room and kissed her aunt on the cheek.

She told her aunt about the accident and the mystery man even though she appeared oblivious to her tale. Aunt Tess continuously folded and refolded the terry towel one of the nurses had placed on the tray holding her in the chair. She mumbled a meaningless assortment of words as Skylar tried desperately to communicate with her. She fed her aunt lunch before leaving the depressing atmosphere of the nursing facility.

As she walked out into the fresh air, she took a deep breath. She wished there were some place else for her aunt. She had tried to keep her at the ranch, but her aunt became violent at times and had pushed Addie down the steps one day when the housekeeper was trying to block the door to keep her in the house. Aunt Tess had also wandered off twice during the night; the last time they had found her walking down the highway.

It had just become too dangerous to keep her at the ranch. Skylar's fervent prayer was that her aunt didn't realize where she was. The atmosphere wasn't appealing to Skylar in spite of the fact it was one of the best skilled-care nursing facilities in Denton, but at least her aunt was supervised and cared for better than they could manage at the ranch.

On the drive home she couldn't help but think about Duke being in a similar place. She couldn't picture anyone that young, and in their right mind, having to stay there. She couldn't shake the nauseating feeling that came over her when she thought of Duke being in a nursing home or at the homeless shelter. Surely there was another answer.

Chapter Four

"What do you think you're doing?" the nurse asked as she walked up beside Duke's bed.

Duke's ears burned with embarrassment as he pulled a fork from between the cast and his leg. "Well, uh…I was trying to get the straw out."

"What straw?"

"Uh…the one I lost down in my cast."

"And just why would a grown man lose a straw inside his cast?" Nurse Jan Ingram crossed her arms and began to tap her foot.

"Well, you see, my leg itches something awful, so I thought I'd scratch it. I was using the straw from my tray…it kinda got stuck, and I couldn't get it out. I was using the fork to try and get the straw."

Duke could see the twinkle in her eyes as Jan tried to keep from smiling. After struggling for several seconds to maintain her professional air, she finally managed to ask, "And just what else do you have stuck down your cast?"

"Nothing else, honest. Just the straw. I don't see what you find so funny. I'm in misery here. I was just trying to get a little relief."

"Well, sticking things down your cast is not the way to get relief. You could cut your leg and make things a lot worse."

"Well, how do I stop the itching?"

"You don't. Itching just goes with a cast. You might try scratching somewhere else. Maybe it will be relieved by sympathy scratching." Nurse Ingram laughed again.

Duke tried to keep a straight face as he asked, "Sympathy scratching? Is that a scientific medical remedy?"

"No, it just sounded good, so I thought I'd say it. You know it works on the same principle as if you have a headache and someone kicks you in the shin. With the pain in your shin, you forget about your headache."

"So if I scratch somewhere else, I'll forget about the itching under my cast. I don't think so." He looked at her, a smile twitched at his lips. "Did you actually go to nursing school?"

Duke watched her assume a stern look, but the twinkle remained in her eyes so he knew she wasn't serious.

"I am offended you would ask such a thing. Have you tried it?"

"No."

"Well then, how do you know it won't work? At any rate, don't put anything else down your cast. I'd have to report you to Dr. Green, you know."

"Sure, Nurse Grouch. Go right ahead and tattle on me. I'm learning that you nurses can be very brutal." Duke smiled at their exchanged banter.

"If you want to be correct, that would be Nurse Cratchett. That's what we, in the nursing profession, call nurses who are difficult to get along with at times. We certainly can be brutal, especially with children and unruly patients. Now promise me you won't poke anything else down your cast, and I'll go get you some Benadryl. That might help stop the itching for a while."

"Scout's honor," Duke held up three fingers. "If I don't behave, you might break my other leg to help me forget the agony this one is causing me."

Jan laughed. "We just might."

****

As Skylar went about her afternoon chores, she couldn't get Duke and his situation off her mind. There just had to be a better solution than a nursing home. Addie and Redigo both found her unusually silent mood at supper a little disturbing because they had told her so without bothering to be subtle.

Skylar didn't know what time she finally fell asleep because she lay in the darkness for what seemed like hours and prayed for this mystery man and his predicament. A thought kept haunting her. She tried without success to shake it off, but her sub-conscious mind kept whispering, *bring Duke to the ranch.* She mulled the thought over. They could take care of him, and when he was well, he could work for her until his memory returned and earn the money to pay toward his medical bills and his daily needs. She knew it wasn't just her decision to make. A lot of the responsibility for his care would fall on Addie and Redigo. She would have to talk with them before she could make a final decision.

Her quiet mood lingered the next morning until Addie forced her to open up.

"Girl, what is wrong with you? You must have somethin' pretty heavy on your mind for you to be so quiet."

Skylar hesitated. She had to try. For some reason, she couldn't let this fellow be carted off to an undesirable place without at least trying to find another solution.

"Well, the man that was hit out on the highway a couple of weeks ago is still in the hospital with amnesia. He's got a broken leg and arm." Skylar stirred the scrambled eggs in the skillet with a whisk.

Redigo took a drink of his coffee before he spoke. "Yeah, I heard. He's in bad shape but what's that got to do with you bein' so quiet?"

"It looks like, since he has no family to take care of him, he doesn't have any place to go to recuperate." She dished the eggs up onto a platter and placed them on the table. After taking her seat, she offered grace before resuming the conversation about Duke.

"What's going to happen to him?" Addie asked as she placed jelly on her biscuit.

Redigo set his coffee mug on the table and took a deep breath. "I really hate to ask this 'cause I figure I'm not goin' to like the answer, but, Skylar, what has that got to do with you? You don't even know the guy."

"Well, I thought, if the two of you would agree, we could bring him out here."

She waited for Redigo to explode.

"I was afraid that's what you were goin' to say." Redigo spooned some eggs onto his plate. He used a little more force than needed.

"I thought when he's on his feet again, we could put him to work. He's gonna need a job to pay-off some of his medical bills."

"Girl, sometimes your heart makes your head soft.

You don't know anything about this man. He could have a criminal background." Redigo took a bite of bacon as he looked across the table at Skylar. The way he bit off a piece of the bacon made Skylar glad she wasn't the strip of crisp meat he chewed on. "And how do you know he could handle ranch work?"

"He looks strong enough to be able to work here." She paused and chewed on a mouthful of scrambled eggs. "That is when he...uh, gets out of his casts."

The clatter of stainless steel against her mother's best pottery made her cringe. She looked up and met Redigo's stare. Her foreman's brown eyes snapped with repressed anger, but he didn't dump his thoughts on her yet. So she moved on in an effort to get her two friends to agree.

"Dan said when they ran his prints they came up empty, so he doesn't have a police record. Besides the nurses all think he's wonderful. They say he's really nice. I thought so, too, when I met him." Skylar hung her head as she stirred her eggs around on her plate. Whoops, she might have said too much too soon.

"You've already met him?" Addie asked before taking a sip of the hot coffee in her cup.

She might as well admit the truth.

"Yes. I went into town yesterday. I met him and then talked to Russ about him. I stopped by to see Aunt Tess on my way home. You know what that nursing home is like. It would be awful for a young man to be in one, besides he wouldn't even be able to get into one since he has no way to pay."

"There's Medicaid," Redigo said.

"Not for him. He has no identification, no social security number. The social services rep has been working on finding somewhere for him to go, but she's had no luck." Skylar prayed she was beginning to make a good case for her request.

"He can go to one of the homeless shelters." Redigo gripped his fork again and shoveled large bites of eggs into his mouth. He chewed a couple of times and swallowed.

"None of them are equipped to handle someone like him. He needs too much care right now."

Redigo looked at her, fork in the air like an extension of his finger. She squirmed under his scrutiny. She wasn't going to like what was coming.

"You're lettin' your kind heart take over your good sense. Skye, you just can't bring every stray you find home."

Redigo had used her nickname. All wasn't lost. "So, unlike the Good Samaritan, you'd just walk by him?"

"Good Samaritan...you pullin' that mess, huh?"

"Yes, I am. I feel God is directing me to do this. Besides, with two broken limbs, what harm can the man do?" Skylar pulled her biscuit apart.

"He could clobber us with his cast and steal our fortune." Redigo picked up his mug of coffee.

Ah, a hint of humor. He was caving in, if only just a little!

Addie spoke up at that point. "That's crazy, you old man. Skylar's right. Someone's in trouble, and it's our responsibility to help. I think we should give it a try. If he becomes a problem, we can always send him to a shelter later."

She had Addie on her side; now it was two against one.

Redigo stood up. "I don't guess anything I'd say now would change your mind. You're gonna do what you want to anyway. I'll be in the barn."

He slammed the door on his way out. His footsteps echoed away as he stomped off the porch.

Skylar looked at Addie.

"That old man'll git over his mad. Do what you need to. I'll make sure the guest room is ready."

"Thanks, Addie. I'll call Russ and let him know we're going to ask Duke to come out here."

Skylar walked to the barn before leaving. Her feet dragged. She didn't like being at odds with Redigo. She hoped to ease his mind about them taking on Duke.

She found him in the office doing paperwork. She sat on the old leather couch beside his desk.

He looked up at her, a frown wrinkling his forehead.

"Redigo, can I talk with you?"

"You're the boss. It's your time."

"So you don't want him to come out here?"

"I don't think it's a good idea. This is a stranger, and you want me to say it's okay for you to move him into the house with just you two women. I just don't like the idea." Redigo shook his head.

Skylar thought for about three heartbeats before an idea popped into her mind. "Okay, what if you bunk in the room I use for an office? Then when he gets the casts off and is able to do for himself, we move him out to the bunkhouse." Skylar smiled. Maybe that would win her foreman over.

Redigo leaned back in his desk chair and laced his fingers together across his stomach. He rocked the chair back and forth. His eyes narrowed in thought as he studied her. She could hear the second hand of the wall clock click the seconds off as she waited for him to speak. Finally he rocked the chair forward and leaned his arms on his desk.

"If you insist on bringing him out here, I guess we could work it that way. At least I'd be in the house if anything were to happen."

"Thanks." Skylar smiled.

****

Skylar drove into town to see Duke.

Her cousin, Russ, was in Duke's room, along with Jan Ingram, when she arrived. They didn't seem to notice her as she stepped into the room. A few seconds later, Russ pulled something that looked very much like a straw out of the cast on Duke's leg. "From this point on, you will refrain from poking objects down into your cast, won't you?"

"Yes. Nurse Cratchett has already given me that lecture."

"Nurse Cratchett?" Russ asked, looking over at Jan.

Duke shrugged and winked at the nurse. "It's a private joke between us, but isn't there something you can do to relieve the itching?"

"Did the Benadryl help?"

"Not much."

"Well, all casts cause itching; that's just the way it is. You could try scratching somewhere else. That might help."

Duke laughed. "My wonderful nurse already tried to

get me to use that solution. I thought since you were a doctor you might have a better remedy."

Skylar caught her upper lip with her teeth to keep from laughing at the scene.

"Just grin and bear it." Russ turned and noticed her standing just inside the doorway. "Well, hello cousin. You didn't waste any time in getting here." The doctor looked back at the patient lying in the bed. "Duke, I understand you've met my cousin. She has something to talk with you about."

"I'm always interested in what a pretty lady has to say." Duke smiled.

Russ looked from Duke to her. "Yes, well Skylar, give me a call later. I've got to finish rounds.

After Russ and Jan left, Duke concentrated his gaze on her. "So, you're Dr. Green's cousin?"

"Yeah, we've been related all our lives." Skylar walked to stand at the foot of the bed.

"Very cute. Now what did you want to talk to me about?"

Skylar frowned as Duke began to scratch his left knee. "Does that leg itch?"

Duke shook his head. "No, I'm just trying that sympathy scratching thing, but it's not helping."

Skylar seated herself beside his bed. "Maybe I have something that will help take your mind off your misery."

"You have an itch remedy?"

"Nothing to help your itch," she laughed. "Have you thought about what you're gonna do when you're discharged?"

A look of dismay clouded his handsome face, and his green eyes lost their sparkle. "I've been told I have very few choices."

Skylar grinned. "Well, I've come to offer you one. I want you to come out to my ranch to recuperate."

Duke stared at her for a long moment. "I can't do that! You don't know anything about me. I don't know anything about me. I couldn't take your charity. I can't pay you. No. I can't do that."

Skylar felt her stomach muscles tighten up as she searched for the words to counter his refusal.

"You can't pay for a nursing home either, and a

homeless shelter is, at best, charity even if they would take you with your injuries. Anyway...what I'm offering isn't charity. When you've recovered, I expect you to go to work for me, if you haven't regained your identity before then. That way you could earn some money for your medical expenses along with room and board. Plus I'd get the extra help I've been needing." Skylar knew she didn't really need another hand, but if she made him feel like he was doing her a favor, maybe he'd agree.

****

"It'll be weeks before I can work. I'd just be a burden until then. How would you take care of me and the ranch? I thank you for your offer, but I just can't accept."

He clinched his jaws together. He couldn't take advantage of the woman in front of him.

"I wouldn't be doing it by myself. I have a live-in housekeeper, Addie. Actually she's more like my second mother. She'd see to you most of the time. Also my foreman, Redigo, lives right on the ranch. He'd be there to help you as well."

Her smile threatened to weaken his resolve. She looked like a little girl expecting a big surprise.

"Like I said...it's real nice of you, but I don't think so. I just can't ask a stranger to take that responsibility."

"I might not be a stranger, remember. You could be my long-lost brother that some villain kidnapped and brain-washed and did plastic surgery on."

She threw one of the fictional pasts he had created back in his face.

"I thought you said you didn't have a brother?" Duke was still trying not to give in to her. Her blue eyes sparkled. He would have to be careful; his will was weakening.

"Maybe you were taken before I was born, and my parents found it too difficult to talk about, so they never told me about you. Now, I would never forgive myself if I turned my brother away when he needed help. You've got to come out to the ranch, or I could feel guilty for the rest of my life. Do you want to have the responsibility of placing that burden on my heart?"

His jaw muscles relaxed.

"I believe you're just a little crazy. Maybe I should be

worrying about your motives instead. Are you sure your ranch isn't the mental hospital?"

Skylar chuckled. "I probably am a little crazy, but the way I see it I'm still the best offer you've got. So I'll be here at ten o'clock in the morning; you be ready to go."

She stood and walked toward the door.

"So I have nothing more to say in this matter?"

Skylar turned and looked at him. "Do you have another plan?"

"No."

He felt tired.

"You just be ready in the morning."

"Why?" His voice came out almost as a whisper.

She stopped with her hand on the door.

"Why be ready?"

He shook his head. "Why are you doing this? What do you get from it?"

Her eyes told him she spoke the truth when she answered him.

"I feel it's what I'm supposed to do, and I'll get the satisfaction of knowing I've helped someone who needs it."

Duke cast his eyes down to his hospital gown, breaking the seriousness of the moment.

"Well, it won't take much for me to be ready to go. I understand I have a boot and a sock. Maybe they'll loan me a couple of these lovely gowns. They could be very fashionable on a ranch, don't you think?"

Skylar burst into laughter. The sound of it replaced the bit of depression that had seeped into his soul.

"Maybe we can do something about that. I'll see what I can figure out; I don't think those gowns will win any prizes with my other hands. You'd never be able to live down the ribbing they'd give you. I'll see you tomorrow."

Staring at the door after Skylar left, Duke decided she had to be either crazy or very special. He believed it was the latter.

He leaned back against the pillows and sighed. Making the effort to remain hopeful and upbeat in front of people was exhausting. He hoped it would be a while before anyone else popped into his room. He needed a rest.

Duke couldn't believe he had let her talk him into

going to her ranch. He'd been a push over. *Am I always like that?* Maybe he should let her know he couldn't leave with her tomorrow. *But where would I go?* Dr. Green had said he would be releasing him tomorrow since he couldn't justify keeping him in the hospital any longer. Actually he would have been sent home days ago, if he'd had a home to go to.

He found himself rubbing his forehead. His head ached again. It must be all the stress. Picking up the control he turned on the TV. Maybe he could lose himself in some make-believe characters' troubles.

Chapter Five

Duke was startled awake early in the morning when the door to his room flew open and the nursing staff walked in. "Hey, wake up, sleepy head," Sherri, his night nurse, called. "You're leaving us today, and we came to say goodbye."

Duke managed to get his eyes open to see most of the nurses who had taken care of him standing in his room. "What are all of you doing here?"

"We're throwing you a birthday party," one of them answered.

"Birthday party? How do you know it's my birthday?"

His heart began to beat a faster. Had someone he knew found him?

"We don't know if you were born on this day, but this is the day you start the rest of your life and leave the hospital. So we decided we'd call it your birthday and give you a party."

His balloon of hope deflated as fast as it inflated. The nurses set a large cake on his table and begin to place presents on the bed around him.

"Now open your gifts so we can cut the cake," Jan stated.

The heat of a blush burned his ears as Duke opened the first gift and found a package of underwear and socks. "I don't know what to say."

"We couldn't let you leave here without being properly clothed. After all, we are nurses. We have a reputation of caring to uphold," Sherri said. "Now open the next present."

In the second box, Duke found a pair of jeans and a long-sleeve, western-cut shirt. "You thought of everything," he noticed they had slit the right leg so it would fit over his cast.

"Didn't you think it was a little strange yesterday

when I measured from your waist to the top of your cast?" Jan asked.

"After all the torture you've put me through, why would I think anything you do is strange? I figured you were measuring me for a coffin."

The next gift revealed a pair of shorts and a T-shirt on which was written, 'Memory Missing. Do you know me?' "You nurses have a wicked sense of humor," Duke said trying to hold back his laughter.

The last was a beautifully wrapped gift. Duke figured it had to be something very special. Opening it, he pulled out one of the dreaded hospital gowns. Snickers filled the room.

"We wanted you to have something to remember your stay with us and also to have something familiar to you since you have no memory of your life before this room," Jan said.

"That's very thoughtful. As I said, you have a wicked sense of humor. I'll treasure this gown. Oh, when I get my bill, will I be charged for this?" Duke asked.

"Probably. That will make it all the more special," Sherri added.

Duke tried to get serious and thank them all for their kindness, but the lump in his throat made it difficult to get the words out.

"Listen, as long as you'll be around this area, just drop by and see us from time to time," Jan said. "When you get your memory back, and you will get it back, we want to know all about you. No matter what evil you may have done."

Her innocent, teasing remark sent a shaft of fear through his heart. His breath caught. The nightmares had left their mark. *Was I an evil person before? Is that why I am always running in my dreams trying to get away from someone chasing me?* He tried to shake off the anxiety as the nurses left. A tremble in his hand told him he hadn't been successful.

****

Skylar was surprised to find Duke dressed and sitting in a wheelchair when she arrived to take him home. "Look at you. I don't guess you'll need the sweat pants and T-shirt I brought along."

"Nope. The nurses bought me some clothes and threw me a little party early this morning."

"You look very nice." Skylar couldn't help but laugh when she read the words printed on his T-shirt. "I guess it never hurts to advertise."

The volunteer helped Skylar get Duke in the truck and put his wheelchair in the back. As they drove, their conversation was relaxed and she told him general facts about the ranch and the people who worked for her.

****

As they neared her place, Duke asked, "Can you show me where my accident occurred? You did say it happened near your ranch, didn't you?"

"Yeah. It happened a few yards across from the entrance to my place." Skylar pulled the truck to a stop when she came to the spot she said the accident happened. She explained the jacket was found on her side of the road.

"You found the jacket over there, but the accident happened here. If that is my jacket, it looks like the driver of the car didn't even start to slow down until after he hit me." Duke's brow crinkled, as he looked the situation over.

"That's true. Do you think someone hit you on purpose? Does anything look familiar?"

"Nothing looks familiar, and I have no idea if it was on purpose or not. Maybe they just didn't see me."

"Or like Dan Tate says, maybe it's not your jacket." Skylar drove the truck back onto the road and turned onto the drive leading to the ranch.

Duke mulled over her last comment as she moved the vehicle down the graveled drive.

An older man and a younger one came out to meet the truck when Skylar pulled up to the house. She introduced them as Redigo and Billy. They got him inside with little difficulty up a ramp that looked like new construction. Duke apologized for being so much trouble but everyone reassured him they didn't mind. He felt unsure of himself. These people were strangers. Why were they being so nice?

Once inside the house, he was introduced to Addie. The middle-aged woman had a sweet smile to go with her short, gray hair. She offered him a warm welcome that seemed sincere, but he guessed he'd have to wait a while to find out for sure.

"Duke, would you like to rest awhile before lunch?"

Skylar's voice called him out of his reverie. He looked up from his wheelchair as she continued.

"Redigo and I have some things to take care of in the barn."

"No. I'm tired of being cooped up in one room. If Addie doesn't mind, I'd rather stay in the kitchen and visit with her. I'll stay over here out of the way." Duke was able to maneuver the wheelchair using his good arm.

"That's fine with me. Not often I have someone to talk to while I cook," Addie said.

As the others left, Duke looked around the kitchen. It had a homey, welcoming atmosphere, but he still wasn't too sure about the cook. Although her greeting had been friendly and warm, he picked up a sense of reserve about her. The odor of food tickled his nose.

"What's that you're cooking? It sure smells good."

"It's a Mexican chicken casserole. I hope you like spicy food." Addie filled a glass with ice water and offered it to him.

"Thank you." Duke took the water. "I'm sure I'll love it. Besides, anything will beat hospital food."

"Isn't that the truth? If they'd just learn to season stuff, it'd help." Addie continued preparing the meal as she talked.

"I agree with you on that." Duke took a drink from the glass he held in his hand. The cold water felt good going down.

"Duke, tell me about yourself, where do you come from?"

Her innocent question stabbed at his missing memory. When would he be able to answer it? He decided to fall back on the joking demeanor he had adopted in the hospital.

"The hospital. That's all I know about myself."

Addie turned as red as a tomato. The knife she wielded while slicing salad greens stilled in her hand. "Oh Duke, I'm so sorry. I completely forgot. I was just trying to make conversation. Please forgive me."

Her sincere apology touched him. He shrugged. "You're forgiven. Don't worry about it. As you can tell by my shirt, it's kind-of become a joke. You know you have to keep a sense of humor about things, or you'll go crazy. So don't worry about offending me."

After lunch, Skylar insisted Duke rest for a while. She and Redigo helped him settle onto his bed, and she handed him the remote for the television. "Good, I was afraid I'd miss Sonny's latest caper." Duke switched on the set to the soap opera he had grown accustomed to watching.

Skylar laughed. "You know those programs aren't the best of entertainment. They're full of sin."

"It does seem that they are, but daytime television leaves a lot to be desired, and compared with these soaps, my problems seem pretty small."

Skylar shook her head as she and her foreman left him alone with his program.

A little more than thirty minutes later, a soft knock sounded at his door. "Come on in."

Addie stuck her head through the doorway. "I thought I heard your TV when I came down the hall."

"Are you a fan of this show?" Duke asked.

"I am when no one's around to catch me. Soap operas are the one vice I haven't allowed the Lord to remove from me yet," Addie confessed.

"Well, pull up a chair. It'll be our secret." Duke grinned. "I got the impression Skylar isn't fond of soap operas."

"No, she's not, but while she is out of the house, I pretty well do as I please." Addie seated herself in the armchair beside Duke's bed. During the commercials, she filled him in on the past lives of the characters, since she had watched this show for many years.

The combination of the trip to the ranch and the painkillers Dr. Green had prescribed put Duke into a drowsy state. He found himself nodding off in the middle of the pop psychologist show that came on next. When Addie noticed, she excused herself and left him to take a nap.

Later that evening, after dinner, he watched TV with Skylar, Addie and Redigo. When the ten o'clock news broadcast ended, Redigo assisted Duke to bed. Although the older man didn't say anything, Duke got the feeling he wasn't happy about the whole situation.

"I'll be in the room next door, if you need me."

Somehow Redigo's offer to help had a tinge of warning shading it.

"Thanks," Duke said.

A couple of minutes later, Skylar stuck her head through the doorway of his room to tell him goodnight before going to her own room. "I hope you enjoyed your first day with us."

"How could anyone not enjoy being with you? I'd say you were the nicest folks I'd ever met, but that wouldn't be much of a compliment, since I don't remember meeting many people."

Skylar laughed. "You are crazy. I'll take it as a compliment. You get some rest; I'll see you in the morning." She started to pull the door closed but paused. "Duke, I'm really glad to have you here."

Duke was glad the light was off when she made the last comment. That way she couldn't see the tears run down his cheeks at her kind words. What were these people made of?

As tired as he was, he had dreaded for night to fall. The days weren't so bad, but the loneliness of the night was hard to take. Every night in the hospital had been the same, at least since he had regained consciousness. He had dreams, and they were always the same. A terrible pain would hit him, followed by lights flashing all around him, and then he would hear loud talking. All that was followed by a sense of being chased, but he never got any further in the dream than that. He wished there were something more in his subconscious to remember. He hated reliving the night of his accident over and over again.

The darkness made the realization of having no one to care even more intense; he felt so alone. As he lay in the darkness in Skylar's home the pain was not quite so intense. Somehow tonight he didn't feel so lost and alone.

****

New York City

It was late; the office had closed a long time before. When the phone rang, the man knew it could only be one person. "Hello."

"I miss you terribly," came a sultry reply.

"Listen, I've told you not to call me at the office." He leaned back against the supple leather of his desk chair.

He heard the hurt in her voice as she answered, "It's late. I knew you'd be alone, and I called your cell. I didn't go through the switchboard. I just had to at least talk to you; I miss you so much. Don't you miss me?"

"You know I do, but we have to be careful. We can't let anyone get suspicious." The man tapped the pen in his hand on his desk. "Where do you suppose he is?"

"I don't know. The private investigator hasn't been able to turn up anything. Maybe he's dead." He could almost hear a smile in her voice when she spoke the last sentence.

"That would be too much to hope for. He's probably out there just waiting to get us." The man stood and walked to the window of his office. He looked down to the street below. "Do you think he knows we were the ones who set him up?"

The woman's voice lost its warmth. "I don't know. Even if he does, how can he prove anything? There's no way he can trace it back to you. Is there?"

"I don't think so, but he is a genius when it comes to computers."

"Let's not talk about him anymore. Why don't you stop by here on your way home? You won't be sorry if you do," she said.

The man paced in his office; the lure of her seductive voice tempted him. "You know I can't do that. What if someone saw us? We can't take the chance."

"How long do we have to wait? I don't know how much more of this I can take."

Her voice was almost whiney which grated on his nerves. "I don't know. I guess until we're sure he's not a threat to us anymore. If we get caught, we could be apart for a very long time. They sure wouldn't let us share a jail cell."

Sounding somewhat annoyed and hurt, she told him good-bye and hung up. As he punched the end button on his phone, he couldn't help but worry. Had he hidden his tracks well enough that no one could trace anything back to him?

Chapter Six

Lazy M Ranch

Skylar helped Addie prepare breakfast. "Addie, thanks for being so nice to Duke yesterday. I hope he wasn't too much trouble."

"He was no trouble at all. I really enjoyed having him around; he has a wonderful personality. You did the right thing by bringing him out here." Addie washed the few dishes that were in the sink.

"I think so, too. I'd hate to know I was alone in the world. It must be awful not to know if you have a family somewhere. The thing that puzzles me though is, if he does have a family, why haven't they put out a missing person trace on him?" Skylar carefully turned the omelet she was preparing.

Addie set four places at the table. "I don't know. Maybe he was on a long vacation, and they don't realize he's missing yet."

Redigo wheeled Duke into the kitchen. "Well, he's all spit and polished for the day."

Skylar noticed several tiny pieces of tissue on Duke's face. "What happened to you? You look as if the toilet tissue roll exploded on your face."

"Well, I'm not good one-handed, and Redigo is not very good at shaving someone else. So this is the result of our combined efforts."

Addie laughed. "Maybe you'd better grow a beard until you recover. At this rate if you keep trying to shave, you'll have to go back to the hospital for a blood transfusion."

Breakfast conversation centered on the horses, as usual. There was talk about the upcoming three-day event.

"I think I'll go out and check with Billy. When I

talked to him last night he said Redigo's Dream was a little off his feed. Then I'm takin' a run into town." Redigo took his hat from the rack by the back door and placed it on his head.

"Sounds like a good idea," Skylar said. "What time will you be back?"

"By noon. Jake can help with our friend here if you need him," Redigo said, indicating Duke.

"I sure hate to be such a burden," Duke said. "Skylar, you could go with Redigo if it weren't for me."

"Actually I couldn't. I have to concentrate on getting Skylark's Son ready for the show. Now you quit feeling guilty. You're not in the way, and we all want you here."

Duke looked a trifle sad. "Say, would you like to go out to the course with me? It might do you some good to get some fresh air," Skylar suggested.

"I'd love to, but wouldn't it be a lot of trouble with me in this contraption?" Duke patted on the arm of his wheelchair.

"Not with the ramp. The ground is very level all the way out to the practice area. We can wheel you out there." Skylar walked behind the chair and placed her hands on the handles.

"Well, what are we waiting for? I'm ready for that fresh air and a look at the next world champion."

****

The crisp morning air was exhilarating as Duke inhaled deeply. It seemed like ages since he had been allowed to enjoy the outdoors. *Did I work outside or in an office?*

As Skylar wheeled him toward the barn, Duke noticed the big, white building looked nice, well kept. The stalls had big doors that split horizontally about halfway from the top. It reminded Duke of the big horse barns dotting the rolling hills of Kentucky. It looked like a barn that would house racehorses, not at all like a barn found on a cattle ranch. As the thoughts passed through his mind, Duke wondered how he would know such a thing. Had he been to Kentucky and seen those barns? How would he know what a barn would look like on a cattle ranch? He knew he wore boots in his past life because he was wearing the left one now, but they didn't look like work boots. He was probably one of those want-to-be cowboys; a drug store cowboy who had never been up close to a real horse.

As they entered the barn, something familiar about the sweet smell of hay mixed with the rustic scent of leather made him feel at home. He knew instantly that he had known this atmosphere before and felt peaceful for the first time in conscious memory.

Skylar wheeled Duke to where he had a good view of the course while Jake led Skylark's Son out onto the dirt of the course. Duke noticed the pride in Skylar's eyes as she walked over and mounted her prized stallion. Skylar slowly paced the stallion around the perimeter of the course several times to warm him up. When the horse was ready, she took him through the jumps. Skylark's Son ran like the wind and his rider handled him skillfully.

Jake had started the stopwatch as Skylark's Son began his last run. Even Duke's adrenaline pumped as he watched the masterful way Skylar controlled the thundering animal. The horse was bred to jump. If given his head, he would have probably gone through the course on his own, but Skylar held him in check until just the right moment. Jake let out a whoop as the stallion crossed the finish line in front of them.

"Man, what a run! His best time ever!" Jake shouted as Skylar walked the animal to a stop in front of him. "If he jumps cleanly at that speed, there's no way he can be beat."

"Don't say that. There's always a chance another horse could be better." Skylar's grin spread across her face as she patted the horse on the neck. "Although it's highly unlikely. What'd you think about my horse, Duke?"

"The horse and its rider are both magnificent. I agree with Jake; you two will be hard to beat."

****

Several days later, after breakfast, Deputy Tate stopped by the Lazy M. "I brought this jacket by." He handed it to Skylar. "No one's claimed it, and I thought if it was Duke's maybe it would jar some memories. He still doesn't remember anything?"

Skylar shook her head. "Nothing. He's keeping a real positive attitude though. I don't know if I could do nearly as well if I were in his situation."

"I hope he's not just a good actor and taking advantage of you and your kind heart," the deputy said.

"Dan Tate, always the skeptic. This man is not a fake."

Dan grinned at her. "I hope you're right." He put his hat on as he stepped off the back porch. "Well, if I can do anything, just let me know. I've got to run; I have to be in court again this morning." Dan walked the short distance to his car. "See you later."

Skylar turned and walked into the house. Maybe the jacket would help if he saw it. She would take it in to him before she went to the barn.

"What are you doing with that again?" Addie asked as Skylar walked into the kitchen.

"Dan just brought it by." Not seeing Duke in the kitchen, Skylar asked, "Where is he?"

"He's in the living room watching TV. He said he might as well try to keep up on world events even if he couldn't keep up with his personal ones." Addie continued with her chores as she talked.

Skylar found Duke watching a local Texas morning talk show when she entered the living room.

When he noticed her standing in the doorway, he said, "I thought you'd already gone out to the barn to give Skylark's Son his morning work-out."

"I was headed that way when Dan Tate stopped by."

A look of concern clouded Duke's face. "What did the deputy want?"

"He brought this jacket by. It's the one I found on the road near where you were hit. He thought if it was yours it might stir up a memory."

Duke took the coat from Skylar's extended hand. She watched as he looked over every inch of the garment. He examined it inside and out, right down to putting it to his nose and smelling it.

"Well?"

"Nothing." He put the jacket on and it fit like it was tailor-made for him. "It doesn't seem familiar to me at all." He shook his head as he took the garment off. "I'll hold on to it for a while and see. Maybe something will come back." A look of sadness was on his face and in his eyes. "You'd better get to work. The boss around here is ruthless. She could fire you if you don't get your chores done."

His effort to joke around his disappointment touched her. She swallowed hard and followed his lead.

"You're probably right. She wants another world champion, you know; I'd better go to work. I'll see you at lunch, if not before."

****

Another day had passed. As far as he knew, everyone else was asleep. Duke tried to keep his mind on the book he was reading, but couldn't seem to keep his eyes off the jacket draped over the chair at the foot of his bed. JBC, the initials monogrammed inside the jacket, haunted him. *Are those my initials? Who is JBC? Is he an honorable man?* There were no answers to these questions in Duke's mind. The deputy's visit this morning had scared him. He worried every time he saw a police officer. Since he didn't know his past, he couldn't get over the feeling he might be on the run from something or someone.

The doctor had told him there was no medical reason for his amnesia. What could he have done or what could have been done to him that was so bad it would erase his whole life from his mind? Sure the accident was bad, but he had lived through it. Why couldn't he remember?

One brown, full-quill ostrich boot. One light brown leather jacket with three initials monogrammed inside. The familiar smell of a horse barn. Not much of a lead to a person's past. He knew the boot was his. It molded to his foot and he was wearing it when he was brought to the hospital. The jacket could belong to anyone.

These thoughts kept running through Duke's mind until he reached the point of mental exhaustion, turned out the light and closed his eyes. He drifted off to sleep; his subconscious came alive.

Skyscrapers surrounded him. The concrete began to close in around him, causing him to experience a feeling of suffocation. He had to escape. Duke began to run; something was after him. He sensed his life was in danger. Looking down at his feet, he thought for this one time he'd trade the comfort of his cowboy boots for a pair of running shoes. He ran faster and faster. His breath became ragged. His chest ached, and he gasped for air. Duke felt an excruciating pain and was thrown into a sea of whirling, colored lights.

Duke awoke with a start and found himself drenched with perspiration. His heart pounded. He thought it would break through his chest wall. He could hardly catch his breath. The fear of being pursued was so overwhelming, even in his waking, that he flipped on the light beside the bed to check out the room. Everything looked the same, but his eyes locked on the brown jacket. Minutes passed before he turned out the light, but for most of the night, he lay awake in the darkness, afraid to close his eyes. Afraid to let the dream return. Afraid.

Morning brought a cheerful Jake to Duke's room. With a groan, Duke answered Jake's wake-up call. It seemed to Duke that he'd only just closed his eyes. A glance at the clock told him he wasn't far from wrong. If he had managed to get a couple hours sleep after that unnerving dream, it would have been a lot.

Duke looked up at the man standing over him.

"You look pretty ragged this morning," Jake said. "What's the matter? Couldn't you sleep?"

"No. I didn't sleep much."

"Well, come to think of it, you'd have a pretty hard time finding a comfortable position to sleep in, what with a broken leg on one side and broken arm on the other. I'll bet them bones are aching pretty good right about now, huh?"

Duke let Jake rattle on as he helped him wash and dress for the day. The dream still haunted him.

Addie looked up with a grin when Duke's wheelchair bumped over the threshold to the kitchen. Her welcoming smile faded just a bit as she looked into his face. Even though he smiled as he said good morning, she must have seen the fatigue in his eyes.

"You didn't sleep well, did you?"

Duke started to make light of it, but Addie's penetrating gaze made him decide to be honest with her, at least as far as his lack of sleep was concerned. "No. Jake noticed that himself. I must not have a good poker face. My bones were achy last night so I couldn't get comfortable."

Skylar walked in on the end of his confession.

"You should have called me when you couldn't sleep. I could have brought you some of the painkillers Russ prescribed. You didn't take any before you went to bed." Skylar walked over to the coffeemaker and poured two mugs of coffee. "I should have thought and left the bottle on your nightstand."

Duke took the mug Skylar handed him. "I haven't been needing them, and I didn't want to wake you up. Last night was a little out of the ordinary; I'll be fine." Duke took a sip of the coffee while trying to think of a way to change the subject. "Where's Redigo?"

"He went to Fort Worth. He should be home sometime this afternoon." Skylar helped Duke get his wheelchair up close to the table. "Everything seems fine with Redigo's Dream, so he felt comfortable leaving the horse in Billy's care for a few hours." Skylar set a plate of pancakes on the table. "Redigo said all that's been wrong with the horse in the first place was he was tired of Billy's company. Redigo's Dream wanted someone with a higher IQ to talk to him."

Duke laughed. "If that's the case, when Redigo gets back, I'll have to tell him I should have taken care of the horse not him."

They all laughed, and some of the tension began to ease from Duke's body.

"Well, from the lack of your tissue freckles this morning, I'd say you might regret Redigo coming back." Skylar seated herself at the table. "You had better watch what you say to him; you know he's half-Indian. He could do more than just nick you if you insult him." Skylar placed a stack of three pancakes on Duke's plate. "Jake seems to have a better hand when it comes to shaving someone else."

Duke grinned as he touched his jaw. "You're right about that. If I don't get this cast off my arm soon, Dr. Green may have to refer me to more than a plastic surgeon if I make Redigo unhappy. I'll save my insults for when I'm in one piece again."

The remainder of that Saturday was typical for a working horse ranch. Skylar and the hands fed and watered the stock, and then exercised the ones in training. Duke watched from the porch for a good part of the day, but when Addie found him dozing in his wheelchair that afternoon, she made him take a nap. Redigo's return from Fort Worth came in the late afternoon and dinner was lively with tales from Cowtown. Duke tried to keep himself awake that night by watching old movies on TV but fell asleep before the first one had been on for more than a few minutes.

Again his dream took him back to a city, but this time, as he was running, he saw himself loosen a tie and toss it into the air. Everywhere he looked he saw signs with large, bright flashing numbers. They surrounded him. He stopped and turned but found no escape from them. The numbers made no sense, but he knew he had to get away. Again, he was startled awake by the feel of excruciating pain and a flood of colored lights.

The same tenseness and panic gripped him as he lay in the dark trying to slow his breathing. Sweat beaded on his forehead. Reaching over, he shook two of the tablets into his hand from the bottle Skylar had left on his nightstand. Maybe they would bring him some uninterrupted sleep.

Chapter Seven

Sunday morning began about the same as any other day, but immediately after breakfast, the whole crew dressed for church. Duke tried to bow out saying he didn't have anything to wear, but Skylar squelched that argument when she brought out a new pair of trousers and a shirt. Redigo helped get Duke into the pick-up and put the wheelchair in the back.

Once at church Duke was overwhelmed with the excitement around him. These people acted like they were at a football game, not at church. They really got excited about worshiping God. After the service, everyone was friendly and made it a point to introduce themselves to him. The thing Duke found the hardest to comprehend was everyone promised they would pray for his health and that he would get his memory back soon.

He didn't know why that disturbed him; maybe he'd never had a close relationship with the God they were talking about. He couldn't even remember going to church, but he did recall some stories from the Bible. He remembered about Noah building an ark for the flood and Daniel in with the lions. Somewhere, he had learned a few things about the Bible; he just couldn't remember where. He wasn't sure prayer would help. He wasn't sure God had time for someone like him, but if these people wanted to pray, then more power to them.

Duke felt restless for the rest of the day. The people around him took the day of rest thing literally. They did as little around the ranch as they could. Had he fallen into some sort of cult? Strange.

****

Monday morning, Redigo and Jake helped Skylar load the wheelchair into the truck, and she drove Duke to Denton for his appointment with Russ. Russ examined Duke and x-rayed his arm and leg. After viewing the film,

Russ decided to put a walking cast on Duke's leg. As he applied the new cast, Skylar asked, "Where were you and Evelyn yesterday? I missed you at church."

Russ grinned. "We did something totally unheard of for the weekend. We escaped. I had Dr. Thompson take my calls, and Evelyn and I drove to Dallas. We got a hotel room and went to the theater Saturday night. I didn't even take my cell phone. No one knew where we were."

"It's about time you two took a little time for yourselves. If I were Evelyn, I'd have probably knocked you over the head a long time ago and kidnapped you."

"Hmm, that's an interesting thought; I'll have to tell Evelyn. We may want to try that one sometime. Of course, I think I'll leave out the part about hitting me over the head."

Russ looked up at Duke as he finished the cast. "Now, I put this walking cast on for you to be a little more independent, but it's not meant for you to run marathons. It'll allow you to move around the house a little more on your own, but don't try too much. Come back next week and I'll check it again. From the look of your arm, we may be able to get rid of that plaster cast and put you into a brace."

"Thanks, Dr. Green. My leg already feels much lighter. It's wonderful to be able to bend my knee again."

Russ and Skylar helped Duke to his feet. He wobbled a little, but with a steadying hand from Skylar and using the crutch Russ handed him, he was able to take a few steps for the first time in weeks.

"This is great. I can't wait to get back to the ranch. That chair has been a pain. With only one hand to use, it's hard to wheel in a straight line."

Skylar watched him as he walked around the room. His smile added wattage to the whole place. She glanced at Russ.

"Don't worry, Russ, I'll make sure he takes it easy."

"At least try to keep him off the backs of your horses. I don't want to have to put casts on the other leg and arm."

"I'll mind my manners, Doctor. I'll save the rides for a while, since I don't remember if I know how to ride. Walking will be a luxury," Duke said.

When they got back home, Duke behaved like a kid as he showed Addie his new freedom. Skylar stood back and watched with a smile as Duke performed his hobbling walk. His walk reminded Skylar of Marshal Dillon's deputy, Chester, as he thumped around the room.

****

The first couple of days after Duke got his walking cast on, he took it pretty easy. It amazed him how little strength he had. On the third day, he got cabin fever and managed to escape from Addie's watchful eye. She was a great lady but had eyes in the back of her head. The barn and horses were calling to him, so he eased his way to the closest stall. A chestnut stallion was stabled there, and Duke had been watching him from the porch for the past week.

The horse appeared on the young side and was pretty skittish from what Duke had observed. As he walked close to the stall, the young stallion eyed him warily while Duke began a soft conversation.

"Hey, boy. What's got you so nervous? This is a great place. They take good care of you here." Duke eased a little closer. "Come here and see what I've got for you."

Duke extended his good arm and tempted the horse with a half-eaten apple. He held his hand flat with the apple in the center of his palm.

The stallion's nostrils flared and his ears twitched back and forth a couple of times. He looked at Duke and appeared to be listening to his soft words. With a toss of his head that sent his long mane flying, the horse walked over to the door of his stall and nibbled at the apple a couple of times before he caught it with his teeth. He chewed hungrily and then sniffed Duke's hand looking for more.

Duke grinned and began to stroke the young horse's velvety soft nose as he quietly talked to the horse. The feel of the animal was so familiar he was sure he'd at least been around horses.

****

Redigo and Skylar were walking back toward the house when they spotted Duke with the new stallion. Skylar drew in a deep breath. Duke didn't know how dangerous that stallion could be. Then she realized the horse was relaxed in Duke's presence. So far Redigo was the only one who'd been able to get that close to the chestnut without him pitching a fit.

Redigo muttered something. "What?" Skylar asked as they neared the barn.

Redigo stood for a few moments looking at the young man talking to the horse. "Duke, you must have some Indian blood in you."

"Why would you say that?" Duke continued to gently stroke the horse's neck.

"Takes an Indian to gentle a wild one like that so quickly."

"Maybe I just talk his language; maybe he just wanted someone with higher intelligence to talk to him," Duke said.

Skylar saw Duke's lips twitch and knew he fought to keep his mirth in check. Then she looked over at her foreman to see his reaction.

"Nope, I'd just say he felt sorry for someone down on his luck." Redigo walked up to the door of the stall.

Skylar grinned. Redigo had finally met his equal.

Addie's voice from the back porch called them all to attention. "Duke, what do you mean walking all the way down to the barn? You looking to break that leg all over again? Get yourself back to this house."

Duke hung his head and tried to hide behind the horse. "Oops. Got caught by the truant officer."

Skylar smiled and opened the stall door for Duke. "Yep. She'll make your life miserable if you don't get back to the house. Come on. Redigo and I were headed that way for a breather anyway. We'll keep you company for a while. Maybe she'll forget about your excursion before we have to get back to work."

****

Duke had been asleep for several hours when his subconscious went to work. Once again the towering buildings and flashing numbers surrounded him, but Duke noticed the numbers were all in the thousands. There was one difference this time. Instead of flashing randomly, they lined up in columns like soldiers and pursued him. He felt an ache in his right arm. When he looked down, he could see something brown clutched in his right hand. He was holding on so tightly his knuckles were white. Before he could escape from the lines of marching numbers, some of them managed to disappear into the brown container he was clutching.

The same sense of fear stalked him, and once again, he was awakened when he saw the swirling, colored lights. When he shook himself completely awake, he realized his broken arm throbbed. Pain pulsed with his heartbeat. As he tried to steady his breathing, he worked at relaxing the muscles in his arm. He stared at his fingers as they peeked out from the end of the cast. What could he have been gripping so tightly in his dream? What was that brown container—a bag, a suitcase? Why would the numbers have disappeared into it?

He lay quietly listening to the stillness. He would have liked to blame these strange dreams on the painkillers. But the first night the dreams occurred here at the ranch, he had not taken anything. The second night he hadn't taken any of the pills until after he'd been awakened by the dream. Again tonight he hadn't taken anything for the pain before the dream started. Duke realized his subconscious was sending him messages. But for the life of him, he couldn't figure out what the recurring dream meant.

****

The next Saturday Addie worked most of the day getting things ready for a barbecue. She issued orders to one and all alike. Russ and Evelyn Green and Dan and Trina Tate were coming for supper, and Addie wanted everything to turn out right. She prided herself on her cooking, and everyone in the area was eager to get an invitation to one of her meals. She told Duke so as she engaged even him in her preparations.

Then Redigo chimed in claiming it was his old family recipe that made his barbecue renowned throughout Texas and most of the rest of the Southwest. Addie argued it was her fixings and desserts that really attracted everyone. Duke thought they were a funny pair.

Duke watched the self-proclaimed master at the barbecue grill. "Smells like the best I've ever had."

"Well, that don't mean nothin'. You don't even remember your own name. So are you telling me you remember eating barbecue?" Redigo asked.

"That's a low blow. Why don't you just kick a fellow while he's down?" Duke acted hurt as he went over and stuck his finger in the barbecue sauce to taste it. "Wimpy stuff. Why don't you add a little pepper to it?"

"That's for you city boys." Redigo lifted the lid on another pot. "This is for the real men."

Duke took the spoon Redigo offered. As soon as the dark sauce hit his tongue, Duke's eyes began to water. It took a few minutes, but he finally found his voice. "That's what I'd call fire sauce."

"Guess I should have mentioned that my daddy was Indian and taught me how to handle horses, but my momma was full-blooded Mexican, and she taught me how to cook." Redigo turned the meat cooking on the grill.

Duke mumbled to himself as he hobbled toward the house. "I'm going to make sure we have enough antacid. It's going to be heartburn city for anybody who eats that stuff. The preacher should use some of that sauce to demonstrate what Hell is like."

****

The first of April was warm and pleasant for an outdoor party. The guests arrived and began chatting. As they sat around waiting for the brisket to finish cooking, Skylar tattled on Duke to Russ.

"He's been down to the barn several times. We even caught him hobbling out to the course twice while I worked Skylark's Son. Would you talk to him, Russ?"

"Yes," Addie said. "Tell him to stay where he won't break that leg again."

"He's a big boy. You women need to stop acting like mother hens." Russ looked at Duke. "But I can understand their concern, so don't try to do too much. It won't be long before we get the casts off. Just remember that right now you're still off balance on the walking cast, so be extra careful."

"Dr. Green, you're not much help," Skylar looked at her cousin. "You were supposed to take my side."

"Sorry, cousin."

"Aw shucks, y'all quit pesterin' the boy. If he falls and breaks his leg again, we'll just shoot him like we'd do one of the horses." Redigo placed a slab of meat on the table.

"Now, Redigo, who was it that dogged the vet for weeks when that yearling you brought home broke his leg? I don't seem to remember you shooting him," Skylar reminded her foreman.

"Yeah, but he was worth money. I haven't found one thing that Duke's good for yet," Redigo said.

Skylar giggled with the rest of her friends. Redigo was beginning to loosen up about Duke. Her foreman seldom bothered to be sarcastic with people he didn't like.

"Money? Who was the horse worth money to? I seem to recall you sold him to the Simpson's kids for twenty bucks. That didn't even cover the vet's first visit." Dan laughed as he reached for his glass of tea.

"Yeah, I remember being consulted to check on the vet's work," Russ said. "First time I've ever consulted on a horse, and for free at that. I never could figure out how to charge for a horse call."

"I don't know why you couldn't. You doctors charge for everything else. Sit in your office for five minutes, and you send people a bill for fifty dollars. You didn't really do nothin' for the horse anyway. I'm the one who finally got him well, usin' my granddaddy's old remedy," Redigo said as he sliced the brisket.

"You would try and take all the credit." Russ reached over and grabbed a sample of the meat Redigo was carving.

Addie came out of the house at that point with Trina close at her heels.

Trina took over the conversation after that, and as they all began to eat, Trina told tales from the beauty shop she owned. She had bits of gossip on everyone who'd been in her shop that week. She glanced over at Duke as she finished one story.

"Duke, what line of work were you in before all your troubles started? Were you a rancher?"

Skylar had her mouth full of food and nearly choked. Trina didn't always think before she spoke.

Before Duke could answer, Dan gave his wife a reprimanding look. "Trina! I told you he has amnesia. Duke doesn't remember anything—nothing at all about his life."

"Amnesia? I thought you said he got amnesty," Trina said in all innocence.

The whole crowd roared with laughter.

Finally controlling his mirth Duke said, "Trina, I may need amnesty when I discover what my past is. So you remind Dan of that possibility if the time comes."

Dan looked relieved at the way Duke handled his wife's innocent blunderings. "Trina, dear, I love you, but you need to put that brain of yours in gear before you engage your mouth."

"Just keep it up, Deputy Dan, and just see what your hair looks like after I cut it the next time."

"Darlin', I'm just teasing. You wouldn't really butcher my hair, would you?"

"Depends on how well you grovel between now and then," Trina said with a waggle of her eyebrows.

The group gathered round the table all laughed at the couple's teasing exchange. Relief flowed through her when Skylar saw that Duke chuckled with the rest of them.

Before the guests left, they all wandered down to the barn for a look at Skylark's Son.

Dan looked over the stallion. "Skylar, are you sure you want to enter this nag in the Houston show?"

Playfully, she threw a handful of hay at her friend. "If you knew anything about horses, you'd know you were looking at the next world champion. You should be begging me to sell you an interest in him so you could make a little extra money when we put him to stud."

"Yeah, but that'd cause the captain to start asking a lot of nosy questions. He'd figure I was on the take if I began coming in with a lot more money than I should have on a cop's salary. It'd cause much more trouble than it's worth."

Skylar's muscles ached when she went to bed that evening, but it was a pleasant tiredness. The day had been fun. The kind of day the owner of a horse ranch seldom had the time for. As she lay in the darkness, she thought about her long-time friendship with Dan. It was nice to have a friend like him.

She chuckled as she remembered Russ asking her about Dr. Scott Mitchum. Russ and Evelyn had set them up a couple of months ago. They had dated a few times and enjoyed one another's company, but he seemed out of place on the ranch. Skylar knew she could never be happy anywhere else, so they had agreed to just remain friends.

She really didn't mind her cousin's interference in her love life. Skylar knew Russ only wanted her to be happy. The only man she'd met in a long time who looked like he belonged on a ranch was Duke. That revelation surprised her. She'd never consciously thought of Duke in any way except as a person who needed help; someone who needed a friend. What did she know about him? Nothing. He knew nothing about himself. For all they knew, he could have a wife and five kids somewhere, but his personality and courage did give him an irresistible charm. Skylar fell asleep with pleasant thoughts on her mind.

****

The next morning Duke felt good, relaxed—more so than in all the time he'd been at the ranch. From the laughter he heard as he made his way into the kitchen, he realized the rest of the household must feel the same way.

"Morning, everyone," Duke said. He sat in his usual place next to Redigo. "Great party last night."

Redigo leaned back in his chair, coffee cup in hand. "Place is never dull when Trina's around."

"Redigo…" Addie gave the older man a pointed look.

"Just speaking a bit of the truth." Redigo's grin flashed at the housekeeper.

Duke wondered how deep the friendship between Addie and Redigo went, but Skylar distracted him as she settled into her chair. She had already dressed for church. Duke's sense of contentment slid. He had been going to church with Skylar and Addie, but to tell the truth he was uncomfortable there. Maybe it was the open acceptance of the people who shared bits of their lives with him. He couldn't do the same and was often at a loss.

Addie's words to Redigo drew Duke's attention.

"You're not dressed for church, old man."

"Nope." Redigo took a piece of toast and slathered it with grape jelly.

"Now…"

"Don't give me no grief about not going to church—

I've got a sick horse to tend."

"Hmmph. Seems to me you manage to come up with more excuses to not attend church than any man I've ever known." Addie attacked her eggs, turning her attention to Duke.

He wanted to bolt, but Addie's eyes pinned him to his chair.

"Young man, you don't look dressed for church either."

Duke tried to swallow his sausage past the lump in his throat. "No, ma'am. I thought I'd stay here and help Redigo." His excuse sounded lame even to him.

"See there, now you've started Duke skipping church."

Duke hated that the atmosphere at the table had turned dark. Maybe he should rethink going to church, but Skylar saved him before he could comment.

"Addie, if we've got an ailing horse, someone needs to take care of it. This is the hands' weekend off. You know what the Bible says about taking care of the ox in the ditch." Skylar looked at Duke as she continued. "It does sometimes take two people to take care of a sick horse."

Skylar was as good as Addie about pinning a man with her stare. With that one look, Duke knew she saw through his excuse. Duke broke eye contact, starting a conversation with Redigo about the horse in need of care.

A short while later, Skylar and Addie drove off with a wave.

Redigo gave Duke a nod. "Ready?"

"Sure." Leaning on the rail, Duke took the steps with care. The walking cast was great but felt a bit unsteady going down stairs. Once on the ground he hobbled a couple steps behind the ranch foreman.

Glancing around at the blue sky above him, Duke decided it would be a perfect Easter in a few weeks, if the weather held. He couldn't believe it had been almost three weeks since he had arrived at the Lazy M. Time had a way of passing without a person realizing it. Duke still had no idea who he was or where he came from, and that bothered him.

In the barn, the ailing mare refocused Duke's attention to the moment at hand. He took a deep breath and stepped into the stall to hold the mare steady while Redigo tended a cut on the mare's foreleg.

Chapter Eight

Monday afternoon, Duke walked into the kitchen and found Addie baking brownies. He reached over and took one of the warm treats from the plate before asking, "Where's Skylar? I want to show her my surprise."

"What surprise?" Addie looked up as he took a bite out of the brownie. She scolded him. "Just like a kid. You can't wait; you have to snitch a brownie behind my back."

Duke noticed the smile on Addie's face and knew she was teasing. "Addie, your cooking is so good I just can't help myself." He took another bite of the brownie. "Where did Skylar run off to?"

"She's in her office." Addie noticed his arm. "You got your cast off. That's wonderful. Go on in. Skylar will be thrilled."

The dismayed look on her face and her mumbling as he stepped into Skylar's small office told him she was angry. She was talking to the computer as though it was alive; the conversation was so animated she didn't notice him enter the room.

"You stupid machine! I should just throw you in the trash. And I would, if you hadn't cost so much money. Money down the drain, I guess." Skylar randomly punched keys on the keyboard.

"Boy, I'm glad I'm not that computer. What did it ever do to you to make you so mad?"

Skylar jumped and looked back over her shoulder when Duke spoke to her. "How long have you been standing there?"

"Long enough to know you have a terrible grudge against an inanimate object. What seems to be the problem?" He walked over and stood behind her chair.

"I bought this machine because it was supposed to make things simpler, but instead everything has become more complicated. I can't make heads or tails of this manual, so I can't get my bookkeeping program set up. This thing is no good to me!"

Duke pulled a chair up beside her at the computer, "Here let me see what I can do." Without thinking, he began to punch keys and in no time at all had the bookkeeping program installed and showing on the screen. "Where are your accounts payable?"

She opened her ledger and silently pointed at the page he wanted. "How did you do that?"

Her question startled him. His mouth felt as dry as cotton. How did he know how to install and run the program?

"I don't know." That was the truth. Duke looked at the ledger she showed him. He did understand what he needed to do with the information. "Do you just want this month's put on, or do you want to go back to the first of the year?"

"The first of the year, if that's possible," Skylar said. Her eyes were wide with amazement at his ability to handle the program.

"No problem. Is this all of them?"

Skylar nodded at his question. Duke began to enter the information. Accounts, amounts, check numbers, balances still due. He did it all with ease.

It took Duke about forty-five minutes to enter the accounts payable for the first three months of the year. When he had completed that, he moved on and asked for any accounts receivable.

"It's amazing how you can do that." Skylar watched as Duke's hands punched the numbers on the keyboard.

Duke didn't understand it all himself. "When I saw the computer, I just knew I could work it. It all came naturally to me. I didn't think about it," he shrugged. "Now what about those receivable accounts?"

"I just noticed. You don't have a cast on your arm."

"Got it off this morning. It's great to have my arm free.

"Are you sure you should be typing? I don't want you to do anything you're not supposed to."

"Dr. Green only said not to lift anything. It feels fine. I'm just a little slow with that hand if you hadn't noticed. It feels pretty stiff, but this should be good exercise.

Maybe it will help limber up my fingers."

Duke began to work on the few accounts receivable and then moved on to payroll. After he entered all the information, he printed a profit and loss sheet for each month. As he stared at the screen with all the numbers lined up in neat columns, something clicked in his mind. Could the numbers in his dream be part of another bookkeeping system he had worked with somewhere? Could possibly be an accountant? He appeared to be familiar with computers and knowledgeable of accounting. Since the numbers in his dream were bright, maybe he had seen them on a computer screen somewhere. Computer screens were bright.

If he were an accountant, why would he have such a sense of fear in his dreams? Had he done something illegal? Maybe stolen money from someone? If he'd done that, he must have hidden it, because he certainly didn't have it on him. What if he had worked for the mob and they were after him? And what about the numbers disappearing into that brown container? Still very little information to help him find his past.

Duke heard Skylar's voice, and it brought him back from his thoughts. He heard his heartbeat pounding in his ears. "What did you say?"

"I said, I can't believe you did that. I've been trying for weeks to make sense of this machine and get my bookkeeping on it. You sit down and in a matter of a couple of hours have it all up and running. You're a genius!"

"Maybe that's who I am. A computer genius. A whiz of modern technology. Maybe I'm a wealthy millionaire who owns a computer design company." Duke laughed, trying to joke away his anxiety.

"Don't laugh. It has been done before. You might just be the inventor of some well known technology." Skylar stood and placed the printouts Duke had given her in the filing cabinet.

"My technology might be well known, but I must not be since no one appears to be looking for me. If I did invent something famous, I could do one of those old American Express commercials and say, 'You don't know me but...'."

"Well, if you did do a commercial maybe someone would recognize you. It might not be a bad idea. Not an American Express commercial, but maybe we could get you a spot on one of the Dallas TV stations and say, 'Do you know this man?' What do you think?"

Duke looked in amazement at the woman standing beside him. "I think you're crazy. That would cost a small fortune."

"Not if we got you on the news. They're always looking for human-interest stories. Why don't we give them a call?"

His hand shook at the suggestion. Was it using his hand so much doing the typing, or was it fear? He gulped.

"I want to find out who I am, but I don't know if I'm ready to go on television. I think I'll put a hold on that idea for a while, if that's okay with you."

"Whatever you say. We could run an ad in the Dallas paper. It gets wide circulation."

Something about all the suggestions for publicity made him squirm. He needed some breathing space.

"I think I'll stretch out for a while. I'm tired."

****

New York City

"The private investigator still has no leads. I don't see how a man can just totally disappear from the face of the earth unless he's dead," the young man commented to the platinum blonde seated across from him in his richly appointed office.

"Don't under estimate Brett. He's very resourceful. I wouldn't buy flowers for his memorial yet," the blonde said as she stroked the man's hand with her perfectly manicured fingernails.

"What does the boss have to say about the situation?" the young man asked. Sweat beaded up on his upper lip. He wiped it away with the back of his hand. Standing up, he strode across the room to the wet bar and refilled his tumbler with expensive whiskey.

"He still believes there was some foul play. He can't believe Brett left of his own accord."

"Maybe it's time we let him make the discovery that his well-trained puppy is an embezzler," the young man suggested, taking a long swig of his drink. The ice bumped against the crystal making it tinkle like high-pitched chimes ringing.

"That's fine by me," the young woman replied. "It's time the boss met the real Brett."

****

Lazy M Ranch

Duke adjusted the covers on his bed for the tenth time. He couldn't get comfortable. His back felt as tight as a spring. He hated for night to come. The strange dreams still haunted him and wouldn't go away. It wouldn't be so bad if they were leading him anywhere. The evening air felt pleasant, so Duke had left the window up in his room. He lay in the dark listening to the call of a bobwhite in the distance and finally drifted off to sleep.

This time when the dream started Duke wasn't racing down a city street. He walked into a large plush office and seated himself behind the huge mahogany desk. He saw himself turning on the computer in front of him. For some reason, he had a little trouble accessing the file. The password had always worked before, but this time the words 'Access Denied' kept flashing on the screen. Someone had changed his password. Finally he gained entry to the file with a different password.

Duke could see himself staring at a screen full of numbers. Something told him the numbers didn't add up right. In his dream, he made copies of all the files, and he saw himself drop the disks into a brown leather briefcase. As the disks disappeared into the briefcase, he began to feel the throbbing pain and see the flashing lights before he jerked awake.

He lay in the dark trying to calm his racing heart once again. The cool breeze from the window swept across his hot brow. Duke got up and pulled on his jeans and shirt and tried to find his way to the front porch without disturbing anyone.

Much to his surprise when he opened the front door, he saw Skylar sitting in the swing. "I didn't expect to find anyone else up at this hour." Duke closed the door as he walked out onto the porch.

"I just couldn't get to sleep. Too much on my mind I

guess."

"What turmoil are you trying to solve?" Duke leaned against one of the posts supporting the roof of the porch.

"Nothing in particular, and a lot of stuff in general." Skylar looked up into his face.

"Well, that really narrows things down." Duke chuckled.

"What are you doing up?"

Duke stood in silence for a long time. Should he confide in Skylar about his dreams?

Skylar must have noticed his hesitation. "Are you okay?"

Duke slowly made his way over to the swing and sat down beside her. He rubbed his leg. He had gotten the cast off earlier that day and his leg felt stiff. He sat quietly for a few more moments. "Something woke me up."

"I hope it wasn't me. I bumped into the coffee table when I walked through the living room."

"No, it wasn't you. I get awakened almost every night." Duke could feel her gaze on him but refused to look her way.

"Is there anything I can do to help?"

"No." He knew his answer had sounded rather curt. "I'm sorry. I didn't mean to be so short with you." He decided to take the risk and tell her about the nightmares. "I keep having dreams. They all seem to be related to each other, but they don't make much sense to me."

"If you'd like to talk about them, I'd be glad to listen." Her voice was soft and sincere.

Duke hesitated before he began to tell Skylar about his recurrent nightmares. "Well, at first I would see myself running through what appeared to be the street of a very big city. Something or someone seemed to be chasing me. Then I kept seeing numbers."

"Numbers? What kind of numbers?"

Duke rubbed the back of his neck.

"I know this sounds crazy, but just columns and columns of numbers. Tonight though it was a little different. Tonight I saw myself in a big office, and I downloaded some files off a computer. I put the disks into a brown leather briefcase. The dreams all end the same. I feel terrible pain and see flashing lights, and then I wake up."

"The pain and the flashing lights are probably your subconscious remembering your accident, but the rest...I don't know. Did anything look familiar? Anything about the surroundings?"

"I know in the first dreams I felt real fear. Tonight, when the dream started, I didn't feel fear. I seem to be very at ease in that office. As I stared at the computer screen and those numbers, a sick feeling began to rise up in me."

"Can you remember anything about the numbers or the computer?" Skylar began to move the swing slowly back and forth as she pushed against the porch with her foot.

"I do remember the password I used to access the file. The first password I tried didn't work, and I remember thinking someone had changed my code. Then I tried another and it worked."

"What was the password?"

"The first one was Lone Star and the second was Texas." Duke finally began to relax with the swaying of the swing.

"Then maybe you're from Texas. Maybe the big city was Houston or even Dallas."

"Could be. With those passwords, you'd naturally think about Texas."

"I have an idea. Why don't we go into Dallas tomorrow and walk around downtown. Maybe something will jar your memory."

"Are you sure you have time for that? The horse show in Houston is Saturday."

"Yeah. Billy can give Skylark's Son his workout. I have some papers that I have to see a lawyer about anyway, and my lawyer just happens to be in downtown Dallas."

"Now that's what I call coincidence." Duke smiled at his beautiful companion under the moonlight.

Chapter Nine

The morning dawned bright and clear. Duke awakened with a lighter mind and spirit. For the first time since waking up in the hospital, he truly felt a small ray of hope. It was the hope he would eventually know who he was and where he had come from. He'd tried not to be too depressed, but the more time that had passed, the more he felt his life might not ever come back. Today's trip to Dallas dangled a golden nugget in front of him.

They took off for Dallas a little after nine o'clock. By eleven o'clock, they had visited Skylar's lawyer and given him the papers. As they left the building, Duke looked around the street. He wanted something to jump out at him and shout, "Hey, you know me. I'm where you come all the time." But nothing on Elm Street did. Sadness pressed in on him as though the tall buildings around him had collapsed.

"Let's walk up the street for a while and see if something seems familiar." Skylar began to move down the sidewalk leading further into the downtown area.

Duke fell in step beside her. "Fine with me."

Skylar pointed out several landmark buildings as they walked, but nothing stirred his memory. By the time they had walked a few blocks around the downtown area, Duke's leg felt like it weighed thirty pounds more than his good one. He realized his limp had become more exaggerated.

"Duke, you look worn out. Why don't we head for the restaurant on the corner and have some lunch?"

Being able to sit down for a while sounded even more inviting than lunch did so he agreed to her suggestion. They timed it just right to beat the lunch crowd and were seated in moments.

Duke and Skylar studied the menus in silence. Skylar finally looked over the top of hers. "Well, what looks good to you?"

Duke shrugged. "I'm not sure. Have you eaten here before?"

"Yes. My father used to bring me here. Everything is good." Skylar laid her menu to the side. "I'm going to have the Chicken Kiev."

Duke laid his menu on top of Skylar's. "Sounds good. I think I'll join you."

The waiter came over and took their orders. As he walked away, Skylar looked across the table at Duke. Her expectant gaze made Duke sorry he would have to disappoint her. "I didn't recognize anything."

He must have let the ache he felt show through. It was the first time he'd really ever let anyone see he wasn't as confident as he wanted everyone to believe. She reached out a hand to cover his. Electricity seemed to jump from his hand to hers.

Skylar must have noticed the spark because she jerked her hand away from his and tried to ignore it as she offered him another smile. "We'll just have to keep trying then. Maybe it wasn't Dallas. Houston's…"

Stopping in mid-sentence, Skylar stared at him. He could almost see her brain working as she made up her mind about something. She motioned to their waiter.

"What are you doing?" Duke asked.

"I'm going to cancel our order; we're leaving for the airport. Love Field is just a little way from here. They have flights to Houston about every thirty to forty-five minutes. We can catch the next available one and be in Houston in less than an hour."

Duke gave her a look of disbelief as another lead weight dropped into the bag that took the place of his heart. "We can't do that."

"Why not?" Skylar stood to her feet.

"Another historical event I remember is 9/11. Skylar, I don't have any identification. I can't get on an airplane."

Skylar sat back down at the table. "I didn't think of that, but you're right. I guess we'll just have to drive to Houston."

Duke looked across the table at the woman so willing to help him. She looked as crestfallen as he felt about not recognizing downtown Dallas. "Maybe someday but not today. You have a ranch to run and a horse show to get ready for. Not to mention, I've about had it for one day; my leg is really starting to ache. I don't think I could walk around another city even if I could get there today."

"Duke, I'm so sorry. I've been so excited about helping you get your memory back that I have probably pushed you a little too hard today. We'll go back to the ranch and then we can work something out about getting to Houston."

****

As they drove back, Skylar glanced at the quiet man sitting in the truck beside her. His face showed his tiredness as he stared out the window at the passing countryside.

"Today was a waste of time," Duke mumbled.

"Maybe not. Just because you didn't recognize anything in Dallas doesn't mean you're not from Texas. There's still Houston, Austin, San Antonio, even Fort Worth."

Duke interrupted before she could say more. "We're not driving to every city in Texas just to see if I recognize something. It's too much of a long shot. There's got to be another way."

"I guess that would be a little impractical." Skylar nodded in agreement. "But if that's the only lead we've got, we may have to consider it."

Duke turned and faced her. "Skylar, you're something else. I'll just remain Duke Green. It's beginning to grow on me."

Skylar sat still for a moment. Today must have been taxing on this man she was trying to help. Another thought came to her. "How would someone go about breaking into a company's computer?"

"Why do you want to know that?"

"You said in your dream you got some files off a computer. If we could get access to the computer, maybe we could track your past."

"Good plan, Skylar. The only problem is we don't know the company's name. We'd have to access every company's computer in the country. I think the FCC would catch up after about the first hundred or so." Duke shook his head and turned his gaze back to the countryside.

"Well, it was just an idea. Maybe you'll get the name of the company in your next dream. Try real hard to see the name of the building you're in okay." Skylar chuckled.

"Sure I will. I'll just write myself a memo, so I'll remember to do that tonight. Wouldn't want to waste time waiting for it to come up randomly."

Duke's half-hearted attempt at a joke fell flat. Tears welled up in her eyes, and she had to blink repeatedly to keep them from spilling over onto her cheeks. This man's situation affected her more than she had realized. She needed to keep her distance. There was a good chance he was married. She had to keep reminding herself that this was an act of kindness like that of the Good Samaritan.

****

Duke gazed around at the crowd, noticing that three-day eventing must be a sport for the rich and famous. The crowd didn't seem to fit the "good ole boy" feeling he got when he was at the Lazy M. These people drove expensive cars and wore diamonds on every finger.

Over a week had passed since Skylar had driven him to Dallas. In her own way, she had managed to get him to Houston after all. Duke was helping Redigo saddle the horses and check the equipment when he spotted Skylar walking across the parking lot in her new riding habit. Dressed like that, in the midst of the other people present, he realized she fit in nicely. There was more to Skylar McCrea than he realized.

Skylar asked Duke to walk with her to the starting area. Just before she mounted Skylark's Son, she bowed her head and closed her eyes. It appeared to Duke that she was praying, so Duke stood silently until she lifted her head.

"Were you asking God for a win?"

"No. Just a safe ride and a safe weekend for everyone. Besides it wouldn't do me any good if I asked Him for a win. You see God is no respecter of persons. He doesn't love me any more than anybody else. He won't help any of us win, but He will watch over our safety."

Duke made no comment as he gave her a leg up. There was a whole lot more to Skylar McCrea than he'd thought.

First I'm Nobody

****

Addie stepped to the door when the caravan returned from Houston late Sunday evening. As they pulled to a stop beside the barn she called, "How'd he do?"

Skylar's trilled her happy reply. "He took a second place."

Duke helped get the horses fed and settled for the evening, thinking back to the weekend. He had not had the time to focus on his own problems. It was good to be busy and to be a part of this group.

Skylar had taken him for a drive around downtown Houston before they had headed home. Nothing about the large city had brought forth any hidden memories. It shadowed the fun of the weekend but didn't fully eclipse it. If he wrote out a list, he knew there would be more items on the positive side. Duke patted Skylark's Son on the neck as he latched the stall door. The warm firmness of the stallion's muscular neck comforted him. Yes. It had been a good weekend.

Lying in the darkness later that night, Duke could picture Skylar as she and Skylark's Son ran the course yesterday. They fit together so perfectly that it appeared as though they were of one mind as Skylar guided her young mount across the obstacles. He compared her to the other women he'd seen in Houston during the day. There had been some beautiful women at the arena, but Skylar had a special radiance around her. Her smile looked somehow more genuine. There was more than that. Her eyes reflected a knowing. Of what Duke wasn't sure since he had no memories to fit it to. One thing he did know was he'd been unable to keep his eyes away from her.

He chastised himself. He shouldn't be thinking about Skylar this way. No one knew anything about him. Without a past, he could not think about the future. Without his permission, his mind went back once more to Houston. This time his mind's eye settled on the picture of Skylar praying beside Skylark's Son. She really believed what she gave voice to. Her faith was real. Duke wondered if this God could help him find his past. Oh, well, he'd think about that later. Sleep finally overtook him.

His mind reached that deep dream-stage of sleep. He

saw himself in an elevator. Several people were crowded around him, but none of them had faces. The elevator doors opened and Duke walked out into an elaborately decorated lobby. He seemed to be in a big hurry as he moved through the revolving doors. He began to race down the sidewalk. Then nothing. A peaceful darkness held him.

****

After finishing her daily Bible reading and prayer time that night, Skylar turned out the lamp. Lying back against the pillows, she thought about the weekend's events. She thanked God for the trip. Most of her thoughts were happy but Duke's dilemma always tainted her happiness. She had prayed and prayed he would have a breakthrough in his memory. She guessed her prayers were being answered in a way through his dreams. She knew God spoke to people through their dreams, so maybe tonight he would learn something new and more helpful than he'd gotten so far.

Skylar smiled as she thought about Duke. He had seemed to fit so perfectly into her world this weekend. He'd made himself at home on the ranch, but he'd been just as comfortable in the different atmosphere of the horse show. He was really the first man since Timothy who had fit so well into all of her world.

Skylar blocked out the thoughts of her former boyfriend right now, and she shouldn't be thinking of Duke as anything but a friend. She knew it was possible he had a wife and family somewhere. Allowing anything more than friendship might lead to problems later. Determinedly she said another prayer to God for strength and patience in waiting for His will to be done. She turned over on her side. Relaxing, as the peace she always felt after her talks with God slid over her, she drifted to sleep.

****

For the first time in weeks, Duke woke up feeling somewhat rested. Suddenly he remembered he hadn't been awakened during the night by his vivid dream of pain and flashing lights. After breakfast, he walked with Skylar to the barn.

"Did you have a dream last night?"

"No, I got a good night's rest for a change." As Duke led Skylark's Son out to the course, his mind flashed back to a big lobby with lots of people milling around. He suddenly stopped, and Skylar walked up beside him. "Wait. I just realized I did dream last night."

"Well, tell me about it."

"I remember being in an elevator with several other people."

"Did you recognize anybody?" Excitement lit up her face.

"No. None of them had faces. It's really kind of strange. I got off the elevator and hurried through this really fancy lobby. When I went through the revolving door, I began to run down the street." Duke paused in concentration. "That's all I remember."

They moved closer to the course. "At least we know we're looking for a building with a revolving door."

"That really narrows it down, Skylar. There shouldn't be more than two or three hundred of those in every city in the United States. We can start looking today." Duke smiled. Her enthusiasm tugged at his heart.

"Well, at least it's something. Can you remember anything you saw outside of the building? Did you see any kind of sign?"

"No. That's all I can remember now."

Skylar sighed. "Oh, well, maybe something will come to you later. Let's get to work." She took the reins from Billy and mounted her horse.

****

Duke was sitting in the front porch swing as the sun was going down that evening. Skylar walked out the door and handed him a large glass of fresh lemonade. "The sunset's beautiful tonight."

"Huh? Sorry, Skylar, my mind was elsewhere." He moved over and made room for her in the swing.

Skylar sat down beside him. "Where was it?"

"What? Oh, my mind...back in my dream. A while ago, I remembered a little more about last night's dream. As I ran out the door I remember glancing up and seeing a big sign. I remember the letters J A C."

"J-A-C? That's all? No words, no name?"

"That's it." His words sounded clipped and sharp in

his own ears. Duke took a sip of his lemonade.

"I'm sorry," Skylar said. "I don't mean to make you uncomfortable. I just want so much for you to get your memory back. Please forgive me." She dropped her gaze to the porch.

Duke sat for a moment looking at the petite blonde beside him. "Skylar, forgive me. Of all the people in the world, I should never be short with you."

Skylar lifted her head and turned to face him. "Duke, in case you haven't noticed, I can be rather pushy. Just let me know if I butt in where I don't belong."

"You...pushy?" Duke laughed. "I guess I'm too touchy at times. I get really frustrated. Forgive me."

Skylar smiled. "Forgiven."

The two sat in silence for a brief time.

"How would you go about tracking down a company?" Skylar asked.

"Phone books, Wall Street listings, census records, things like that."

"Could you do it with a computer?"

Duke's eyebrows pulled together. "If you had the right computer and equipment."

"A friend of mine teaches computer programming at the University of North Texas. You think they might have a computer that would do it?"

"Probably." Duke looked at Skylar and wondered what was going on in that pretty head of hers.

"You want me to call her?" Skylar smiled.

"I have no objection if you call your friend."

"Not just call her to talk to her. Call her to see if you can use her computer. Maybe you could come up with a company to match the JAC."

Duke stood and walked to the edge of the porch. "You think she'd let me?"

Skylar moved to stand by Duke. "I know she would. She loves mysteries."

"Well, this is a major mystery all right. I guess we could give it a try. There shouldn't be more than about a million companies with those letters in their name."

"Duke, you think so positively all the time. You really need to think more conservatively."

Her enthusiasm was contagious. Duke's spirits lifted.

****

"Dixie, thanks so much for helping us. It's really great of you to let us use the system. This is Duke Green. Duke, Dixie McCall."

"It's my pleasure. Mysteries are my passion. You should see my library at home. Now let's see what we can come up with." Dixie sat in front of a glowing computer screen.

"All I remember are the letters on a sign. J-A-C is all I could see in my dream."

Setting up the computer for a search, Dixie began specifying the range they needed to cover. Telling the computer to list only the companies in cities larger than 100,000 people, she struck the key that began the search. After a few moments the computer's screen flashed and a list of several thousand records popped up.

Duke realized this could take hours. "In my dream, it seemed as though I ran forever surrounded by skyscrapers. Have the search start with cities of at least 500,000." That produced a list of 150 names.

"That thing won't give us a list of which ones of those companies have revolving doors on their buildings, will it?" Skylar's voice had a hopeful edge to it.

Dixie shook her head. "That'd take a much more specific search range than we have to go from."

As they looked over the list, they found only 15 companies in Texas. Skylar looked unhappy. "These are spread all over the state. That leaves 135 strung out across the rest of the country. This could take years to track down. How do we start?"

"Duke, do you remember anything else? Something more specific?" Dixie asked.

"In one dream, I did access a computer, and I remember the passwords."

"Well, that would only help us if we could hack into the computers of all these companies which is kind-of out of the question." Dixie smiled.

"Thanks for all your help anyway. I'll take this list and study it. Maybe something will strike a cord." Duke folded the paper and stuck it in his pocket.

"Thanks, Dixie. Let me know if I can return the favor somehow." Skylar followed Duke to the door.

"Just keep me informed so I don't drive myself nuts trying to figure this out. Good luck, Duke."

Chapter Ten

New York City

"Mr. Jacobs, I just wanted to update you on what our men in the field have been able to find out," the FBI agent told the tall, gray-haired man seated behind the desk.

"I hope your men have been able to find out more than that pathetic private investigator I hired three months ago," the older man stated. "Mr. Douglas, this is my daughter, Victoria, and the acting vice-president of the company, Jordan Matthews. I wanted them to hear your findings also."

"Well, your man had tracked the suspect to Chicago but had been unable to come up with any leads from there. Our men located a cab driver who recognized the photo and remembered driving the suspect to a large discount store near the airport. It took some doing, but we interviewed every employee in the store before finally finding a girl who remembered him," the agent told the group.

"So, what good does that do us?" Jordan asked.

Douglas noticed Matthews tapping a pen against the palm of his hand.

"Every lead helps. Just let me finish, please," Mr. Douglas stated.

The older man behind the desk reprimanded his young colleague and instructed the agent to continue.

"Well, this girl remembered him because he went into the dressing room and put on a pair of jeans and a western shirt. When he came out, he told her he wanted to wear the clothes and asked her to cut off the tags. He handed her his suit and told her to give it to Goodwill. She noticed the suit because it was an Armani. She became suspicious and called security. She was afraid he had stolen the suit and was going to try to walk out of the store without paying for the new clothes. Security followed him. The suspect picked up a couple more pairs of jeans and shirts, some underwear and a backpack and then paid for it all. Leaving the store, he got in a cab and went to a hotel near the airport."

"So where did he go next?" the older man asked.

"That's all we've got so far. He didn't check in at the hotel, at least that anyone remembers. We've shown his picture all over the airport to every flight attendant we can find, but no one remembers him. There's no record of a Brett Carlisle buying a ticket; he'd have to have some fake identification to use another name. We've checked the bus terminal and trains. Nothing. After buying the clothes, he got very good at covering his tracks," the agent told them.

"Could he be dead?" Victoria asked.

The agent looked at the young woman asking the question. "That is a possibility. But so far we've not been able to turn up anything in the John Doe department either. This fellow's either very good or very lucky." The agent paused and took a sip from the water glass sitting in front of him. "We have people watching his family, too. Nothing there either. He hasn't contacted them."

"You are continuing the search, aren't you?" Jordan asked as he stood and began to pace the room.

"Naturally. We won't stop until we get him. There's a lot of money involved," Special Agent Douglas told him.

"I still find it hard to believe Brett stole from me," the older man said as he ran his fingers through his gray hair.

"The evidence is rather conclusive against him, sir," the agent stated.

"I know. Thank you, Mr. Douglas. Please keep us informed. Now if you'll excuse me, I have business to attend to."

The gray-haired gentleman stood and shook hands with Douglas before the agent left the room. FBI Special Agent Douglas closed the door behind him. The short hairs on the back of his head stood up. He rubbed the back of his neck. That was an interesting exchange. Very interesting.

****

Lazy M Ranch

Billy and Jake were headed out to feed the herd of cattle when a tire went flat on the pick-up they were driving. Jake stopped the truck and the men got out to survey the situation. Billy walked to the driver's side of the truck and pulled the back of the seat forward to remove the jack. Seeing a briefcase behind the seat, he picked it up and turned to his partner.

"Where'd this come from?"

Jake was puzzled for a few moments. "Oh, I found it beside the road a few weeks ago when I was mending fence. I picked it up, threw it behind the seat and forgot it."

The men placed the case in the front seat, went about their job of changing the tire and then feeding the livestock.

Arriving back at the main barn, Billy indicated the briefcase. "What do you want to do with this?"

"Just leave it here. We'll give it to Skylar later. We've got hungry horses to feed right now."

Skylar and Duke walked out to the barn and greeted Billy and Jake, "Morning guys."

"How's it going?" Skylar inquired.

"Fine, Skylar. By the way, we found this." Jake began to explain as he reached inside the pickup to retrieve the briefcase and hand it to her. As he finished his story, Skylar fumbled with the latches that refused to open. Without a word, Skylar and Duke turned and raced back toward the house leaving Jake mystified at their disappearance.

****

Dashing into the kitchen, Skylar pulled open a drawer in the cabinet and reached for a screwdriver. Duke placed the briefcase on the table and explained to Addie where it had come from. "It's got the same initials as the jacket Skylar found."

"Jake said he found this near our fence just across the highway from where Duke's accident happened. Both of them have got to belong to Duke. It's just too coincidental," Skylar finished. Excitement quickened her breathing.

Pushing the tip of the screwdriver beneath the right latch, Skylar began to try to open it. Addie's voice interrupted Skylar's efforts. "Wait. Why are you prying that open?"

"It's got combination locks, and we don't have the combination."

"Don't you think we should let the authorities do that? After all, it might not belong to Duke."

Skylar glanced over at Duke before answering. "Maybe there's some identification inside that will trigger Duke's memory. I think he should have the first look inside."

Duke stared back at Skylar. "It might also hold something that will tell us I'm in trouble with the law."

"If it does we'll deal with it later. Meanwhile, I'm going to open it. Jake found it on my property. I have a right to know what's inside," Skylar said.

Then with a grunt, she gave the screwdriver a vicious upward thrust. With a twang, the latch sprang open. Encouraged by her success, Skylar attacked the other latch, but it proved much more stubborn. Duke took their makeshift pry bar from Skylar's hand and continued her efforts. Their reward came a couple of minutes later as the last latch relinquished its hold.

With nothing standing in the way, he slowly opened the case. At first glance, the contents looked disappointing. An ordinary manila file folder contained a computer printout with columns of numbers and a computer disk. A small cell phone was the remainder of the case's contents.

Taking the disk out Skylar asked, "Do you think my computer would let us into the files on this disk?"

"I don't know, but we could try."

Taking the case and its contents to her office, Duke turned on the computer and loaded the disk. An error message flashed onto the screen drowning their hopes. "Well, I guess it was too much to ask."

While he had been trying the disk, Skylar had taken the file folder out and begun to search through the printout. When the computer failed to read the disk, she turned back to the printout. Realizing it was opened to the middle, Skylar turned the pages until she reached the

beginning. Centered on the first page was:
Jacobs Industries
Year-End Financial Statement
January 31—4:45 p.m.

"Duke, look!" Skylar thrust the sheaf of pages into Duke's hand.

Duke read the words on the page. Raising his eyes back up, he saw Skylar waiting, her blue eyes open wide in expectation. A bitter taste filled his mouth. Duke didn't know what he'd expected when they opened the case. He guessed he'd been waiting for his memory to miraculously come back, or for something in the case to be waiting to tell him exactly who he was and what his life was like. That hadn't happened. The words on the page told him little more than a telephone book would have. He thrust the pages back to Skylar and sat down at the desk.

"What's wrong, Duke?"

"This means nothing to me."

"It's something new, something more than you had before. And look, this printout is a year-end statement for this company. Duke, it's full of numbers. This has got to be connected to your dreams. You said they were filled with columns of numbers, large numbers. Maybe this is what your mind was trying to make you remember." She pulled up another chair and perched on its edge.

Taking the printout back from her, Duke scanned through the pages. His heart seemed to flutter as his brain began to process the information in front of him. "Skylar, you're right. These numbers don't balance out; there's something fishy about this whole report. It looks as though someone has been skimming from this company."

"There's got to be something else here. All businessmen carry business cards with their names on them. There's bound to be one here."

Duke reached into the top of the briefcase and pulled out another file folder. It was filled with more reports from the same company—quarterly reports. Skylar took the case and nearly stripped out the lining looking for anything else that would give them information. Duke shuffled through the pieces of paper in the folder until one brought him to a halt. He read the message typed there and then read it again. What did it mean? Had he written it, or had it been delivered to him?

He stared at the small sheet of paper, blotting out Skylar's presence until she nudged in beside him to read the memo.

To: All Department Heads
Re: Budget Meeting
There will be a budget meeting of all departments on February 5. Please make sure your calendars are clear.
Brett

Almost in a whisper, Skylar asked, "Is that you? Are you Brett?"

At first Duke couldn't make his voice work. Then, "If this case is mine, I guess so."

"But Brett what?"

"I don't know." The paper shook in his hand.

"Brett Jacobs? Could this be your company?"

"Your guess is as good as mine, but if this briefcase and the jacket are mine, I don't think my last name is Jacobs. My last name should start with the letter 'C'. Remember the initials are JBC."

"That's right."

Duke focused his attention on the five printouts spread around on the desk. They were like magnets. He couldn't keep his hands off of them. Opening the first one for the past year, he lost himself in the columns of numbers.

****

Skylar sat quietly for a while until she noticed the clock. Jumping up she rushed out to the barn. Pausing only long enough to tell Addie what they had discovered, Skylar hurried through the morning's chores. Two hours later, she returned to the office to find Duke still engrossed in the computer printouts.

The small cell phone lay on the desk by her computer. Picking it up, she examined it. She finally came to a realization. "Duke." He remained glued to his pages. "Duke."

"Huh?"

"We could trace the number of this cell phone, couldn't we? I mean there's no number on it, but it could be traced by one of the cellular phone companies, couldn't it?"

Skylar's fingers feathered over the buttons on the cell phone. Just as her index finger poised over the power button, Duke's hand reached out to stop her.

"Don't!" came his hoarse command. "The battery is probably dead, but just in case it's not, don't turn it on."

Startled, Skylar looked into his face.

"If these reports are from a company I own, then I must have stumbled onto someone stealing from me. If I don't own the company, then I could be the person trying to do the stealing."

"What stealing?"

"I've been comparing these reports. The first two quarters seem to be okay, but the last two seem irregular. If what I'm seeing is correct, someone is mishandling this company. Someone high up in the administration."

"What does that have to do with this phone?"

"I'm either on the run because I discovered a theft, or I am the thief and have been discovered. That phone is probably being checked regularly and carefully. If we try to trace the owner, it could lead right back here. If we try to use it, the same thing could happen. That might put you and everyone here in danger."

"But it could give us your whole name."

"I'm not ready to chance discovery for that information yet. In fact, I should leave. What we've learned today tells me I'm involved in something you should stay away from. You've done enough for me."

He started to rise when Skylar's hand restrained him. "No, not yet." At his questioning stare Skylar continued. "Only the two of us know any of this. All Addie knows is we've found some papers and a cell phone. We've got some more tracking to do yet."

"But..."

"Duke, we've forgotten the information we got from Dixie's computer. Maybe there's something there that can help us, now that we know the whole name of the company. Before, we were looking for a company called JAC. Those are the first three letters in Jacobs. Come on we've got to give it a try."

Skylar retrieved the list of companies. There were four Jacobs Industries scattered across the United States.

"The only one that seems possible from this list is the one in New York City," Duke said. "I guess the only thing for me to do is head to New York City and see what I can find out."

"Wait a minute," Skylar said firmly. "You can't just traipse off to New York with just a financial report to go on. You've got to get more information."

"Just how do you propose I do that?"

Skylar thought for a moment. "Isn't there some way you could find out if the Jacobs Industries in New York is the right one?"

"The only way to do that would be to break into their computer system, and that's illegal," Duke pointed out. "If I'm not the one embezzling and I'm caught hacking into a company's computer, I could get sent to jail for...I don't know...years probably."

"If you work for the company or own the company, then it wouldn't be illegal to get into the computer system, would it?"

"I guess not, but I'd have to have the right-set up to do it. Your dial-up Internet service just won't let me do what I would have to do."

"Dixie has access to the proper set-up."

"Skylar, I don't want Dixie getting into any trouble for helping someone who may be a criminal. I can't bring her into it."

"We could just ask her to let you use the computer for a short time. That way she could truthfully say she had no knowledge of what you were doing, if she ever had to defend herself."

"You've been a big help to me, Skylar, a life-saver really, and I appreciate everything. But if this turns out bad, then both of us may wind up in the state pen."

"I believe in you and don't think you're a criminal." Skylar smiled at Duke. "I'll call Dixie and see when we can use the computer."

****

Skylar completed her call to Dixie and once again picked up the cell phone. "Couldn't we just turn the thing on and see who and what numbers are in the directory. You'd probably have your family listed."

A big lump rose in Duke's throat. Was he really ready

for that information? Gently he took the phone from Skylar and pushed the power button. Pushing another button he brought up the contact list. It was empty. The phone log was empty also. Apparently he had deleted everything in the phone, if in fact it were his phone. He didn't know whether to be relieved or not.

****

"Dixie, thanks so much for letting us use your computer again. Duke hopes that if he gets a little more information on some of those companies it might trigger something." Skylar steered her friend away from the computer where Duke had seated himself.

"I hope it helps. I'm sorry I don't have time to do the work for him," Dixie said.

"Oh, that's okay. Duke is pretty good with a computer. He set-up mine at the ranch. It didn't take him anytime at all to get all my bookkeeping on and ready to go. I think he can manage," Skylar commented as she looked back over her shoulder to see Duke engrossed in his work.

For the next hour, Skylar talked with her friend while Dixie checked the work of her students. Periodically, Skylar would glance Duke's way. She couldn't tell from his expressionless face if he was being successful or not. Finally she noticed Duke rise from his chair and head their way.

"You get what you needed?" Dixie questioned.

"I did learn a little more about some of the companies. Thanks for your help, Dixie. I hope we didn't cause you any trouble," Duke said. "Skylar, we'd better get out of here and leave her to her work."

"Yeah. Thanks again, Dixie. I'll let you know if we turn anything up," Skylar called as Duke urged her out the door.

"Yeah, we'll let you know if the FBI puts out warrants for our arrest and yours, too, for aiding and abetting a criminal," Duke whispered as he and Skylar walked toward her pick-up.

She stopped in mid-stride. "What do you mean by that?"

"Not out here. Get in."

Once inside, Skylar could wait no longer, "What did

you find out?"

"I don't own the company. It's owned by Lawrence Jacobs. There's a James B. Carlisle listed as vice-president. It appears he could be the crook. And it appears he could be me. The J.B.C. fits."

Skylar wasn't sure what she saw in Duke's eyes. She sensed sadness, maybe fear; she didn't know what else. She just knew they had to get back to the ranch where they could sort things out.

Chapter Eleven

Once behind closed doors in Skylar's office, they began to sort through the information Duke had gotten. He had copied the master program off the Jacobs Industries computer and now loaded it onto Skylar's computer. Then Duke downloaded the financial records he had copied. Skylar watched over his shoulder as he sorted through the maze of accounts.

"Well?" Skylar questioned.

"There's certainly been some crooked bookkeeping, and it all points to this James Carlisle," Duke said with a large lump growing in his throat. He shoved the desk chair away from the desk and jumped to his feet.

"That doesn't mean you're James Carlisle."

He thumped the brown case lying on the desk. "Well then, explain how his briefcase got here." Then he shoved a finger at the computer screen. "Look, the names of the companies listed on this financial statement are the same ones on the list I found in the briefcase. It appears that Carlisle was taking kick-backs," Duke pointed out.

"Maybe you're not Carlisle. Maybe you're the comptroller for the company and found out what Carlisle was doing. You confronted him with it, and he threatened you. You grabbed his briefcase and ran. Maybe he threatened your life, and you had to get out of town to sort things out until you could get the proof you needed to turn him in."

"I think you're grasping at straws," Duke murmured. "Skylar, I've got to get away from here. From the amounts that have been stolen, I'm sure this Jacobs fellow has called in the police, and they've probably called in the FBI. It won't be long before they track me here. I've got to go. I can't put you or anyone here in danger."

"Look, if the FBI was in on this, don't you think Dan would have heard something by now?"

"Probably. I guess so." Duke scratched his head and walked away from the computer. "Oh, Skylar, I don't know. This is all such a mess." He sank down on the couch opposite the desk. "I don't know what to think." He rested his head in his hands. Seconds passed. He raised his head and looked into her eyes. "I just know I can't risk putting you in danger when you've been so good to me. Now I've cracked into a company's computer and downloaded files and made you an accessory."

"Whether you're Carlisle or the company's accountant, you would have had access to all this information, so that's not really stealing."

"Skylar, you're grasping at straws again."

"Maybe I am, but I just can't believe the man I've come to know is a thief," Skylar sighed as she looked at him. "Maybe they caught this Carlisle fellow by now. He's probably in jail, and they're wondering what happened to you."

"Maybe, but I can't know that for sure. I certainly can't call the company and ask." Duke stood and walked over to the window. Options raced through his mind. He cast each one out as unworkable. "No, Skylar, the best thing is for me to leave. Disappear. That way you won't know anything should the cops show up on your doorstep." Duke turned to look at Skylar. "You'll just be an innocent person who tried to help your fellow man and had it backfire on you."

Skylar shook her head. Duke saw tears filling her eyes. He had to give her credit—she held them back.

"Duke, I don't want you to go."

He watched as she swallowed hard before continuing. Her face took on the look of determination he had seen as she worked with an unruly horse.

"What would you do? You still don't know who you are. You have no one to help you."

Duke shook his head and began to put all the printouts into the briefcase. His spine stiffened. "I'll figure all that out later, but for now I've got to get out of here. I got into the company computer without any trouble, but someone may figure out I was in it. When they do, they can trace it right back here to Dixie, and then to you. I can't let that happen. If I leave now, maybe that will keep you and Dixie out of trouble."

Duke finished putting the disks and printouts into the briefcase. He picked it up and held it in his arms since the case wouldn't latch anymore. He walked toward the door without looking at Skylar.

Skylar grabbed his arm. "Wait a minute. No one knows anything yet. We leave for Virginia next week. Stay. Go with us to Virginia, and then you can decide what to do. You're too emotional right now to make a decision."

Duke let her suggestion sink in; it had merit. Today was Friday. They would leave early Monday morning. Maybe nothing would happen over the weekend. Jake and Billy had found the briefcase on Monday, but Dixie couldn't give them any computer time until today. This week had drawn out with the speed of a turtle crossing an eight-lane Dallas freeway. Duke had spent the week analyzing every scenario possible. Today, with all this new information spinning in his head, it was almost impossible for him to think rationally. He could use a few days to plan his strategy, and besides, Virginia was closer to New York.

Duke sighed and then finally spoke. "Okay, I'll go with you to Virginia. That will give me a few days to think." He looked directly into Skylar's eyes as he spoke. "I'll go with you, but I may not come back with you. You have to promise me you'll go along with whatever decision I make, or I'll leave right now."

Skylar must have seen the seriousness in his eyes.

"Whatever you say. I think it'll be the best thing for you. You do need time to think."

Duke's head pounded. He hoped it was the right decision. He'd never forgive himself if Skylar got into trouble because of him.

****

"Addie, I'm sorry, but do you mind cleaning up by yourself? I've got a headache, and I think I'm going to go lie down for a while," Skylar said.

"Of course I don't mind, honey." Addie opened the door of the dishwasher. "But is there something wrong between you and Duke? You both were really quiet during supper."

"Nothing's wrong. I just have a headache."

Addie flinched at the sharp words flooding Skylar with guilt. She walked over and placed her arm around Addie's shoulder. "Addie, I'm sorry. I didn't mean to snap at you. I'm just going to try to get rid of this headache."

Addie turned and gave Skylar a brief hug. "Don't worry about it, honey. Can I bring you some aspirin?"

"No. I have some in my bathroom. Thanks though."

Lying across her bed, Skylar couldn't keep the tears from flowing down her face. Poor Addie. She had no business speaking to the dear woman that way. Addie didn't deserve that kind of treatment after all she had done for Skylar through the years.

The stress of Duke's situation was getting to her. So she did the only thing she could. She prayed God would intervene in Duke's situation. She asked God's forgiveness for any wrong they might have done, and she asked her heavenly Father to allow her help Duke. In the short time this man had been in her home, she thought she had come to know him pretty well. He might not have a past, but the person she had come to know just couldn't be a thief. *Even though he had no memory, wouldn't his personality be the same?* The man she knew was caring, gentle, and wouldn't hurt anybody. He just couldn't be the crook.

She wanted so much for everything to work out for this handsome stranger in her life, but more than anything she wanted him to come to the saving knowledge of Jesus Christ.

Skylar wiped the tears from her eyes and picked her Bible up from the nightstand. She would seek comfort in God's word and keep praying diligently for God's guidance.

****

Addie finished in the kitchen and joined Redigo in the living room.

"Well, I guess I'll turn in early," Redigo said as he lay the newspaper on the coffee table. "I thought Duke would get back, and I could talk him into a game of dominoes. He's been gone a long time; he must've decided to walk into town."

"Did you notice anything out of the ordinary at

supper?" Addie asked.

Redigo pulled off his glasses and looked across at her. "What'da you mean?"

"Well, Skylar and Duke were both really quiet."

Redigo relaxed back onto the couch. "Yeah, I noticed. Skylar didn't even seem interested in our trip to Virginia. That's not like her. Did somethin' happen today?"

Addie shrugged her shoulders. "Well, they went into town this morning. Said they were going to see Russell; something about a final check-up for Duke. I wondered about that because I thought Russell had already released Duke. Then when they got back, they locked themselves in Skylar's office for the rest of the afternoon and didn't come out until I called them to supper."

"Duke's acted a little strange all week. Well, maybe not strange, just a little distracted. I figured it had somethin' to do with that briefcase." Redigo propped his booted foot on top of the paper lying on the coffee table. "I think he's feelin' a little down, and I can't blame the boy for that. Not knowing nothin' about yourself, that's got to be awful."

Addie reached for the remote control and turned the sound down on the television. "I guess you're right. If that is what's bothering Duke, then it's bothering Skylar, too. You know how she is. She sometimes cares too much." She shook her head and a faint smile crossed her face. "She's always brought strays home. Only difference this time is this is a two-legged stray."

"Yeah, and I'm afraid that this time our Skylar has found herself carin' in a little different way. I've seen the way she looks at Duke." He scratched his head and then propped his head on his fist. "I'm afraid we're in for some rough water. What'll happen if those two should fall for each other? They don't even know whether or not Duke has a wife and a bunch of kids somewhere."

Addie grinned at her long-time friend. "Why, Redigo, I didn't know you were so observant about matters of the heart. I'd noticed Skylar and how she lit up when Duke would walk into the room, but I had no idea you would notice such a thing," she teased.

"I notice lots of things, you old woman; like you didn't bring me my after supper cola. You getting' forgetful old woman?"

"So your after supper cola is more important than our girl?"

"Not more important but about equal to." Redigo chuckled and then became serious again. "I just hope Skylar's not in for a broken heart."

"Well, I don't know what we can do to prevent it." Addie stood to her feet. "Even if Duke left now, we couldn't stop her heart from breaking. I think it's too late for that. We'll just have to pray that Duke gets his memory back and that he's not married so everyone will live happily ever after."

As Addie walked out the door toward the kitchen, Redigo called, "This is one time I hope you and your romantic ideas work out right."

After Addie returned with Redigo's drink, he turned the sound back up on the television and watched the news for a short while before he stood to leave. "I'll see you in the mornin', Addie."

Redigo left the room, feeling Addie's stare on his back. It wasn't often his emotions surfaced enough to embarrass him. He hoped he had been able to keep her from seeing the tears stinging his eyes as they discussed the possibility of Skylar getting a broken heart. The young woman had become like a daughter to him over the past twenty years.

****

Duke sat down on the edge of the porch. There were so many things running through his mind. He knew he should leave, but the thought of leaving Skylar behind was almost more than he could bear. He knew he had no right to think of her in any way except as a friend, but that was getting harder everyday.

Looking up at the sky, Duke whispered, "God, are you up there? If you are, would you listen to me?" Duke was afraid, if God did exist, he wouldn't listen to him. He didn't know if he'd ever believed in God. To him it didn't seem right to turn to God now when everything in his life was a mess. Duke couldn't help but wish, and maybe it was more than a wish, maybe it was a prayer. Whichever, he sure wanted Skylar's scenario about him being the one to catch Carlisle instead of him being Carlisle to be true, but God didn't answer him. Only the sound of one of the mares nickering in the barn floated on the night air.

Saturday was rather uneventful. Redigo, Jake and Billy worked to get everything ready to leave early Monday morning. Duke tried to help but was so distracted Redigo finally sent him to the house.

On Sunday morning, Duke tried to get out of going to church with Skylar, but her insistence won out. Duke still could not put his finger on what the feeling was that came over him when he worshiped with this little congregation. He guessed it was just love. They all made him feel welcome and a part of their community.

The preacher talked about a God who loved you no matter what you had done. Duke wondered if that was really true. He didn't understand how God could love him, a man without a past. But then he figured God was the only one who knew if he was this Carlisle fellow. He also wondered if there was some way to get God to reveal that information to him.

After lunch, Duke spent the rest of the day trying to avoid everyone. Skylar finally caught up with him out in the barn.

"You can't avoid me all week, you know. We'll be traveling in the same vehicle. It's a long way to Virginia, so you might as well talk to me."

Duke refused to look at the woman standing beside him. "I don't know what to say."

Skylar kicked at the dirt with the toe of her boot. "Well, we used to be able to communicate. Let's just talk like we have since we met."

Duke walked over and picked up a pitchfork and began cleaning one of the stalls. "Everything's changed. It's harder now." He could feel himself hardening inside, like lava cooling in the ocean.

"Yeah, some things have changed, and I know it's hard for you." Skylar walked over and sat down on a bale of hay near the stall. "But I don't believe for one minute that you stole anything from anybody. You're just not that kind of person."

Duke stopped pitching out the soiled hay and looked at Skylar. "Look, you don't know what kind of person I am. You don't know me at all."

Skylar met his stare. He could see steel in those blue eyes.

"No, I may not know your background, but I know your personality. I think I may even know your heart." She stood and closed the distance between them. "Duke, you're a good person. You're kind and gentle. You wouldn't hurt anyone, and you wouldn't steal from anyone either." Tears began to fill her eyes.

The sight of her tears cut through his heart like a knife. The last thing he wanted to do was cause her pain. He couldn't have what he wanted. He didn't have the right to pull her into his arms. They didn't have much time left. He ground his back teeth together. What kind of a creep made a woman like her cry? For now he would at least pretend to forget about his dilemma.

He took a deep breath before speaking. "I'm sorry, Skylar. Let's forget about me and concentrate on Skylark's Son." He forced a smile on his face as she wiped her tear-stained cheeks.

"That's a pitiful excuse for a smile, and I doubt you're going to forget your troubles." She shook her head at Duke. "But thank you for the effort."

She left him, walking with her head high like one of her prized stallions. He didn't think tears came easily to her. Their exchange had cost her, and it was his fault. He slammed the side of his fist against the doorframe of the stall he had been cleaning. The pain vibrated through his fist to his arm, his newly healed arm. That wasn't the smartest thing he'd ever done.

****

New York City

"Mr. Jacobs, we finally tracked down the flight attendant we'd been looking for. You know, the one who was working the LA flight out of Chicago the day our boy was tracked to the discount store. Seems she had gotten married and had been on an extended honeymoon. Oh well, that doesn't matter. She's sure she saw Brett Carlisle on the flight that day. She remembered him because she thought it was strange that a man who was unshaven, dressed in jeans and a western shirt would be carrying a fancy briefcase and a backpack. She even alerted the pilot. She was afraid the briefcase contained a bomb."

"What else did you find out?" Jacobs asked Special Agent Douglas.

"That's it. I figure he's left the country. We're dealing with a smart man here. He probably had a phony passport and I.D. all set up. He knew at some point things would get too hot for him, and he would have to leave in a hurry. I'm sure he was prepared. After all this time, the trail has gotten pretty cold. We won't stop following up whatever leads we can get, but the situation looks pretty hopeless. Of course, if he tries to access that Swiss bank account, we can track him then. But who knows? He may have had more than one account. That one was so easy to find it may be one he set up to lead us off his trail."

"So, you're saying the FBI is stopping the investigation?" Jacobs inquired.

"No. We're still watching his family. We hope he'll eventually let them know he's all right. I'm just telling you with each day the trail gets colder and our chances of catching this guy get slimmer."

Just as the agent was finishing his sentence, the intercom on Mr. Jacobs' desk sounded. "Yes, Maggie, what is it?"

"Adam Carlisle on line two for you."

Jacobs groaned as though he was in great pain.

"Mr. Jacobs, are you all right?"

"I've just been dreading this call. Adam Carlisle is Brett's father. The two of us go back to college days together."

"Well, if you're such good friends with him, maybe you could pump him for a little information. Try and find out if he's heard from his son," the agent said.

After a long sigh Jacobs mumbled, "My vice-president is on the run because he stole from me. Now I'm supposed to pump his father, who just happens to be my best friend, for information. This is beginning to sound like a plot to a James Bond movie, and I don't think I like it." Lawrence Jacobs reached for the phone and answered. "Adam, I've been expecting your call." He listened as his friend demanded to know about his missing son.

"I don't know where your son is, Adam. You haven't

heard from him?"

Carlisle's voice held a bitter tone. Jacobs sighed deeply and wished this nightmare would end. "I'm sorry the FBI is hounding you. I'll have a word with them." He eyed the agent standing before him.

"Someone embezzled money from me, and right now, everything points to Brett." Lawrence Jacobs held the receiver away from his ear as his friend, probably his former friend, yelled at him. "I'd never have thought it of Brett either. But the evidence..."

Adam cut him off with another tirade.

"Look, I'm willing to listen to his explanation, but he has to show up to give it to me. At this moment, nobody has any clue as to where he's gone. What are we supposed to think?"

Frustration tinged his words with anger. His tie felt like it was choking him. He tugged it loose. His forceful retort must have gotten through to Adam. His friend's reply was apologetic in tone.

"Adam, I understand how you feel. Brett's been like a son to me. I want this mess straightened out as much as you do so I'm doing everything I can."

Adam spoke only a moment more before ending the conversation.

"I'll be the first to call you if I hear from your son. I want your promise you'll do the same." He listened as Adam made his own promise. "I'll talk with you soon."

Jacobs dropped the receiver onto its cradle and turned his attention back to Agent Douglas.

"The next time that man calls me, you'd better have given me something concrete to tell him and have the proof, the unshakeable proof, behind it to eliminate or convict his son in this matter."

The FBI agent returned his stare. "Then I better leave and get moving. I'll talk with you soon, Mr. Jacobs."

The door closed with only a click behind the agent. Jacobs went to the refreshment bar and poured a glass of water. He gulped the whole glassful in a couple of swallows and then threw the empty glass across the room. The resulting crash of glass against wooden paneling was only mildly satisfying.

Chapter Twelve

Duke and Skylar followed behind the horse trailer as Redigo pulled through the entrance to the arena. Duke felt as though he had seen very little except the back of that trailer for the last three days as they made their way from Texas to Virginia. It was a relief when Redigo pulled to a stop in front of the stables, and he could get out to stretch his legs. The trip hadn't been bad. Duke and Skylar had been able to talk freely when they were alone in the SUV and had even managed to talk about something other than his past.

The gentle breeze caressed his face as he flexed his weary muscles. The pennants on the ridge of the stable roof fluttered in the wind while the weather vane slowly rotated. The sweet smell of hay filled the air as Duke watched Redigo walk Skylark's Son around the grounds in front of the stables so the horse could stretch his legs. Activity in front of the long row of white buildings increased as other horse trailers began to arrive and other trainers exercised their horses.

"Something wrong?" Skylar asked as she walked around the truck to stand beside Duke.

"No. Just getting the lay of the land," Duke told her.

"Let's get the horse taken care of, and then we can go to our motel to get cleaned up."

While the men stowed the gear and got Skylark's Son fed and bedded down for the evening, Skylar went to the office and checked in. Returning to the stables, she called, "You boys about finished? We're all checked in, and I'm ready to get cleaned up and then get something to eat."

"We're all done here. Billy's gonna stay with our champion tonight, so the rest of us can go on to the motel," Redigo said as he exited Skylark's Son's stall.

Duke sighed his relief. Food sounded good.

****

"That sure was good. Not as good as Addie's cookin' but a lot better than hamburgers," Redigo said as he pushed his chair back from the table.

"Yeah, a person can sure get tired of fast food." Skylar picked up her glass of iced tea.

"I guess I'd better go back out to the arena and check on Billy and Skylark's Son. Then I'm gonna turn in," Redigo announced. "You two goin' back to the motel now?"

"No. I thought if Duke wasn't too tired I'd get him to take me to the carnival downtown on the square. It's such a pretty evening, and I'd like a little fresh air and exercise."

She cast a playful glance Duke's way.

Duke finished taking a gulp of his iced tea before answering. "That sounds good to me. After three days on the road, a little fresh air would be nice."

Redigo stood to his feet. "Duke, have you got your key to the room? I don't want to have to wake up and let you in later." Redigo tossed a tip on the table as he warned, "And you'd better be real quiet, too, we have to be up early in the morning."

"No, we don't," Skylar said as she looked up at her foreman. "We have tomorrow off."

Redigo laughed. "Just wanted to see if you were payin' attention, and tryin' to find a polite way to tell this young man to get my girl home early."

With a huge grin on his face, Duke glanced over at Skylar and then looked at Redigo. "I promise to have her home before sun-up, sir."

Redigo pointed his finger at the young cowboy. "You'd better have her home long before that if you don't want to be starin' down the barrel end of a shotgun."

Skylar grinned when Duke raised both his hands in the air and promised to have her home early.

Music, laughter and squeals of delight greeted their ears as Duke and Skylar turned the corner onto Main Street. The lights from the Ferris wheel blurred as it turned round and round. The salty smell of hot popcorn and sweet odor of candy apples filled the air as they strolled toward the midway.

They heard the carnival barker as he chanted his spiel trying to entice the customers to buy tickets to the musical revue. "I wonder if this show is anything like the music shows in *Roustabout* with Elvis?" Skylar joked.

"You've got to be kidding! Elvis? Wasn't he a little before your time?" Duke asked.

"Elvis transcends time, but I'm amazed you know who he is."

"As you said, Elvis transcends time and apparently memory," Duke said as he softly began to sing, "Memories, pressed between the pages of my mind."

Skylar began to tremble with laughter. The folks around the couple began to stop and stare as her laughter became louder. "Hey, Pretty Mama, you need to get control of yourself. You're making us a spectacle," Duke said giving a very bad impersonation of Elvis.

Skylar laughed until her sides began to ache. After finally gaining her composure, they bought two tickets and went inside to see the show.

"That show was pretty bad," Skylar said as they walked out of the tent.

"Oh, I don't know. I thought the woman who sang the Patsy Cline medley hit at least three right notes," Duke snickered.

"But Elvis and Frank Sinatra would have both thought the guy who did it 'His Way' should have done it more 'Their Way'," Skylar added, laughter rippling in her voice.

"Okay, what next?" Duke asked as he stared off into the distance.

"How about the Ferris wheel?"

"Do you scream like a girl when you get on a scary ride?"

"I'm no 'fraidy cat'," Skylar boasted. "The scarier the better is what I always say."

"We'll see about that," Duke said.

He took Skylar's hand and led her toward the huge wheel. It was an unconscious move, but she felt a thrill at his touch.

The wheel slowly turned and stopped to allow the passengers to board. Skylar seated herself on the worn leather seat as Duke got in beside her. A young man secured the bar in front of them before cautioning them to remain seated throughout the ride. The wheel began to slowly ascend as the other customers boarded.

"Wow, the view is spectacular! Look at all the lights," Skylar said as she looked down on the scene below.

She turned her head to see him watching her.

"You look like an excited child. You really like this kind of stuff, don't you?"

The wheel began to pick up speed and Skylar laughed in delight. "You bet! A carnival makes you forget all your troubles, and for a few hours, a person can be a kid again."

Duke placed his arm around her and pulled her close to him. Without thinking, Skylar moved comfortably into his embrace. As the wheel went round and round so did Skylar's heart, and she was certain it wasn't from the excitement of the ride. She knew the man next to her was making her heart and her head spin.

The Ferris wheel came to a stop and Duke took Skylar's hand to help her from the seat. "Now what?" he asked.

She left her hand in his warm grasp. "You pick this time."

"How about that?" Duke said as he nodded toward a whirling ride.

Skylar stopped in her tracks. "You mean the scrambler?"

"You're not chicken, are you? I thought you said the scarier the better." Duke teased.

Skylar swallowed hard and prayed she wouldn't get sick. Trying to sound brave she said. "Of course not. Let's go."

Wind blown after their ride, but happy, the two decided to follow the sounds coming from a bandstand on the other side of the square. As they got closer, they saw couples dancing under the stars to the sounds of the big bands of old. Swaying to the beat of the music Skylar looked up at Duke and asked, "Do you know how to dance?"

"I don't know if I do or not." He grinned as he spoke the words.

"Well, let's find out." She took his hand and pulled him toward the makeshift dance floor.

After a few turns around the floor, Skylar

commented, "Not bad for a cowboy."

"Well, thank you, ma'am, I do my best."

The soft music surrounded them. Skylar thought about some old movies she had watched with Addie and could almost picture herself with Duke dancing at the USO during World War II. They had only been on the floor a couple of minutes when Duke stopped and said, "Why don't we go try our luck with some of the games on the midway?" Skylar felt a bit surprised by his sudden change in plans but followed him as he walked away.

Later that evening, Skylar clutched the teddy bear close to her heart as she lay in bed thinking about the night. Duke had won her a stuffed bear by shooting basketballs into a hoop. She had teased him that maybe he had played professional basketball. They had laughed and teased each other all evening. It had been good to get away from reality for even a moment. As much as Skylar hated to admit it and as hard as she was trying not to let it happen, her feelings deepened for Duke everyday. She knew they could never have a future until Duke had a past.

"God, help! You know how I feel about Duke. I can't hide my feelings from You. I'm falling in love with the man, but in my head, I know nothing can come of it until we know just who Duke is. Please help us find his past, no matter what his past may be. Father, let me remain just Duke's friend for now. Please help me to keep my feelings in check until it's okay with You for me to express them. One more thing, please help Duke. He needs You in his life. I think he needs to come to know You as Father." Skylar prayed.

****

Duke quietly entered the motel room. Redigo had left the bathroom light on and the door cracked just enough so he wouldn't stumble in the darkness. He couldn't get Skylar off his mind, as he lay alone in his bed that night. Duke remembered listening to the music as he guided Skylar around the dance floor. He had noticed the other couples; most of them were older. He envied them their past, their memories. He found himself lost in dreams of tomorrow. In those dreams he could see Skylar's face, but he had no right thinking about tomorrow when he had no yesterday.

He knew the best thing for her would be for him to get out of her life. Actually, he knew it would have been better for her if he had never come into her life, but it was too late for that now. Duke had to be honest with himself; he knew he had feelings for her and was afraid those feelings were growing deeper than mere friendship. He knew he couldn't go back to Texas with Skylar. This would have to be good-bye. He would have to make his way to New York and see if he could find the key that would unlock his past.

"God, I don't ask anything for myself, but would You please take care of Skylar? And could You please repair any damage I've done to her? Let her forget all about me." He hoped Skylar's God was listening to him like the pastor at her church had said and that He would grant his prayer.

Saturday morning, Duke led Skylark's Son out of the stall into the cool morning air.

"I'll saddle him if you'll throw me that blanket," Redigo called.

Turning to pull the blanket off the rail, Duke saw Skylar walking toward them. Her face beamed as she approached her prize stallion. Skylark's Son was in first place after the dressage phase of the three-day event. Duke hoped she would carry home the winning prize because then maybe she wouldn't think too much about him when he finally told her goodbye.

Chapter Thirteen

The Lazy M

Addie was mopping the kitchen floor when she heard a car door slam. Looking out the back door she saw Dan Tate walking toward the porch. "Good morning," Addie called as she stepped out onto the porch. "What brings you out our way on a Saturday morning?"

Dan removed his hat as he greeted Addie. "I need to talk to Duke. Is he around?"

"No." Addie sensed a serious tone in Dan's voice. "He went to Virginia with Skylar and Redigo. Can I help you with something?"

Dan hesitated a minute before answering. "No. I need to talk to Duke." He began to twirl his hat in his hand. "He is coming back with them, isn't he?"

"Why, of course." Addie stepped to the edge of the porch. "They should be back Wednesday or Thursday. I can give you a number where you can reach them."

Dan shook his head. "No. It can wait."

"Dan Tate, have you found out something about that boy's past? If you have, you need to let him know. You know how hard he's been trying to remember. Don't go making him suffer any longer than he has to."

"What I've got to tell him can wait. I'll check back with you Wednesday." Dan put his hat back on his head and walked to his patrol car.

There was something about Dan's visit that troubled Addie. The thought plagued her all day as she went about her work. The more she pondered on it the more she couldn't help but think that what Dan had to tell Duke was bad news. Had it been something good, he would have wanted to let Duke know right away. The way Dan had asked if she was sure Duke was coming back with them bothered her. Addie wasn't expecting Skylar to call her again before Sunday. She didn't know if she should try to get in touch with Skylar before then or not. She finally decided to wait because she knew the whole thing could be just her imagination. No use in getting everyone upset about something that might be only an old woman's overactive imagination.

****

Virginia

The last event was scheduled late enough that Skylar could go to the early service at church. She talked Duke into going with her.

He teased her a little on the way. "Since you're now tied for first place, I guess you're trying to get the advantage over your opponent by going to church."

Skylar grinned as she replied, "I might be tempted to try, but what if my opponent is attending church today also?"

Duke winked at her. "You're much prettier than that ugly old boy who's riding against you. You could probably play on God's sympathy if you tried."

"Duke Green, you're shameful. You'd better ask for forgiveness before we leave the church this morning."

Duke enjoyed the service, but he didn't get the feeling of belonging he had gotten each time he had attended Skylar's small church in Texas. Duke realized he would not only miss her when he left, but he would miss that congregation of people also.

Walking along the long row of stables back to Skylark's Son's stall Duke felt a hand grab his arm and heard a female voice say, "Brett...Brett Carlisle. What are you doing here?"

Stopped cold in his tracks by her touch and the shock of hearing himself addressed by the name he only knew from the briefcase, Duke found himself speechless as the stranger continued to babble.

"Tori said you wouldn't be able to make it this weekend."

With his head spinning, the woman's words rang at him from a distance. She was rambling on about some woman named Tori and something about just getting back from Europe. Duke was startled back to reality when the irritating woman asked him why he was dressed like a stable hand.

Trying to hide his panic, Duke managed to mumble something. "You must have me confused with someone else. Please excuse me; I've got work to do."

The woman held his arm a moment longer while she added, "Please forgive me but you look just like a friend of mine. If you had a clean shave and an Armani suit, you'd look just like Brett Carlisle."

"I'm not him," Duke snapped as he pulled his arm free and all but ran through the crowd. His pulse thundered, drowning out the noise around him. Coming to the end of the building, Duke ducked around the corner and leaned back against the wooden wall. His breath came in rapid gasps. He waited a few seconds before chancing a glance around the building. The woman was no longer in sight. He couldn't wait any longer. Time was up.

****

Skylar could see the tension in his face as Duke arrived at the stall. He kept watching the stall door. When the horse in the next stall kicked the wall, Duke jerked his head up and the color drained from his face. Skylar approached him and very quietly asked, "Duke, what's the matter? Did you remember something?" She laid her hand on his arm. He shook it off and returned to adjusting Skylark's Son's saddle.

"No. Everything's fine. You've got to get ready because the event is about to start."

"I'm not going anywhere. You're shaking like a leaf and look as though you've seen a ghost. Now tell me what happened."

Skylar's tone must have convinced him because he finally gave her an answer.

"I just got stopped by a woman who called me Brett Carlisle."

She could see the fear in his eyes. "What did you do?"

"I told her she was mistaken. That I wasn't…him." His voice broke.

"Do you think she believed you?"

"I don't know. Apparently this Brett character wouldn't be caught dead in clothes like these, so maybe she bought it. The fact is I've got to go now. When she gets back to New York, or wherever she comes from, she will probably tell everyone about seeing Carlisle's double. Whoever is looking for me will be able to put two and two together. I've got to get to New York and try to get some information before it's too late."

Skylar grabbed his arm with both hands. "You can't leave. Not yet."

"Skylar, I don't have a choice. I've got to go now." Duke tried to pull free of her grasp but she held on tightly.

"If you leave now, I'm going with you. I won't ride. We'll just leave."

Duke looked at her and must have seen her determination.

"You mean that, don't you? What would you tell Redigo?"

"Nothing. I'll call him later, or leave him a note or something." Skylar looked down at the ground.

"I can't let you can't do that."

She looked back up into his eyes. "Well, then you wait until after the event. We can talk it over then and come up with a plan." When he hesitated, she continued, "Duke, promise me you won't leave until we have a chance to talk, or I won't ride."

He hesitated until she thought she would scream.

"I promise." He finally said.

"Stay here. I won't be gone long."

Reluctantly, Skylar took the reins in her hands and walked away toward the start of the last event. She glanced back over her shoulder and saw Duke leaning against a post. Worry etched lines in his face. Her heart broke for him. There had to be some way to help him.

"Dear God, we need you now more than ever," she whispered as she placed her foot in the stirrup and mounted her trusty steed.

She was glad Skylark's Son was trained to run the course with little help from her. Today the horse would have to take charge, and she would try to stay in the saddle.

****

Duke walked up beside Redigo to watch Skylar take

the jumps. He should have stayed in the stall, but he'd felt like such a coward hiding there. He'd already been spotted. Once he gathered his scattered courage, he headed for the arena. Just as he glanced her way, the horse faltered and a general gasp ran through the crowd. He felt his heart stop until she regained control. If anything happened to her today, Duke would never forgive himself. He knew he was the cause of her wandering mind.

His knuckles turned white as they gripped the top rail of the fence separating him from the floor of the arena. The time that passed seemed like hours before Skylar and her well-trained mount finished the course. It had been a clean run—no thanks to him. There were three more riders to go, and only one of them stood a chance of knocking Skylar out of first place.

Redigo and Duke met Skylar as she walked Skylark's Son off the field. Duke's pulse was pounding so loudly in his ears he could hardly hear Redigo speaking to her.

"What happened to you out there? You lost your concentration. You know how dangerous that can be."

"That's why I have you. Even if my concentration gets broken, my horse is trained by the best, and he knows exactly what to do," Skylar said as she flashed Redigo a smile.

Duke watched the exchange. Her smile didn't reach her eyes.

"Flattery will get you everywhere, but only for today. We'll talk about what's botherin' you later," the foreman told her. Redigo took hold of Skylark's bridle and walked him around the barn to cool him down.

When Skylar looked at Duke, her smile faded. Duke sent her a half-hearted smile of his own.

A few minutes later, when the event ended, Skylar had taken first place. While she was receiving her trophy and having pictures taken, Redigo took off to call Addie to tell her the good news.

"I'll take care of the champion; you go relax," Billy told Skylar, after the photo session as he took the reins of the horse. She walked over and plopped down on a bench under a large oak tree. Duke strolled over and sat down beside her. They saw Redigo as he came out of the stable office and headed toward them.

"I need to talk to the two of you." The older man approached the bench.

"What's on your mind?" Skylar asked. "Is something wrong at home?"

Redigo propped his foot on the bench and leaned down closer to Skylar and Duke. "I called Addie to give her the good news, and she had some news for us. Seems Dan Tate came out to the house yesterday askin' to see Duke. He wouldn't tell Addie what it was about, but she said he seemed worried Duke might not come back with us. Now Addie seems to think what Dan has to say is not good news, or he would have told her or called Duke here. When she offered to give him the phone number, he told her it could wait."

Duke and Skylar looked at one another.

"Okay, which one of you wants to tell me what's goin' on? You found out somethin' before we left Texas, didn't you?" Redigo pushed.

Skylar began to deny everything when Duke interrupted her. "Skylar, he has a right to know." He glanced around them. "I'll tell you, but could we go back to the motel where it's less crowded?"

Once back at the motel, Duke told Redigo everything he knew—from his first dreams to the woman recognizing him.

"What's your next move?" Redigo asked.

His voice took on the rough edge Duke had heard at times when the foreman shifted into his serious, no-nonsense mode. Duke began to pace the floor. "I've got to get to New York and see what I can find out. Maybe something there will trigger my memory."

"That could be dangerous. If they spot you, you'll be arrested before you get a chance to prove your innocence," Redigo stated as he pulled a bottle of water from the ice chest.

Duke turned to look at Redigo. "From the evidence I have now, I'm not innocent." Duke seated himself on a chair in front of the window. "I'd just like to be able to remember being a thief before I go to jail for it."

Redigo covered the short distance and took the chair across from Duke. Looking him in the eyes, he stated,

"You're no more a thief than I am."

Duke shook his head. "I don't know how you know that."

The older man banged his fist on the table separating him from Duke. The sound startled Duke, and he turned his attention back to Redigo.

"In the past few months I've gotten to know you pretty good, and I'm a good judge of character. You're no thief!"

"I wish I could be sure of that," Duke said as he slumped in his chair. "But I've got to find out for sure. I'm leaving. I can't risk getting the two of you any more involved than you are right now. I can never repay you for all you've done for me." Duke found it difficult to keep his voice from trembling as he spoke, and he fought hard to keep the tears back. Redigo had been the last one to allow him to feel welcome at the Lazy M. Now he was adamant in his belief of Duke's innocence.

Skylar had kept quiet so far, but now she spoke. "I'm going with you."

"No, you're not!" both men said in unison.

"Yes, I am." She stood and looked at the two men. "You might be recognized. I can go into places you can't because no one knows me up there. Besides no one will be looking for a man and woman. It'll be a good cover for you."

The argument continued for a few minutes before Redigo broke in. "Skylar, you're right. Duke needs someone to go with him, but not you. It wouldn't look right for the two of you to be traveling alone together. I'll go."

"I don't need either one of you." Duke stood to his feet and began to pace around again. "Do you realize that if they have a warrant out for me, you would be aiding and abetting a criminal? You could go to jail with me. I'm going alone!"

"Suspected criminal," Skylar said.

"What?" Duke stopped pacing.

"You're only a suspected criminal, and we don't even know you are Brett Carlisle. Besides, we don't know that's what Dan wanted to tell you."

All Duke could do was stare at her. *Did she really*

believe what she said?

"You can either take me with you, or I'll follow behind you," Skylar stated firmly as she walked to stand in front of Duke. "But I'm going to see this through to the end. I have too big a stake in you to stay behind." She turned to look at her foreman. "And, Mr. Redigo, sir, we're not going on some romantic interlude. Duke's in trouble and needs help. I'm only going along because I know I can help him out."

Duke looked over at the foreman as he spoke. "Redigo, talk some sense into her."

Redigo shook his head. "Son, I've known this woman most of her life, and once she makes up her mind no one on earth can change it." He then addressed his young boss, "Skylar, people will assume your traveling with Duke is a romantic trip."

Skylar sat down on the side of the bed and faced Redigo. "The people who know me will know that nothing wrong will be going on between us."

Redigo gave a snort. "You've got more faith in people than I have, young lady."

Duke refused to let his life sully the reputation of the fine woman who had taken him in when he needed a place to live.

"Skylar, I'll let Redigo come with me, if you'll go home where you'll be safe," Duke bargained as he sank back down into the hard-backed chair by the window.

"No." Skylar said as she looked from one man to the other. "I need Redigo to make sure Skylark's Son gets back to the ranch safely. He's the only person that can take care of everything back in Texas. Besides, it'll be easier to explain why you and I might have decided to take a few days to ourselves than why you and Redigo wanted to stay in Virginia and spend a little time together."

Her rationale made sense, but Duke still wasn't happy. He couldn't help but think it was too big a risk for Skylar to take. The three talked until late in the night. They reasoned that since Dan hadn't alerted the authorities in Virginia to Duke's whereabouts, he probably wouldn't make any move until Redigo got home and the deputy found out Duke wasn't with him.

Redigo suggested he could make sure he didn't arrive back at the ranch until Thursday morning. That would give Duke and Skylar three full days to see what they could uncover before the authorities were alerted. Duke hoped Redigo's plan worked as he tossed again and again on the bed that became more uncomfortable as the night stretched out. They needed all the time they could get.

Chapter Fourteen

Skylar pulled the SUV onto the interstate just as the sun rose up over the horizon. Neither she nor Duke had been able to eat much for breakfast. The prospect of what might be ahead of them filled both their minds, spoiling their appetites.

Silence stretched between them as the vehicle rolled over the miles. She squirmed in her seat. "What's our plan for this escapade?" Skylar finally asked, hoping to start some conversation.

"What do you mean?" Duke asked. "I thought we were going to try to get some information about my past."

Out of the corner of her eye, she saw him glance over at her.

"Sure we are, but we need a plan. You know, like on all the detective shows. We can't check into a hotel under our real names. We have to think up assumed identities and develop a plan to get into Jacobs Industries to get information."

"What are you trying to do, really confuse me?" Duke laughed. "I already have an assumed identity, and now you want to give me another one."

"This is serious. We have to have a well thought-out plan." Skylar tried to choke back her own laughter.

"Well, I guess we can be Mr. and Mrs. Smith but as far as getting into Jacobs Industries, why don't we cross that bridge when we get there."

"Okay, but why don't we pose as brother and sister. That way we can get separate rooms without raising suspicion when we check into motels. We can tell people we're looking for our birth mother who put us up for adoption when we were babies."

"Doesn't the Bible have something in it about lying?" Duke grinned.

Skylar gave Duke a sidelong glance. "Yes, it does.

However, desperate times calls for desperate measures, and since this could be life or death for you, I'd say we need a cover."

"Okay, so we'll be John and Jane Smith, brother and sister."

"That sounds reasonable, but Smith?" Skylar shook her head. "That's not very original. Surely we can come up with something better than that."

"I don't think it's the name that will matter. We'll just have to convince folks we're related when we look nothing alike." Duke said as he pushed a button to change the station on the radio.

Skylar grinned. "Oh, I don't know. I think our noses sort of look alike."

"Well, on that aspect alone we should be able to convince people we're identical twins."

"Maybe we won't have to explain it to many people." Skylar said as she changed lanes to go around a slower-moving van.

After a day of driving settling down for the night was a welcome respite. The motel rooms were clean but nothing fancy, as Addie would say. That thought crossed Skylar's mind as she set her overnight bag on the bed. Duke put her other suitcase on the table in the room.

His voice interrupted Skylar's thoughts. "Well, it's getting late. I guess we'd better turn in."

"Goodnight, brother Wixson."

"By the way, when we stopped and looked in that phone book to find us a name, whatever made you choose that one? I'm not even sure how to pronounce it. I'll have to stop and think every time I introduce myself to someone," Duke grumbled.

"That's the nice thing about a name. You can spell it and pronounce it anyway you want to." Skylar started to pull her toothbrush and toothpaste from her bag.

"Well, I want to spell it S-M-I-T-H and pronounce it Smith," Duke quipped as he moved toward the door.

"Come on now. Don't pout. You've got to get with the program; we're in the spy game now."

"Okay, 007, I'll see you in the morning. Remember, if you need anything, I'm two doors down." Duke opened the door and glanced back over his shoulder. "You keep this door double locked. You don't know what kinds of scoundrels are roaming this neighborhood."

"Yes, brother dear." Skylar followed him to the door and secured the locks as soon as he had gone.

****

Duke glanced at the clock beside the bed. Sleep wouldn't come no matter how hard he wished it. He had just begun to know what it was like to have a peaceful night's sleep when all this new evidence crept up on him. Now he was back to the sleeplessness. *What is my life?*

His thoughts turned to Skylar. He knew he was falling in love with her, but he had no life to offer her. Duke shook his head trying to get rid of those thoughts. He couldn't let his emotions overtake him now. He had to find his past before he could have a future, but if the evidence he now had were true, his future would be behind bars. He sighed softly. It was going to be a long night.

The next morning found them in a little restaurant across the street from the Jacobs Building which afforded Duke and Skylar a protected view of the main entrance. The two had been sitting, watching and waiting for a while on Tuesday morning, and Duke's mind had wandered into blankness. Skylar had talked, but he had only half-listened as the waitress had served their breakfast.

At the gentle touch of her hand on his arm, he lifted his eyes and focused on her blue ones. "Huh?" He only then realized she must have been speaking to him, and he had failed to answer. "I'm sorry, Skylar," he apologized. "What did you say?"

"I just wondered what we should do next," she said as she pushed her food around on the plate.

"I don't know." Duke looked out the window at the large building across the street. "I hoped seeing the building would make me remember something, but it's as though I've never been here before," Duke replied softly.

"I'm so sorry." Skylar reached across the table and covered his hand with hers. "You've been through so very much over the past few months; you must be completely depressed at not regaining your memory."

The waitress appeared and asked them if they

needed anything else. Duke watched as Skylar smiled politely and shook her head. Leaving the check, the waitress moved on to her next customer.

"Let's go back to the motel and decide what do to next," Skylar suggested.

Duke's intense focus continued on the comings and goings across the street. People had begun arriving about an hour ago, and he had tried to survey each face. He was about to agree to Skylar's suggestion when he noticed a young couple stop outside of the window where he and Skylar sat. The couple held hands and seemed to be thoroughly entranced with one another. The blonde reached up and pulled the well-dressed man's head toward her own and gave him a long kiss. As they parted the blonde's face turned so that Duke could see all of it. The world felt as though it was tilting, and he clutched at the table as if to keep from falling off.

****

Skylar reached for the check and glanced out the window. She noticed a man and woman standing facing each other. The woman gave the man with her a passionate kiss and then looked into their window as if checking her make-up before walking across the street to the Jacobs building. The young man watched her enter the building and disappear. Skylar was surprised when he followed the young woman's path. Something about the whole incident didn't feel right. It was as if the couple didn't want people to know they were together. Skylar turned to comment about it to Duke and became alarmed.

Pain and horror were written all over him. Duke's knuckles were white from the tightness of his grip on the edge of the table. He stared at the same scene she had been watching.

"Duke! What is it?" she whispered.

"I...I don't know. I just suddenly got this really sick feeling. Let's get out of here."

Duke's hasty retreat was almost alarming. He seemed to be running away from something. Could he have recognized the young couple? Skylar was hesitant to question him. She would give him some time and space; maybe he would confide in her later about what had suddenly come over him.

The silence was so loud when they got back to the motel that it was almost deafening; she could bear it no longer. He had followed her into her room. They had wandered around the streets for hours after leaving the diner, and Skylar's feet hurt. Sitting down on her bed, she slipped her shoes off and massaged her aching feet. Reaching for the remote, she flipped on the television just as the last chords of theme music faded away. "Oh, I'm sorry. We seemed to have missed your favorite show." Skylar said, hoping to joke him out of his depression.

"That's okay. I can always call Soap Opera Update to find out what happened," Duke said.

Her spirits lifted a bit when he managed a little grin. "You mean there is actually a number you can call to find out what happens on these, uh, shows?"

"My good woman, I'll have you know these shows are serious business. Addie would be offended if she knew you thought she was silly." Duke sat down in the padded chair beside the bed. "Whoops. I forgot and let Addie's secret out. Now she'll never forgive me for telling you she watches some of the soaps on TV." Duke managed to look contrite at his slip of the tongue.

"Now I didn't say Addie was silly. I said these shows were silly." Skylar pushed a button on the remote and changed the channel once again. "And don't worry about letting Addie's secret vice out. I've known for a long time she watches them when she thinks I'm not around. I figure that's her business. She's over twenty-one."

Duke wiped his hand across his brow. "Whew, I'm really glad you already knew. I'd hate to think Addie would be mad at me forever for letting you know her secret. She might not ever let me have any more of her peach cobbler." With a scowl on his face, he questioned Skylar. "But, still, if you think the shows are silly, what do you really think of the people who watch them?"

Skylar stood up and walked over to the table and poured herself a glass of water. "Hey, how did I come to be on trial for my opinion of soaps? You watch them, not me. You and Addie have to deal with your own vices."

"You'd better watch what you say 'cuz your words can be misconstrued," Duke teased.

Skylar set her glass on the bed table and looked at

Duke. His mood change lightened her heart. She slipped her feet back into her shoes. "You know what? I'm hungry. Why don't we get something to eat?"

"I'd think you were just trying to change subject if I wasn't hungry myself."

Duke's sweet grin settled on his face for the first time in hours. Skylar's heart gave a small lurch as she grabbed his hand and pulled him to his feet. The disturbing scene from the diner could wait for another time.

****

Skylar rolled over and glanced at the clock. She was afraid she had overslept but it was still early. She had just picked up the phone to call Duke's room when she heard a soft knock of her door. She looked through the peephole and saw Duke.

"Just a minute." Skylar pulled on her jeans and T-shirt before opening the door.

"I've got breakfast. Let's eat while it's still warm."

Skylar cleared the small table in her room, and Duke took the coffee and breakfast sandwiches from the bags.

"This tastes pretty good for fast food," Skylar said after she took her first bite.

"It's from that little coffee shop across the street." Duke took the lid off his coffee and sipped the hot liquid.

They ate in silence for a while before Skylar spoke. "Well, what do we do today?"

"I don't know." He took a bite from his sandwich before adding, "Maybe if I got inside the building something would be familiar."

Skylar wiped her mouth with the paper napkin. "That's pretty risky. How do you propose we do that without you being caught?"

Duke looked into Skylar's eyes. "First of all, I don't propose *we* do it. I'll do it."

Holding his gaze she said, "I thought I had made myself clear. We're in this together. Now, no arguments." She picked up her sandwich. "So what's your plan?"

"You are one stubborn female," he mumbled just before taking another sip of his coffee.

"Yes, I am. Redigo warned you about me," Skylar smiled. "So let's get down to planning."

Duke leaned back in his chair. "I thought I, excuse

me, we could wait until late this afternoon and then dress up like we're cleaning crew and go into the building. We should be able to stroll around without being too conspicuous."

Skylar looked across the table and wrinkled her brow, as her thoughts became words. "We need to do something to disguise you better."

Duke's eyes widened as he asked, "Just what do you suggest?"

She placed her elbow on the table and tapped her cheek while deep in thought. "Well, the beard you've let grow looks good." She laughed. "I don't blame you for growing one while your arm was in a cast. You lost nearly enough blood those first couple of days at the ranch to need a transfusion."

Duke scratched his jaw. "I've been thinking about shaving it off. It's itchy."

"I'd keep it a while. Probably if you worked in a big company you didn't have a beard at that time." She thought a few more seconds before she added, "Maybe if we dyed your hair?"

"I'm willing to try anything," Duke nodded in agreement. "How do we get it done?"

Skylar smiled. "That's no problem, I can do it. It would be less risky anyway, if I did it." She stood and walked to the mirror and ran her fingers through her hair. "I think I'll dye mine, too. After all, once Redigo gets back home, the authorities will probably be looking for me."

They found a discount store and bought the necessary products to dye their hair. Then they bought clothes for their disguise as janitors before returning to the motel.

"Have you ever done this before?" Duke asked as Skylar pulled the instructions from the box of hair dye.

"Well, not exactly, but it doesn't appear to be too hard. I've watched Trina do it lots of times. Come on, sit down." Skylar continued read the instructions as she pointed to the straight-backed chair she had positioned in front of the vanity.

"Why don't you, uh, do yours first?" Duke asked.

"It'll be all right. Sit down. Look, it has picture

instructions." Skylar began to apply the solution to Duke's hair. "Now we just have to time it. Let's see...we're supposed to leave it on for twenty minutes," Skylar said as she wrapped the plastic cap around Duke's head. "Just to make you feel better I'll go ahead and do mine while you're waiting."

"That's a little encouraging. At least you're not gonna wait to see if my hair falls out or something before you do yours."

Skylar repeated the steps on her own hair and joined Duke in front of the TV. They got so involved in a program they lost track of time.

"This stuff has been on ten minutes too long," Duke shouted as he looked at his watch.

"Keep your voice down." Skylar stood and tried to calm him. "That shouldn't hurt. The color will just be a little darker that's all. Now hurry up and go wash it out so I can wash mine."

In just a few minutes, Skylar heard the bathroom door open and looked up from the program on TV. Duke stepped through the door; he looked horror-stricken. His hair was the most horrible shade of green she had ever seen. The sight made her double over with laughter.

"I fail to see the humor in this," Duke growled as he looked into the mirror. "What do you propose to do about this mess?"

Through her laughter Skylar blurted out, "Wash mine...before it turns that color, too." With that she ran into the bathroom and closed the door. She could still hear his bellowing over the rush of the shower. A few minutes later she reappeared, trying not to let her relief show through in the form of a grin, but it was extremely hard to hold back.

"Why is yours a pretty dark brown and mine this split-pea green?" Duke moaned as he ran his fingers through his hair.

"I don't know. It must be some kind of weird body chemistry reaction you're having." Skylar brushed through her now dark brown tresses. "Get the phone book. I'll call a salon and ask them what I should do."

Except for her own voice, the room was silent as she discussed the situation with the woman on the other end of the phone call. "I see. If you think that's the best way. Okay."

"Well?" Duke crossed his arms and scowled at her.

"They told me a couple of things I could do but strongly suggested that you come in and let them try."

"To top off the humiliation of having green hair, I'm now supposed to walk into a beauty salon full of women to get my hair turned another color." Duke's shoulders slumped and he shook his head.

"That's it." Skylar shrugged. "Unless you want to let me try again." She began to laugh once more as she looked at Duke's pathetic expression.

"What a choice," Duke muttered.

"Well, you could leave that way. I'm pretty sure you wouldn't have been into punk rock working for Jacobs Industries. So they probably wouldn't be expecting to see you with that lovely shade of green hair." She tried to choke back the laughter. "It could help with your disguise."

"Yeah. It would immediately draw everyone's attention to me when we walk in the door." He picked up his cap and pulled it on his head. "Let's go and get this over with so we can take care of business later. Time is getting short."

Duke kept mumbling to himself as he strode out of the door and headed for their SUV. Skylar followed him still snickering at his green hair. It was the exact shade of green that had been on some kid in an old movie she had seen on cable a few weeks ago.

"Hey, it looks good," Skylar commented as Duke walked into the reception area a couple of hours later.

"Let's get out of here. I've had about all I can take for one day," Duke grumbled as he grabbed Skylar's hand and pulled her toward the door.

She giggled as quietly as she could even as he dragged her out the door.

Chapter Fifteen

Duke and Skylar walked into the lobby of the Jacobs building as if they belonged there. Nobody was about to notice the couple's presence. They walked straight to the elevator and pushed the button for the top floor, where all of the executive offices were located. When they exited the elevator, most of the offices appeared to be empty. Skylar felt like an amateur spy as they walked into the reception area. Duke pulled a trash bag from his back pocket and began to empty the contents of a wastebasket into it.

"What are you doing?" Skylar asked as she stared at him.

"We're janitors, aren't we? I'm just trying to make it look good."

Skylar glanced at their surroundings. "But, Duke, the place is empty."

"Yeah, what if someone comes in? It needs to look like we're doing something."

Duke grabbed the trash bag and started down the hallway glancing at nameplates on the doors. Skylar followed behind him and shook her head while she worked to control the laughter that threatened to bubble back to the surface from deep inside of her. Duke had a point. They shouldn't be drawing attention to themselves at this point. When they reached the end of the hall, they heard voices coming from behind a door marked Boardroom. Duke shoved her into an empty room across the hall.

"They must be having a late meeting," Duke commented as he eased the door closed.

"Yeah. Why don't we get out of here while the gettin's good," Skylar whispered.

Duke walked over to the desk and picked up the nameplate. "Well, I guess I haven't been replaced." He turned the nameplate around to show Skylar what he held in his hand.

"James Brett Carlisle." She felt her eyes grow wide. They had stumbled into the right office without even trying.

****

Shaking off his initial shock at seeing the name he had come to believe was his, Duke began to survey the office. He walked behind the desk and sat down in the big padded desk chair. This chair might have been comfortable to him at one time, but right now it felt like it was a hot seat, maybe even the electric chair. He looked through the drawers as Skylar watched from her post by the door.

"Duke, hurry. Let's get out of here before we get caught."

Duke looked up at her for just a moment before he continued to look through the drawers of the desk. "You're the one who wanted to be a spy."

"I'd rather do it in a safer place than this." Skylar opened the door just a crack and peered up and down the hallway. Then she closed it again. "Duke, hurry."

Her voice was a harsh whisper. Duke noticed the picture sitting on the top of the desk. His breath stopped as he recognized the girl in the photo. It was the woman he had seen through the window of the diner yesterday. He sat in stunned silence for a moment and then forced himself out of the chair, hurrying to the door.

"What are you waiting on then?" He asked Skylar as he opened the door. "Move it."

****

A heated discussion was in progress inside the Jacobs Industries' boardroom. Victoria Jacobs, daughter of the owner, major stockholder, and member of the board, sat back in her chair listening to the discussion going on around her. Her anxiety about the outcome of this meeting caused her stomach to clinch. So much depended on Jordan moving into Brett's place.

"I still don't believe Brett could have been so dishonest. There must have been something pushing him to make him embezzle from the company," Lawrence Jacobs pronounced loudly to those gathered in the room.

"Larry, that's not the point in question here. Carlisle needs to be replaced. Who will be the one to take over his position? My vote is for Mark Stillman. He's got a lot of potential," Tom Farris said.

Victoria held her breath.

"Stillman's not seasoned enough to handle it all," her father said.

Now was the time to make her suggestion. "What about Jordan?" Victoria asked. "He's older than Mark and much more knowledgeable. After all, he's the one who discovered the discrepancies in the accounts after Brett disappeared."

"Yes, Tori, he is intelligent and handles himself well. He also works long hours, but I'm not sure he's the best one for this job," her faher replied to her suggestion.

She started to speak again, but the other woman in the room spoke up before she could.

"Edward Thomas is next in line for promotion," Cynthia Gold reminded the board.

A murmur of agreement followed. "But, Father, I really think you should give Jordan the chance. He deserves some sort of reward," Victoria said. The muscles in her neck tightened up. Her head began to throb. If she pushed too hard, someone might become suspicious.

"We could divide Carlisle's duties between Thomas and Matthews for six months and make a final decision then," recommended Jeffrey Nichols, board secretary.

Nodding his head, her father asked, "All in agreement to Jeffrey's motion?" All the members of the board signaled their approval, except Victoria.

As her father looked directly at her, she, too, gave her acceptance of the motion. Her approval was unwilling. Jordan wouldn't like having to wait another six months to finally take over, but he'd just have to live with it. Any real protest at this point would make her father wonder about her, and they couldn't afford that right now.

****

Duke seemed to be distracted that evening back at the motel, but Skylar figured it was because he was trying so desperately to remember something. She didn't push for information.

"Duke, where do we go from here?" Skylar asked, when she could stand his silence no more. "Do you need more time in New York?" She finished throwing away the take-out containers and sat down at the table across from him.

"No." Duke shook his head. "I've probably gotten all the information I'm gonna get from here. Redigo will be home sometime tomorrow. I figure by tomorrow night, at least, there will be an army looking for me." Duke paused for a moment and then looked at her. "Skylar, you've got to let me go on alone. You're not in any trouble yet. If you go home now, you won't be. If you stay with me, we may wind up in adjoining cells."

Skylar looked down at the table before turning her gaze back to Duke. She was about to get tired of his objections. She used her toughest boss-voice when she spoke again.

"I thought we had this all settled. I'm staying. Now what do we do next?"

****

"You are one stubborn woman, aren't you?" Duke stood and walked over. He turned off the television. "We need to get out of New York. Redigo's going to mention we talked about going down to Florida, but the authorities will probably blanket the whole east coast area with their announcement just in case. Especially since New York's where I apparently lived. I guess we'd better head west early in the morning."

"West to where?"

Where? Where? The word echoed in his mind as he rubbed his temples. "I'm not sure. We've just got to disappear. I hate to say it, but we're going to have to dump your SUV."

"Why?"

"If you're with me, they're going to be looking for both of us and your vehicle. Plus it's equipped with On Star and can easily be found when the authorities realize that."

"But I don't have On Star activated anymore."

"Skylar, that doesn't matter; your vehicle still has the equipment and can be tracked," Duke pointed out. "We're going to have to find some other way of traveling which leaves us with another problem."

"What problem?"

"Money." Duke answered as he sat down on the edge

of the bed.

"Oh. Well, I guess we'll just have to visit some ATM machines along the way."

A thought from deep in his mind emerged. "I think we'd better do it all here in New York and get as much as we possibly can this one time."

"Why would we need to do that? There are ATM machines everywhere."

"Yes, but you can be tracked pretty easily that way, too. The electronic age makes everything faster, including tracing down banking activity. Using the ATM machines will leave a trail like a giant neon sign flashing 'Here They Are'. No, I think we'd better get as much as we can and then leave town. We need to find some place to leave the SUV though."

"We could sell it. That'd give us quite a large stake," Skylar offered. "After all, it's almost new."

"There are a couple of problems with that. To get as much as it's worth, you'd have to go to a reputable dealer and show him all your credentials. That would leave a big clue for the FBI or whoever. If we took it to a not-so-honest dealer, we wouldn't get much for it. Looking for some place to sell it will take a lot of time and there isn't much time left to waste. We'll just have to abandon it somewhere."

He watched her nibble on her lower lip for a moment before she finally spoke. "We can't just abandon it on a street out in the open—too noticeable."

"Yeah. That's right. Where could we put it so it wouldn't be noticed?"

****

Lazy M Ranch

It was mid-afternoon on Thursday when Redigo and Billy pulled the trailer into the Lazy M. Addie heard the truck and walked out onto the porch. "Where's Skylar and Duke?" she called as Redigo stepped from the cab.

Now the deception would start. Addie couldn't know about Duke. The fewer people who knew, the better. Swallowing hard he told her the story the three of them had agreed upon. "They decided to stay on a few days. Said they might even head down into Florida."

"But what about Dan? He wants to talk to Duke. Did y'all forget?"

"No, we didn't forget." Redigo took on a solemn look as he opened the back door for Addie to enter the house. "Listen, Addie, don't ask questions, and when Tate shows up, let me do the talking. Right now I can't say no more." He walked to the sink and washed his hands before pulling a cola from the refrigerator. "Skylar and Duke are fine, so don't worry. There are just some things Duke has to work out before he comes back."

"But..."

Redigo spoke again before Addie could get any more out. "You've just got to act natural." Redigo sat down at the kitchen table. "Like the two of them stayed to get better acquainted. Like maybe they're falling in love." The foreman stopped talking and listened carefully. "That's Tate's car now. Remember act like nothing is out of the ordinary and let me do most of the talking."

****

Addie stared at Redigo's back as he walked out the kitchen door. What on earth was that man talking about? Addie looked out the window over the sink; there was no car in the drive. She grabbed two plates from the cupboard and took them to the table. As she set them in place, she looked out the bay window facing the long drive leading to the house. Addie studied the horizon. Not even any dust. She placed the flatware and a napkin beside each plate.

Redigo had some unusual ways about him, but right now Addie questioned his stability. The man must be going daft, hearing things where there was nothing to hear. Addie turned to attend to the pot of beans she had cooking on the stove.

What does he mean I should keep my mouth shut? That man knows I don't spread gossip. And I'd never say anything about Skylar to get her in trouble. Addie picked up a hot pad, opened the oven and took out a pan of Mexican cornbread. Setting it on a trivet, she cut the hot bread into squares and stacked them on a platter.

What happened in Virginia anyway? Addie opened the oven door and slid the peach cobbler in to bake. *Should put this thing in the freezer the way Redigo's been acting. He doesn't deserve his favorite dessert. He better be telling all he knows when he gets in here for his dinner.*

She transferred the pieces of chicken fried steak from the skillet to a platter and set it on the table with the red beans, rice and cornbread. As she did, the sound of an approaching car caught her attention. Addie looked out the bay window again. *How did that man do it?* It had to have been at least five minutes since he walked out the door announcing the arrival of a vehicle, and he had been right—it was Dan. *There is no way he could have heard the deputy's car that far away.*

Curious as to what Redigo was about to tell Dan, Addie checked the stove and then walked out to the porch, just as Dan pulled his patrol car to a stop beside Redigo's pickup. Addie shook her head. Redigo's ways were too strange sometimes.

****

"How'd it go?" Dan called as he walked toward Redigo.

"How do you think? Skylark's Son won the whole thing, just like we expected," Redigo smiled as he stepped toward the deputy.

"I guess Skylar is still flying high," Tate remarked. "Is she in the house?"

Redigo faced the officer, looking him straight in the eyes. If he was going to convince him that all was as it should be he had to be able to face the man.

"No. She and Duke have kinda been sparking, and they decided to stay out there for a while. To get to know one another a little better without any outside interference, at least I think that's what she said." Redigo did his best to show the proper amount of indignation as he continued his deception. "I don't know what's got into that girl. A handsome, mysterious face comes along, and she forgets everything we tried to teach her."

Tate's frustration was evident to anyone who bothered to watch his face, and his voice reflected it.

"Did Addie tell you that I needed to talk to Duke?"

Redigo managed to have a puzzled look on his face as he asked, "Something happen? You get some news on him?"

Tate pulled off his hat and ran his hands through his

hair. "Do you know how to get in touch with them?"

Redigo shook his head. "No, nothing other than her cell phone." Redigo propped his foot on the bumper of the trailer. "They said they were heading down the coast. Skylar will probably call in a couple of days." The foreman paused before adding, "Dan, what's going on?" Redigo hoped Dan would tell him what he knew.

Giving a long sigh, Tate put his hat back on his head. "Redigo, when Skylar calls tell her to get away from Duke. I got some evidence showing that Duke is an embezzler. He could be dangerous because he's on the run. His amnesia could all be a hoax."

Redigo's temper slipped. "I don't believe he's dangerous for one minute. If you're any kind of detective, you'd know that, too. I also don't believe that Duke is a thief."

"I'm not sure I do either." Tate shook his head. "He seemed like a real nice fellow, but that's not the point. He's a wanted man. I've stalled as long as I can. I have to let the FBI know what I know." The deputy adjusted his sidearm as he continued. "They'll put out an all points bulletin on him and Skylar, too, since she's with him. When you talk to her, tell her to get Duke to turn himself in and for her to get herself home. Do you understand?"

"I'm not stupid, Deputy. I don't want my girl in any trouble. I'll talk to her when she calls. Though I can't say when that might be." Redigo hoped his bluff carried a ring of truth to it.

The deputy looked the foreman in the eyes. "Will you let me know when she calls?"

Holding his gaze, Redigo answered. "I'll let you know whenever I know anything new." Redigo watched as the deputy walked back to the patrol car and drove off, leaving a trail of dust billowing behind him. He raised an eyebrow. Dan hadn't indicated he would call Skylar on her cell himself. *Strange.*

Redigo turned and caught Addie's determined look. If the FBI only knew how that woman could worm information out of a person, they'd hire her for sure. He dreaded the next few minutes but decided to go ahead and get it all over with so maybe he could enjoy the meal Addie had been preparing. That is if she let him have anything to eat after he told her what had happened in Virginia.

Chapter Sixteen

The doors of Philadelphia Memorial Hospital slid silently open, allowing a young couple to exit and get into a waiting taxi. The tall, bearded man leaned forward and said, "Bus station, please," before settling back against the vinyl-covered seat.

The dark-headed woman beside him smiled as their eyes met. "Where are we going?"

"Wells River, Vermont," came Duke's hushed reply.

"Why there?"

"I heard this old couple talking while I waited for your sandwich in the hospital cafeteria. The old man was describing the delicious pancakes and maple syrup they had at a small cafe there. It was just down from a little motel. Pancakes and maple syrup sounded good. I think I'll have some for breakfast tomorrow." Duke grinned.

"That's some reason to go to a town," Skylar said as the yellow cab wove in and out of traffic.

"And you have a better place to head for?"

A few minutes later, the taxi pulled to a stop in front of the bus station. Duke paid the fare as the two climbed out. They walked inside and located the ticket counter.

"Two tickets for Albany, New York, please."

"One way or round trip, sir?" The ticket agent questioned.

"One way," Duke answered.

"Names?" the agent wanted to know.

"Nick and Nora...Wixson." Duke almost stuttered out the last name Skylar had decided upon.

"Address?"

Trying to keep calm, he recited the fictitious address Skylar had made him memorize. The zip code almost got him in trouble though.

"No, Nick, it's 90054 not 90045. You'll have to excuse my brother; he's dyslexic. He always reverses those last two digits." Skylar said to the ticket agent, smoothly correcting his mistake.

As they walked away with their tickets, Skylar whispered, "I thought we were going to Wells River?"

"We are."

"Why are we going to Albany? We just left New York."

"We're trying to confuse anyone who might be tracking us, remember?"

"So then how do we get to this Wells River place?"

"We take another bus. It'll take a while, but that's okay. It'll give us lots of time to plan and think." Duke picked a couple of chairs in a row as far away from the other waiting passengers as possible. He dropped their suitcases in an empty chair and settled into the one next to it. He motioned with his head for Skylar to take the remaining seat.

"If you say so. I've never been on a bus trip before. It'll be an adventure." Skylar settled into her seat and glanced around at the other passengers.

"Some adventure," Duke grumbled to himself hours later as he searched for a way to stretch out his long legs so he could try to get some sleep. Looking over to his left, he watched Skylar as she slept. *How could she do it?* The constant movement and sway of the bus kept jerking him awake. The way this trip was going he wasn't sure what day he would finally get to eat those pancakes. They'd been on this bus for seven hours now and were only halfway there. They stopped in every tiny, little town. Wiggling again, he finally found a somewhat more comfortable position and drifted off to sleep.

The dream began with him running and numbers chasing him. Tonight, though, a blonde woman's face suddenly cropped up in the middle of his dream. She talked, but Duke couldn't understand her.

"What?" he demanded. "What are you telling me? I don't understand you!" came his loud cry.

****

Duke's cry startled Skylar awake. "Duke! Wake up." Skylar whispered as she tried to shake her partner awake. His continued shouts were waking people all around them. She tried again, "Duke, you've got to wake up now!" With a last push, Skylar managed to capture Duke's attention. Looking around them, she tried to defuse the situation. "I'm so sorry. He was recently traumatized, and sometimes he has terrible nightmares," Skylar explained. Her excuse sounded lame even to her.

As the rest of their fellow travelers grumbled and returned to their sleep, Skylar turned to Duke. "Are you all right?" By now, Duke had finally managed to drag himself out of his dream and focus on her.

"Yeah, I'm fine," Duke reassured her as he repositioned himself. "I just had another one of my dreams."

"Tell me about it. Did anything new happen?"

"Just the same old stuff. I wonder if anyone has noticed your vehicle yet." Duke said.

He shifted his eyes away from hers. There was something he wasn't telling her. She decided to let it alone for the moment.

"I doubt it. The hospital parking garage will be a safe place. People sometimes stay in the hospital for weeks. I bought a thirty-day parking pass, so it will be at least a month before the parking garage owners try to find me. And since you disconnected the battery cables, On Star can't locate the vehicle for anyone. You know, when my mother was in the hospital, I didn't move my car for over a week."

"What about food?" Duke wanted to know. "What did you do about that?"

"There is always a cafeteria in the hospital. I ate there, or Dad would take me out. The larger hospitals, like Philadelphia Memorial, are almost like small cities. The ones down in Houston are connected by enclosed walkways to the buildings across the street. There are shops and restaurants all within walking distance. You don't really need a car there."

"But what about the out-of-state license plates?" Duke worried.

"Often there are cars from different states at a large hospital. People from all over go to visit their relatives. I don't think that will make much difference."

"It seems logical."

Duke closed his eyes and leaned his head back

against the seat. He looked like he wanted to drift back to sleep. Skylar leaned her head against her own seat. She wondered what he might have seen in his dream that he didn't want to talk about. It wasn't long before she fell back to sleep herself.

****

With a blast of black exhaust, the bus pulled away leaving Duke and Skylar alone on a quiet street of Wells River, Vermont. It was a small town. They could almost see the entire village from where they stood. Below them lay a quaint-looking motel nestled against the side of the hill. Picking up the suitcases, they walked the stiffness out of their legs as they headed for the motel.

Checking-in went quickly. Tossing her suitcase on the bed, Skylar flopped down and moaned out loud. "Oh, this feels so good!"

"I think I'll go to my room and do the exact same thing. I'll see you whenever."

Duke fell asleep without any problem and then the dream began. There she stood. The girl in the picture. Duke's mind kept flashing from the picture he had seen in his office to the picture his memory held of the same woman kissing another man on the street as they paused in front of the diner. The dream continued in a muddle of confusion but nothing cleared up. Once again he saw the woman speaking, but he couldn't understand what she said.

He began to call out to her in his dream. "What are you saying?"

Duke jerked awake to find Skylar standing over him shaking his arm.

"You were dreaming again," she told him as he shook his head and tried to brush away the cobwebs. "Duke, is the dream still the same? Is it the one you were having at the ranch?"

"Yes and no." Duke sat up on the side of the bed—glad he slept in a T-shirt and lightweight sweat pants. She was dressed in a pair of pajamas with clouds scattered on them and had pulled a blue robe over those.

"What do you mean?"

She knotted the belt of her robe as she waited for him to explain.

"You know when we were in my office at the Jacobs Building?"

Skylar nodded as she sat down in a chair beside the bed.

Duke continued. "Well, there was a picture sitting on the desk. The woman in the picture happened to be the one we saw kissing that man in front of the diner."

"So you must know her."

Duke ran his fingers through his hair. "I must have known her pretty well. Now her face is showing up in my dreams. I keep seeing the photo; then I see her kiss that guy. She appears to be trying to tell me something, but I can't hear her."

"And that's when you begin to yell."

Duke nodded. "Wait. How did you get in here?"

Skylar motioned with her head to the other side of the room. A door between the rooms stood open.

"You must not have checked the lock on your side. When I heard you yell, I unlocked my door and knocked, but you didn't answer. I grabbed the knob and started to rattle it. The knob turned in my hand, so I came on in. Go on with your dream, who do you think she might be?"

Duke stood and walked over to the sink. He turned on the water. "I don't have any idea." He began to wash his face with the cool water from the faucet.

"She must have been someone special since you had her picture on your desk."

Duke dried off his face and then turned to look at Skylar. He leaned back against the vanity cabinet. Her face reflected his fears, and she continued to voice her thoughts.

"She could be your wife." Skylar rose, walked to the window and opened the curtain. "But why was she kissing another man? She's not being very faithful." She shifted around to look at him. "You've only been gone a few months, and she's already found someone new."

His mouth went dry. She voiced what he had refused to say himself. She clamped a hand over her mouth when she realized what she said.

"I'm sorry, Duke. I shouldn't have said that. That was very insensitive of me."

"It's all right. Maybe I didn't put the picture there."

Duke dropped the towel on the cabinet. He felt empty inside. "Someone else could be using my office now. Maybe the man she was kissing is using that office. The picture could belong to him."

Skylar's smile trembled as he watched.

"That's possible," she said. "Of course if someone else is using your office, why haven't they removed your nameplate?" She groaned out loud. "I just did it again, didn't I?"

"Yeah, well..." Duke glanced at his watch. "Do you know what time it is? We must have been really tired. It's almost six. The sky's already getting light."

"Well, I guess we can get dressed and go try some of those pancakes that drew you to this quaint town," Skylar said as she walked back toward her door.

Wells River turned out to be just what it appeared—a peaceful little town. Most of Saturday, Skylar and Duke walked around enjoying the scenery. Then they watched a little television before going to sleep that night. Duke dreamed again, but this time he didn't cry out and wake Skylar. The blonde in his dream didn't talk; she just gave him a spiteful grin.

When he awoke, he lay in the darkness trying to make some sense of the whole thing. *Who could the woman be? His wife?* She seemed to be very attracted to the young man they had seen her with in New York. Maybe she wasn't Duke's girl. Maybe the young man had been using his office. The idea was as hollow as it sounded. He didn't know much, but he knew the woman in the picture was connected to him. Another nail had been pounded into his casket. This wasn't going to turn out well in the end. He knew it.

****

At first, Duke thought the pounding he heard came from his heart as he struggled to wake from deep sleep. Skylar's muffled voice managed to penetrate his foggy brain after a few seconds.

"What? Something wrong?" Duke threw the bedcovers off, and his feet hit the floor with a thud. Heart pounding, he stood and took a wobbly step toward the door.

"Nothing's wrong. Just giving you a wake-up call. We

have to get ready for church."

"Church?" Duke dropped back onto the bed. "You woke me up for church?"

"Yes. It's Sunday and I always go to church." Her light laugh trickled through the closed door.

Duke brushed his hand over his face. *Didn't the woman know how to use a phone?*

"I'll be ready in a little while."

"Okay. Hurry though, so we'll have time for breakfast."

Duke groaned and flopped back, letting his eyes close while he waited for his heart to return to its normal rate. A short while later, he stood in the shower letting the warm water wash away the last vestiges of sleep. Less than a half hour after Skylar had pounded him awake, Duke knocked on her door, clean-shaven and dressed.

Skylar opened her door and her fresh, clean appearance took his breath. She had pulled her hair into that clippie thing she liked, letting it cascade to her shoulders. The dress she wore complemented her curves in a modest way. If she had applied any makeup, Duke couldn't tell. She had the natural look of a young girl.

"Morning." Duke smiled at Skylar, and she returned it. "Which church are we going to?"

"The little one across the street from the café."

Skylar closed her door, and they stepped off the sidewalk.

"But that's a different denomination from yours."

"Doesn't matter."

Skylar's strides were long and steady, almost matching his. If she had worn heels instead of flats, she would have been just about the same height as him.

"Why doesn't it matter?" He adjusted his steps to hers.

"God shows up in any church where the people love Him. He loves everyone. Denomination doesn't count. Now come on. My stomach is growling, and my taste buds are longing for some more of those pancakes with maple syrup."

"I think I'm going to try the waffles today." Duke laughed. "Don't want to get in a rut."

Skylar smiled and slipped her arm in his.

As they strolled toward the little restaurant, Duke questioned her statement. *Could God love him?* A man whose past is questionable, to say the least. *Could God really care about him?* He longed for an answer to that question, but he didn't know whom to ask.

The small church they attended that Sunday worshiped in a more reserved, formal manner, but Duke liked the different atmosphere. The minister spoke about the same love of God Skylar talked about so often. He said all a person had to do was ask and God would come into his life. According to him, Jesus stood at the door of your heart and knocked; all you had to do was open the door. Duke knew he felt something tugging at his heart. He had the urge to step out into the aisle at the pastor's invitation. He held himself back. *Could the urging have been Jesus? But how would he know if it was?*

"Well, how did you like the service?" Skylar asked him as they walked away from the church.

"It was different, but I enjoyed it."

"Me, too. It's amazing how God can use almost any form of worship to touch people."

Duke couldn't get the morning's service out of his mind. He felt full of restless energy and needed to work some of it off. A long walk should help. Skylar sat in a white, plastic chair in front of her motel room when he walked outside later that afternoon.

"I'm going for a little walk. I'll be back soon."

"Care for a little company?"

He looked down into her beautiful face. She had fastened her darkened hair back with some sort of long clip. It ruffled in the soft breeze. He liked her natural color better.

"If you don't mind, I'd like to be by myself for a little while. Nothing personal. I just need to think."

She smiled at him. "Sure. No problem. I'm enjoying the peace and quiet out here."

His wandering about the little Vermont town brought him to the church they had attended that morning. Staring at the white frame building, he felt an urgent need to speak with the minister. Duke surmised that the little house next door to the church might be where the minister lived. He timidly knocked on the door. A short, gray-haired woman answered in just a few seconds. Duke asked to speak to the preacher, and the lady with the kind look asked him in. As he stepped across the threshold he had a strange feeling his life had reached a turning point. For the first time in a long while, he felt no fear—only a sense of hope.

Chapter Seventeen

Skylar watched as Duke strolled down the street in the direction of the church. His need for time alone came as no surprise to her. There had been little private time for either of them during the past few days. She could use some alone time, too. She went in the room, pulled out her Bible and began to read. She read for a long time before turning to God in prayer. A couple of hours later, she glanced at the clock on the nightstand. She began to get concerned. Duke had been gone a long time. What could have happened to him? Where could he have wandered? She walked to the door thinking she would walk in the direction Duke had headed. Just as she reached for the knob, it opened and he stepped into the room.

"Where did you go off to? I was getting worried since you were gone a long time." She paused and got a good look at his face. "You look different. What on earth happened?"

A broad smile covered Duke's face. "Nothing on earth, this came directly from heaven. Skylar, I just spent the last couple of hours with the minister we heard this morning. I told him everything...well, almost everything. He said that no matter what I had done God still loves me. He loves me, Skylar! He really loves me!"

Duke's expression was like a little kid at Christmas who had just gotten the best gift ever, and actually he had. Duke had just been born again. He was a little kid in Christ. "Oh Duke, that's wonderful!" Skylar gave him a big hug.

"Should I give myself up? I'm confused because I know God doesn't want us to break the law."

Skylar stepped back and looked up into his face again. "No, He doesn't want us to break the law, but He doesn't want us to be abused by the law either. Let's wait a while longer. Give yourself more time. I know you'll get your memory back now. Just ask God to give it to you. He will, Duke. I know He will."

Skylar and Duke talked until late in the night. She shared some of her favorite Scriptures with him, and like an eager child, he tried to absorb everything. They also made plans to leave Wells River the next day.

"I really hate to leave here." He sounded wistful.

"Me, too," Skylar said. "I really like the pancakes."

Laughter filled the air as Duke looked into her eyes. "Well, that is a number one reason to stay in a place."

"You can't find good food just everywhere and we both know eating is important."

Duke nodded. "Very. Pancakes like those can't be found just anywhere, but the atmosphere here may be what makes them so special. What do you think?" Duke grinned at her.

She smiled back in response. She felt a real sense of comfort. God's presence surrounded her and filled her with peace.

****

Finally realizing that the night grew short, Skylar and Duke parted company. Duke couldn't squelch the smile that covered his face as he opened the door and walked out into the cool spring air. Skylar seemed more content and relaxed tonight than she had in weeks. Looking up to the heavens, Duke realized how different they looked tonight. The stars had never seemed brighter. The heavens were alive and a testament to a Living God.

He began to walk toward the little river that ran just behind the motel, and as he did so, he began to speak softly. His words flowed from his heart without conscious thought. "Father God, I feel such a peace tonight. It's almost as though I don't have a care in the world. Or maybe it's because I finally know You're in charge. I don't know what the future holds, but I'm not afraid. I do ask that You reveal my past to me no matter what it is." Duke paused for a moment before continuing. "I just came to know You this afternoon, and already I'm asking You for so much, but Brother Ferguson said You would help me find myself." Again Duke stood quietly and listened to the water as it gently rippled over the worn rocks. "One last thing, Father. Please help me remain a gentleman with

Skylar. You know my feelings for her, so there's no need pretending with You. Just help me keep my wishes in check until I know if I have a right to proclaim them to her." Duke once more looked heavenward, "And Lord, please don't let Skylar be hurt by me or my situation."

****

Pulling her towel from the rack, Skylar could see Duke's face in her mind. For the first time since they'd met, the torment in his eyes was gone. As she dressed for bed she began to pray softly. "Father, please help Duke remember his past no matter what it is." The sincerity in her prayer surprised her. At first she had wanted Duke to remember, but for weeks her feelings for him had somewhat changed her prayers. She had still prayed for him to remember, but she always added for him to not be married, especially since Duke had begun dreaming about the woman in the picture from that office. "God, You know how I feel about Duke, but I'm going to put that in Your hands. Please help me accept the future no matter what."

****

Sleep came easily for Duke that night. As his mind drifted into that deep place where dreams are made, he began to see himself sitting behind the desk in Brett Carlisle's office focusing on a computer screen. Someone had made it look as though he had embezzled a large sum of money from the company. At that point, Duke awoke but not in the usual cold sweat.

He reached for the phone and rang Skylar's room.

"Hello," came her sleep-filled voice.

"Skylar, wake up! I remember something!"

He heard a click coming through the phone line.

"What did you say?"

He sat up on the side of his bed. "I had another dream, and I actually remember something!"

"You do. What?"

"I know I'm Brett Carlisle. I could see myself sitting at my desk in that big office. I saw the computer screen with all the numbers. I didn't do it, Skylar! I didn't steal from the company. Somebody tried to frame me. It was a dream, but when I woke up I knew. I am Brett, and I know I am innocent!"

"Oh Duke, that's terrific!"

He heard her pause. When she spoke again, he thought he heard a little sadness coloring her question.

"Did you remember anything else?"

"No. That's it. I don't remember it all...but God showed me I'm innocent, Skylar." Duke let out a relieved sigh and plopped back on the bed. "Skylar, I give my life to Him and in less than twenty-four hours He lets me know I am Brett Carlisle *and* I'm innocent!"

"That settles it."

Her voice sounded cheerful again.

"Settles what?"

"God showed you you're not a thief. We have to keep moving now until God reveals more of your past to you. Maybe you will remember who the real crook is."

Duke lay in the darkness after their phone conversation and thanked God for His mercies.

****

New York City

"Our man's not dead," FBI Special Agent Douglas announced as he stood in front of Lawrence Jacobs' massive desk.

"How can you be sure?" Jacobs asked.

"A sheriff's deputy in Texas has seen him," Douglas explained.

"Seen who?" Tori Jacobs had been about to step into her father's office from Jordan Matthews' office when she had heard the agent being announced by her father's secretary. She had chosen to wait a few seconds just inside the portal to see what she could learn, but his announcement that Brett was still alive made her want to be in the middle of the discussion.

"Tori, come in and sit down. Special Agent Douglas has some news on Brett," Lawrence Jacobs said.

She took a seat and then waited impatiently as the FBI agent continued his report. She wound her fingers together to keep her hands from shaking. She tried to regulate her breathing so it wouldn't get out of control. Focus. Focus. Focus. She chanted it over and over in her mind.

"Well, seems our boy was hit by a car and received multiple injuries. He supposedly has amnesia."

"You think he's faking amnesia?" her father asked.

"According to the doctor, he wasn't faking at the time it happened, but if the act was working for him, he might have kept it up even if his memory returned."

"Where's he been all this time?" Tori questioned.

"Seems the owner of a horse ranch took him in. He's been working on the ranch since he left the hospital."

"When do you pick him up?" her father wanted to know.

"Well, that's the problem. He went to Virginia to some kind of horse show with this woman, and when it was over, they didn't return home."

Neither man noticed the look on Tori's face as she asked, "What woman?"

"Oh. The owner of the ranch is a woman," the agent said.

"Brett's been living with a woman all this time?" Tori asked, choking back her anger.

"I don't have any details about their living arrangements. I would guess they must have something going between them, since they decided to extend their trip. We have an all points bulletin out on both of them. They are supposedly heading down the coast toward Florida, but we have notified all police agencies from Florida to here. We'll get him," Douglas said.

His confidence irritated her.

Special Agent Douglas left the massive office without Tori noticing. Her mind wandered back to a cocktail party she had attended just yesterday afternoon. Barb Maddox had cornered her and told her some ridiculous story about seeing a cowboy who looked just like Brett. "Tori, you just wouldn't have believed it. If you'd taken him out of those jeans, put him in a pair of Dockers and given him a shave, he could have been Brett's double." Tori could still hear Barb's high, shrill voice telling her about the bearded cowboy. Now Tori knew it hadn't been Brett's look alike; it was Brett.

Her father coaxed her out of the chair. He pulled her into his arms and hugged her. Her mind felt frozen. Was everything coming to an end? Her father's concerned voice drew her attention back into the room.

"Honey. I know it hurts for you to think of Brett with

another woman. But if he has amnesia, he doesn't remember you. Let's wait until they bring him in to pass final judgment. I still find it hard to believe Brett would steal from me."

At least her reaction hadn't been taken for what it was. She had to remember to keep up the act. She had to play this like the hurt woman in his life, the woman who still believed in her fiancée's innocence. Mentally shaking herself from her reverie, she told her father about the encounter with Barb Maddox.

"Did Barb say he acted like he recognized her?" Jacobs asked.

"No. She said he just gave her a blank stare and told her she had the wrong man."

"Maybe he's not faking," Lawrence mused. "Maybe he really does have amnesia."

"Maybe."

Tori left her father's office, when she could, and rushed straight back to Jordan's office. She had the presence of mind to go down the corridor and return through the boardroom entrance so she wouldn't be seen.

****

Lazy M Ranch

"Hello," Addie answered the telephone as she wiped the bread dough from her hands.

"Addie, it's me," Skylar said. "How's everything there?"

The worry Addie had been harboring came to the surface. "Are you all right, Skylar? Where are you?"

"Sure, Addie, we're fine, but we're, uh, moving around a bit. Is Redigo around? I really need to talk to him for a minute."

"Skylar."

"Really, Addie, I only have a couple of minutes."

With a sigh of exasperation Addie punched the hold button and buzzed the barn. When Redigo answered, Addie explained who was on the line. "Redigo, you tell those two to get themselves back to Texas. I want Skylar home and Duke back here where we can help him."

****

Redigo's reply was a harassed snort as he poked the

button that would let him talk to Skylar.

"Skylar, Dan was out here looking for Duke Thursday. He's got an APB out on the two of you. Seems Duke really is this Brett feller."

"Yes, we know. Duke remembered a little more last night. He's not guilty, Redigo. Someone's trying to frame him."

"How do you know that?"

Skylar relayed Duke's dream to Redigo.

"That's great. Now you two can come home," Redigo said. He relaxed a bit and tilted his chair back.

"Not yet."

"Girl, what do you mean not yet?" He demanded, dropping his chair into an upright position again. "What's keeping you from heading home now?"

"Duke doesn't remember everything. He still doesn't know who's trying to make him look guilty. We need some more time."

"Skylar McCrea, didn't you hear me? The whole country is looking for you two. Staying out there could get you hurt. Use your head, girl!"

"I've got to go. We'll call you again."

"Skylar, don't you hang up!" ordered Redigo even as the electronic click of the connection being cut reached his ear. "Stubborn female," the angry foreman hissed as he slammed the receiver back on its hook. Glancing up he saw an equally stubborn Addie standing in the doorway, waiting for him. "Guess I'll have to wait a while longer for a piece of her peach cobbler," Redigo muttered to himself. He tried to figure out what he could say to mollify Addie as he moved toward her, since he had not had any luck in getting Skylar to head for home.

****

The gentle rocking of the bus had lulled Skylar to sleep almost immediately after they left Burlington, Vermont. From the emotions that had played across her face, Duke knew what that call to Redigo had done to Skylar. He prayed his newfound God would get them through this quickly. Duke glanced at his watch, and then realized time didn't matter because it would be days before they reached Denver. He prayed that the search for Skylar and himself would be concentrated on the East

Coast for a time yet.

Chapter Eighteen

Uvalde, Texas

Clayton Carlisle sat on his porch with his feet propped up on the railing. The mug of coffee in his hand had long ago stopped steaming as his thoughts wandered. His thoughts were on his nephew, Brett and the phone call he had received from his brother Adam. Adam's phone call still rankled. They'd never been really close, not even as boys, but the way Adam had attacked him yesterday had caused Clayton to react badly. He knew better. You keep your cool when handling an angry man. Adam was just taking out his frustration on Clayton.

The problem was Clayton was just as frustrated about Brett as Adam. A long time had passed since Brett had disappeared. Clayton knew the more time that passed without any clue as to what had happened to his nephew lessened the chances of finding him alive. A flicker of regret again passed through his mind. If he hadn't retired last year, he could've been down at Ranger Headquarters keeping an eye on the reports for himself. As it was, he had to depend on his buddies to keep him informed.

The portable phone at his side jerked him out of his reverie as it shrilled at him. "Carlisle here. What? When?" Clayton sprang to his feet with a speed which would have convinced anyone not knowing him that he was a much younger man. His long stride carried him quickly into the den where he reached for the pad and pen on his desk. "Where did you say the ranch was located?" Nodding Clayton continued to fire questions at the caller on the other end as he made notes. "Thanks, Randy. I owe you one. Tell the boys they'd better keep a closer eye on that fax machine. I should've known about this Friday when it came in."

"Rosa!" Clayton shouted to his housekeeper as he

settled his gray Stetson on his head and ended the call.

"Sí, Señor." Rosa said as she stepped into the den to answer her employer's call.

"I won't be home for supper." Clayton announced as he reached for his keys and headed for the door.

"Sí, Señor."

****

Denver, Colorado

Duke woke Skylar as soon as the bus pulled to a stop in Denver.

Her voice sounded sleepy as she asked, "Are we nearly there?"

"We're here, sleepyhead."

When the bus driver opened the door, a man in a dark-blue suit stepped onto the bus. "Ladies and gentlemen, due to a security issue we ask that you please step into the bus station and have your ID ready to show. We're very sorry for any inconvenience..."

The remainder of the man's speech drifted by Duke. They were caught. His lungs felt flat, empty. Skylar's hand sought out his. She clasped it tightly as the passengers began to stand and exit the bus.

The two of them watched as a team of black-jacketed men walked around the bus. Large letters that read FBI were plastered across their backs. Duke watched out the window over Skylar's shoulder.

"I guess I'm hotter than we thought," came his whispered attempt at levity. The sad look on Skylar's face told him he'd failed.

"We might as well get in line. No need to delay this any longer," Duke said as he rose from his seat. He looked down into her beautiful, blue eyes wide with fear. "You could stay here and let me go alone. It's me they're really looking for. Maybe if they take me, they'll be satisfied."

With a shake of her head, Skylar rejected his offer. "No, we go out together. I'll stay with you as long as I can." She stood to join him in the aisle.

That said the two of them began the slow procession down the narrow aisle to the exit. As they neared, they could see a pair of dark-suited men checking papers, and with each step, Duke prayed silently. He held her hand in his as they inched forward. Turning his head, he could see her face. Her eyes were closed, and her lips moved. She must be praying as well.

His prayers were for this to all end without Skylar or anyone else being hurt. They were only two steps away from being the next in line to have their papers checked, when the radio one of the two men held burst into life.

"Michaels, the terrorist has been located at the airport. Repeat. The terrorist has been apprehended at the airport. Cease all activity at the bus station and report at once to our location here. Marks out."

Suddenly, the men were gone.

They had been saved. Skylar looked up at Duke. He could feel the sweat on his face. A tremble he couldn't control in his hand conveyed his relief. As quickly as they could, they left the bus station. Once outside they found a remote a spot where they collapsed wearily against one another.

****

Lazy M Ranch

"Don't tell me she hasn't called yet," Dan Tate barked.

Addie noticed Redigo appeared to be at a loss for words, so she chimed in, "She did call, but we were out of the house. There was a message on the machine early this morning. She said they were getting a lot of sun and they would be out of pocket for a few days. Said something about renting a boat and spending a little time out at sea."

"She didn't say where they were or leave a number where they could be reached?"

"Now, Dan, when you were courtin' Trina, did you want the old folks to always know your whereabouts?" Addie grinned.

"Look, I've got to have something concrete to tell the sheriff. He's been keeping the FBI from putting out wanted posters for Skylar on my say-so that she's an innocent by-stander. If she doesn't call soon and either come home or get Duke to turn himself in, they'll have no choice but to consider her an accomplice." The deputy shook his head and turned to leave. Looking back he called, "You will convince her to come home when you talk to her, won't you?"

"When I get to talk to her in person, you can bet she will get a piece of my mind," Redigo assured him, finally finding his tongue.

For Redigo's ears only Addie whispered. "You better be careful, old man, giving someone a piece of your mind. You don't have that much to spare."

With the deputy safely in his car and backing away, Redigo asked, "When did you take up lying, old woman?"

"I didn't exactly lie. There have been messages on the answer machine when I had left the house before. I just didn't tell Dan when Skylar left the message."

Redigo snorted. "This twisting of the truth is okay for you to do?"

Redigo had her there. She could feel her face grow hot with embarrassment as she realized what he was pointing out to her. "No, not exactly. I'll have to ask for forgiveness, but I know those kids need help and not necessarily from the police. You looked dumb-founded, so I thought I'd better say something."

"Well, however you came up with that tale, you made it sound pretty convincing."

Redigo looked down the long drive. Addie glanced down the drive as well and saw another car making its way toward the house. "Now who could that be?" Redigo stomped off the porch without bothering to answer.

****

Just as Clayton pulled his car onto the Lazy M's driveway, a Denton County Sheriff's car passed him heading the opposite direction. Clayton's trip had him somewhat out of sorts. By the time he had driven into San Antonio the day before and talked in detail with his buddy at Ranger headquarters about his nephew, it had been late. He missed the last flight to Dallas. It annoyed him that his visit to the Lazy M Ranch had to wait until Tuesday. Clayton knew someone here had to have some answers, and he didn't intend to leave until he got them.

As he parked his car and opened the door, a short woman opened a screen door and walked into the house. Noticing a man standing out by the barn, Clayton began to walk in that direction.

The man he walked toward eyed him. He appeared to be Hispanic, but when he spoke there wasn't any trace of an accent. The man's high cheekbones sent a subtle sign he probably had some Indian blood in him also.

"Can I help you?"

The man's stance indicated he would not take any attempts at subterfuge well.

"I'll get right to the point; my name's Clayton Carlisle. I understand my nephew Brett Carlisle worked here for a while."

"No one by that name's been here far as I know," the man said.

"He used another name—Duke Green." Watching the other man carefully, Clayton hoped for some sign of acknowledgment but saw none.

"Before I talk to anyone, I like to make sure who I'm talkin' to," the man demanded.

Pulling his wallet from his back pocket, Clayton took out his driver's license and handed it over. "If that's not enough, how about this?" Clayton removed a small wallet from his vest pocket and handed it to the discerning man in front of him.

Looking at the Texas Ranger's badge, the man asked, "Are you here as a concerned uncle, or are you on official business?"

"Technically I'm retired. I just want to find my nephew and get to the bottom of this mess."

Extending his hand in greeting, the man said, "Name's Redigo. I'm the foreman around here. Come on in my office and let's talk."

Clayton followed the foreman into a small office beside the barn. "Pull up a chair, and I'll pour us a cup of coffee. You take anything in yours?"

"No, just black," Clayton answered as he surveyed his surroundings. Taking a mug of the dark brew from his host, Clayton asked, "Tell me what you know about my nephew."

"Well, first of all, he don't know he's your nephew. Duke don't remember much about his past."

"What do you mean by 'much'?"

"He just remembered that he is this Brett Carlisle, and that he's innocent. Says someone's trying to frame him."

Clayton relaxed a little, leaned back in his chair and placed his left ankle on his right knee. "So you've spoken to him recently?"

Redigo leaned back in his desk chair. "Why don't I start from the beginning?"

Clayton only nodded occasionally as Redigo recalled the events of Duke's coming to the Lazy M and everything he knew up to this moment.

Clayton looked across the desk at the man who had been relaying him this story. "You have no idea where they are?"

"I don't know where they are, but I'd bet you they're not on the East Coast." Redigo took a sip of his coffee.

"Why did Skylar stay with him?"

Redigo smiled. "Skylar never deserts a friend—no matter what. When they left, Duke was so confused and upset he would have probably given himself away in no time. She thought he needed her."

Clayton nodded. "She sounds like a good woman."

"The best," Redigo told him. "She's been running this ranch since she was nineteen-years-old and her folks were killed in a car wreck. You don't have to worry about her, Mr. Carlisle. She can take care of herself and Duke, too, if she has to."

"Please call me Clayton." He leaned forward and placed his coffee mug on the desk. "Brett can do a pretty good job of taking care of himself. Or at least he could before he moved to the big city." Clayton stood and walked to the window in Redigo's office. "He used to spend the summers with me at my ranch. He was a good hand even when he was a kid."

"Now I know why ranchin' and workin' horses came so easy for him," Redigo said.

Clayton chuckled, "Yeah. The boy has a way with horses. He wanted to be a rancher, but my brother had other ideas. Adam didn't think ranching was a good enough occupation for his son. Insisted he go to college and then helped him get this high-powered job in New York." Clayton turned to look at Redigo. "Now look where it got him. He's on the run and doesn't even remember that he has family who cares and will help him." The

Ranger couldn't stop the moisture filling his eyes as he continued, "Redigo, I've got to find them. I can help him clear himself. I know I can if I can just talk to him."

"When Skylar calls, I'll tell her about you. We'll both help if we can. I knew Duke was no thief. He's a good man."

"That he is. Funny you should call him Duke...that was my nickname when I was with the Rangers; we called Brett Little Duke." A smile covered the Ranger's face. "Thanks for helping Brett."

****

Somewhere in Colorado

"Who did you say we are today?" Duke asked as the bus pulled away from the station.

"Lee and Amanda Barkley."

"Oh yeah. If someone calls my name, would you please punch me? It was much easier when I didn't have any identity; now I have too many," Duke grumbled as he turned to look out the window.

"After Grand Junction, where are we going?" Skylar asked in hushed tones.

"Oh, I don't know. Just on west I suppose." Duke stretched his legs out as best he could. "I sure wish God would reveal a little more to me. Then maybe we could just go home."

"He will in His own time," Skylar said as she picked up her overnight bag. "He's never late in doing things. Remember that."

Duke turned in his seat and looked into Skylar's eyes. "He's never late by whose clock?"

"His clock. You just have to learn patience." Skylar reached into her carry-on bag and pulled out her Bible. "Here do some reading."

Duke took the book, and opening it, he lost himself in his reading.

"Duke, let's get out, stretch our legs and get something cool to drink."

Startled, Duke looked up and noticed the other passengers standing in the aisle waiting to exit the bus. Duke handed Skylar the Bible and got to his feet. "Okay, I guess we could use a break."

Once outside Duke scanned his surroundings. The bus had pulled to a stop by what looked like a general store and across the street sat a gas station. "Not much of a town, is it?"

"Well, I wouldn't call it a booming metropolis," Skylar agreed. "But look at it this way, they probably don't have much of a police force either."

Duke pulled two colas from the cold box and handed one to Skylar. They browsed the store for a few moments before Skylar moved off to look at something across the store.

Duke paid no attention to her until one of the other passengers poked him in the side and said, "I think your friend is calling you."

Looking a little annoyed, Skylar once again called to him. "Lee, would you come here, please?"

Somewhat embarrassed Duke walked to Skylar's side and whispered to her. "I told you I couldn't remember my name."

Ignoring his statement Skylar called his attention to an item on the small bulletin board, 'Mountain lodge, rooms for rent. Inquire at counter'. "Could be a nice place to find some peace and quiet. And maybe get a memory back."

"Could be, but a lodge could be really expensive."

"It won't hurt to ask about it." Skylar walked over to the counter. The man there gave her all the information they needed about the lodge. "We'll take two rooms." Looking at Duke, she drawled, "Brother dear, would you please go and get our luggage off the bus while I get us registered?"

"But..." Duke began, only to be interrupted by Skylar's thick southern drawl, "Now Roy, you go on, and I'll take care of registering and paying the man."

Duke's mind began spinning as he left the store. *Now she can't even remember who we are, she called me Roy. I thought I was Lee.* Duke got to the bus driver just in time. The driver acted a little aggravated but got their luggage out before speeding off.

****

"Well, Roy and Dale Cartwright. You're brother and sister?

"That's right," Skylar nodded.

"I hope these rooms meet with your approval," the old gentleman said as he showed them upstairs. "The bathroom is just down the hall; you'll find clean towels and washcloths in the linen closet. If you need anything just let me or Stella know." The little man handed them the keys to their respective rooms and then walked down the hall. "Stella will have dinner ready about six. See you in the dining room, until then feel free to wander about and explore the territory if you'd like."

Skylar thanked him for all his help and then turned to look at Duke. "You looked puzzled. Is something wrong?"

She opened the door to her room. He followed her inside with her suitcase, and she closed the door behind him.

Duke shook his head. "You're getting as confused as me. I thought we were Lee and somebody Barkley. Now Mr. Wheeler just called us Roy and Dale something or other."

Skylar set her overnight bag on the bed. "We were Lee and Amanda, but that was on the bus. Now we're Roy and Dale Cartwright." She smiled and whispered, "When no one's around we can be Duke and Skylar."

"Are you sure?" Duke moaned as he started for the door to go to his room. "Maybe I'll just call you Jane and you can call me John, as in Doe."

Skylar laughed.

"Lord, give me a better memory so I can not only remember my past but remember who I am in the present," Duke mumbled as he left her room.

"Did you say something?" Skylar asked as she followed him to the door.

"Just praying," Duke said as he walked on down the hall.

Duke and Skylar went downstairs a couple of hours later to join Stella and Tom Wheeler for dinner.

"So where are you kids from?" Stella Wheeler asked, once grace had been offered at the dinner table.

"We grew up in Texas," Skylar said as she took the plate of roast beef offered to her by Mr. Wheeler.

"It's nice to see a brother and sister traveling

together. Don't see that very often," Stella said.

Skylar smiled. "Well, my brother has been through some very rough times lately, and I thought it would be good for him to get away. I decided to go with him since we don't get to spend a lot of time together." Skylar picked up her glass of water and took a sip.

Duke focused on Skylar, wondering how she came up with these stories with such little effort.

"Mr. Cartwright, what do you do for a living?"

It took several long moments before Duke realized the older man was talking to him. He stammered, "Please call me...Roy." He took a long drink of his iced tea so he could compose his thoughts. "I, uh, work on a horse ranch."

"Now, that's really work. I did some ranching in my younger days before I met Stella and settled down to married life."

Mr. Wheeler took off with tales of his younger days, relieving Duke of the effort of having to remember who he was at the moment and preventing him from having to make up more lies. Guilt about the lies pricked at his mind.

After dinner Duke and Skylar walked out onto the front porch. He sighed his relief at being alone with her.

"I thought I had really blown it in there when I didn't realize he was talking to me."

"You made a quick recovery, though." Skylar walked over to the edge of the porch and looked out across the mountains. "This is an incredible view."

"Yes, it is."

He moved to stand beside her.

The lodge sat about halfway up the side of an Aspen-covered mountain. From the porch, they could see a lake below them and more mountains to the east. God's hand was all over this beautiful creation. Duke breathed in the fresh air. How good it was to be able to relax for a while.

The squeak of a door hinge needing oil brought Duke's attention back to the moment.

Tom Wheeler stood in the open doorway.

"Excuse me, but I wanted to invite you both to join us for our devotion time." He hesitated only a second. "Don't feel obligated; we only wanted you to know you're welcome."

Skylar looked up at Duke, and he nodded his agreement. She answered for the two of them.

"We'd love to join you."

Stella Wheeler had already seated herself in one of the rocking chairs when they got to the living room. Tom Wheeler sat beside her in the matching rocker. A set of padded club chairs had been placed across from the rockers. Skylar and Duke settled into those.

Tom Wheeler's baritone voice was easy to listen to, and Duke found himself concentrating on each word. When he read Hebrews 13:5, the verse came alive in Duke's mind. *Did Got really mean that?* God would never leave His followers alone. Feelings of being alone had taken him over during the past few months. No memory of friends or family left him filled with a sense of emptiness. Skylar and the rest of the Lazy M crew helped shove his feelings away at times. Even so, most of the time, he felt disconnected.

In this verse God was promising to be there for him—always. Joy at the knowledge moved through Duke's body from head to toe.

"Son, that's a bright smile you have there. Did something in that passage get your attention?" Mr. Wheeler asked.

In his joy, Duke decided to share his newfound faith with this couple. "Yes, you see...I just recently accepted Jesus as my savior, and the part in that verse about God never forsaking me is very comforting." Duke looked down at his boots. "With no memory, I have to depend on someone telling me facts about me. It made me feel alone a lot of the time. Now I know I've always got Someone, no matter what."

Stella Wheeler stopped rocking her chair. "That not only comforts new converts, but those of us old in the faith find it comforting also. But, what do you mean about no memory?"

Duke's throat clogged with emotion at the woman's question. He couldn't speak. Skylar must have seen the 'deer-in-the-headlights' look that came upon his face, so she spoke for him.

"As I said at dinner, he's had a rather traumatic

experience recently. He was in an accident and left for dead. When he woke up, he had no memory of the past. He still doesn't remember much. He's having a tough time right now."

Skylar's warm hand touched his.

"Oh, son, I'm so sorry," Stella said. She reached over and took Duke's other hand. "Would you mind if Tom and I pray you would get your memory back?"

Duke fought to keep his tears at bay. He cleared his throat. "No ma'am. I need all the prayers I can get."

Before he could understand what was happening, Stella, Tom, and Skylar gathered around him. They began to call upon the Lord to restore his memory to him and to restore all that had been taken from him. Duke felt like someone was whispering in their ears telling these people how to pray for him. His body flooded with peace. A warm silence floated through the room as their prayers ceased.

Duke broke the stillness when he said, "You people have the kind of relationship with God that I want. You really seem to know Him as a loving Father."

Skylar's hand still clasped his.

"We do." She smiled. "We may or may not have an earthly father, but we will always have a heavenly Father. The Bible says God loves us even more than our earthly father."

The emotions that had filled him overflowed. He found a tissue being pressed into his hand by Stella.

"How do I get that feeling, that...that relationship?

"You've got to get to know Him," Tom Wheeler answered. "And the way you do that is to read His word. The more you study the Bible, Roy, the more you'll learn about God and what he wants for us, His children."

"Can we keep doing that while we're here?"

"Why, that would be wonderful!" Stella said, before anyone else could.

"Stella and I always start and end our day with devotions. We just don't usually invite our guests to join us, but you two are welcome."

Duke wondered why the Wheelers had decided to include them and couldn't let this wonderment go. "Why did you decide to ask us to join you tonight then?"

Duke saw Tom look at his wife before he answered. A

smile passed between them.

"We both got the feeling we needed to have you with us. Stella shared her feelings while we were doing the dishes. I'd had the same urge, so we followed God's leading."

Duke's grin came from his soul. "I'm glad you did."

"Me too, son. So we'll see you in the morning."

"Tomorrow will be great." Duke stood to his feet and shook hands with his new friends.

****

New York City

"Why didn't you come by, or at least call me, when you got back to town yesterday?" She didn't bother to try to hide her agitation as she spoke into her cell phone. She paced in front of the windows stretching across the living room in her apartment. The view of Central Park added to the value of the apartment, but at the moment, she could have been looking at a brick wall for all its value to her.

"It was late when I got in. Besides, we're supposed to be playing it cool for a while, remember?"

She didn't like it when he was right. She whirled away from the window and marched to the kitchen. Pulling open a cabinet door, she took a glass and filled it from the bottle of wine sitting on the counter. She swallowed a large mouthful before she asked, "Well, what do you think about the news?"

"What news?"

"That Brett's alive." She swallowed again and a satisfied grin eased across her mouth. She knew something he didn't. Seconds ticked by while she waited for her partner's answer. His voice came at her filled with suspicion.

"How do you know that?"

"The FBI got a lead on him. He's been in Texas this whole time. He's supposed to have amnesia."

She heard him release a huff of air before he replied.

"That's almost as good as him being dead."

"Not if he recovers from it, and if he does, you're sunk."

His next words sounded like the snarl of a tiger.

"Don't you mean we're sunk?"

She gasped. "I didn't have anything to do with it."

His laugh was evil. "And just who do you think will believe that after they find out about us?"

The woman's hand shook as reality sunk in, white wine splashed down the front of her silk dress; she could be held as an accomplice.

Chapter Nineteen

Houston, Texas

Julia Carlisle's fingers trembled as she dialed her brother-in-law's phone number. Her voice quivered as she heard his husky answer. "Clayton, it's Julia."

"Where are you?"

She spoke softly. "It's my garden club day so I'm at a friend's and it's okay to talk." She worked hard to keep from crying. "Clayton, have you...have you heard anything?"

The silence made her think she had lost the connection.

"Clayton?"

"He's alive, Julia. Brett's fine."

"Thank you, God," she prayed. Tears spilled down her cheeks. She sank onto the chaise lounge in Marla's guest room. "Where is he?"

Again there was silence. Clayton wasn't telling her something.

"Tell me."

He cleared his throat. "I don't know where he is specifically, but I know he's okay, now, physically. He was in an accident after he left New York."

Julia's breath caught, and she gripped the phone tighter. She waited.

"He's been on a ranch outside of Denton the whole time. He's recovered from his injuries."

"Why...didn't he call us?"

Clayton's pause tightened her nerves. There was more.

"He's got amnesia."

Julia's breathing accelerated. "He's got brain damage? He doesn't remember any of us?" Her voice had risen in volume.

"Julia, calm down. The doctors say there's no apparent brain damage, but the trauma of the accident has given him amnesia."

He stopped her interruption before she could voice it.

"But...he has started to remember bits and pieces. He knows he is Brett Carlisle and that he's innocent. He knows he was set up to take a fall, but doesn't remember who or why."

Julia lowered her voice and her breathing slowed down. "I always believed he wasn't guilty. My son couldn't do what Larry said he'd done." She swallowed. "Then you've spoken with him."

"No."

"But why not?"

"Julia, he's running. I'm getting feedback from him through the foreman of the ranch where he's been living since leaving the hospital. The foreman doesn't know where he is right now."

She jumped to her feet and began pacing the room. "Do you believe this foreman? Clayton, we've got to help him. Adam and I will go to Denton. We can be there in a few hours."

"No. You can't. I need you to keep Adam there."

"But..."

"Julia, your whole family is being watched. Sit tight. I have a plan I think will help Brett get out of this mess. Don't let that hot-headed brother of mine fly off the handle and mess things up before I can get everything in place."

Julia chuckled for the first time in weeks. "I thought I was talking with the hot-headed brother."

Her brother-in-law's deep-throated laugh reached her ears.

"Hey now! You know what I mean. Don't let him bring the FBI to my door."

She smiled. "Then go do your job and get my boy out of this trouble."

"I'll do the best I can," he promised.

She punched a button on her phone and slid it closed. Her head bowed. At least she knew her precious son was alive.

****

Western Colorado
The sweet fragrance of mountain air filled Duke's senses as he walked along the trail leading to the small lake south of their lodge. The sun burst over the mountain, and its rays made diamond-like sparkles on the water below. He knew God was alive and well in Colorado. His beauty surrounded Duke.

He sat down on a fallen tree trunk in the peaceful silence that was broken only by the occasional sound of a bird's sweet song or the rustle of the Aspen leaves being kissed by the cool breeze. The only flaw in this painting was the missing facts of his life. He knew no more about himself than he did when they left Wells River days ago.

"God, I don't understand. Am I not listening to You or are You not talking? Why are You not revealing more of my past to me?" He paused in his prayer to listen to the piercing call of an eagle. "Skylar says You're never late, that You're always on time. God, if You could tell me what time you have, I'd be happy to set my watch with Yours."

With a heavy sigh, Duke stood and began to walk back to the lodge. His spirits lifted as he topped a small hill and caught a glimpse of Skylar. The sun's glow caused the red in her natural color to show through the dark brown rinse she had put on it. She looked relaxed and content sitting in a double rocking chair with her feet propped up on the porch railing. She grew more appealing every day.

She pushed against the railing and rocked the chair as she called to him, "You must have been up bright and early."

Duke tried to ignore the fluttering inside him caused by the sight of her. He offered up a short prayer for strength.

After walking up the steps of the porch, he sat down on the railing. "I took a hike down to the lake. It's beautiful this time of day, and if you hadn't been so lazy, you could have seen it, too."

"What do you mean, lazy? It's barely seven o'clock now."

Her frown was ineffective because her eyes sparkled with shared teasing. She dropped her feet to the porch with a thud.

"How about a cup of coffee? Stella's got breakfast about ready. I think I could snatch you a piece of cinnamon toast if you can't wait."

"Coffee sounds great, but I can wait for breakfast. Keep your seat. I'll grab a mug and come back to join you."

With a large mug in hand, Duke sat next to Skylar. He took a careful sip of the steaming brew. His mind drifted to Texas and the Lazy M.

"Why haven't Redigo and Addie ever married?"

Skylar coughed and sputtered as she almost choked on her coffee.

"Are you okay?" he asked.

"Yeah, but where did that come from?"

Duke stared off into the copse of trees in the distance. "I was thinking about the ranch and the two of them. I just wondered why they never married."

"Duke, they're just friends. They don't feel that way about each other."

He turned and looked at her. "Don't tell me you've never noticed the way they look at each other. They're friends all right, but I'd say they have deeper feelings, too."

Skylar's brow furrowed.

"I never thought about them that way. Do you really think they're in love with each other?"

Duke put his long legs on the porch railing and leaned back against the chair. He shrugged and smiled. "I'm not sure they have ever admitted it to themselves, let alone to each other, but I'd say there is definitely a chemistry between them."

"When we get back to the ranch, I'll have to pay more attention. I might even play Cupid. Hmm. Romance at the Lazy M. That has a nice ring to it."

Her smile had a wistful quality to it. "Has there never been romance at the Lazy M?"

The question slipped out. He didn't know whether he wanted to hear her answer or not.

"Sure, my parents were very much in love."

"But what about Skylar McCrea?" Did he no longer have control over his mouth?

She blushed. "Maybe...a long time ago."

Duke looked away. He'd hit a tender spot.

"You don't have to tell me. It's not fair for me to pry, especially when I can't share my own past with you."

She paused and took a long drink from her mug.

"That's okay. It would probably do me good to talk to you about Timothy." She took a deep breath as he watched. "I thought I was in love with him, but my big mistake was in thinking he loved me." She sighed. "That was another time God had to love me through a bad stretch in my life."

"I can't believe any man couldn't love you." Duke closed his eyes. He couldn't look at her. He wished he could take those words back.

"Umm, thank you, but Tim didn't feel that way. It was about five years ago. We had dated about six months, and I was head over heels for him. Every moment was special. He fit into my life so perfectly. He said he loved the ranch and came out to help with the horses. I knew he was the one God meant for me, or I thought he was."

Her voice cracked, and she cleared her throat. "Valentine's Day was going to be a special time. He said he had a big question to ask me." She laughed but it didn't carry any mirth with it. "I was all ready to accept his proposal." She shook her head. "He made one all right, but it wasn't the one I had anticipated. He wanted me to let him move in with me at the ranch."

Duke wanted her to stop. He cringed as he realized the pain it caused her to tell him her story. He picked up her hand and wove his fingers through hers.

"Stop, Skylar. Don't tell me any more."

She shook her head. "No. I want to finish it. I'd made it clear from the beginning I wouldn't have sex before marriage. I'm old-fashioned, I guess, but I still believe in saving myself for the man I marry."

Duke was speechless. Her confession floored him. His memory of his own life might be missing, but he knew in this day and age that it was rare for a woman to still be a virgin at eighteen, much less at twenty-eight. Here he'd been praying for God to keep him a gentleman where Skylar was concerned. With her strict belief, she had enough fortitude for both of them.

She continued her story.

"Seems he didn't believe in marriage. His parents had divorced, and both of them remarried...a couple of times. His stepfather, at the time, was only a couple of years older than Tim. That didn't set well with Tim."

She shrugged. "I thought, when I refused him, he would be miserable like I was and come back to me. After several days, when I hadn't heard from him, I nearly gave in to the temptation to tell Tim I'd live with him." She paused and sipped the last of her coffee. "But I couldn't. No matter how much I loved him, I couldn't give up the standard I'd set for my life. If I lived with him, I would have been selling myself short and going against God's word."

She sighed and looked at him. "So, now you've heard the story of my life. Kind of dull, isn't it?"

He didn't know what to say. Everyday this woman amazed him. She had more character than anyone he knew, and he knew this would remain true if he ever remembered the rest of his life. "Did you ever hear from him?"

"Yeah, I saw him with his new love a couple of years ago. Her father owns a large ranch on the other side of Fort Worth. He built Tim and the girl a house to live in on his ranch. Seems he's a liberated father and doesn't expect a man to marry his daughter. She looked about six months pregnant when I saw them."

Loving the wrong man had hurt her. He slipped his hand away from hers and stood up. Stella called to them from inside the lodge, saving him from having to comment. Breakfast waited on them.

"Come on. Let's fill up on Stella's great cooking." His smile was weak, but it was the best he could manage. He opened the door and waited for her to walk through ahead of him. She did and held her head high.

Duke wasn't blind. He knew how Skylar felt about him, and he was pretty sure she knew his feelings for her. Right now they couldn't put voice to their feelings; they might never be able to do so. Following her through the doorway, he asked God not to let her be hurt again.

****

Lazy M

Deputy Dan Tate stared at Redigo. "From the look on your face, I'd say you still haven't heard from Skylar."

Redigo returned the young man's stare. He hadn't heard from the owner of the Lazy M, so he didn't have to lie. "Nothing. Not a word."

Dan twirled his hat in his hands. "The sheriff called me into his office this morning. He said if I came back empty-handed today that the FBI would put out a warrant for Skylar, too. For aiding and abetting a fugitive."

Redigo looked down and kicked a small rock with the toe of his boot. "I guess they gotta do what they gotta do." He paused a moment to get control of the anger bubbling to the surface. He looked back into the face of the deputy. "Dan, off the record, Duke's not a thief. I believe if he has enough time he can prove it. I'd bet that's what Skylar thinks, too."

He saw Dan nearly drop his hat.

"Are you telling me you have heard from them?"

"I'm not sayin' anything like that. It's just that…you know Skylar. If somethin' or someone is in trouble, and she thinks she can help them, she'll do it and hang the consequences."

Dan pointed his finger at Redigo. "Listen to me. Don't you get involved, too. It's bad enough to know one of my best friends is fixin' to be wanted by the FBI, and I can't do a thing about it. Don't go adding another person to that list."

Redigo smiled at the deputy's ferocity. It reminded him of a bulldog he'd known once. "I won't do anything you wouldn't do in my place."

Dan snorted at him and shook his head. "That's what has me worried. Look, as far as anyone is concerned, I know for a fact you and Addie know nothing about Skylar and Duke's whereabouts or their plans. Just be careful, and tell Skylar to do the same."

"I will."

The deputy nodded at him, placed his hat on his head and scuffled his boots through the gravel, sending dust into the air. He gunned the engine of his patrol car and the tires threw more dirt into the air as he sped down the drive.

Redigo shook his head. Skylar better hurry up and get back here. Things were getting worse by the second.

Chapter Twenty

Duke got out of the old pick-up and helped Skylar down. "Thanks for the ride back to town."

Tom had gotten out of the truck and walked around to stand with Duke and Skylar. "Glad to do it." He extended his hand to Duke. "Hope you folks enjoyed your stay."

"We certainly did," Duke said as he shook the older man's hand.

"Son, you keep reading the Word and reaching out to the Almighty and He will restore everything you've lost." Tom paused for a moment and then added, "but in His own time."

Duke grinned, "I'm slowly learning about His own time."

"Just keep learning." Tom turned to Skylar. "Did you enjoy yourself?"

Skylar looked at the older gentleman and smiled. "Yes, I did. It was peaceful and quiet out there. We both got some much needed rest." She gave Tom a hug. "I believe God placed you and Stella in our path." She looked up at Duke and then back at Tom. "You have given Roy some much needed parental-type guidance; I thank you for that."

"It was our pleasure. And both Stella and myself will be praying that all will work out for your brother."

With a wave, Tom Wheeler drove off. Duke stepped inside the general store and spoke to the clerk. He checked the bus schedule and told Duke the time the bus would arrive. Walking out the door, Duke saw Skylar at the pay phone, so he hurried to join her.

"We expected that," Skylar said. "What? Wait a minute." She motioned for Duke to come closer. "Duke listen."

He leaned his head down and placed his ear on the

other side of the phone.

"Go ahead, Redigo," Skylar said.

Redigo's voice came over the line.

"I said I've met Duke's uncle. Seems we might have gotten a break. Clayton's a retired Texas Ranger. I've told him everything I know about Duke and the situation. We've come up with a plan. Where are the two of you right now?"

Duke turned away from Skylar and the phone. More pieces of his life. At least he had some family, and, from what Redigo said, this uncle was willing to help him. Duke offered a prayer of thanks. God was putting something together here.

****

"We're on the way to Grand Junction, Colorado," Skylar said.

"How are you traveling?"

"By bus."

"That won't do. Clayton and I need you back here in Texas as quick as you can get here. A bus will take you too long. Where's the closest airport?"

"There's one in Grand Junction, but..."

"Then go there and catch a plane," Redigo instructed.

Skylar didn't say anything.

"Skylar, are you still there?"

Her voice came out soft and shaky. "Yes."

"What's wrong?"

"We, uh, can't fly."

She heard him muttering under his breath and figured she didn't want to know what he was saying.

"And why not? You runnin' out of money?"

"We've got plenty of money for bus tickets, but I don't know if there's enough for plane tickets."

"I'll send you more then."

"That still won't help, Redigo." She leaned against the glass wall of the phone booth.

"Why can't you fly back here?"

"Redigo, I'm trying to explain. Duke doesn't have any picture identification. No ID, no purchasing plane tickets."

Skylar listened to the sound of his breathing while Redigo thought for a moment.

"I keep forgetting about that." He paused again. "All right, girl, I can get my cousin in Colorado to buy you tickets and have them waiting for you in Grand Junction. What name shall I have him use?"

She sighed. He still didn't understand. "Won't work either. They check your ID before you board the plane to make sure you are the person whose name is on the ticket."

Redigo's groan came through the phone line.

"Hmm. Wait a minute...let me think."

Skylar twirled the phone cord.

"Hang tight there. Give me that phone number."

Skylar read it off to him.

"I'll call you back in a few minutes."

She hung up the phone. Duke walked over to her.

"What did he say?"

"He's checking on something. Uh, how much time do we have before the bus leaves?"

"About an hour."

Skylar watched as Duke paced around the outside of the phone booth. He had his hands shoved in his jeans pockets, and from time to time, he bent to pick up a small rock and throw it against the side of a dumpster near them. She leaned against the side of the phone booth. She was getting tired of waiting all the time. When the phone rang, she pulled it off of the hook so fast she almost dropped it.

"Yes?"

Redigo's voice came over the wire with an air of confidence. "All right, girl, I called my cousin in Colorado. He'll pick you up at the bus station in Grand Junction."

"You have a cousin in Colorado?"

"I have cousins everywhere," Redigo laughed.

"Okay. Tell him we're traveling as John and Marlena Rogers." Skylar smiled as Duke let out a loud moan.

"What's the matter with Duke?"

Skylar snickered. "Oh, nothing."

"Okay. He'll pick up John and Marlena Rogers," Redigo confirmed. "Do you have enough money to get you back to Texas?"

"Maybe, but isn't it a little dangerous for us to come back to Denton?"

"That's exactly the reason you'll be heading for El Paso. My Colorado cousin, Juan, will take care of you for tonight. Tomorrow he'll take you back to Grand Junction, and you'll get on the bus for El Paso. When you get there, my cousin, Julio Gomez, and his wife, Juanita, will get you a car and give you some more travel money. Julio will give you the rest of your instructions when you see him."

Skylar leaned her forehead against the cool metal of the phone box. When would this all stop? The urge to scream made her clinch her hands.

"My cousin and his wife will have a sign for John and Marlena."

"I think you'd better make that sign for Luke and Laura Evans." Skylar smiled.

Duke's groan came from behind her. She glanced at him and saw he had slumped against the side of the store and was shaking his head. She giggled.

"Did I hear Duke groan again?"

"Yes." She giggled again.

"Is something wrong with him?"

"No, he's just…tired. It's a long story."

"Tell me when you see me then."

"Will do. So don't forget, Luke and Laura Evans in El Paso."

"Is all this really necessary?" Redigo asked. "Skylar, you have a world class imagination I never knew about. All right, Luke and Laura it'll be. Julio and Juanita will be waiting."

"Thanks, Redigo. I don't know what I'd do without you."

"Shucks, girl. Lookin' out for you is part of my job. You tell that rascal, Duke, he's got a good man in his uncle. We'll get him out of this yet. You two take care."

"I think this is a little above and beyond your job description. Give my love to Addie. I can't wait for a bowl of her peach cobbler."

With a snort Redigo returned, "You and me both. Since you two have been gone, that woman's been more cranky than that old red hen of hers settin' on a nest full of eggs. Blames me for all this mess, I reckon. I haven't had one of her desserts since I got back without you. See you soon."

Hanging up the receiver, Skylar turned to face Duke and burst out laughing. He had his hands on his forehead and was muttering to himself. "First I'm nobody, and then I'm Duke, and then Brett, followed by who remembers what. Now I'm doomed to more names. Lord, is this a part of Your plan, to have this crazy woman drive me totally nuts? I didn't think I was that bad. Help!" He extended his arms and looked up into the sky.

Grabbing one of Duke's arms, Skylar tugged him away from the phone booth. "Come on, Lee, I see our bus coming down the road."

"But, aren't we Roy and Dale?" Duke sighed and fell into step beside Skylar.

Skylar shook her head. "That was in the store. The bus is coming, so we're Lee and Amanda again."

"Please! Just call me brother, and I'll call you sis." Duke begged as the bus pulled up to a dusty stop.

"Hey. I'm being nice. I let us go back to Lee and Amanda. I could have come up with a couple more different names, you know," Skylar whispered as the bus driver opened the door and stepped down.

Minutes later the bus rumbled slowly away from the station. There were only a few passengers on board, so Duke asked Skylar about the bits of conversation he'd overheard. "So you've become a wanted woman now."

A grin played across Skylar's lips. "If you mean have they issued a warrant for me, too, then, yes, I am a wanted woman. I guess we can try to relax until we get to Grand Junction."

Chapter Twenty-One

Juan was waiting at the bus station in Grand Junction just as Redigo had said. The three got into his car before much conversation ensued.

"You two are probably hungry," Juan said.

A rumble in his stomach at the mention of food made Duke realize he indeed was ready for something to eat.

"That would be very nice," Skylar said.

Juan pulled into a fast food restaurant and ordered burgers, fries and drinks for all of them and then pulled back out onto the road.

"I know you folks are tired of riding, so I apologize for yet another ride. My home is about a hundred miles from here. We will spend the night there; tomorrow I will drive you into town to the bus station and put you on a bus for El Paso," Juan told them.

Duke listened as Skylar made easy conversation with the man. They talked about Redigo, and Juan told her his childhood memories of his cousin.

Duke tried to stretch out his long legs in the cramped space of the backseat. He laid his head back, and his thoughts went back to the mountain lodge. He had felt so at peace there. Now, out here in the real world, his peace had fled. What would tomorrow hold? What was the plan Redigo, and this uncle he couldn't remember, had in mind? Duke's mind was on overload. Thinking about it all made him more confused, so he fell into a restless sleep.

For the first time in days, the nightmare returned. He wasn't running through the streets of the big city but was standing in front of the blonde, and she was yelling at him. He stood stone still as she yelled words he couldn't make out. He wanted to vomit or run away, but he couldn't do either one. He began to yell back. Someone shook him, pulling him away from the blonde woman.

Duke opened his eyes to see Skylar stretched over

the back of the seat looking at him.

"You were having another nightmare."

Duke didn't speak but sat up in his seat and tried to shake himself awake.

Skylar turned back around and replaced her seatbelt. Duke heard her trying to explain some of their situation to Juan without telling him the whole story. How Duke longed for this whole long nightmare of his life to end. How he longed for the peace he had found by that little mountain lake.

****

El Paso, Texas

There were no unusual activities going on at the bus station as Skylar and Duke stepped off the bus. Within seconds, they spotted a man holding a cardboard sign with the name Rogers printed on it.

Skylar walked over to the man. "Julio Gomez?"

"Sí, señorita." Julio pointed to a waiting car across the street. "This way, please." A pretty woman of Hispanic descent sat in the driver's seat. Their luggage was stowed in the trunk, and the car discreetly pulled away from the curb. Julio introduced his wife Juanita as their driver.

As Juanita drove, Julio explained the rest of their travel plans. "When you get to Laredo, you are to go to the casa of an hombre named Carlos Ramirez. He will take you the rest of the way to your Tío Clayton's." Julio handed Skylar a large wad of money. "My cousin, Redigo, asked that I give you this."

"But Julio, surely you've made a mistake. This is too much. It is much more than Redigo said he would send." Skylar held her hand up in protest.

"Sí, señorita." Julio nodded his head. "But Juanita and I have owed Redigo a debt for a long time now. He has stubbornly refused to allow us to repay him for a loan he made us many years ago when we were first married. We started our grocery shop with his money and have done very well. When he told us of your plight, Juanita and I knew this was a way to repay him for his kindness. It will give us much pleasure for you to accept our gift."

Knowing it would insult the generous couple to refuse any further, Skylar humbly took the money from

Julio. "We will remember your generosity always."

Juanita maneuvered the car to a stop behind an older model car. Julio turned to the couple in the backseat. "This is the car you will take to Laredo. It has been living in Mexico with Juanita's sister. We are told it has been an excellent car. There is a map and directions in the glove compartment. A phone number is written on the map for Señor Ramirez. He will be expecting you sometime after tomorrow evening." Julio handed Duke the keys.

Juanita stepped out of the car carrying a basket. "Here Señorita, I have packed some food for you. Your trip will be a long one, and you will need refreshment. I have included some of my homemade sweets. I hope you will like them."

The humble Mexican couple standing before them would be the picture Skylar would see each time she heard the story of the Good Samaritan from now on. Impulsively she hugged Juanita before taking the basket from her. "Muchas gracias, señora."

Duke extended his hand and clasped the older man's. "Thank you for all you have done for us."

Duke and Skylar smiled broadly as Julio ushered them into the waiting car. "Vaya con Dios," came the blessing of the Hispanic couple as Duke pulled away.

Skylar's eyes flooded with tears as she turned to wave good-bye to another set of new friends. "Lord, please don't let them get into any trouble because of us."

"Amen," Duke finished for her.

****

Somewhere in the mountains of West Texas

Darkness had long since fallen as Duke drove the weary miles away from El Paso. "I don't remember a mile being this far before," Duke quipped as Skylar awoke from her nap.

Skylar stretched her arms out in front of her. "Ah, but this is Texas remember? Everything's bigger in Texas. That's got to include miles. You about ready for me to take over?"

"Yeah. I think I'll crawl in back and stretch out a little. Let me find a place to pull over."

The change in drivers was made quickly, and Skylar

soon heard Duke's tired snore coming from the back seat. The moon rose as she drove, and Skylar alternately prayed and sang hymns to help pass the time. The radio in the car refused to work, so it was of no help in keeping her awake.

It had been a couple of hours since Duke had given the wheel over to her when she noticed a car pull onto the highway behind her as she passed a low-sitting billboard. When the car caught up and stayed behind her, Skylar felt sure she knew what was going to happen next. Sure enough, after a few moments, red and blue lights began flashing from the top of the car behind her.

Her heart felt as though it rose to her throat and was choking her. Skylar slowed down and prepared to stop. "Lord, please, not now. Not after this far."

The change in their speed must have woken Duke. He sat up in the back seat and glanced out the back window. "Skylar, you weren't speeding were you?"

"Not unless this speedometer is wrong. I've been very careful to keep it just about five miles an hour below the speed limit." She brought the car to a complete stop. "I don't know what's wrong."

The span of time that it took the Texas Department of Public Safety trooper to exit his vehicle and walk to her car felt like hours, but in reality was only a few seconds. Skylar rolled down her window as the trooper approached. "Good evening, Officer."

The state trooper shined his flashlight onto Skylar's face. "Good evening, Ma'am." He then moved the light to the back seat. "Where are you two headed?"

Skylar fought back the waves of fear flooding her. She tried to remain pleasant. "We're on our way back to San Antonio. My brother and I have been on a vacation. We stayed a day longer than we had planned, so we're driving through. I was letting Clark sleep for a while so he could take over for me later. Did I do something wrong?"

"Did you know you have a tail light out, Ma'am?" the trooper questioned.

"No. I didn't realize that," Skylar said. Being able to tell the truth released some of her tension. But that rush left her light-headed.

"May I see your license and proof of insurance, Ma'am?"

The hand Duke had placed on her right shoulder as the trooper began his inquiry tightened slightly, and Skylar knew Duke was as anxious as she. *God, please help,* she prayed as she reached for her purse.

As slowly as she dared, Skylar began to sort through her wallet to find the items the Texas trooper had requested. Her hand stilled as she came to the license, and she had to force her fingers to grip it. With a tug, it came free of its snug compartment, and Skylar fingered through the rest of her cards looking for her insurance card. Skylar watched as her hand extended itself toward the trooper. Just as he reached for the two pieces of condemning plastic, the trooper's radio crackled to life.

An exchange of information took place, and as quickly as he had appeared, the Texas DPS trooper left. His last words hung in the air. "Be sure to stop and get that light repaired as soon as possible."

When at last she could breathe again, she noticed Duke's ragged breathing. Her wide-open stare met his in the rearview mirror. "Thank you, Lord," they both whispered at the same time.

****

It seemed that every station they passed was closed, but daylight was fast approaching so they wouldn't need the lights for a while. Duke began to search through the basket Juanita had packed for them.

He pulled out a sandwich and offered Skylar one. "No thanks, I'm getting really thirsty though and could use a trip to the ladies' room."

Duke swallowed the bite of sandwich in his mouth. "The sign a mile back said there was a truck-stop about five miles ahead. We could stop there, get something to drink and have the light repaired, just in case we don't make Laredo before nightfall."

Skylar drove the car into the service area of the truck-stop. Duke left to ask the attendant to fix the taillight before joining Skylar in the restaurant. After ordering a hot breakfast, they sat back, tried to relax and drink the coffee the waitress had set before them.

"How much longer before we get there?" Skylar asked

as she slumped back in the booth.

"I don't know. Since we're trying to avoid the interstates as much as possible, it will take us longer." Duke tried to stretch the kinks out of his neck.

Skylar sipped her coffee. "I think, since that little heart-stopping episode with the state trooper, you're right. We'd be better off avoiding them. The local police probably won't get the bulletins on us quite as fast, and maybe they won't look at them as closely."

"I hope you're right." Duke looked up and spotted a local police officer coming through the restaurant door. Did they have to test that theory so soon?

Duke tried to watch the officer without being obvious, while they finished the breakfast sitting on the table in front of them. Each time he dared to glance at him, the deputy seemed to be staring directly at them.

Duke leaned across the table and whispered. "Skylar, we better get out of here."

Skylar asked no questions. Duke dropped enough money on the table to cover the cost of their meal and the tip, and then placed his hand on Skylar's arm escorting her outside to the car. He paid for the repair, and then got in behind the wheel of the car.

Panic stretched his nerves taunt. Duke drove off at a much faster pace than he should have.

"Duke, what's wrong?"

He could hear fear in her voice.

"That police officer back there. He followed us out of the diner and got into his car. From the way he was studying us, I get the feeling he recognized us."

Skylar turned and looked out the back window. "I got the same impression. I was hoping I was wrong."

"We'd better do a little praying." Duke kept a close eye on the rearview mirror. He saw Skylar look back at him.

"I've already been working on that."

Duke was just beginning to feel at ease when he saw a black and white patrol car pull in behind them as they passed through another small Texas town. He carefully watched the speedometer to monitor his speed. He made an extra effort to obey all the traffic laws, but the patrol car still appeared to be following him. Just as Duke reached the outskirts of the town, the officer turned on the flashing lights.

"Skylar, they've got us." Duke moaned. "I broke no laws, so he's got to have an idea of who we are. That officer at the truck-stop must have radioed ahead."

Skylar hesitated only a moment before she said, "Lose him!"

Duke glanced quickly over at Skylar. "Are you sure that's what you want?"

"We haven't got time to discuss it. We're too close to give up without a fight. Now let's go for it."

Duke pressed hard on the accelerator and the vehicle responded without hesitation. The officer stayed right behind him. Taking a sharp left turn, Duke headed the car eastward. After several more turns, at speeds only a NASCAR driver should hit, he managed to lose the officer. Driving for about another thirty minutes, away from the direction they actually wanted to go, Duke felt secure enough to get back on course. Skylar sighed beside him.

"Would you hit me if I ever make a statement like I need some excitement in my life? The past few weeks of knowing you have given me enough excitement to last a lifetime."

"Skylar, I'd give anything if you weren't caught up in this mess with me. I just pray that some day I'll be able to make it up to you for all the trouble I've caused." Duke turned his head to look at his companion.

For just a moment their eyes met. "I'm sorry, Duke. It's not your fault. I guess I can always keep you on as a ranch hand and work you until you drop."

"If my past will allow me to have a future as a ranch hand, I might just let you do that."

Chapter Twenty-Two

Their detour had cost them several hours, but they finally pulled into Laredo about mid-afternoon Sunday. Duke stopped at a small grocery store and used the pay phone to call the number written on the map. A man named Carlos arrived at the store approximately ten minutes later and had them follow him to his home. As soon as Duke and Carlos took the luggage from the old car that had brought them on this leg of their journey, a young Mexican man jumped in and drove the car away.

Once inside the house Carlos began to explain, "Pedro is taking the car back to Mexico where the officials won't be able to trace it."

Skylar squeezed into a chair on the backside of the kitchen table. If it had been much closer to the wall, she'd never have fit. "Can't they trace the license plates?"

Carlos grinned. "Not really. The Texas plates that were on the car were...well, shall we say borrowed? The car will now have its original Mexican plates."

Skylar's mouth dropped open. The older man explained how they had switched plates with a car that had been abandoned in a junkyard across the border. Julio, it seems, had gotten a current inspection sticker and window tag for the car.

Skylar placed her hand over her heart. She thought it might beat out of her chest. "You mean we were driving a stolen car?"

"No, ma'am, the car was not stolen." Carlos smiled and then poured them all another cup of coffee. "The tags were just borrowed, and they will be put back in place as soon as Pedro gets the car home. The two of you will be my guests this evening, and we'll leave for the Eagle's Nest before dawn."

"The Eagle's Nest?" Duke asked.

He looked as puzzled as Skylar felt.

Carlos sipped his coffee and then smiled. "It's a hunting and fishing lodge that your Uncle Clayton owns in the Texas Hill Country. We've been using it for years."

She watched Duke run his finger around the rim of his coffee mug. "By we, do you mean I've been there?"

Carlos smiled as he answered. "Many times, Little Duke."

Skylar almost choked on the coffee in her mouth. "Little Duke?"

"Yeah. I know the name doesn't fit him now, but when he used to spend the summers with Duke, that's what we all called Clayton, Brett here took every step his uncle took, so we called him Little Duke."

Duke stood and walked to the kitchen window. "Tell me about my uncle."

Carlos gave a hearty laugh. "Trying to explain Clayton Carlisle is like trying to explain the wind. He got the name Duke because he reminds people of John Wayne. He's a tough character, but the best friend a person could have. He's always had a soft spot for you, Brett. Even more so since his son was killed while serving in the military."

Skylar's heart broke as Duke continued to look out the window. What must he be feeling?

"Have you ever met my parents?"

"Yes. But Brett, I'd rather your uncle fill you in on family history."

Duke finally turned around and looked at their host. "Sounds funny to be called Brett."

"I'm sorry." Carlos walked over and placed his mug in the sink. "But it would seem strange for me to call you Duke, since that's what I usually call your uncle."

Duke's smile warmed her heart.

"I'll try to remember to answer when you say Brett. Just yell at me again if you don't get my attention the first time. After traveling with this woman and using all the aliases she thought up, I will practically answer to anything though."

Skylar relaxed her grip on the coffee cup. At least he could still joke.

****

The sun was just coming up as Carlos and his two

very tired passengers turned onto Highway 83 heading toward Uvalde.

Carlos glanced sideways at Duke. "You two probably drove pretty close to your uncle's ranch when you came through this part of the country. I'm sorry you had to drive all the way to Laredo, but we thought that was best, since you didn't remember how to get to the Nest. We wanted to cover all our bases."

"This is new country to us. We didn't exactly come this way." Duke grinned.

Again Carlos glanced at him. "How'd you come?"

Duke looked over at Carlos. "We kinda skirted clear around San Antonio."

"That was way out of your way. Did you have trouble?"

"You might say that." Duke laughed. "We picked up a shadow just outside Dryden, and I took a more northeasterly course to throw them off. Drove a long way out of our way but didn't pick up any more tails."

"Well, at least you finally made it, and I can assure you that you're safe as long as you stay with me or Clayton."

Carlos stopped at a tiny country store. "You can get out and stretch your legs if you'd like. I'm gonna buy some fishing bait and a few supplies, just like I normally do." Carlos glanced back as he got out of the car. "Oh, by the way, if anyone asks, Brett you are my nephew, Tony, and Skylar is your wife, Judy."

Duke moaned as he stepped out of the pick-up. "Oh, just great! Another name I have to remember."

Skylar laughed. "Don't worry Tony, when we get to the Eagle's Nest you can pick out whichever name you like best and stick to it."

"I'm not sure which one that should be. At this point I'm more confused about my identity than ever before." Duke shook his head and walked away from the store.

"Thanks, Joe," Carlos called as he left the store. "Let's get a move on, you two. We've only got about an hour to go."

****

The Eagle's Nest was a rather large log-house nestled among a grove of trees. For the last forty-five minutes of the drive, Duke had noticed they didn't pass any houses.

"This is a long way from anywhere," Duke observed.

"For the last thirty minutes, you've been on private property—your Uncle Clayton's property." Carlos parked the truck. "That's him standing on the front porch."

Clayton rushed to the truck as soon as Carlos stopped. The minute Duke stepped from the cab the tall gray-haired man grabbed him and gave him a bear hug.

"Brett, it's so good to see you. I thought for a while I might never see you again. But thank God, here you are." The man took a few steps back; he seemed to be examining Duke. "You look the same except for your hair. I seem to remember that it was dark blonde."

"Just part of our clever disguise." Skylar extended her hand. "Hi, I'm Skylar McCrea, and my hair is usually not quite this dark either."

The old Ranger greeted Skylar and then looked back at Duke. "I like the original color better."

"Me, too." Duke laughed. "But believe me this color is better than the green she turned it at first."

"Green? How'd that happen?"

Duke explained and laughter filled the air as Clayton showed his guests inside.

"There are four bedrooms upstairs. You can pick whichever one you like. I know you must be tired." Clayton looked once again at Duke. "And I know you must have a million questions."

An hour later Duke decided to go back downstairs. He had tried to rest, but couldn't stop his mind from running wild. To his surprise Skylar was already there, nestled in an overstuffed chair listening to Carlos and Clayton as they told her about building this oversized cabin.

Clayton noticed Duke as he came down the stairs.

"Come on in, son. We were just telling Skylar how we got a little carried away when we started to build our little huntin' cabin here."

Duke scanned the room with his eyes. "I wouldn't call this a cabin. I'd call this a lodge."

"You helped build it." Clayton moved over and stood beside Duke. "We worked on it for years. You were just a kid when we started, but you played gofer and even pounded a few nails. By the way, which room did you pick?"

The question confused Duke. "Back left."

Clayton and Carlos looked at each other and laughed at him.

"Brett's still in you whether you remember him or not. You completed that room your last summer with me before you left for college. It's your room."

Duke saw Clayton swallow like there was a lump in his throat and then walk to stand in front of the big fireplace.

"That's the deer you killed when you were fifteen hanging on the wall in the room you picked. Your mother wouldn't let you put it in her house, so you brought it up here and created a room around it. Everything in there has a special meaning to you. Even the quilt on the bed was made by your grandmother."

Duke seated himself on the couch. "Tell me about my parents. Do they know I'm here?"

Clayton shook his head. "They don't know you're here, but they know you're safe. The FBI is keeping close tabs on your folks and may even have their phone tapped, so communication with them is nil."

Clayton strolled over to the kitchen and poured himself another cup of coffee. "Anybody else want any coffee?"

Clayton filled Carlos's cup with the dark liquid and then sat down in a big rocking chair. "Your mother, Julia, is one of the sweetest ladies I have ever had the pleasure of knowing, besides my own late wife, Norma. You favor your mother. Your sandy hair and green eyes." Clayton paused and gave a long sigh. "As for your father, Adam's a business man. He took a small company and made it into a million-dollar business. I guess you'd say he's a workaholic, but he has provided well for Julia and you three kids."

Duke looked at his uncle. "I have brothers, sisters?" Siblings? That was a surprise.

Clayton nodded and smiled at Duke. "One sister, Krissy. Well, her real name is Kristina, and a brother, Jeffrey, but we call him Jeff."

Duke was quiet for several moments. His voice

choked as he asked, "Am I married?"

He heard Skylar gasp softly, as she, too, waited for the answer to his question.

Clayton looked at Skylar and then at his nephew. "Not to my knowledge."

Duke sighed deeply. He looked at Skylar as he asked his next question. He wanted an answer but dread filled him as he waited. "Did I have a woman in my life?"

Clayton sipped from the cup he held in his hand. "Brett, for the last four or five years I haven't heard much from you. After you finished at the University of Texas, your father got you a job in New York with his old college buddy, Lawrence Jacobs. You've lived up there for quite a while. We sorta lost touch." Again the man glanced over at Skylar as if to gauge her reaction to the answers he gave to Duke's questions. "Your mother told me, about a year ago, that you and the boss's daughter kinda had a thing going. I think the girl's name is Victoria."

Duke watched as the color drained from Skylar's face. He tried to keep his face from showing any emotion. "But as far as you know, I hadn't married her?"

Clayton smiled. "As far as I know, and I think your mother would have told me if you had. I hope I would have been invited to the wedding."

Duke began to pace the floor. "You said my father got me a job with his friend in New York. If my father owns such a big company, why didn't I go to work for him?"

Clayton laughed. "You and your father didn't have the closest relationship. You didn't exactly want to go to college, but he forced you into it. So, I guess to spite him, you refused to work in his company. Your brother Jeff works with your dad."

"What about my sister?" Duke stopped his pacing and stood in front of the fireplace next to his uncle's chair. He crammed his cold fingers into his jeans' pockets. A shiver ran down his spine.

Clayton looked up at him. "She's married and has two kids. Her husband also works for your dad."

"Sounds like I'm the black sheep of the family."

"Sorta. But a nice black sheep. You always had a mind of your own."

Clayton grinned at him. It didn't make Duke feel

much better.

"If I didn't want to go to college and then work for my father, what did I want to do?" Duke walked back over and sat down on the couch.

"You wanted to be a rancher." Clayton looked into Duke's eyes. "But your father had different ideas. So you finally went along with him." Clayton rose, took his coffee mug and set it on the bar between the kitchen and the living area of the cabin. "I think that's enough background for now. Brett, do you remember anymore about this crime you're supposed to have committed?"

The tightness in his chest eased up. He was glad his uncle had put a stop to his questioning. He had heard as much as he could stand to think about, for a while anyway.

"No. I just know I am Brett Carlisle and I'm innocent. I remember finding where someone had misappropriated funds. It looks like I did it, but I know I didn't."

Duke joined his uncle at the kitchen bar. "Someone must want me out of that company and out of New York, because the amount of money missing would put me in jail for a long, long time."

Clayton went across the room to his desk and pulled out a large file folder.

"This is information on all the major employees of Jacobs Industries. It tells their work history and as much about their private lives as we've been able to come up with so far." He handed the folder to Duke. "Look through it. Maybe something will jar your memory."

Duke began to scan the file. "You must have some kind of connections to be able to get this kind of information."

"Don't underestimate a Texas Ranger, even a retired one."

For the rest of the evening, Duke combed through the papers Clayton had given him. Nothing was familiar. He read information about his boss, Lawrence Jacobs. He was a shrewd businessman. A few of his deals might have been a little questionable when he started his illustrious career, but he seemed to be forthright now. Duke read over and over profiles on these people that he should know, but nothing opened a door for his mind. His head pounded. Duke had just stretched out on his bed with the meaningless information when he heard a soft knock on his door.

"Come in."

Skylar stuck her head through the opening. "It's getting late, and you still haven't eaten."

"I'm not hungry."

"Still no memories?" Skylar moved through the door and stood next to his bed.

"Nothing."

Skylar smiled. "Why don't you put that away? You're exhausted. Get some rest."

Duke closed the folder. "I think I'll do that. Besides, all my memories so far have returned in my sleep. Maybe God will show me something new tonight."

"Maybe so. I'll go and leave you to get some sleep then."

The door closed with a soft click. The only reminder of her was the light scent of vanilla Duke had come to know.

The night was a restless one for Duke. Sleep eluded him. He tossed for hours thinking about the family Clayton had told him about, trying hard to remember. He wanted, no needed, to have a memory of this uncle who was working so hard to help him. What about his mom and dad? He had a life once. A family, a brother and sister.

He heard the clock on the mantle downstairs chime the hours away—midnight, one, two. Throwing the covers away from him, he got up and paced the room.

"Dear God, please give me memories of my childhood and growing up with these people."

Duke looked out the window into the moonlit night. He spotted movement in the brush. A couple of jackrabbits in search of food. Duke thought about the woman he was supposed to be interested in.

"What about Victoria, Lord? Did I love her? Were my feelings for her anything like what I feel for Skylar?"

If he had loved this other woman, how could he not remember her? Duke didn't understand how a person could love someone as much as he had come to love Skylar McCrea and not remember it.

He prayed and paced until his leg ached. He crawled back into his bed and sleep finally overtook him.

Morning had come too soon. His body ached all over. Duke walked outside onto the large porch. Even though he was tormented by his lack of memory, Duke began to feel peace like he had felt back at the lodge in Colorado. Maybe it had something to do with the outdoors. He looked over the land stretching out before him. It made him feel rested. Skylar stepped out onto the porch and handed him a cup of coffee. Together they looked over the view.

Clayton stepped through the door behind them. "I never get tired of looking at that." He walked up beside Duke. "I've got to head back to the ranch. I got a phone call late last night. Seems there's some young, eager-beaver FBI agent in town snooping around. I'd better go see what's up for myself."

"Is everything going to be okay for you?" Skylar asked.

Duke saw she wore a look of worry.

"If the time ever comes when I can't out think some tenderfoot FBI agent, it'll be time for me to hang up my spurs for keeps. Don't you two worry." Clayton patted Duke on the back. "I'm just on a fishing trip. Carlos will stay here. I'll check in with y'all later."

Duke's uncle tromped down the steps and settled into his truck. Duke watched it drive off into the distance leaving a dust cloud hanging in the air. His future hung around him like that cloud of dust. What would happen to it? Would it drop to his feet and be trampled on, or would it be blown away by a strong wind? Time alone held the answers.

Chapter Twenty-Three

Uvalde

Clayton watched from the porch as the dark sedan wound its way up the long drive. Sure took him long enough to get here. Clayton had been home for a couple of hours now, plenty long enough to phone in to Ranger headquarters. Randy Cooper, the local Ranger dispatcher, had told him the FBI had just found Skylar's vehicle on Saturday. Skylar and Brett had stashed it in the parking garage in that Pennsylvania hospital two weeks ago. It was about time for the FBI to show up on his doorstep.

****

Special Agent Douglas stepped out of his car and looked at the man sitting on the porch. He didn't look so tough. The Rangers he'd talked to must have really exaggerated on this one. These local cops thought they were pretty big stuff, but Douglas hadn't found it too difficult to get information when he needed it.

The agent walked up to the porch. "Good morning. Are you Clayton Carlisle?"

Clayton rocked back and forth in the big chair on the porch. "Yep."

"I'm Ralph Douglas, Special Agent for the FBI." He stepped up on the porch and extended his hand to Carlisle.

"Got any proof of that?" Clayton asked as he took the agent's hand in a tight grip.

Momentarily taken aback at having his identity challenged, Douglas reached into his inside breast pocket and withdrew a black leather case containing his badge and ID.

Scrutinizing the information for a moment, Clayton leaned back in his chair and propped his feet up on the rail. "Mighty long way from home, aren't you?"

"Yes, it sure is hot in Texas this time of the year." He replied as he wiped the sweat from his forehead with a crisp white handkerchief. "Have you heard from your nephew lately?"

"Well, let me see. I think I remember talking to Jeff sometime last month," Carlisle said.

Douglas' temper simmered just beneath the surface. Was the Ranger as stupid as he acted? "Not him. Your nephew, Brett Carlisle. The one wanted for embezzlement and unlawful flight. We've found out he's probably somewhere in Texas heading for his hideout in Denton."

Clayton continued to rock but kept his gaze directed at Agent Douglas's face. "What are you doing in Uvalde, then? It's a far piece to Denton from here."

"We were informed by the local police in Dryden that he and his accomplice had been spotted driving through there on Sunday." Douglas again wiped the perspiration from his brow. This old Ranger seemed to have lost his edge, if he had ever had one.

"They didn't catch 'em?" Clayton laughed.

"No. The locals got outrun and lost Carlisle and Ms. McCrea outside of the town. They were driving northeast though, so we believe they were returning to her ranch."

"Why aren't you trailing after them? Uvalde's not exactly on the way to Denton."

"We know Carlisle has spent a lot of time down here with you." The agent tried to remain calm as he leaned against one of the posts on the porch. "We thought he might have panicked and turned this way, expecting you to help them."

"I haven't been close to that one for four or five years. Besides I hear from my brother that he's supposed to have amnesia or somethin'. Don't think he'd remember his way here, if that's true. Probably wouldn't even remember me either." Clayton dropped his feet with a thud on the porch.

"You're right, if he really does have amnesia; I'm just not convinced of that fact. I think he's using it as a ruse, especially now that he's run from the law, but we'll catch him."

The FBI agent rephrased his question and asked about Brett once more. "Then he hasn't phoned you or come by here in the last couple of days?"

"No, sir, I haven't talked to Brett on the phone for almost a year now. Like I said before, it's been over four years since he set foot on this here porch."

Agent Douglas looked at Clayton. He shook his head. *Unbelievable.*

"Then the FBI can count on you to inform us if you do hear from him? As a law official, you know the penalties for withholding information pertinent to an official investigation."

Douglas saw Clayton Carlisle's face tighten up. He checked a smirk that wanted to come out. *Got him.*

"Mister, I'm retired, not brain-dead. I think I remember a few things from the olden days."

Disappointment replaced the smugness he'd felt. The older Ranger failed to lose control and tell him what he wanted to know. Douglas spun on his heel and marched down the steps of the porch. He turned once again to look at Clayton. He held eye contact. He wouldn't be the first to look away.

"Well, then, I'll be expecting to hear from you as soon as you hear from your nephew. Good day."

****

Rosa walked out of the house. Clayton smiled at her.

"Señor, I heard a car drive up. Will you be having company for supper?"

"No, Rosa. It'll just be us tonight." Clayton laughed at his housekeeper's question.

"You seem to be in a much happier mood since your visitor came. Did he bring you good news about Señor Brett?"

"Yes, Rosa; in a way, he did bring me some good news; although, he doesn't realize it yet. I think it's gonna take him a while to figure out just what he did let me know."

"That's good. Supper will be ready shortly."

"Thanks, Rosa." Clayton propped his feet up on the porch rail and smiled. He reached for the small cellular phone tucked beside him. Just as well let Carlos and Brett know they weren't in any immediate danger of being located. He didn't want that young Skylar to lose any more sleep either.

****

"Okay, Clayton. We'll see you then." Carlos hung up the phone.

Duke looked at Carlos. "What did he have to say?"

"He had a visit from the FBI. They think y'all are heading for Denton, but they were checking on Clayton to make sure." Carlos picked up a dishtowel and began to dry the dishes in the drain rack. "Clayton said the agent he'd spoken to had been the one to question Randy and the others at headquarters. They haven't seen you since you left for New York City, so that's all they could tell him. Apparently that's the same information the agent got from your uncle." Carlos laughed. "The agent needs a little more training on interrogating witnesses and digging up information. Seems he asked Clayton if he'd spoken to you on the phone or seen you at the ranch. That's pretty good. Clayton didn't even have to tell a fish story."

The information lightened the mood at the cabin. Skylar and Carlos worked together to make their supper while Duke poured over the file his uncle had left with him. Still nothing new popped into his holey memory. He rubbed his tired neck as Skylar called him to the table. Skylar blessed their food, and then the three companions began to eat.

Duke set his tea glass on the table. "Is Clayton coming back out to the Nest tomorrow?"

"He didn't think so. He wanted to wait and see if the FBI was satisfied with what they have gotten so far from him. Said unless something came up he'd probably not be back for a couple of days." Carlos picked up a forkful of mashed potatoes. "He doesn't want the FBI to get smart enough to have him tailed. That'll also give us some time for things to cool down around here. After that, he'll be back out so we can work on plans for figuring out the rest of this mess." Carlos took his last bite and then pushed back from the table. "Man that was good."

"Sure was." Duke dropped his napkin beside his plate. "Guess I'll get back to that file."

Skylar stood to help clear the table. "Did you come up with anything new this time?"

Duke shook his head. "Not yet.

"Then why don't you forget it for tonight?" She placed

the dishes on the cabinet. "I think you need some exercise. You've been cooped up inside too long today. The sun's going down so why don't we take a walk down to the river before it gets too dark?"

A walk would relax him a bit and loosen up the tight muscles in his legs and back. Skylar's bright smile cinched the deal. "Sounds good. You're on."

Skylar turned to Carlos. "When I come back, I'll take care of these dishes."

"Don't worry about the dishes. I'll take care of those few things before a rattler could shake his tail twice. You two go on for your walk."

The heat of the day was dissipating rapidly as the sun sank lower. A gentle breeze sprang up and made their trip down to the river enjoyable. The roar of the river as it made its way downstream was inviting. Duke and Skylar walked along its edge for a long while in companionable silence.

They paused by the water's edge about a half mile from the cabin. Duke's mind had been on his situation as they walked. The woman beside him had put herself through a lot over the past months for him.

The sky filled with a deep orange glow as the sun took a final dip to extinguish its light. Skylar's face glowed with her own radiance as well as the sun's rays. *I am going to have a lot to ask God to forgive me for.* He stepped closer to Skylar. But now that he knew he wasn't married, he wished just once he could allow himself to hold her in his arms. How he wanted to learn what it would be like to kiss her. Surely God wouldn't frown too much on an innocent kiss.

****

Skylar's thoughts had been on Duke's past a large part of the day. Especially the part that had to do with the woman named Victoria. At least he wasn't married, but if he is engaged, he might as well be. Skylar wished Clayton had been more informative about Duke's personal life. Something about the way Clayton's voice had lost its warmth when he spoke of the distance that had grown between Duke and him told Skylar that it had not been to Clayton's liking. She wondered what had happened between them.

Skylar glanced up at Duke. She knew from the look on his face that he wanted to kiss her, and she had to admit she wanted that, too. *What would be the harm of one little kiss?* She moved just a little closer to Duke as she gazed into his eyes. Duke reached for her and she stepped into his arms. It was as wonderful as she had dreamed it might be.

Chapter Twenty-Four

New York City

Special Agent Douglas paced as he waited outside of Jacobs's office. He wasn't accustomed to being kept waiting, but Jacobs's secretary had been adamant about not letting him go straight in when he arrived. The phone buzzed, and the secretary spoke quietly into the receiver.

"Mr. Douglas, you may go in now." Maggie said. "Mr. Jacobs is ready to see you."

Douglas smiled at the attractive young woman as he entered the large office. Jacobs's secretary walked over to her boss's desk and stood quietly to his side. Lawrence Jacobs's daughter, Victoria, was seated to the left of the huge desk on a plush sofa. Jacobs was discussing something with his daughter, and Douglas fumed as he was kept waiting even longer.

Victoria nodded as Lawrence Jacobs looked up and said, "Yes. What did you find out in Texas? Was it Brett? Where is he now?"

Agent Douglas's stare was cool as he turned it toward Maggie.

Jacobs followed the agent's gaze as it centered on his secretary. "It's all right. Maggie knows everything that goes on in this company anyway. She's aware of the situation with Brett."

"As you wish. Carlisle was spotted with the McCrea woman in a small town in west Texas. I've been to her ranch, and the people there don't know anything helpful. In fact, they seemed genuinely upset not to have heard from Ms. McCrea." Douglas sat down in a chair in front of the big desk. "As I told you yesterday, we located her SUV on Saturday where they dumped it in Pennsylvania. When they were seen in Dryden, they were driving an older model vehicle, hoping not to be noticed I assume.

Probably stolen. The plates were traced back to a car that belonged to a man who has been dead for five years."

Douglas paused briefly. "I then flew down to Uvalde and checked out Carlisle's uncle. Clayton Carlisle was a dead end also. That ex-Texas Ranger was not the hot-shot I had been lead to believe. Not any brighter than most of those back woods, country yokels. We are keeping a closer eye on him for now, just in case his nephew does contact him."

Jacobs leaned back in his chair. "I'm not so sure about your assessment of Clayton Carlisle."

Douglas crossed his legs and smiled. "Trust me; I know my job. Did you have any more information about what your accountants have come up with in regard to the missing funds?"

"The figure we first gave you looks like it might double, possibly triple." Jacobs shuffled through some papers on his desk. "Digging deeper into the confused records, my accountant has been able to account for at least a half a million in missing funds. He said it might go as high as $750,000 before he's through."

Douglas made some notes on a pad he pulled from his pocket. "I'll keep in touch. When I have more information I'll let you know." He stood to his feet and shook hands with Mr. Jacobs. "Good day."

****

Eagle's Nest

"Yep, I gave that FBI agent my best imitation of a country bumpkin. He left thinking I was some doddering old man barely able to feed myself. I don't think he left anyone behind, but just in case I rode out this morning like I was going to check the herd and detoured to borrow Chester's jeep." Clayton chuckled. "I would like to see Douglas's face when he realizes what happened at the ranch. That would make a pretty picture."

Clayton watched Skylar as he talked. He could tell she had deep feelings for his nephew, and he was pretty certain Brett cared just as much for her. Clayton knew in his heart this woman would be better for Brett than the one he'd taken up with in New York. Skylar would complete Brett. Given a chance, Clayton had a gut feeling these two young people would end up together. Maybe when this ended, his brother would realize how wrong he'd been in trying to mold Brett into something he wasn't meant to be. Brett didn't belong in the city, living a fancy life, any more than Clayton did.

****

New York City

"Hello."

"Where have you been?" the woman demanded, ignoring the groggy sound of his voice.

"Out of town. What's your problem?"

"My problem is the amount of money you stole!" She threw the green velvet pillow that was annoying her across the room with such force it knocked a bottle of perfume off the vanity. Too bad it hadn't been his head.

"Not stolen, re-appropriated. What's wrong with the amount?"

"I thought you were just hiding a few thousand. Just enough to make Brett look untrustworthy. A half a million is a little more than untrustworthy, don't you think?"

"Maybe I did just hide a few thousand. Maybe Carlisle really is a thief," the young man chuckled.

"Cut the sarcasm. What did you do with all that money?"

"It's taken care of."

"And just what do you mean by that? With this large of a sum and if Brett manages to prove his innocence some day, you'll be in too deep to get out."

"I won't be the only one in trouble, honey. You're in just as deep."

"Just how do you figure that? I haven't done anything. You've done it all!"

"I may have done it, but I made sure the trail will lead to you, too, my dear!"

The woman's breath caught. She clutched at her chest. What had she gotten herself into?

****

Eagle's Nest

Just knowing he had a family and a place to belong

helped Duke relax. The problem of proving he was innocent didn't seem so overwhelming since he'd met his uncle. A deep sense of security and well-being flowed over Duke as he prayed that night. When he finished, he drifted off to sleep.

Duke didn't know how much time had passed as he jerked upright in bed. *What had awakened him? Was it another dream? No, he hadn't had a dream. A sound?* Nothing but silence surrounded him. Then he realized what it was. He remembered. He remembered being Brett. He remembered everything right up to the time he had walked into his office at Jacobs Industries and discovered someone had been stealing from the company. His memory was back!

Oblivious to the time, Duke ran out into the hallway and yelled, "I remember! I'm James Brett Carlisle! I'm the son of Adam and Julia and the brother of Krissy and Jeff. I'm the Executive Vice-President of Jacobs Industries in New York City and I'm in real trouble!"

Carlos walked from his room into the hallway. "What's all the commotion?"

Skylar appeared a moment later. "You remember?" Oh Duke, that's wonderful!"

She ran into his arms, and he hugged her.

"I've got to go tell Uncle Clay." Duke smiled down at Skylar.

Clayton rubbed his hands through his hair as he joined the group assembled in the hall. "Tell me what?"

Duke watched over the top of Skylar's head as a smile as wide as the Rio Grande snaked its way across his uncle's face.

"Wait a minute. You called me Uncle Clay! You remember, don't you?"

"Everything." Duke released Skylar to embrace his uncle. "Even how badly I've treated you for the past few years. I just got so homesick every time I talked to you that I quit calling; I felt so guilty." Again the two men hugged. "I knew I couldn't blame my father for the way my life had turned out and talking to you just made me more unhappy with myself."

Clayton's smile was forgiving. "That's all behind us now. Let's get on with the business at hand, once we have that solved you can decide about your future and forget your past."

"I don't think any of us can get back to sleep now," Skylar said. "Why don't I make us some coffee and we can talk more?"

"Good idea." Clayton agreed as he placed his arm around Duke. "Let's go catch us a thief, Little Duke."

"I'll vote for that, Big Duke." The two men walked down the stairs.

The group sat around the kitchen table. Clayton looked at Duke. "Okay, now that you remember Jacobs Industries and the employees, try to figure out who might have set you up."

Duke related how he had gone into his office and discovered the missing funds in four different accounts when he had started compiling his information for the annual board meeting.

Clayton's face showed signs of confusion. "Why hadn't the losses been noticed before then?"

Duke shook his head. "I don't know. I wondered that myself. When I compared the financial statements I'd been given at the end of each quarter, the first two matched what was on the computer, but the third quarter was off." Duke took a sip of his coffee. "The one given to me at the board meeting for that quarter and the one on the computer were completely different."

Clayton leaned back in his chair and scratched his jaw. "So someone in the accounting department could be behind the whole thing. At the very least, they had to be in on it."

Duke placed his elbows on the table. "I thought about that, but I don't think that's true which is why it looks like I did it. You see, the accounts in question all belong to me. I personally oversee them. The bank statements come directly to me, and I send them to the comptroller."

Duke looked around the table to see the reactions of the other people in the room before he continued. Their faces still showed support.

"Most of the time, I don't really pay any attention to them; I just have my secretary make copies and send them on to the accounting department."

Clayton thought for a moment. "Did you send the

copies or the originals to the accountant?"

"The copies. I kept the originals in a file in my office."

Skylar said, "Well, all we have to do is get the originals and compare them to the statements."

"The originals show the losses." Duke looked at Skylar. "Apparently someone altered the originals of the statements before sending them to the accountant, so they would show nothing out of the ordinary. All of it together makes me look as guilty as sin."

"Okay, the bank statements come to you." Clayton ran his hands through his thick hair. "Now, just guessing, your secretary probably opens all your mail unless it's marked confidential."

Duke nodded and Clayton continued. "You gave them back to your secretary to make the copies and forward them on, right?"

Duke nodded again.

"So, who else could get to them?"

Duke leaned back in his chair. "Almost anyone. Allison puts the copies in an envelope addressed to the accounting department and puts it in the out-box for the runner to pick up."

"Okay, whoever set you up would know approximately when to expect the bank statement and be watching for it. The culprit could pick it up after Allison copied it, alter the original, make a new copy and send it on."

"That really narrows it down, Clay," Carlos said, taking a drink of his coffee. "Anyone in the office could pick up that envelope."

Clayton nodded. "Anyone could have done it, but what we have to figure out is who had a motive. Who wanted Brett out of the company?" He looked at Duke. "Brett, who might have wanted your job?"

Duke thought for a moment, "Jordan Matthews."

"Who's Jordan Matthews?" Clayton asked.

Duke started to speak, but his mouth felt as dry as sand. He looked around the table and focused on Skylar. Darkness seemed to crowd his eyesight.

"What's the matter, Duke?" Skylar asked.

Duke sat in frozen silence. Until now, he had only thought about everything to the point of discovering the crime. Now he remembered what happened after that. Dizziness overcame him, and he began to feel sick to his stomach. He couldn't look at anyone, especially Skylar.

He tried to force his breathing to regulate. A voice came from beside him, "Son, what's wrong?" He raised his eyes enough to see his uncle squatted down next to him. Duke could hear voices but couldn't find his own. All he could see was Victoria's face. Her laugh was disgusting, and her screams, as he had left that day, chilled him to the bone.

Someone placed a cold, wet cloth on his forehead.

Duke began to shake his head trying to get the images out of his mind.

"Duke, talk to me," Skylar begged.

She held the cloth to his head; his hands clutched together into fists. He wanted to crawl inside a barrel and pull the lid down.

"Tell us what's wrong."

Her caring tone only exploded the guilt, spreading it through his mind like shards of flying glass. Duke finally found his voice. "I'm okay. Just give me a couple of minutes."

Leaning forward, he pushed away from her and rested his head in his hands. He had to get every thing sorted out in his mind before he could tell the people in this room about what he had just remembered, especially Skylar.

Duke rose to his feet. He wobbled and grabbed hold of the table for support. "I need a little fresh air."

Skylar moved to stand beside him.

"I'll go out with you."

"No! I need a few minutes to myself." He pushed passed her and ran out of the room to the front porch. The screen door banged against the wall with a sharp thud.

Duke almost fell down onto the porch swing. He could hear his uncle telling Skylar to leave him alone for a while, that he might need to sort something out. *Sort something out?* Yeah, that was right.

His mind refused to let go of the last scene he'd remembered. His body shuddered and he felt like ice water pumped through his veins. With the picture of his last memory stuck in his mind, he suddenly knew for sure who had set him up, Jordan Matthews. He'd wanted Duke's job ever since Lawrence had assigned Jordan to be his assistant. Duke had just never known to what great lengths the man would go to get it.

A sick feeling flooded him again as he remembered how he'd gone home after finding the account errors. He had gone to his apartment hoping to find an ally in the woman he was to marry, but instead he got concrete proof, in his own mind, that Jordan Matthews wanted to replace him. He remembered how he felt when he opened his bedroom door and found Jordan in bed with Victoria. Duke didn't know how long he'd been standing in the doorway when the amorous couple finally spotted him.

Victoria's mocking laughter echoed in his ears, like he had just heard it. He covered his ears with his hands, trying to block out the sound. He remembered turning to leave. Victoria grabbed her robe and followed him down the stairs, all the way to the front door. She hurled insult upon insult at his masculinity as she reminded him her father would believe her story over his.

"Oh, Father in Heaven, how can you ever forgive me for all this? I was living in sin with Victoria. I was living with her and planning to marry her, but not because I loved her. I was doing it just to make her father happy and secure my position at Jacobs Industries. When I gave my life to You, I didn't know what that life was. I may not have stolen the money, but look at what I have done." Duke hung his head in dismay.

He sat for a few moments in silence with horrid thoughts filling his mind. Skylar's soft voice drifted out the door. Skylar! He moaned.

"Dear Lord, even if You can forgive me, what about Skylar? She believes in the sanctity of marriage and has saved herself for her husband. She will never want me after she finds out about my relationship with Tori."

That thought paralyzed him. For months he had thought of little else except getting his memory back. Now he almost wished he was still Duke Green and not Brett Carlisle. He didn't know how long he had been sitting outside, but he knew he couldn't stay on the porch forever. He knew if he didn't go back inside soon, Skylar would come looking for him.

****

"Don't you think someone should check on him?" Skylar asked as she walked toward the front window trying to get a glimpse of Duke.

"If he doesn't come in soon, I'll see about him. I don't know what he remembered, but it really hit him hard. I don't know when I've ever seen him so pale."

Just as Clayton finished his statement the front door opened, and Duke entered the room. His face was void of any traces of humor. His skin was still pale. He didn't make eye contact with any of them.

Skylar rushed to him. "Duke, are you okay?"

He sighed deeply as he looked into her eyes. "I'm fine."

He lied. To her. The lies he had told before hadn't been directed at her. This one was for her and Clayton and Carlos. A wall of ice seemed to keep her from reaching him. She stepped back. Tears rushed to her eyes.

Clayton spoke for her. "Son, you look tired. Come to think of it we're all tired. Let's all try and get a little rest. We can continue with this later."

Skylar climbed the stairs behind Duke. His shoulders slumped, and he walked like a man in his nineties. She started praying.

****

Duke went to his room to lie down, but he couldn't sleep. Thoughts of that last afternoon in New York kept running through his mind. Being framed as an embezzler seemed to pale next to what he had remembered earlier. He thought back to the standards he had tried to live his adult life by. Even when his father refused to allow him to live with Uncle Clayton after high school graduation, he had attended college and had given it his best. After college, Uncle Clay had asked him to take over management of his ranch, but once again Duke had allowed his father's disapproval to sway his decision. He accepted a position in Jacobs Industries from his father's old friend. Lawrence Jacobs was a good man, and Duke admired him both as a person and as a businessman. Even though it was not the job his heart really desired, he gave it his all.

Duke wondered why he had lowered his standards so

much as to sleep with a woman he didn't love. That wasn't the way he had been raised. Now he realized he had only asked Victoria to marry him because it would make her father happy. Lawrence Jacobs had never made a secret of the fact he wanted him to take over as CEO of the company one day. Lawrence would probably pass the reins of leadership over to him even if he weren't going to be his son-in-law, but had been thrilled when Victoria and Duke had announced their engagement.

Another thought crowded into his confused mind. Since Victoria and Jordan were so intimate, it was possible she was in on the scheme. What would that do to Lawrence if he found out his daughter was a thief? More guilt and remorse filled Duke's thoughts. Lawrence had never been anything but kind to him, always treating him like a son. He cared for Lawrence Jacobs, even if he didn't love Victoria.

Ever since he had admitted to himself his feelings for Skylar, he had prayed there was no wife waiting in his past for him. He had prayed he would be free to express his love to her. Well, he wasn't married, but neither was he free. There had to be some way he could make everything right without hurting any more people. He had to pay for all the pain and trouble he'd already caused. He would have to figure something out.

When Duke finally joined the others downstairs later the next morning, he managed to not say anything new. Uncle Clayton was content to believe Jordan Matthews was the criminal, and he and Carlos discussed various ways to prove it. Their first order of business was to get as much background on Jordan as possible. Clayton planned to return to the ranch the next morning.

Duke closed his feelings down and refused to let those around him see his pain. He'd caused them enough pain of their own. He could see it in their faces, but he hardened his heart to it. Skylar was the hardest to keep out. He knew she realized something was bothering him, but she refrained from pressing him about it. He figured she thought he would tell her when he was able to sort everything out in his head. He had made the mistakes; he would pay for them.

Duke needed a plan. He isolated himself all day from

the others and worked on developing a plan. Late that evening he had sorted it all out. He had to put it into effect without wasting any more time. Uncle Clay would stop him if he didn't move on his plan without delay.

A couple of hours before dawn the next morning, Duke left the cabin to head for San Antonio to turn himself in to the authorities and plead guilty. He had reasoned that if he took all the blame the sordid details would never have to come out. Duke made his way to the side of the house away from the bedrooms. He had managed to move one of the four-wheelers there the evening before without being caught.

He moved the vehicle's gears into neutral and pushed the four-wheeler. He wouldn't be able to start the engine until he got around to the other side of the hill about a mile down the drive. He thought it would be safe to start it up then. If Uncle Clay or Carlos noticed the sound, they would think it was one of Clay's friends, who often went spelunking in the caves on Clay's property.

Sweat broke out on Duke's face as he worked to push the four-wheeler across the uneven terrain beside the gravel drive. He concentrated on the details of his plan. Lawrence Jacobs would never have to know his daughter had stolen from him. Most of all, Skylar would never have to know what a bum he was.

A half mile later, Duke sat down on the vehicle to catch his breath. He used the sleeve of his shirt to wipe the sweat away from his face. Looking back toward the cabin to catch a final glimpse, he decided he was far enough away to risk pushing the four-wheeler the rest of the way along the more even surface of the gravel drive.

Taking a deep breath, he continued his trek. Skylar could remember him as Duke Green and forget Brett Carlisle ever existed. The only part he regretted was Jordan Matthews would get away with everything, but he knew Lawrence would see through that young man's façade in time. Lawrence Jacobs was too shrewd a businessman and too good a judge of character to let Jordan fool him forever.

Judging he was far enough away, Duke turned the key and started the engine. He shifted into drive and took off. He increased the four-wheeler's speed until he could barely hold the curves. If anyone had woken up and realized what he had done, Duke couldn't chance them catching up with him too soon. He had to reach the main highway and find a ride into town. He had to.

****

Clayton rose early. He was eager to get home and start compiling a file on Jordan Matthews. The thought of starting an investigation awakened the spirit of the Texas Ranger inside Clayton. You might be able to retire the man, but no one could ever retire that spirit no matter how hard they tried. Clayton just wished his nephew wasn't the reason he was back in the proverbial saddle again. The coffee was almost ready when Carlos joined Clayton downstairs.

Carlos retrieved mugs from the cabinet. "When do you plan on coming back?"

"Should be back in a couple of days. I'll get Randy to run another check on Matthews and see if he can turn up anything new. I doubt we'll get any more than we got the first time, but we'll see." Clayton poured coffee into the mugs on the counter. "I'll probably wind up having to go to New York myself and do a little snooping. I doubt the man has a criminal background, and the only way I'll be able to find out anything personal is to go looking on my own." He took his coffee and sat down at the kitchen table. "But I'll come back up here before I go. Maybe after a couple of days that nephew of mine will feel more like talking."

"He's gone!" Skylar yelled. "Duke's gone!"

Clayton abandoned his coffee and caught Skylar as she slipped down the last two steps.

"Calm down," Clayton said. "He's probably just gone for a walk."

Skylar shook her head and handed Clayton a note she held crumpled in her hand. Clayton read Duke's familiar scrawl:

I'm sorry for everything. For all the trouble I've put everyone through. After I finally remembered my past, I decided that what I'm about to do is the best thing for everyone. I can't allow innocent people to be hurt. Get on with your own lives.

Skylar, always remember Duke Green, but please try

to forget Brett Carlisle.

Tears were running down Skylar's cheeks. She sobbed against his chest, "We've got to find him."

Clayton looked over her head at Carlos.

Carlos said, "He's gone to turn himself in; and probably not to the local boys either."

Clayton nodded. "You're right. He's headed toward San Antone." Clayton pushed Skylar away from him and looked at her. "I'm going to see if I can catch him before he gets there. You two wait here in case he has a change of heart and comes back."

With tears still staining her cheeks, Skylar said, "I want to go with you."

Clayton put a hand on each of the young woman's shoulders. "Skylar, you can't go with me. I'm not supposed to know you, or know where you are. How would I explain you being with me? And besides you're wanted, too."

It took some convincing to change Skylar's mind, but she finally relented.

"Just find him before he does something stupid," she sniffed, "and bring him back."

Chapter Twenty-Five

San Antonio, Texas

The desk sergeant eyed him. "You're who?"

Brett pulled his hat from his head and sighed. "Brett Carlisle. I think there's a warrant out for my arrest."

"You think there's a warrant out for your arrest, and you're just walking into the police station to turn yourself in?" The silver-haired sergeant laughed.

Brett nodded his head.

The sergeant placed his elbows on his desk and leaned forward. "And just what is it you're wanted for?"

Duke looked the man in the eyes. "Embezzlement."

The sergeant just sat staring at him for several long seconds. "Embezzlement, huh? Well, that's different. Most guys that come in here looking for a night's lodging and a hot meal claim they beat up their wife or some fellow in the bar. Embezzlement, that's a good one. A white-collar crime. I like that." The sergeant laughed again. "Now why don't you go on home and make up with the wife?"

Duke placed both hands on the sergeant's desk and leaned forward. "I don't have a wife. I'm wanted for a crime!"

The sergeant gave Duke a stern look. "Look, fella, if you've run into some bad luck I can give you the name of an organization here in the city that you can contact. They'll help you out with whatever you need."

Duke shrugged in disgust. "What does a person have to do to get arrested around here? If you'll just run my license number through your computer, I'm sure you'll see I'm telling you the truth."

"I don't know what the joke is, but I'll go along with you. Give me your driver's license." The sergeant stood up and extended his hand for the license.

"I don't happen to have my license with me but I do

have my number." The sergeant typed the numbers into the computer.

Duke waited for what seemed an eternity. The desk sergeant's face grew pale and then flushed with what Duke figured was embarrassment.

"Well, you're right. You're a wanted man, and it's my duty to inform you that you're under arrest."

Stepping from behind the desk, the officer took Duke's arm to lead him down the hall and into the lieutenant's office. All traces of humor disappeared from his voice as the sergeant began to read Duke his rights.

A tremor ran through Duke's body. *What is going to happen to me now?* He'd never seen the inside of a jail before; he'd keep his nose out of trouble as a kid. He sighed. Now he was going to find out if jail was anything like it was portrayed in the movies and on television.

When the Sergeant knocked at the open door, a middle-aged man wearing a navy-blue suit looked up from the papers he was working on. "What's the problem, McDonald?"

Sergeant McDonald ushered Duke further into the room. "Well, sir, you see this man just walked into the station and gave himself up. This is Brett Carlisle, and he's wanted for embezzling from a company in New York."

The man removed his glasses and looked at Duke while he addressed the desk sergeant.

"He just walked in and gave himself up?"

"Yes, sir. Beats all I've ever seen in my thirty-five years on the force."

Duke listened as the two men discussed the unusual circumstances of his arrest. When the man introduced to him as Lieutenant Jefferson had finished looking over the computer printout the sergeant had given him, he asked Duke if he wanted an attorney present before he was questioned.

After Duke declined, the lieutenant told him to sit down. "Well, Mr. Carlisle, after all these months, what made you decide to just walk into the San Antonio Police Department and give yourself up?"

Duke explained about his amnesia and that he had just gotten his memory back.

"Well, that's wonderful." The officer's comment

sounded sarcastic. "What about the woman you were on the run with? Let me see," the officer commented as he glanced down at the papers he held. "Oh yes, Skylar McCrea. Where is she now?"

Duke shifted in his chair. "She wasn't involved; I used her. I needed money, and she had some. When her money ran out, I sent her packing. She was of no use to me any longer. She didn't know anything about me, or who I really was."

The lieutenant stared at him for several longs seconds. "I remember reading about you now. You're Clayton Carlisle's nephew. Were you headed here to get his help?"

Duke shrugged. "I thought about going out to his place, but I knew if I did, he would just make me turn myself in. He's a real stickler for the law, so I decided to save him the trouble." Duke paused for a moment. "Besides we haven't seen much of each other in the last few years."

"McDonald, process him. I'll let New York know we've got their man."

****

After the sergeant led Brett from his office, Jefferson picked up the phone. He had to smile as he thought back to Brett Carlisle's reply about his uncle. He had known Clayton Carlisle for years. Clayton was about the best he'd ever seen at catching a criminal and had been known to use some questionable methods in doing his job. He'd never known the old Ranger to break the law, but he had sure bent it from time to time. He also knew the man would do anything he could to get his nephew out of jail. He flipped through a Rolodex and located the number he wanted. Picking up the receiver, he punched in the numbers.

"Is Clayton home?" Jefferson asked when a woman answered.

He left no message when she gave him a negative reply. Dialing another number Jefferson asked to speak to Ranger Harris

"Harris, I need to talk to Clayton Carlisle. Do you know how I can get in touch with him?"

"As a matter of fact, he's standing right here. Hold

on."

The older man came on the line. "Jefferson, what's up?"

"Clayton, your nephew just walked in here and gave himself up. I thought you'd want to know."

"I'll be right there."

Lieutenant Jefferson heard a click and the line went dead. He dropped the receiver on its cradle and shook his head. This was going to be interesting. Another flip of his address file brought the next number to his eyes. Yep, this was going to be interesting. He punched in the number for the local FBI office.

****

Duke was staring out the window when Clayton walked into the interrogation room. "So you got your memory back, and now you've completely lost your mind!"

Turning to face his uncle, he saw the hurt and disappointment on Clayton's face. He winced as the pain cut him like a knife. He steeled his mind to keep it on track.

"I thought this was best. There's no way to clear me, so I'd just rather face the music now and get it over with."

Clayton moved to stand in front of Duke, almost nose to nose.

"So now you're an expert on criminal justice. How do you know there's no way to clear you?"

Duke backed away from his uncle. "Just let it alone. Believe me; it's for the best."

"You can give up if you want to, but I'm not about to forget it."

Clayton closed the distance, and Duke held his ground.

"I know you're innocent, and I'm going to prove it!"

The old ranger turned to the door, slamming it on his way out causing the window to rattle.

Duke's shoulders slumped as though the weight of the world sat on them. Depression tried to crush his soul. He had little strength left to fight it.

****

Clayton sat on his front porch at the ranch thinking through the whole situation. He had talked to Carlos and told him and Skylar to just sit tight for the present. He was pondering the next move when he noticed a car coming up his drive. He had known it wouldn't take his brother long to get here once he found out about his son.

Adam Carlisle stomped up the steps to the porch. "I should have known when you said everything was fine and not to worry that something bad would happen."

"It's good to see you, too, Adam," Clayton stood to greet his brother and sister-in-law. "Julia, are you okay?"

Julia hugged him. "I guess so. Just stunned by the recent turn of events. Clayton, can you shed any light on what's going on?"

Clayton motioned for the two of them to sit down and dropped into his chair. "Have you seen him?"

Adam sat across from him. "We went there first."

Clayton looked his brother in the face. "Did he tell you anything?"

Adam shook his head. "Not much. Just said this was for the best and to just let everything play out naturally. He said less people would be hurt this way." Adam paused. "Did you have him turn himself in?"

"No. He had just gotten his memory back and was so excited. We were discussing the missing money and trying to figure out who might have set him up. Then all of a sudden he turned real pale and quit talking." Clayton looked at Julia as he continued. "He apparently remembered something that disturbed him, and from then on he said very little. That was Thursday morning." He took a deep breath. "Then some time during the night he left. The next thing I heard was from Lieutenant Jefferson at the police department. Brett had turned himself in."

Julia pulled a tissue from her purse and wiped her eyes. Her sorrow saddened him.

"Did Brett tell you why he did it?"

Clayton shook his head. "No. Just told me what he told you. Said for me to just leave it alone."

His sister-in-law stared him down. "You're not going to, are you?"

Clayton smiled. "Of course not. He didn't take that money, and I'm gonna find out who did. It'll be a little harder now, since he's clammed up, but I'll still get to the bottom of it."

Adam stood and walked to the edge of the porch. "The mighty Texas Ranger rides again." His voice was loud and angry. "Just how do you propose to free my son now?"

Clayton rose and faced his brother. "I have a lead and I plan on following it."

Adam didn't give him an inch. "Well, Lone Ranger, what's your lead?"

Julia reached up and put her hand on Adam's arm. "Adam, calm down. Getting upset at Clayton won't help Brett. You know he can do more for him than we can. Now just listen."

Adam paced the porch for a few minutes. His battle with his temper played across his face while Clayton waited.

"Clayton, I'm sorry. What have you got, and can I help?"

Clayton sat back down in his rocking chair. "The only lead he gave us before he stopped talking was about a fellow named Jordan Matthews. I've run a check on him, but he has no criminal background. I need to get to New York and get some personal information on him."

Adam took his chair again. "Maybe I can help with that. If I can convince Larry that Brett's innocent, maybe he'll help us."

Clayton thought for a moment. "Maybe you could. Since you and Larry are personal friends, you could probably get more out of him than anyone else. When can you leave?"

Adam looked at his wife. "First thing Monday morning. I'll take Julia back home and talk with Jeff and Krissy to let them know what's going on."

Clayton smiled at his brother. "Well, it's getting late now. Rosa will have supper ready in a little while. Why don't you two eat and then stay here tonight? You can fly back to Houston first thing in the morning."

Julia looked at her husband and then at Clayton. "We'd be delighted. Thank you, Clayton."

At the dining table later, Julia sipped her iced tea. "Tell me about this woman who took care of Brett when he was sick and who was on the run with him."

"Skylar." Clayton's face was stretched with a smile as

he began to tell them about the young woman. "She's terrific. Stuck by Brett when most people would have dropped him like a hot skillet. She's the reason he was able to get back here."

"She certainly made a good impression on you," Adam said.

Clayton smiled. "Not only me but on your son as well."

Julia laid her fork on her plate. "What do you mean?"

"They're in love." Clayton laughed. "I don't think they've acknowledged their feelings to one another yet, but it's pretty obvious."

"No doubt they've probably acknowledged something." Adam scowled as he picked up his glass of iced tea. "After all, they have spent a lot of time together."

"I'm afraid you're jumping to wrong conclusions there, brother." Clayton dropped his napkin on the table and pushed his chair back. "Skylar isn't that kind of girl. She's a Christian, and it seems your son has met this Jesus of hers also."

Adam pushed his chair away from the table and crossed his legs. "You honestly believe a man and a woman can spend as much time alone as these two have and sex not become an issue?"

Clayton laughed again. "I didn't say it wasn't an issue, but I don't believe Duke and Skylar have slept together."

Julia smiled. "Maybe our son has found an old-fashioned girl like his mother." Julia looked at her husband. "You and I didn't have sex until after we were married. It was common back in our day for a girl to be a virgin when she got married. I'd like to believe there are still some girls left in the world who believe the same way."

Clayton stood and stepped over to assist Julia with her chair as she got up from the table. "I think your son found one when he found Skylar McCrea. Or rather when she found him."

Clayton couldn't help but notice that no one seemed to be questioning him about his statement that his nephew had met Jesus.

Julia walked toward the door. "We're overlooking

something. Now that Brett has his memory back, what about Victoria? They were engaged, you know."

Adam followed his wife from the dining room. "I was trying to forget her." Adam mumbled to himself. "I hope he will do the same."

"I thought you'd approve of the union." Clayton walked into the living room behind his brother. "Especially since you and Lawrence Jacobs are such good buddies."

Adam took a seat on the couch. "My liking Larry doesn't mean I have to like his daughter. I regret the day those two met. Victoria is nothing but a spoiled brat."

Julia sat down beside her husband. "Maybe that's why Brett got so quiet. Maybe he remembered his love for Victoria, and now, with Skylar in the picture, maybe it was too much for him." She paused and looked at Clayton. "He's torn between the two of them. He doesn't want to hurt either one so he's sacrificing his own freedom."

Clayton sat down in his easy chair. "I don't really think that's why he gave himself up. I don't know the reason he did it, but I don't think that's it."

Chapter Twenty-Six

New York City

Special Agent Douglas sat in the armchair in front of Lawrence Jacobs desk. "Just wanted to let you know Brett Carlisle has been apprehended. He's in custody in San Antonio."

Jacobs stood and began to pace around the office. "When did they catch him?"

"They didn't catch him; he turned himself in sometime on Friday. I don't have any other details but I'll know more when I get back. I'm leaving for Texas this afternoon."

Just as the FBI agent was leaving, Victoria Jacobs entered her father's office. "Did you have something new to tell my father?"

"Yes, but I'll let him fill you in. I have to catch a plane. I'll talk to you when I get back." Douglas left the executive's office and closed the door behind him.

****

Victoria looked at her father. "What's going on?"

"Brett's been arrested. They have him in custody in San Antonio."

Victoria embraced her father. "I'm sorry, Daddy. I know you had big plans for him. I'm sorry he hurt you."

"I still can't believe he stole from me; the thought of him behind bars makes me sick to my stomach." Lawrence sat down at his desk and rested his head in his hands, leaning his elbows on his desk. "Honey, I can't imagine how this must be affecting you. You've held up beautifully but I know your heart must be broken. After all, you're in love with the man."

Victoria turned away from her father in order to hide her true feelings. "I'll be okay. I'm just worried about you." She paused; she had to maintain control of her voice and her emotions. "Why don't you take the rest of the day off? Surely Jordan could handle whatever is on the schedule for today."

Lawrence opened the file folder on the desk in front of him. "I may take off after lunch. I just can't right now. I have to finish checking these proposals. After all, I've lost enough money. I can't afford to lose anymore or I'll be out of business."

Victoria whirled around to look at her father. She hadn't really thought about what losing that much money would do to his business. "A half million dollars won't shut down Jacobs Industries."

"No, the half million Brett stole won't close us down." Lawrence pulled his reading glasses from his face and leaned back in his chair. "But Tori, we lost all those accounts. They've pulled their business. If I don't bring in some new accounts, you may see a big downsize coming for this company."

It wasn't until this moment that Victoria realized the magnitude of what had taken place. She wouldn't be able to stand it if her father lost his company. It would be devastating to him, not to mention what it could possibly do to her lifestyle. Until now, she had only thought about herself and what she wanted. Now she realized that what was supposed to have been a simple plan, and gone off without a hitch, had turned into something extremely complicated. Victoria returned to the present when she heard her father's intercom sound.

"Send him in."

Just as Victoria stood to leave, the door opened and Adam Carlisle walked in. His presence dominated the room. His six-foot plus frame and the look on his face would have frightened anyone not knowing him. Victoria knew him, and that made her even more uncomfortable about his visit.

Adam shook hands with Lawrence. "Larry, I need to speak with you." He turned to look at Victoria. "In private please; I'm sorry, Victoria." Adam walked over. "I know you must be having a difficult time right now. But it will all be over soon, and my son will be free to make his own explanations and apologies, if necessary."

Victoria managed to mumble something and then left

the office. *What have I done?*

****

As the door closed behind Victoria, Adam turned back to face Lawrence. "Larry, I'm sure you know by now that Brett has been arrested."

Jacobs stood and walked to the small sitting area in his office. "Yes, the FBI agent on the case told me just a short time before you got here."

Adam seated himself on the brown leather sofa, opposite of his friend. "I hope you realize the wrong man is in jail."

"Are you sure about that, Adam?"

"Of course I'm sure! I know my son. He would never do anything like this. Brett's one of the most honest people I know." Adam stood and began to pace the room.

"Everything points to him."

Adam stopped pacing in front of his friend. "Evidence can be made up. You know that. Somebody framed Brett." He punctuated his words with his index finger and then began to pace again.

"Does he know who would try to do something like this to him?"

Adam paused. He prayed he could continue his bluff. He couldn't let his guard down now. He had to continue to be firm and show no fear. So with a conviction he didn't really feel he looked Lawrence in the face. "Jordan Matthews."

From the look of surprise on his friend's face, Adam could tell he was shocked at the accusation. "You can't be serious. Matthews is ambitious, but I don't think he'd go so far as to set Brett up so he could take over his job."

Adam sat back down on the sofa, gripping the arm to keep his hand from shaking. "You don't believe Matthews would set Brett up, but you're willing to believe Brett would steal from you?" Adam paused to let what he had just said soak in. "Are you sure Matthews is not that ambitious? How much do you really know about him?"

Lawrence shrugged. "I know he graduated from one of the finest schools in the country, and he comes from a good family. I had a complete background check done on him." Lawrence got up, went over to the bar and poured himself a drink. He offered one to Adam. He refused and watched as Lawrence took a large swallow of the alcoholic drink. "He does his work. I've never had any complaints about him."

"Well, a short time ago, you would have said all those things about Brett, but now you're ready to throw him to the wolves." Adam kept his gaze on his friend.

Lawrence was silent for a long moment before he spoke. "What is it you need from me?"

Adam let out the breath he'd been holding and began to feel somewhat at ease. "All the background information I can get on Jordan Matthews and for you to keep it just between us. And I mean just between us. No one else can know Matthews is under suspicion, not even your daughter."

Now Lawrence paced the room. "Why should I go along with this? Why should I help you try to clear Brett?"

Adam's anger exploded out of him. "Because you know me, Larry, and you know Brett. Deep down, you know he wouldn't have betrayed you this way." Adam fell silent as he watched his friend wrestle with what he had said. He also attempted to calm his anger.

Finally, after several long moments, Lawrence spoke. "I should be able to get you what you want. Jordan is in line for Brett's job, so if I start looking into his background a little more carefully no one will think anything of it. How soon do you want all this?"

Adam moved across the room to stand beside his friend. "Yesterday."

Lawrence gave a light chuckle. "I can get you everything we have in his personnel file this afternoon. You'll have to give me a few days on the rest."

The two old friends shook hands. "Thanks, Larry; I knew I could count on you. I'll come back by here about two o'clock. Will that give you enough time?"

"That will be fine." Lawrence paused. "And Adam, I hope you're able to clear Brett. You're right—I've never been able to accept the fact that he did this."

****

San Antonio

Duke waited in the interrogation room he'd been led to fifteen minutes before. The stark gray walls sprinkled with dings and pits along with the metal grating imbedded in the windowsill covering the filthy panes of glass foreshadowed what his future would be like. Chills ran down his back. The manacles binding his wrists rattled when he put his elbows on the heavy metal table in front of him. *What are they waiting for? Who wants to talk with me now?*

The door opened. Duke looked up to see a trim, balding man in a black suit enter the room. He pulled out the chair on the opposite side of the table and seated himself. He placed his briefcase on the table.

"Mr. Carlisle, I'm Special Agent Ralph Douglas of the FBI. I understand you do not wish your lawyer present during my questioning."

Duke nodded his head. "That's right. I'll answer whatever questions you want to ask."

The agent opened his briefcase and removed a yellow legal pad. The snap of the latches springing open echoed in the room. He pulled a pen from his pocket.

"Lieutenant Jefferson said you just waltzed right in here and turned yourself in."

"Yes, sir."

"Why, after all these months, did you just suddenly decide to do that?"

Duke let his gaze fall to the table. "There was nowhere else to go. I was tired of running."

"What happened to the woman? Your accomplice? What was her name?" Douglas paused a moment while he looked through his notes. "Oh yes, Skylar McCrea, wasn't it?"

Duke had to make this convincing. He raised his head and looked across the table at the agent. "She was not an accomplice to anything. Skylar is innocent. She was nice enough to take me in when I was hurt and didn't remember anything, not even my own name." Duke paused and took a deep breath. He repeated the story he'd made up and given to Lieutenant Jefferson.

The agent laughed. "How is it possible you needed money? You embezzled over half a million dollars. What did you do with all of it?"

Duke didn't have a quick answer for this one, so he just told the truth. "I don't have it."

Agent Douglas stood and walked to the window. He looked out through the bars. "Then where is it? You know it will probably go easier on you if you return the money."

The agent's questions came out in a tone as cold as the room felt.

"I can't return it. I don't have it."

The agent turned to face Duke. "Then who does? Your girlfriend?"

Duke slammed his hands on the table. "No! It's gone I tell you. I don't have it. I can't return it because I don't have it! As you may or may not realize, my girlfriend is, or at least was, Victoria Jacobs. Do you think she would be involved in stealing from her father?"

Duke's last statement froze the agent in place. His eyes scanned over Duke's face. His expression was impossible to interpret. What was he thinking?

The agent walked to the table and stood beside Duke. "What did you do with the money, Carlisle? A half million dollars doesn't just up and walk away by itself."

Duke looked up at Douglas. "I spent it! Okay!"

"On what?"

Duke shrugged. "I don't know. A little here and a little there. You know how it is. Money goes fast these days."

Douglas chuckled, but it was without humor. He sat back down in the metallic, straight-backed chair. It looked like it and the rest of the room had been painted from the same bucket of gray paint.

"You blew a half million dollars, and you don't remember what you blew it on?"

"That's right; I don't remember."

Douglas shook his head but kept his gaze on Duke. "That's odd. Because when we did a background check on you, you had not made any lavish purchases. You hadn't taken any trips. As a matter of fact, you worked six days a week and usually spent the seventh day at home watching TV. So when did you spend all this money?" The agent sneered at Duke. "Oh, I know. You gave it away to charity, right?"

Duke hung his head once again. "Look, what does it matter what I did with it? I just don't have it, and I can't return it. So that's that."

"You'll forgive me, Mr. Carlisle, if I don't believe you, won't you?" The agent paused. "I don't think you were dumb enough to just blow that much money. If you went to all the trouble to steal it, I think you had a purpose for it. Now if it's in a Swiss bank account, just tell me and we can recover it. Like I said, it'll go easier on you if you return the money."

"I don't have a Swiss bank account." Duke balled his hands into fists. "I don't suppose I have a bank account of any kind since I emptied out the only one I had when I left New York." He stared at the agent. "I can't return the money! I don't have it!"

"Maybe a little more time in your cell will sharpen your memory."

Special Agent Douglas shoved his chair back, stood, and jerked the door of the interrogation room open. "Guard."

In only a few seconds the uniformed policeman appeared. "Sir?"

"Take Mr. Carlisle back to his cell." Douglas put the pad back in his briefcase. "I'll continue with this later."

The guard hooked his hand under Duke's arm and tugged. Duke got up and let the guard take him back down the hallway. The chains clinked together as he walked. At his cell, the guard removed the manacles; the cell door lock snapped open and then slid shut with a thud behind him as Duke stepped inside. The guard walked away without a word. Duke stood in the middle of the cell and looked out through the thick bars. His feet moved like he had weights packed all over his body. *Will I ever feel light and free again?*

The more Duke thought about the interview with Special Agent Douglas the more fear he felt. He felt smothered, but his fear was more for Skylar than for himself. Agent Douglas didn't seem to be buying the story he was giving them. What if the authorities were hard-nosed enough to continue to pursue charging her as an accomplice?

"Lord, please protect her. She didn't ask for any of this. She was only trying to help someone she believed in. Don't let her pay for my sins. Please."

He stretched out on the cot, his mind still a swirl of

confusion. He couldn't sleep without dreaming about Victoria and her barrage of insults after he'd caught her with Jordan.

Skylar was never far from his thoughts either. He once dreamed of having a life with her, but that was all gone now. His sinful past was too bad to be forgiven by a woman like her.

These four walls were his future now, and they were just what he deserved. After a few years behind bars, everyone would forget all about him. At least that was what he prayed would happen. He knew he didn't deserve any special favors from God, but he was hopeful God would honor his request for the people he loved and cared about to go on with their own lives.

****

Agent Douglas threw his key on the table in his hotel room. For months he'd run this investigation. He'd probed into every aspect of Brett Carlisle's life. He thought he knew the man pretty well by now, but the man he interrogated this afternoon did not fit the profile he'd developed. The Brett Carlisle he'd come to know through his investigation was a smart man, and, up until this incident, had a perfectly clean slate. There wasn't even anything on his record from when he was a teen-ager. If a man like that stole money and then decided to turn himself in, he'd return the money. It just didn't make sense. *How could he not know what happened to all that cash?* It just didn't add up.

Carlisle was lying, but he couldn't figure out why. *Who is he trying to protect? Is it the money he wanted to hang onto?* The jigsaw pieces of this puzzle just weren't fitting together to form the picture he had created.

Chapter Twenty-Seven

New York City

Victoria's mind reeled as she hurried to Jordan's office. Adam Carlisle being in her father's office made her nervous. With Brett in jail, things should be calming down, not getting more confusing. Why wasn't Adam at home working on getting Brett out of jail?

Her breath came in rapid gasps as she neared the private entrance to Jordan's office. Surely he hadn't realized that taking so much money would have affected the company so adversely. What if their plan caused her father's company to collapse instead of moving Jordan into Brett's position?

With a shaking hand, Victoria turned the knob and pushed the door open. The sight of Jordan in a compromising embrace halted her in the middle of a step. Her breath whooshed out of her lungs like she had been punched in the stomach. Her vision narrowed down, and she seemed to be looking through a long, dark tunnel. The only sounds she heard were like rushing water being momentarily shut off and turned on again. How long she stood there Victoria didn't know, but she finally managed to suck in a breath and re-inflate her lungs.

Anger overcame her. "What is going on here?" She walked into the office. "Jordan, what do you think you are doing? Who is this bim...?"

The sight of Maggie's face stunned her into silence again. *What is happening here?*

Jordan looked at Maggie. His voice was soft, tender like the one he used with her. *How could he?*

"I think you'd better go, Maggie. I'll talk with you later," Jordan said.

Victoria watched as the beautiful blonde left the room. "I'm waiting, Jordan. Just what was that episode all about?" She paused but Jordan didn't speak. "Come on, I'm waiting."

Jordan straightened his tie. His movements so slow that Victoria edged toward hysteria. Her hands itched to adjust it for him. She'd fix that tie and the neck to go with it. He reached out to take her manicured hand in his, but she jerked it away. His touch sent icicles speeding through her body.

Victoria kept her stare on Jordan's eyes. "Well, what excuse do you have for what I just saw? And just how long has this been going on?"

Jordan tried to get close to her again, but she stomped away putting a wing-back chair between them. That didn't stop his move toward her. He slid around the chair and wrapped his hand around her upper arm, squeezing it to hold her still.

"Tori, how do you think I got all of the information I needed to put this scheme together?"

His voice was sweet, enticing. With his other hand, he began to stroke her arm, a light, feathery touch.

"But what about all the stuff I got for you?"

She tried to brush his hand away, but the stroke of his soft fingers on her arm began to draw out some of the anger bubbling away inside her. Again Jordan reached for her hand, and this time she allowed him to take her hand in his. Jordan moved a fraction closer and began to slide his other hand soothingly down her back. A look of adoration plastered itself on his face.

"Tori, the information you got was necessary, but I needed things you couldn't get access to easily. Things only your father's secretary could get without suspicion."

Victoria stiffened. "So you decided to seduce Maggie into helping you, too."

Jordan grinned. "Do you know of any easier way to get information from a woman?"

At his last words Victoria tried to pull away from his embrace, but by now he had managed to lock her into his arms so she couldn't break free easily.

"So you use all of us to get you what you want." Victoria said through clenched teeth as she struggled to free herself.

"Not you, Tori. What I feel for you is real. I'd never

use you." Jordan whispered into Victoria's ear as he drew her closer. "Maggie doesn't mean anything to me; she's just a means to an end. She's not special like you."

She allowed his words to soothe her. It was what she wanted to believe. No, she *needed* to believe them. When Victoria relaxed, Jordan let his grip on her ease up.

When he spoke again, he used his pet name for her. "Tori, what was so important that you rushed in here without letting me know you were coming?"

"Important?" Victoria then remembered why she had come to Jordan's office. "Oh, Jordan, Brett's been found. He's in jail!"

Jordan smiled. "Well. It's about time the FBI did its job. Now maybe things will get settled around here."

He dropped his arms, and Victoria was able to walk away from him.

"But, Jordan, I still don't understand why you took so much money. Especially now that the company is in so much trouble." Victoria turned toward Jordan. "What if Daddy has to declare bankruptcy?"

"Tori, what are you talking about?"

Victoria looked up into Jordan's face. "Then Daddy hasn't discussed this with you?"

His impatience showed in his voice. "Tori, tell me what you know."

She moved to the couch and sank down gently into its cushions. "Daddy says we've lost a lot of clients because of the embezzlement. People are afraid to trust us any more." She looked at Jordan. "You didn't mean for this to happen, did you? You didn't know this would happen when you took so much money, did you?"

****

He angrily muttered a few words under his breath and then tried to reassure her. "Of course not." Jordan sat down on the couch beside her, his mind racing. He'd not planned on this complication. He had to think.

The woman babbling on the couch was giving him a headache. "Look, Tori, I need to do some more planning. Why don't you go on home and let me work. I'll call you later."

"But, Jordan, can't you just give the money back now? Wouldn't it help ease the clients' minds to know you found the missing money?" She gave him a tremulous smile.

He'd paid off some large debts with a portion of the money, and then he'd managed to tuck away the rest. With the freedom having that money gave him, he almost blurted out, *Not on your life!* But he restrained himself. "I can't yet."

Victoria gave him a worried look. "Why? What's happened to it?"

Jordan tried to soothe her emotions. "Nothing's happened. It's just tied up right now."

Victoria jumped up off the couch. "Tied up? How? Where?"

Jordan got to his feet and attempted to embrace Victoria. "I invested it, so Lawrence wouldn't lose any of the interest it would draw while it was out of his accounts."

Victoria calmed some with that lie.

"Oh. But when do you think you can get it released?"

Jordan watched Victoria move away from him "Tori, I'll get it when it's time."

"Jordan, you are returning the money, *aren't you?*" Hesitating only a moment, she pushed a little harder. "You can't keep it. It's Daddy's money."

An evil sneer curled Jordan's lip. "Not right now, it's not. Right now I have control of it, and if you know what's best for you, you'll erase this whole conversation from your mind. Don't forget, the way I've set all this up you'll be incriminated, too, if I'm found out." Jordan had tired of trying to placate Victoria. He walked over to her and looked deep into her eyes. "So if you don't want to end up dressed in drab gray every day, you'd better hope I can find some way out of this snafu."

The fear on her face let him know she would let herself be dragged back into his web once again. It was all he could do to not smirk as her attitude changed from demanding to mellow.

"All right, Jordan. I'll leave this all up to you, since you have promised to protect Daddy's interests." She slipped into the husky, whispery voice she used when she tried to wheedle him. "You were so smart to think of something like putting the money where it would be safe and yet profitable." She placed a gentle kiss on his cheek. "Thank you for taking care of Daddy. You're right; I should go. You will call me when you figure out what to do, won't you?" Her voice quivered.

Jordan jerked her into an embrace and kissed her before assuring her he would call soon. As the door closed behind her, he sank into his plush desk chair and pondered the scene he'd just participated in. Victoria was becoming hard to handle. Perhaps he'd have to find a little more of the money than he had originally planned on. It also might have to be a bit sooner than he'd thought. Lately he had begun to feel he might never have to return the money, but with Brett turning up those plans had been shredded.

He hoped his threats of involving Victoria, should his plan collapse, would keep her from telling everything she knew. She had seemed ruffled when he'd hit her with that reminder, so she probably would keep her knowledge to herself. She had fallen in love with him after all. He'd already duped enough women to know how to control them.

He'd better check on the other woman in this little play. Reaching for the telephone receiver, he punched in Maggie's extension number. Now he had to soothe her ruffled fur and see how much damage control was needed there. He might still need Maggie to escape unscathed.

****

Staring at the closed door, Victoria forced herself to unclench her hands. She had a horrible feeling about all this. She needed time to think and someone to talk to. Someone she could trust. Checking her watch she decided there was enough time to find Dexter before he drove them home for the day. He'd be able to help her sort out the mess she was in right now. Her father's chauffeur had always been able to help her out of her troubles.

She pressed the down button at the elevator. Most definitely Dexter would help her. He'd been the one to help her when she had needed to be driven home after one of the wild parties she had attended. He had been the one to carry her upstairs and had gotten Velma to put her to bed. He'd even seen to it that Velma never said a word to her father. Dexter was the one person in the world she could always count on and trust. He had always been there for her, even when her own father had been too busy with his company. Stopping at her office only long enough to phone for Dexter and gather up her purse, she rushed for the elevator.

****

Dexter looked down at the beautiful young woman on the bench beside him. A man thirty years her senior, he felt for Victoria as an indulgent uncle would. He'd questioned his actions from time to time where she was concerned because he'd hidden a lot from her father. At times, he thought he should have let her escapades be found out, but somehow couldn't bring himself to let her face the consequences her behavior warranted. Every time he'd decided to leave her on her own, she would smile at him with that trusting smile just as she had when she had been two and his convictions had caved in. He knew she had him twisted around her little finger.

Yet, she had always treated him with respect and had always remembered his birthday with some gift. When she was a young child, her gifts had been drawings or some such other bit of childish endeavor. Later as a young girl, she had bought him gifts for his birthday and Christmas from her allowance. Velma had told him of how she saved for those special presents for him.

Now she was presenting him with a dilemma he couldn't fix. He guessed life for Victoria might have been different if her mother had lived. Instead, her father's employees had raised her. A chauffeur and a housekeeper were poor substitutes for loving, doting parents. Mr. Jacobs had put his life into his work after his wife's early death. In doing so, he let a tiny little girl wander around in the world—lost and seeking a haven of love. He and Velma had taken over out of their own love for the little girl, but that was in the past. Their love couldn't fix this hurt.

"Miss Tori, I told you to stay away from Jordan Matthews. I knew he was trouble from the first. Mr. Brett was the right man for you."

Victoria turned her pouting face to Dexter. "You're probably right, but he was so stuffy. He never wanted to party with me. He worked all the time, just like Daddy."

She got a far away look in her eyes. "Jordan is like me; he likes to have fun. If you'll remember, that's where I first met him, at one of Daddy's cocktail parties."

Dexter dropped the pretense of formality. "But, Tori, how did you ever let him talk you into becoming involved in this scheme? Surely you don't hate Mr. Brett that much."

Victoria began to cry. Her tears pierced his heart.

"Oh, Dex, I don't hate him at all. I just wanted out of the engagement and knew Daddy would never forgive me for dumping Brett. He's the son Daddy always wanted. He's almost a clone of Daddy."

Dexter placed his arm around her shoulder as she continued to speak.

"I knew if I married Jordan, he would never stand a chance of taking over the company with Brett still there. I wanted Jordan to have Brett's place, and the only way to do it was to discredit Brett. Jordan was right about that."

Dexter handed the young woman his handkerchief. She dried her eyes before she continued.

"I never thought he would have to spend more than a couple of days in jail at the most. Daddy was supposed to have gotten upset but drop the charges and fire him. Jordan was to pretend to find the money where he had hidden it and make Daddy grateful." Victoria looked up at him, tears still clinging to her lashes. "But then Brett walked in on Jordan and me at the apartment. I said some really hateful things to him and he disappeared."

Dexter shook his head in remembrance of Tori's reaction to being caught with Jordan. Victoria dropped her gaze to the ground.

"I just found out Jordan took $500,000 instead of $50,000. Today he told me the money was hidden away in investments, but I'm not sure he will return the money. I'm afraid he will keep it and let Brett take all the blame."

Leaning into his embrace, she continued.

"I can't tell Daddy what's going on to get Brett off because then Jordan will be in trouble, and if his threat is real, I'll be implicated, too! They'll throw me in jail, and Daddy will hate me." She started to cry once again. "How do I get out of this mess, Dexter? You've got to help me!"

She flung her arms around him, tears streaking

down her cheeks. As he worked to comfort her, Dexter tried to think of a way out for her, but the only thing he could come up with was for her to go to her father.

When her sobbing stopped, she blotted her face, blew her nose and then looked at him.

"Tori, I've protected you for a long time now. Maybe that was a mistake, but you have to face your father with this one." When she began to protest, he stopped her. "You know your father would never allow you to go to jail. I don't care what you've done, or what he's not done for you, in the past; Mr. Jacobs loves you. He's the one you really should have been going to with your problems all these years. I'm just an employee."

Throwing her arms around his neck again, she hugged him tightly. "No, you're not. Not to me. I guess you're right; I'll have to talk to Daddy this time."

Dexter stood to his feet. "All right then, let's go. I'll drive you back to the office."

A look of panic crossed her face, and she blanched. "Now?"

He nodded his head. "Yes, now. Before you lose your courage."

He extended his hand to assist her to her feet. As she rose, Victoria slid her arm through the crook of his elbow and clung to him. The drive back to the company offices was much too short. When he opened the door to help her out, he nearly caved in. The look she wore on her face made him feel she was on her last march to the gallows.

"Tori, would you like for me to go with you?"

She seemed to gather her courage around her as she shook her head. "No, I don't want you to be any more involved in this than necessary. You've given me good advice, now I have to face up to my mistakes. Maybe it's time I finally grow up a little. Thank you for being my friend, Dexter." After she took several steps toward the revolving door, she hesitated. Turning back to look at him, she called with a little quiver in her voice. "Dex, if I'm in jail when your birthday gets here, tell Velma to look in the back of my closet. Your present is there."

Dexter gave her a big smile. He nearly crushed the expensive cap he held in his hands as he murmured to himself when she passed through the revolving door. "Mr.

Jacobs better not let you down, or he'll have a hard time explaining it to me."

Chapter Twenty-Eight

Uvalde

Clayton watched as the dust rose up behind the sedan speeding up the long drive to his ranch. The sun was setting and cast deep orange and pink fingers through the summer clouds. Randy had told him Douglas had questioned his nephew another time that afternoon. The old Ranger expected the FBI agent to call on him again before he left with Duke for New York. He was happy to see his instincts hadn't failed him.

Before the dust could settle around his car, the agent walked up the steps to the porch. Special Agent Douglas stared at Clayton for a few long seconds before he spoke. "Your nephew's not guilty."

Clayton stopped his whittling. He pushed his Stetson back slightly with the tip of the knife. "Figure that out all by yourself?"

The corners of Clayton's mouth twitched as he tried not to grin while Douglas proceeded. "What I haven't been able to figure out yet is who he's protecting by claiming to be guilty and why."

Motioning to the chair beside him, Clayton nodded in agreement. "I haven't figured that part out yet myself."

"I also haven't decided why you pretended to be a dumb country lawman for me either." Douglas smiled. "I did some background checking on you during the past several hours I spent in San Antonio. I was talking with the bureau chief, and he made some comments about you being one of the most respected law officers across the nation. The police at the jail have about the same regard for you. I guess I'll have to admit you outwitted me."

Clayton laughed. "Rankled you a bit, huh? When you realized it, I mean."

"You could say that."

"Well, son, I learned a long time ago that bullying your way about unfamiliar territory wasn't usually the best way to handle people." Clayton started to whittle once again. "Oh, there's a time when you've got to push hard to get what you need. However, if you've got the time to ease into the situation by being friendly and appear a little on the dumb side, you often get more information faster."

Douglas sat back in his chair. "So what did you learn from me?"

"More than you learned from me, I bet." Clayton smiled.

"Since I learned absolutely nothing from you, that wouldn't be hard to top."

Rosa appeared at that moment carrying a tray loaded down with a frosty pitcher of cold lemonade and two glasses filled with ice. Clayton raised an eyebrow at her unexpected entrance.

Rosa glanced at her employer. "I thought you might need a little something cold and sweet to help settle your differences. Mr. Brett needs us all working on his side right now."

Setting the tray down, she turned and went back to the house. Clayton merely shook his head. "Now that's one person I'll never be able to figure out. In all the years she's kept house for me, I've never been able to learn how she knows what she knows." Clayton handed his guest a glass of lemonade. "But she's right. Brett needs everyone he can get on his side right now." Clayton smiled at Douglas. "Including a young, smart-aleck FBI agent I know. You willing?"

Douglas nodded his head and then took a sip of the cool liquid. "I don't know why, and I should keep my nose out of this, but, yes, I'm willing. I hate to be wrong, and this one will turn out wrong the way it's going down now. Where do we start? You think you can get your nephew to talk?"

Clayton shook his head. "I've tried." He paused a moment before continuing. "I just don't know what got into the boy. All of a sudden he just shut up tighter than a starving mutt's mouth on the first bone he's seen in a week. Wouldn't tell us anything."

The agent looked at Clayton. "Do you feel confident enough to share what you know with me?"

Clayton grinned, as he looked the young lawman in the eyes. "Well, I believe you really want to help him, or at least find the person who is guilty, but there are a few particulars best kept to myself right now."

"I understand. Why don't I ask a few questions, and you tell me what you can?" Clayton nodded his agreement and the FBI agent continued. "The girl who was on the run with your nephew, is she in on any of this?"

The ranger shook his head. "Skylar? No, the only thing Skylar McCrea is guilty of is trying to be a Good Samaritan to someone who had become a friend of hers."

The agent stood and walked to the edge of the porch. "You know legally she's in a mess, but if the right agent interrogated her, he might find she was just an innocent victim." He paused and turned to face Clayton. "After she was cleared of the charges against her, maybe she would be able to shed some light on the situation."

Once again Clayton was surprised by the young man's change of attitude. "Tell me, Douglas. What made you decide after all these months of pursuing my young nephew, that he was innocent?"

Douglas leaned against one of the posts on the porch. "Well, you're a lawman. You know you can form a pretty good assessment of the kind of man you're after when you start putting all the evidence together." He took another sip of his lemonade. "I knew Brett Carlisle had to be a very smart man. I also knew he had never been in any kind of trouble before in his life, so something had to have snapped in him to make him turn criminal."

Clayton interrupted the man. "Did you find anything that might tell you what made him snap?"

"To be honest, I didn't try to find a reason that he might have done the crime. The evidence was and is so strong against him that it really didn't matter why he did it."

There was silence for a few moments. "Your nephew said he and Victoria Jacobs were an item, but I don't see how that could tie into this mess." He paused again, "Unless..."

"Unless?"

"Well, I am not very good when it comes to matters of the heart, but I would have bet money there was something between that uppity Ms. Jacobs and Jordan Matthews. What if Carlisle found out about them and that made him snap?"

Clayton set his glass on the small table beside his chair. "Interesting thought." It was even more interesting to Clayton than he wanted to let on at this time, so he steered the agent back to their previous line of conversation. "I've known all along my nephew was innocent, so why don't you finish telling me why you decided he wasn't guilty."

"In my interrogation of him, you would have thought he was some ignorant boob. He said he didn't have the money and didn't know what happened to it." Douglas let out a breath and shook his head. "Said he just spent it. Yet he can't tell me what he spent it on. Just doesn't add up that a man as smart as Brett can't remember what he spent a half million dollars on."

Clayton crossed his legs and began to slowly rock his chair. "But since he never had the money, he naturally doesn't know where it is, or if it was spent on anything."

"True." The agent nodded. "The other thing that convinced me is that since he turned himself in, if he had been guilty, he would have returned the money, too. So whom is he covering for?"

"That's the half million dollar question," Clayton sighed.

Douglas sipped his lemonade for a while before speaking. "Did he give you any clues at all?"

"At one point he did mention the only person who might want to set him up was that fellow named Jordan Matthews."

The agent nodded his head in agreement. "Matthews does strike me as a man who's very ambitious." The man paused a few moments and then added, "Maybe he's a little too ambitious."

Clayton sighed heavily. "I figure Matthews is the best place to start. The more we can learn about him the better."

"I'll get right on it. I can get his personnel file immediately."

Clayton waved his hand at the agent. "No need. Already got two copies of it. I got it weeks ago, and my brother Adam got another copy when he went to New York to see Jacobs."

"Well, I'll see what else I can dig up." Douglas stood to his feet. "In the meantime, what about Miss McCrea? If I can get her cleared, maybe she can get Brett to talk, since they're supposed to be friends."

"Can you be back out here tomorrow about three?" Clayton smiled. "I might be able to locate her for you, and I can turn her over to you here if you have to take her in."

Douglas extended his hand. "See you tomorrow at three."

****

San Antonio

Sweat poured from Duke's forehead as he awakened from another nightmare. He could still hear Skylar's voice telling him how terrible he was and how she could never forgive him.

"But, Skylar, I love you," Duke whispered to the emptiness that surrounded him. "God, for the first time in my life I fall in love, but there's no way I can have the woman I love. How did I ever get myself into such a mess?"

When he realized sleep wouldn't come, he sat up on the edge of the lumpy cot that was his poor excuse for a bed. As he sat with his head in his hands, he heard a loud commotion coming toward his cell. An officer stopped in front of his door. As he unlocked and opened the door, another officer shoved an unruly young man into the cell with Duke.

"Brought you a roommate, Carlisle."

Duke looked at the dirty young man. The kid swayed, and Duke could smell the stench of alcohol from across the cell. Just as he stood to assist him, the young man collapsed to the floor. The kid was about Duke's size. He had to struggle, but he managed to get the boy up on his bunk. The rank smell of cheap whiskey almost made him sick to his stomach as he crawled up onto the top bunk to try to finish a restless night.

****

Uvalde

Carlos and Clayton drank coffee in the big ranch kitchen.

"Are you sure we can trust this young agent?" Carlos asked.

Clayton nodded after taking a drink from his cup. "I'm sure. He's convinced that young scamp is innocent. Maybe, with all the resources of the FBI and the Texas Rangers, we'll be able to find a way to clear him."

Rosa left the kitchen with the ring of the front doorbell. Within moments, Carlos and Clayton joined Special Agent Douglas in the study.

Douglas looked around the room. "Well, where's Miss McCrea?"

Clayton walked further into the room. "She'll be down in a minute. Did you find out anything new?"

"I called the office and asked them to do a thorough background check on Matthews." Douglas sat down in one of the overstuffed chairs in the room. "To justify it, I told them I thought he might be an accomplice. So far the only thing new we've found out is that Matthews was a little overextended on his credit, but recently he paid off some of his credit cards."

"Would that amount to a large amount of money?" Clayton asked.

"It was several thousand," Douglas explained.

The men looked toward the door as Skylar's soft footsteps sounded on the tile floor in the hallway. They dropped their conversation just before she came into the room.

Clayton moved to where she stood. He took her hand and ushered her into the room. "Skylar, come on in. I'd like for you to meet Special Agent Douglas from the FBI."

****

"Hello, Mr. Douglas." She extended her hand to the agent. "I understand you want to question me."

Skylar didn't know just what to expect. She was afraid she might have spent her last night in freedom for a while, but right now, that didn't matter. For the moment, all she could think about was Duke being locked away, and the fact she hadn't seen him in days.

Douglas stood to his feet and shook hands with her.

"Yes, Miss McCrea. I do have a few questions. Why don't we sit down?

Douglas pointed toward the large leather couch, and Skylar made herself comfortable for what she felt would probably be a long interrogation.

"Miss McCrea, did you know Brett Carlisle was a wanted man when you took off on the run with him?"

"Well, I didn't know it for a fact but..." Skylar was interrupted by Douglas before she could finish her sentence.

"That's just what I suspected. Carlisle kept everything from you and used you as a cover. I'm sure you didn't even know his real name."

Skylar shook her head. The agent was answering his own questions.

"Well, I didn't at first but..."

Once again the FBI agent interrupted. "That's what I thought. You were just an innocent young woman being used by the man you had fallen in love with."

Skylar was confused. This interrogation wasn't going anything like she had assumed it would. Mr. Douglas wasn't giving her a chance to completely answer any of his questions. She looked at the two other men in the room. It looked to her as if Clayton and Carlos were finding it hard to keep straight faces. What were these three men doing?

"Miss McCrea, I don't think the FBI has a case against you, especially if you can help us catch the real thief."

In spite of her surprise, Skylar managed to ask, "What are you talking about?"

"The charges against you will be dropped since you were an innocent victim..."

This time Skylar interrupted him. "But I've tried to tell you I'm not."

Skylar was stopped once again as the agent spoke.

"Now you don't have to say anything else, Miss McCrea. I have all the statement I need from you." Agent Douglas smiled. "I'll get that all charges against you have been dropped on the wire this afternoon."

Skylar looked toward Clayton. "Clayton, what's he talking about? He didn't get a statement from me. He won't let me talk."

Clayton sat down beside Skylar and smiled at her. "Why, Skylar, Special Agent Douglas just did one of the best jobs of interrogating an innocent bystander that I've ever witnessed. Couldn't have done better myself."

Agent Douglas spoke again. "Miss McCrea, I will need you to accompany me into San Antonio. Maybe if you talk with Brett, you can get him to confess and tell us where the money is."

Now Skylar was even more confused. "But I thought you thought Duke...uh, Brett was innocent?"

The agent looked at her. "It doesn't matter what I think. Officially he has confessed to the crime, and I have to do everything in my power to find out where the money is." He hesitated for a moment. "Plus, I have to convince my superiors you're not guilty of any of the charges against you. So if I take you in to confront Mr. Carlisle, then maybe we can help each other."

Douglas uncrossed his legs and leaned forward in his chair. "He has already told me you knew nothing. I can't just allow you to go visit him because then it might look suspicious. However, if I take you in and happen to leave you alone with him for a few minutes while I take care of some paperwork, maybe you can get him to talk to us. Then we may be able to find out who really stole the money."

"How about I just go along for the ride?" Clayton offered.

Relief filled Skylar as the agent readily agreed.

Chapter Twenty-Nine

San Antonio

Skylar paced in the hallway. She knew Duke was just beyond that closed door. She didn't feel comfortable about the plot Clayton and Agent Douglas had come up with. They wanted her to go in there and convince Duke she was being arrested as his accomplice. They hoped that to protect Skylar from the humiliation of imprisonment Duke would tell everything he knew. *How can I lie to Duke?* She loved him. This just didn't feel right to her.

"Father, what do I do here? Help me, please."

****

"I've already told you everything I know." Duke walked back and forth across the floor in the little room.

"I know that's what you say, but I thought you might change your mind if you had to confront your accomplice." Douglas crossed to the door.

Duke turned to stare at the FBI agent. "My accomplice? What are you talking about? I never had an accomplice."

Douglas opened the door without saying a word to Duke. "Miss McCrea, you can come in now."

Duke's heart stopped as Skylar walked into the room. It took all the will power he had not to walk over and take her in his arms. She looked so scared and helpless.

"If you two will excuse me for a few minutes I have some paperwork I have to take care of. I'll be back shortly." Douglas left the room and closed the door behind him.

Duke and Skylar stood looking at one another for what seemed like an eternity before either one spoke.

"How have you been?" Skylar asked.

Duke took a couple of steps toward her. "Okay. How about you?"

Skylar moved a few steps closer to him. "Fine. Just worried about you."

Duke stopped and looked into her eyes. "Don't worry about me. I just decided it was time for this mess to be over, but what does Douglas mean? He said you were my accomplice."

Panic flew across her face as he watched. She stammered as she spoke.

"They think I knew all about you when I helped you."

She averted her eyes from his close scrutiny.

"I did know you were wanted."

He walked closer to her and tried to console her. "You did know I was wanted, but you were just trying to help a friend. I told them I tricked you."

Tears began to flow down Skylar's cheeks. Duke stepped to where she stood and pulled her into his arms. "Skylar, just go along with my story. Tell them I tricked you to go along with me, and I dumped you when I was through with you."

She sniffed as she talked into his chest.

"Duke, don't try to protect me. You're not guilty, so as soon as we can prove your innocence, both of us will be free." She looked up and held his gaze. "Then we'll be free to share our feelings for each other."

For the second time, in all the months they had been together, he could not control his desires. He lowered his head and captured her lips with his. Skylar returned his kiss with equal emotion. When the kiss subsided, she held him as if holding on for dear life.

"Duke, I love you."

She had finally given voice to the words he had hoped she would keep buried deep inside her. Those words were like an arrow through his heart. He wanted to tell her he loved her, too, but that would be unfair.

Duke pushed her away and walked to the window. "We can't do this. Skylar, there is no future for us. I'm not Duke anymore. I'm Brett, and I have to pay the consequences for my life."

Skylar moved to his side. "But you don't have to go to jail. You're innocent."

Duke looked at her. "But we can't prove that. All the evidence points to me. Just let me take the blame, and we can put an end to this."

"If you would just talk to your Uncle Clayton and tell him everything you remember, he might be able to prove you're innocence."

Duke's voice rose. "Skylar, forget it! Just let me do things my way. It's best for everybody. I'll tell Douglas again that you're innocent."

"What if you telling him I'm innocent isn't enough? What if I'm still arrested as your accomplice?" Skylar grabbed his arm as he tried to move away from her. "Are you going to let me go down, too, without trying to save me?"

He could hear the hurt and anger in her voice. No, he couldn't let her go to jail. What was he supposed to do now? Before he could answer her, Douglas walked back into the room.

"Well, do you two have anything new to tell me before I book Miss McCrea?"

Duke moved to stand in front of the agent. "Skylar didn't do anything to be booked for! She helped me when I didn't have any memory. When we set out on the run, I still didn't know the details of my past. As soon as I remembered everything, I turned myself in. She's innocent. Please don't make her pay for my stupidity."

Douglas opened the door once again, and Clayton walked into the room.

"Brett, your uncle and I believe you're innocent," Douglas confessed. "We want to help you, but we can't do that unless you help us."

"I don't know anything else to tell you." Duke looked around at the group of people assembled in the room.

Clayton moved to stand in front of him. "What about Matthews?" Clayton paused. "What can you tell us about his personal life that might help us prove he's the kind of guy who would set someone up?"

Hesitantly he murmured, "I don't know anything about him personally. We just worked together." He turned his back on his uncle and walked to the window, praying they would all leave and let him be. He only had control of his determination with a fingernail. If they didn't leave soon, he'd break.

****

Clayton knew his nephew too well. He knew he was holding something back. Maybe if he could talk to him alone, he could get Brett to confide in him.

"Douglas, would you mind giving me a few minutes alone with my nephew?"

Douglas nodded his head. "I'll go finish up the paperwork." He looked at Duke. "Brett, I'll be taking you back to New York tomorrow, so tell your uncle all you can now."

Duke looked at Skylar. "What about Skylar? Will you be taking her with us?"

"I'm dropping all charges against her." Douglas opened the door for Skylar to pass through.

Skylar stopped and looked back at Duke, her tears drying on her cheeks. "You'll always be Duke to me. Please help us help you."

Tears filled Duke's eyes as he watched Skylar leave the room. The door closed, shutting her away from his eyes.

His uncle spoke. "The two of you can have a life together when we get you out of this mess."

"No, we can't," Duke stammered. He turned away from his uncle's knowing look.

"I don't like to blow my own horn, but, nephew, I've always been able to get my man," Clayton said. "Now tell me what you didn't want Skylar to hear."

Duke turned to face his uncle. "How do you always read my mind? I've never figured that one out, but somehow ever since I was a child, you've always known what was going on in my head."

Duke sighed. He might as well come clean. He told his uncle about finding the shortages in the accounts and then finding Victoria in bed with Matthews.

"So Victoria cheated on you with Jordan." Clayton sat down in one of the chairs at the small table in the room. "Interesting."

Duke plopped down across the table from Clayton. "Yeah. She was probably in on the whole set-up with him. The woman I was supposed to marry helped frame me for embezzlement."

Clayton raised his eyebrows. "Think Victoria might talk to save her own skin?"

Duke shook his head. "Look, we can't involve Tori."

Clayton leaned forward. "Why would you want to protect her? She was unfaithful to you."

Duke hung his head. "I don't care what happens to Tori, but I do care about Larry. He has always treated me like a son." He raised his head and looked at his uncle. "Tori is all he has. It would break his heart if he found out she was in on a scheme to steal from him."

Clayton shook his head and leaned back in his chair. "Son, I don't understand you. Jordan, and possibly Victoria, set you up to spend a great number of years behind bars, and you don't want us to go after her because it might hurt her father." Clayton paused. "And you want me to just accept that?"

"I don't see how we're gonna prove Jordan set me up." Duke stood and began to pace the room again. He bet he could do it with his eyes closed, as many times as he had marched across the small distance. "But if you can find a way, I'm all for it as long as you keep Tori out of the picture. Larry has enough trouble. From what I could tell when I broke into the company computer a few weeks ago, the half million dollars is not all Larry lost." Duke stopped and stared out the window. "There are several large accounts that have pulled their business from Jacobs Industries. Larry stands a real chance of losing everything he has worked for all these years. I can't be the cause of him losing Tori, too."

"One more question then, why didn't you want Skylar to hear this? You did nothing wrong."

"Tori and Jordan were at our apartment. I had been sharing an apartment with her for several months. I was living in sin with another woman." Duke continued to look out the window. Guilt washed over him in waves again. "How could Skylar ever forgive me for that?"

"You've known Skylar McCrea for months, but I don't think you really know her. I've just known her a few days, and even I know she's in love with you." Clayton's voice was as stern as Duke had ever heard it. Clayton joined him at the dirty window.

"Brett, I believe God tells people that they have to forgive one another, or He won't forgive them. I know Skylar believes in God, and I figure she would forgive you.

Besides that all happened before you met her or her Jesus."

Duke glanced over at his uncle. "How do you know what God tells people to do?"

"Just because I don't go to church doesn't mean I haven't read the Bible on occasion." Clayton smiled. "You know how your Aunt Norma loved Jesus and tried for years to get me to go to church with her."

"Yeah, and I know how you always had an excuse." Duke watched his uncle. "Some of my best excuses for getting out of doing something I got from you."

"Uh, yeah, well, some things you should have ignored about me."

His uncle cleared his throat, and then hit him between the eyes with another deep question.

"Are you sure you're afraid Skylar can't forgive you, or is it that you can't forgive yourself?"

Duke fell silent. He was at a loss for how to answer that one. "I'm not sure of anything right now except that I'm probably going to jail for a very long time. I don't want Skylar to know anything about this conversation, and I don't want her to come back to jail to see me." Duke walked away from Clayton. "She might as well start trying to forget me and get on with her life. Send her back to the Lazy M. Redigo and Addie will take care of her."

Clayton laughed. "I'll do my best, but that young lady has a mind of her own. You tried to send her home once and didn't have any luck, remember?"

Duke nodded his understanding as a police officer came into the room to escort him back to his cell.

Chapter Thirty

New York City

Lawrence Jacobs stared aimlessly out the window. The pouring rain seemed to match the low mood he was in. How could Victoria have been so stupid as to be duped by someone like Jordan Matthews? The question now was what was he going to do about it? To tell the FBI what he had recently found out could put his own daughter behind bars. He loved Brett like a son, but could he sacrifice his only daughter, his only child, to save Brett? It was a dilemma no father should have to face.

The buzz of the intercom startled him from his thoughts. "Yes, Maggie, what is it?"

"Adam Carlisle, on line two."

Lawrence had been putting off calling Adam, but now he had to tell his old friend something. He picked up the black receiver and took a deep breath. "Adam, sorry I haven't gotten back to you, but I have found nothing new on Jordan. Nothing that would help free Brett at any rate."

Adam's tone became very downhearted. "I was just hoping for a miracle. You will keep trying, won't you?"

Lawrence Jacobs lied to his old friend. "Sure. If I turn up anything, I'll let you know."

"Listen, Clayton told me to ask you about Matthews' personal life. Does he have a girlfriend or any vices that you know of?"

The question panicked him. His legs trembled so that he had to lower himself into his chair. He had to tell Adam something that might keep the nosy Texas Ranger from finding out about Victoria. "The only thing I know about him is he likes to collect expensive art objects. Probably spends more money on that sort of thing than he should." Lawrence took a deep breath and then added,

"Adam, I hate to cut this short, but I'm late for a meeting. I'll call you if I think of anything else."

Lawrence held the receiver to his chin for several minutes before replacing it on its cradle. He had just lied to the best friend he ever had. What a mess. At this rate he would probably lose his daughter, his company, and his best friend.

****

The New York City jail wasn't much different from the one in San Antonio—just bigger, more crowded and dirtier. Duke knew he had better get used to life behind bars. He just wished he could be a little choosy about roommates. The drunk in Texas was better than this one. He hadn't found out for sure why this man was in jail, but if it wasn't for murder, he felt sure it at least had to be for major assault. If he slept while the man was in the cell with him, it had better be with one eye open.

****

"Did Jacobs say Matthews just likes expensive art or that he indulges in expensive art?"

Clayton asked his brother. He listened intently as Adam answered his question. "Yeah, that might be helpful; if he is prone to overindulge, then we might come up with something. Let me give Douglas a call. We'll see what we can come up with. I'll let you know as soon as I know something."

Immediately after he broke the connection with Adam, Clayton dialed the number the FBI agent had given him. He tapped his fingers on the desk as the phone rang on the other end. *Come, on. Come on. Someone answer.* Finally he heard someone pick up the receiver.

"Douglas? Clayton Carlisle here. I just talked with my brother. He had a discussion with Lawrence Jacobs and it seems Matthews has a real passion for fine art, expensive art. Reckon, that's what the charges were for on those credit cards?"

"That's very possible."

"Think we might come up with an overly-priced art object to sell?"

"Let me see what I can do."

Clayton hung up the receiver and drummed his fingers against the top of the table. Waiting was not his long suit. Clayton needed to get some fresh air. He strode to the back door and grabbed his Stetson. "Rosa, I'm heading for the barn. I'm going for a ride."

"Sí, Señor."

Carlos and Skylar had left yesterday after Clayton had talked her into going back to her own ranch for a while. He promised a million times to call her with any new information. He didn't want to make that phone call until he had a little more concrete information. A short ride while he waited for Douglas to call back would help. He rode through the hills on the back part of his ranch. As he rode, the clean, fresh air began to clear his head and a plot to catch Jordan began to form.

"If the boy really has a problem, that's the way we can trap him." Clayton reached down and patted the horse's neck. His horse was a good listener. "That's it, old girl. We'll beat him at his own game. If Douglas has no luck, I reckon brother Adam can come up with some fancy artwork we can sell to a chump. We'll set him up." Clayton headed Bessy back toward home and the barn.

Bursting through the back door, Clayton yelled. "Has Douglas called yet?"

"No, he hasn't." Rosa turned from her job at the sink. "And that's no way for a gentleman to enter a house."

Clayton picked up the petite Mexican lady and spun her around the kitchen. "Who *ever* accused me of being a gentleman? Anyway, Rosie, my friend, I think I've finally got it."

"Got what?" the housekeeper asked.

"A way to get Brett out of jail."

Rosa looked at him. "I hope I'm not supposed to know what you're talking about."

Clayton grinned as he grabbed a fresh baked cookie from the counter. "No, you're not. If we put my plan into effect, get ready for a few houseguests. There'll be a few people here to help plan the thing."

Rosa went back to her baking. "Just how many do you suppose?"

Clayton quickly figured in his head. "Probably six or seven."

He had just started down the hall when he heard the telephone ring. He rushed into the study and picked up the receiver just in time to hear Douglas ask to speak to him. "I've got it, Rosa. Douglas, what did you find out?"

Clayton sat down on the edge of his desk. "He has spent thousands at art galleries, but the FBI doesn't have a budget for expensive art. Fifty grand is about the most he's ever spent on one object. We'll have to have something so expensive he'll have to dip into the till to get the money to buy it." Douglas paused, "Where do we come up with something like that?"

"I've got a plan," Clayton informed him.

"What kind of plan? Tell me about it."

Douglas sounded eager to hear Clayton's plan.

"No, not yet. I don't want to talk about it over the phone. How fast can you get to my place?"

"I can clear my calendar and be there tomorrow morning," Douglas answered.

"That will be great. Call me with a specific time when you have it. Either Carlos or I will pick you up. See you then."

Clayton then made three other phone calls before telling Rosa to get the extra bedrooms ready.

****

"Okay, Clayton, what's the plan?" Redigo asked.

"Well, there doesn't seem to be any way for us to prove that Jordan set Brett up to take a fall, so we have to make Jordan admit it," Clayton informed the group assembled in his study the next morning.

Carlos looked across the room at him. "And just how do you propose we do that?"

Clayton smiled. "We pull a sting on the young man."

Carlos grinned from ear to ear. "Sounds like old times. Let's get started."

Skylar was the only woman in the room. "Just what do you mean by a sting?"

Clayton sat down behind his large desk. "Well, Matthews likes expensive art. We're gonna sell him what he likes." Another big smile crossed Clayton's face, he leaned back in his chair and propped his feet up on the desk.

"Boss, that sounds good, but where do we come up with something expensive enough to sell this fellow? I don't think your taste in western art will do much for that city slicker," Carlos said as he sat down on the couch.

"I've got that problem solved," Adam Carlisle said as he entered the room.

Skylar walked to stand in front of Clayton's desk. "You mean we're gonna try and sell Jordan Matthews a work of art?"

Clayton looked at Skylar. "You bet we are, and it's something expensive enough and desirable enough to get him to access that money out of his greed to have it. When he gets it, Douglas will be waiting on him. Pow! Matthews is arrested for a crime he actually committed and Brett is free. Free to get on with his life." Clayton gave Skylar a smile when he made his last comment.

Douglas finally spoke up from his seat on the couch. "I wondered where I fit into this. I can't officially be connected to a sting operation the bureau hasn't set up. So I don't want to know any more of the details." Douglas stood up to leave the room. "Just call me when it's time for me to pick our boy up. That way I can say I was acting on a tip and Matthews won't be able to use any legal maneuvering to get out of the arrest." Douglas smiled. "I wish you all the best."

"We'll call when we need you," Clayton told the agent. "We won't discuss any more details right now. I'll get Ruben to drive you to the airport after lunch."

****

New York

Duke walked around the exercise yard. The days had begun to run together. The past several days seemed like forever. Skylar was continually in his thoughts. He couldn't help but wonder if Uncle Clayton had been right. He had read in the Bible about forgiveness and that a person had to forgive seventy times seven. If God can forgive anything, and a believer has to forgive to be forgiven, Duke was on safe ground with God and with Skylar, so what was his problem?

Was Uncle Clayton right? Can I not forgive myself? He knew Skylar might be hurt when she learned of his past activities, but maybe she would forgive him. He wished he had someone to talk to. Another believer. Maybe a minister, like the one in Vermont who had led him to Jesus.

Duke had no more than sat down at one of the picnic tables in the outdoor enclosure at the jail, when a young man in a pair of slacks, a sport shirt, and a baseball cap walked up to him. Obviously this man wasn't one of the prisoners or a guard.

The young man extended his hand. "I'm Clifford Stamps. Mind if I sit down?"

Duke grasped the young man's hand and introduced himself as he offered the man a seat across the table.

Duke looked at the young fellow. "You're obviously not a prisoner."

Clifford smiled at Duke. "No. I'm the pastor of a church down the street from the jail. My church sponsors a ministry here." He paused as he looked around the exercise yard. "I try and visit the men several times a week, especially the new ones. You know, to find out if there is anything I can do for them. Brett, do you need anything?"

Duke smiled. "God sure doesn't waste time in answering some prayers."

"What do you mean?"

"I was just asking for another believer to talk to and here you are. It's pretty amazing."

The young pastor laughed. "Yes. God is amazing. What do you need to talk about? I've got all the time you need."

Duke felt comfortable with the young minister and began to tell him his story—every detail.

Clifford pushed his cap back on his head. "Sounds like you've been through a great deal. I'm so happy you found Jesus there in the midst of your troubles. You know He's always right there in the middle of everything we go through." Clifford propped his arms on the table and leaned forward. "But tell me, since He brought you this far, why would you think He has forgotten you now?"

Duke shook his head. "I just don't see any way out of this mess. Jordan set me up good, or at least I'm ninety-nine percent sure it's Jordan. I don't see any way to keep myself out of prison."

The young minister held Duke's gaze. "You don't have to see a way out. God doesn't need your help. He just needs your faith and trust. He has ways unknown to man."

It amazed Duke that this young minister seemed to believe his story. "You really believe God could come up with a way to get me out of here and get me and Skylar together? Even after what I've done?"

The minister's expression sobered. "I've been in this jail ministry for a while now. Every offender I've met has given me the same story. They all proclaim they are innocent of the crimes they've been accused of."

With the minister's words, Duke's stomach felt as though a large brick had just dropped into it. His assessment of this man believing him was all wrong. *Why would God answer my prayer with a man like this?* He was so depressed he almost missed the minister's next words.

"I don't know why I believe you, but I do. I also don't know what you think you've done that would make God punish you in this way. You are innocent of embezzling." The minister once again had Duke's attention. "Brett, let me tell you something. As far as the living in sin with Victoria, when you accepted Jesus he forgave your sins and made you white as snow."

Duke could only stare at the man sitting across from him. No one, outside of his family and Skylar, had truly believed him. But now here was a man he had only met a short time ago who believed his claim of innocence. Duke sat transfixed, listening to every word the minister said.

"Brett, Jesus got rid of all the ugliness in your life that was there before you accepted Him. He erased your past. As far as God is concerned you're a virgin, as clean as the day you were born." Clifford paused a moment. "The Devil is the one who keeps reminding you of your past. If he can keep you beat down, he thinks he can steal you back from God. Don't let the Devil win! Remember; greater is He who is in you than he who is in the world. Tell the Devil to get under your feet and then stomp the fire out of him."

Duke was overwhelmed with what Pastor Stamps had just told him. How could he be a virgin again after Victoria? "To God, I'm really clean?"

Clifford smiled and tried to assure him. "God forgives

and forgets."

"Do you think a person could forgive and forget? I mean, could another person forgive and forget my past?"

Brother Stamps smiled. "If you're talking about Skylar, well, I've never met her. But from what you've said about how she took you in and helped you until you got your memory back, I think she's the kind of woman who can forgive and not hold a grudge." The preacher turned and propped his foot up on the bench. "Brett, give her the benefit of the doubt and tell her. I have a feeling she won't let you down. If she can't forgive you your past, she wasn't the one in God's plan for you. If that happens, God will give you the strength to accept it and go on with your life. I don't think you'll have to worry about that though."

Duke leaned on the table. "And when I start feeling guilty, that's the Devil?"

Clifford nodded. "Yes. That's Satan. He knows our weak spots and goes after us. The Devil is a liar; remember that. When he tells you things that are against what God says in His Word, rebuke him and tell him to get behind you. You follow the teachings and promises of the Lord. Just call on the name of Jesus. The Devil has to bow at that name."

Duke smiled at his new friend. "I thank God for sending you to me today. I'm still a baby Christian; there's so much I don't know. Thank you for taking the time to talk with me."

"I'll be back, and on Sunday, I hold services in the chapel at two in the afternoon. I'll see you then if not before."

The two men shook hands before the pastor walked away. Duke watched him until he was out of sight. His spirit felt lighter than it had in months. He began to walk and pray.

Chapter Thirty-One

Uvalde

Clayton once again assembled the amateur task force in his study. He looked around the room at each one of them. What was he thinking? Cold chills zipped up and down his back. What if one of them got hurt? He had no option at this point. The authorities in New York were convinced they had their man. Douglas was on their side, but no one else in the FBI believed Brett's story. His Ranger buddies would back him up, but they would be risking their jobs if they were involved. He'd already pushed the envelope by asking them for information.

This was the only way to break the case. He couldn't risk putting his nephew through a trial; there was too much evidence stacked against him.

"Okay, where do we start?" Adam wanted to know. "How do we set this thing up?"

Clayton looked across the desk at his brother. "First, we need someone to let it be known this Ming vase is available and for sale."

Adam sat in an armchair in front of the desk. "It can't be me; he's seen me."

Clayton shook his head. "His other weakness is pretty girls." Everyone in the room turned to look at Skylar.

Carlos spoke up. "So we find out where he likes to go to relax and have Skylar there. She gets in a conversation with him and then spills the beans about her somewhat questionable ties to a rather unscrupulous art dealer."

"I couldn't have said it better myself," Clayton admitted. "Adam, do you think you might make another trip to New York and find out a little about Jordan's habits."

Adam pressed his tented fingers to his lips for a

moment. "How about I take Skylar with me and introduce her as my new assistant. I could see to it that she is introduced to Matthews."

"I like that even better, but we need to know if she will actually do this or not."

Skylar finally spoke. "I didn't know there was any question. You know I'll help—if it will help Duke."

Carlos propped his feet up on the ottoman in front of his chair. "Okay, Skylar hooks our fish; then what?"

"Then there's the middle man who shows up with a picture of the item," Clayton said.

"I can do that," Carlos offered. "Then Redigo can be 'The Man'."

"You can be the middleman, but I'm 'The Man'," Clayton stated. "Redigo can be my bodyguard. I want the pleasure of hooking this fish."

"How soon are we going to do this?" Adam wanted to know.

Clayton looked across the desk at his brother. "How soon can you and Skylar leave?"

Skylar stood and walked to stand beside Adam, "I can leave anytime you would like, Boss. I just need to stop and buy a couple of expensive-looking outfits, so I'll fit into New York society."

"You'd better make those sexy-looking outfits." Clayton's ears grew hot as he said it.

"Be careful how you talk about my girl," Redigo warned.

"She's got to appeal to Matthews," Clayton shot back.

Everyone else in the room laughed, breaking the tension.

"Now where will we set up this sting? New York?" Carlos asked.

Clayton mentally took back control. "Okay, let's fine tune." The room grew quiet as he began it lay out the plan.

****

New York City

"Adam, I'm glad you stopped by," Lawrence Jacobs said as his friend entered his office.

"Well, I'm here to see Brett, of course, and talk with a

couple of attorneys on his behalf; plus I have a little business here that needs taking care of. Elise can do that while I'm busy with Brett."

Adam paused and introduced Skylar as his assistant, Elise, to Larry. Then Jordan Matthews walked into Lawrence's office unannounced. Adam could hardly contain his excitement.

"Oh, Lawrence, I'm sorry; I didn't know you were with anyone. I have those figures for you," Jordan said. Adam watched as Matthews turned his eyes from his boss to the lovely young woman in the room.

"Jordan, you've met Adam Carlisle, haven't you?"

Jordan walked over to shake hands with Adam. "I sure have. How are you Mr. Carlisle, and may I say I am so sorry about the unfortunate events with your son."

Adam's anger threatened to choke him, but he shook hands with the young executive. What he really wanted to do was punch him in the mouth. "Jordan. May I present my assistant, Elise Hall."

A lewd smile slid across his face as Jordan greeted Skylar.

Adam banked his anger and glanced at his watch. "Larry, I have a couple of things I want to run by you. How about your young executive taking my assistant to lunch?"

"I would love to take a beautiful lady to lunch," Jordan replied.

Skylar smiled and stood to leave the office with Jordan. The plan was falling into place better than expected. Adam could wait for his anger to be avenged.

****

"Miss Hall, how long have you been working for Mr. Carlisle?" Jordan asked as they stepped into the elevator.

"I've only been with Adam a short while." Skylar gave him her warmest smile. "And please call me Elise."

The two continued with small talk while they walked to a small restaurant a couple of blocks down the street from Jacobs Industries.

"Jordan, tell me about yourself," Skylar said after they were seated at a small table in the back of the restaurant.

Jordan Matthews proceeded with a long dissertation

about his college training, his many attributes and how he had landed the job with Jacobs. He continued with his hopes for the future and how he saw himself eventually as the CEO of Jacobs Industries, although he considered his job a stepping-stone. He expected bigger and better things to happen in his life—beyond Jacobs Industries. His inflated ego disgusted her. Skylar lost her appetite by the time he stopped talking about himself.

"Jordan, that sounds very ambitious, and even though I just met you, I know you will go far in life. But tell me, do you have any interests outside work?"

The waitress delivered their food at that moment, so Jordan waited until she finished serving them before he answered. "I'm really very busy but occasionally I get to take a beautiful woman to lunch."

Skylar smiled as she picked up her fork to stab a piece of lettuce from her salad. "I'm sure you have no trouble in the romance department; you're such an attractive man." She placed the bite of salad in her mouth to try to replace the awful taste his last words had given her.

After a few moments she continued, but she had to play this carefully. She smiled. "Oh, surely a man as sophisticated as you would have some outside interest. I, myself, love the world of art. I am only a small time collector, but sometime in the near future, I hope my circumstances improve enough to allow me the luxury of having more fine art in my home."

"You're an art connoisseur?" Jordan smiled as he picked up his water goblet.

"No, not exactly. I appreciate fine things and have a very limited collection."

"That's such a coincidence. I have a limited collection of fine art." Jordan took a sip of his water and set the glass back on the table. "I'm afraid that's a weakness of mine."

"Really?" Skylar smiled after wiping her mouth with her napkin. "What do you collect?"

"My weakness is Ming vases. I don't know why they appeal to me so, but they do."

Skylar leaned back in her chair and tried her best to look astonished. "I can't believe this. I have a passion for them, too. I think mine stemmed from the fact my grandmother had one very beautiful Ming, and I so coveted it, but my cousin inherited it when Grandmother passed away."

"What a shame! Right now, I only have three. I refuse to buy one unless it is really rare. I can't stand those cheap imitations." Jordan took a bite of his steak.

"Oh, I know." She leaned forward to give him the impression she valued his every opinion. "I have a friend who thinks she owns a real Ming, but I know it's a fake. Someone ripped her off big time." Skylar took a sip of her iced tea.

"How long will you be in town? I would love to show you my small, but exquisite, collection." Jordan smiled.

The way he nearly drooled when he looked at her filled her with revulsion. Skylar forced herself not to gag. She tried to concentrate enough to give him a smile that appeared enticing. "Is that anything like inviting a girl up to see your etchings?"

Jordan raised his right eyebrow in surprise and tried to look affronted. "Of course not. Honestly, I didn't mean anything by it. It's just so rare I find someone who shares my love of art."

Skylar returned his gaze and flashed a smile at him. "Well, we are supposed to be here a few days, so I might be able to slip away for an evening."

"That would be wonderful," Jordan said, still gazing into Skylar's eyes.

Playing the vamp was harder than she had anticipated. How much longer would she have to suffer through this?

"Actually, I will probably have a lot of free time this trip. I'll conclude the business Adam needs me to take care of tomorrow. So I will just be waiting around for his wife and him to finish finding a lawyer for that son of theirs." She shoved another bite of her grilled chicken salad into her mouth. She made it a small one. She had to force her food to go down.

Jordan's eyes narrowed as he took another bite of his steak.

"Do you know Brett Carlisle?"

"Not really. I met him a couple of times." That was

nearest to the truth Skylar had told since she started her conversation with Jordan. She didn't really know Brett; she knew Duke Green.

"Well, from all the evidence I've seen, it looks like Mr. Brett Carlisle will be in jail for a long time; I don't think his father can buy his way out of this one."

Jordan's smug look deserved to be wiped off his face. Skylar's hand itched with the urge to slap it away. Instead she gripped her fork with such intensity she thought it might bend.

Skylar stabbed a large forkful of her salad and then another. She had to calm herself before she tried to speak again. She chewed and swallowed and then drank half her glass of water before she could rein her temper in again.

"Adam and Julia contend that Brett is innocent."

"Yeah, well, let's see them prove it." Jordan took another drink of his water. "Let's not talk about Brett Carlisle. There are other subjects much better suited for lunch with a beautiful woman."

Before they parted company for the day, Skylar and Jordan made a date for the following evening. As he left her in Lawrence Jacobs outer office and walked away, Skylar allowed herself to shudder. She couldn't wait to get back to her hotel room and shower. She felt dirtier than she ever had in her life, and she'd been covered in an awful lot of black Texas dirt during her lifetime.

****

Skylar fidgeted in her chair. Waiting was the hardest thing to do. She wished she and Jordan could have made a date for this evening. She wanted to get all this over with so Duke would be free. She thought about his name for a minute. She didn't know if she would ever be able to think of him as Brett. In the note he had left at the Eagle's Nest, he had said for her to remember Duke, not Brett. That wasn't going to be hard. Every time anyone called him Brett, her mind replaced it with Duke.

Skylar glanced across the room at Julia Carlisle. She sat on the couch in the hotel room with a glazed look on her face. They had been attempting to keep one another company while Adam talked with lawyers. They had to cover all the bases in case their sting operation didn't have the outcome they prayed for.

Skylar stood. "Come on, Julia. Let's get out of here for a while."

Julia looked up from the magazine page she had been staring at for the past fifteen minutes. She lounged against one arm of the camelback sofa, covered in a soft yellow and blue striped fabric.

"Where will we go?"

Skylar grabbed her purse from the oak library table in the entry. "I think I need something sweet and chocolaty and very fattening. It'll help me get through the waiting."

"I'll be right with you. Let me get on my shoes."

Skylar and Julia managed to find a local ice cream parlor that fixed them up with gigantic hot fudge sundaes. They consumed the sweet treats so rapidly they almost got brain freezes. Instead of going straight back to their hotel, they decided to do some shopping. Skylar and Julia walked through several stores, but their hearts just weren't in it.

The sun was setting as they arrived at the hotel lobby. Once back in the living room of their suite, they each dropped onto matching sofas. Julia's face appeared as sad as Skylar felt. Skylar didn't have the energy to speak. Julia must have felt the same way as they sat in silence for a long while. It was Julia who spoke first.

"I don't think I've ever thanked you for helping my son when he was injured, as well as with everything else. You're a remarkable woman."

Skylar didn't feel remarkable, so she admitted honestly, "When I asked Duke, I mean Brett..."

"Don't worry about calling him Duke. I got used to hearing Clay call him Little Duke when Brett was a boy. It actually fits him. Go on."

With a smile Skylar continued. "I felt as though it was something I was supposed to do." The puzzled look on Julia's face caused Skylar to elaborate. "I knew it was what God wanted me to do. Duke needed a place to go and people who would take care of him. It's not hard to do what God asks of you if you trust Him to guide you."

Julia stood up and stared at Skylar. "You mean you've done all of this out of a sense of Christian duty? He means no more to you than that?"

Skylar could hear the skepticism in Julia's voice. She didn't know how to proceed. Getting to know Duke, falling in love with him and being privileged to be with him when he had found his Savior had been a great blessing to her. She wasn't sure how to go about explaining all that to his mother. She said a silent prayer for God to direct her words.

"Duke means much more to me than that, but that was how God directed our meeting. I love Duke as a brother in Christ." Skylar paused. She could feel a flush spread across her face. Her eyes darted to the landscape hanging on the wall above fireplace mantle. "But I've also fallen in love with him."

Julia moved slowly across the room and perched on the sofa next to Skylar. "I see. You and Brett have plans for the future then."

Skylar shook her head. Her sadness deepened. "For a short time I felt that's where we were heading, but since Duke has regained his memory, something in him has changed. He's pulling away from me. The last time I saw him he was so distant I could hardly believe it. I'm not sure, but he may have realized he still loves Victoria."

"Tori?"

Julia's voice came out full of disbelief. Skylar looked at the older woman. Something akin to shock widened her green eyes. Duke's eyes. Skylar stood and walked across the room to the window looking out over the wide expanse of Central Park. A patch of green in the midst of the mountains of concrete and steel. It soothed Skylar's wounded soul a bit.

"Yes. I've been praying God would change the feelings in my heart if that's true, but so far they've only grown stronger." She sighed. "Right now I feel I'm supposed to be here helping get him out of this mess. What happens after that, I'm trying to leave up to God." Skylar drew the curtain back and looked out at Central Park Lake. "But it's hard. I have problems sometimes letting go of things and letting God do His job."

Skylar risked a glance at Duke's mother. She dreaded seeing the pity in her eyes. Instead, she saw Julia reach for a tissue and wipe the tears from her cheeks. Skylar left the window and sat beside Julia, taking the woman's cold hand in hers. There had been no pity in Julia's look, only the crushing fear of a mother for a child in trouble.

****

Julia clutched Skylar's hand and buried her face in the tissue in her other hand. The honesty with which Skylar had been speaking touched her heart. In the world today, it was hard to find anyone with the complete convictions of a belief in Christ such as Skylar was demonstrating. Her feelings were spoken with such joy and reverence she had no doubt this young woman truly tried to live a Christian life.

She felt ashamed. She was a good woman. She and Adam attended a church in Houston regularly... truthfully would be more like when it was convenient. She believed in God and remembered a time way back in her youth when she had accepted Christ. But through the passing years she had put all that low on her list of priorities. Julia hoped her eldest son had the sense to see what a wonderful person Skylar was. This was the woman he needed to make a life with, not Victoria Jacobs.

Julia had never felt comfortable with the thought of Victoria as her future daughter-in-law, but she had kept quiet. She'd seen too many marriages where the in-laws caused children to be estranged from their parents. She had been determined not to be a part of those statistics. Well, if Brett couldn't see the forest for the trees, she might have to get out an ax and chop down a few trees. She straightened her shoulders and wiped the last of her tears away.

"I don't feel his loving Tori and not you is the problem, Skylar. Mothers can see some things their children don't see fit to talk about." Julia took both Skylar's hands in hers.

"Brett doesn't love Tori; I don't think he ever did. Oh, he might feel affection for her, but I think he loves Larry more. I think his engagement to Tori was his way of making Larry happy. I think my son has been a man lost, and that was his way of settling."

Julia continued, "He has not been truly happy since he agreed to follow his father's wishes for him. Adam and he agreed, after a long period of verbal disagreements, that he could have a year of working on Clay's ranch when he finished high school after which Brett would go to college and get a business degree."

Julia sighed heavily. "He was never meant to be a businessman. I've known that for a very long time. It's caused me many nights of sleeplessness. Adam and Clay have had a lot of arguments of their own because of Brett. Adam wouldn't admit it, but he's jealous of the relationship Brett and Clay have always had. Maybe all of this will clear up things between them, too."

Julia smiled at her own comment. Some of the tension fell away. It was going to be all right. She knew that now.

****

Skylar had watched and listened to this woman's words. Julia's features softened and relaxed as she talked, drawing Skylar in. When Julia started to rise and move away, Skylar placed a restraining hand on her arm. "Julia, would it be okay with you if I said a prayer right now?"

Julia offered an assenting nod and tears filled her eyes as Skylar watched her. The two women sat hand in hand while Skylar asked God for the strength and patience to wait through the next few days.

When she ended with "...and Lord, give us acceptance for whatever You have in store for us. Let our hearts be filled with peace at whatever outcome You have planned," Skylar saw tears flowing down Julia's cheeks. Skylar pulled a tissue from the box on the rich oak end table and handed it to her companion.

After a few seconds Julia sniffed and said, "I wish I had the faith to let go of the control of my life the way you do. When this is all over, I want to know more about the kind of relationship with God you have. You're a special young woman."

Skylar blushed. "Not really, Julia, but I'll be happy to share what I know with you."

Chapter Thirty-Two

"You have a lovely apartment, Jordan," Skylar commented as she gazed around the living room of his contemporary apartment. "And those vases are stunning."

"Thank you," Jordan smiled as he handed Skylar a glass of sparkling water. He walked across the room to admire his small collection of Ming vases. "Some day I would really like to own a vase with significance."

Skylar smiled as she stood beside him. "I suppose you would like to own a vase like the one that sold recently for over ten million dollars."

Jordan laughed. "Right." Then he turned to face Skylar, "Seriously, Elise, I would love that, but my lack of funds prevents me from shopping in those circles."

Skylar turned and walked to the French doors which looked out at the New York skyline. Jordan Matthews lived well and probably considerably above his means, hence his need to embezzle.

Jordan opened the doors. "The view is much better from the terrace."

Skylar followed him outside. The cool breeze did little to calm Skylar's nerves, but she said a silent prayer and proceeded to carry out her part in the plan.

Jordan turned to face Skylar. "Elise, how long did you say you would be in New York?"

Skylar gave Jordan a sidelong glance and then turned her attention back to the skyline. "I thought I would have to stay until Adam and his wife were ready to go back to Houston, but he is sending me home tomorrow."

Jordan leaned closer to her, "So we only have tonight."

She couldn't stop the giggle, "That sounds like a line from an old movie."

A flush covered Jordan's face. He cleared his throat

before he tried to speak. "I just meant...we don't have much time to get acquainted." He adopted what Skylar figured he thought of as his shy young man persona. "And I would really like to get to know you better, Elise Hall."

Again Skylar had to fight laughter, but she didn't want to lose...what was it Clayton had called Jordan? Oh yes, their mark. "I would like to get to know you better, too, Jordan."

The man turned and leaned forward. Skylar knew he was trying to kiss her. She had to think fast. She scooted to the side as she said. "Jordan, back to your collection of vases. Would you like to add to it?"

Jordan looked perturbed as he answered.

"Of course, but I won't add to it just to have quantity; I insist on quality."

Skylar seated herself on one of the chairs on the terrace and then looked up into Jordan's face. "What if I could put you in touch with a dealer who...well shall we say, sells at cost?"

Jordan's interest was very evident from the look on his face. He took the seat next to Skylar. "What do you mean 'sells at cost'?"

"Let me just say, I know someone who has access to numerous pieces of fine art at bargain prices."

"Is he reputable?"

Skylar gave him a warm smile. "His pieces are authentic."

"But is he reputable?"

Again she smiled at Jordan. "What's more important—the reputation of the dealer or the authenticity of the piece?"

"Well..."

"Jordan, if your funds are limited, but your tastes are not, sometimes you have to look for different ways to have what you desire." Skylar stood and strolled to the edge of the terrace. "Just last week I saw a picture of a Ming vase that I would have given my eyeteeth for, but it was just out of my range."

"You saw a picture and were willing to buy from a picture?"

"I've purchased from this dealer before. His merchandise is good, but this one was just too expensive."

She turned to face Jordan. "Would you be interested?"

"How expensive are we talking about?"

"A million," Skylar smiled.

Jordan stood to his feet. "Elise, I don't have that kind of money...what did the vase look like?"

Skylar took a deep breath, trying to steady her nerves. "You know the vase I spoke of earlier that sold for over ten million?"

Jordan nodded and Skylar continued. "Well, it is similar to that. It's early fourteenth century Ming.

"And he just wants a million?"

Again Skylar smiled. "Well, I explained that he sells wholesale."

Jordan leaned against the terrace railing. "So, if one buys from this man, you can't sell what you buy to a reputable dealer."

"If you buy from this man, you're buying because you love the art, not because you want to buy and then sell to make money."

Skylar looked at Jordan's face. He looked so eager he was nearly drooling. "I know the price of the vase is steep, but Jordan, if you could only see the picture, you would absolutely fall in love with the piece."

"I would never buy a piece from just seeing a picture of it, even if I could get my hands on that kind of money."

"I am sure we could work something out.If you're interested, after you see the picture, you put up, shall we say, earnest money and you will be shown the actual piece."

Jordan shook his head. "Still, a million dollars...that's out of my reach."

Skylar took a deep breath. She didn't want to lose him now. "A million is the asking price. Like anything, there is bargaining room."

Jordan sneered. "I've heard this type of dealer doesn't bargain."

Skylar shrugged, "Jordan, money talks, and this man can't hold on to the merchandise forever; he has to move it."

Jordan moved back into his apartment and stood in front of his small collection of vases. "What if he's already sold the vase?"

"I could easily find out." Skylar stood in the doorway between the living room and terrace. She had him hooked! She wanted to shout, to dance, but she had to remain calm. "Are you interested?"

Jordan turned to look at her and simply said, "Yes."

Skylar walked to where her purse lay on the couch and pulled her cell phone from its pocket on the front. She dialed Clayton Carlisle's number.

When the retired Texas Ranger answered she said, "This is Elise Hall...is the Ming vase still available?"

"Skylar, you've hooked him?"

Clayton's voice sounded so much like Duke's when he got excited.

"Yes, I have someone interested in the vase."

"When will you be here?" Clayton asked.

"He would, of course, want to see the real thing." Skylar paused as if listening to the party on the other end of the connection. "Yes, I know. He looks at the picture, gives you twenty thousand in cash and will be taken to see the vase."

"You're in the room with him, I presume."

"Yes. I will be back in Houston tomorrow. Oh...yes, I see. I may be able to talk him into coming with me. If I am able to do that, could you hold off and have your man come to my apartment?"

"Oh, apartment. Yes, we got you one. Brett's brother, Jeff, and his wife agreed to let you use their apartment. Jeff will pick you up at the airport and take you to their apartment. He will be another employee of Adam's, which actually he is," Clayton said with a chuckle.

"I will call you later to let you know what time to come to the apartment with the picture." She closed her cell phone, breaking the connection with Clayton.

"They still have it, but there is someone else interested in it. Can you come to Houston with me?" Skylar asked.

"Did I hear you say I would have to have twenty thousand up front just to see the vase?"

Skylar walked to stand beside Jordan, placing her hand lightly on his arm, "Would that be a problem?"

Jordan began to pace the room. She could tell the wheels in his brain were turning. "No, I could get that, but it's a lot to lose, if I decide I don't want the vase."

"It is a gamble, but we never get what we want, if we're not willing to risk a little to get it."

Jordan crossed back to stand in front of her.

"What if I want more than just the vase?"

His voice sounded a little husky. She had to move with care. Skylar forced herself to look up into his face. "That's a gamble also, but one that could be explored."

Jordan leaned down and gave her a soft kiss on the lips. Skylar cut the kiss as short as she could without showing her repulsion. "How about getting something to eat?" she suggested.

The man smiled. "So you're a woman who has to be wined and dined first."

"Well, one has to keep up her strength."

"If I feed you dinner, will you still be here for breakfast?" he wanted to know.

Skylar walked away so she would be out of Jordan's reach and he couldn't see her face. "That would be appealing, but actually, Adam is expecting me this evening. He has some things he needs to go over with me before I go back tomorrow." The she added, "He wasn't too happy I had made a date with you, making him wait until later this evening to work. We have to finish his task before I leave in the morning."

Disappointment showed in Jordan's voice as he spoke, "So our evening will be cut short?"

Skylar looked at her watch. "Yes, I really should be going now…but if you go to Houston with me, who knows…"

"What time does our plane leave?" Jordan closed the distance between them and kissed her again.

Skylar gently pushed him away. "Jordan, I really have to get out of here. I need my job. The plane leaves at noon." She picked up her purse off the couch. "Will that give you enough time to get the cash you need?"

"The cash won't be a problem but a ticket on the plane might be."

"You won't need a ticket. We'll be flying back on Adam's private jet."

"Where do I meet you?"

Skylar smiled. "I'll pick you up at your office at ten-thirty." She hurriedly left his apartment before he had a chance to kiss her again.

****

"We're leaving at noon," Skylar said as she sat down on the couch and kicked her shoes off. "I hope that's okay."

"That's fine," Adam said as he reached for the telephone. "I'll let Chad know to have the plane ready."

"When will you and Julia be coming back to Houston?" Skylar asked after Adam got off the phone with his pilot.

"That depends on how this set-up goes. I hope when we return to Texas, we have Brett with us."

Julia smiled and added, "That is our prayer, Skylar, and again, thank you so much for helping our son."

"It's my pleasure." Skylar returned the woman's smile. "I need some help from you. Clayton said Jeff would pick us up at the airport and take us to his apartment, and I would pretend it was my home. Since I've never been there, could you draw me an outline and tell me about my temporary home? Maybe even show me a picture of Jeff so I recognize him, since we are supposed to both work for Adam?"

Julia pulled some paper from the desk drawer and sat down beside Skylar on the couch. The women spent the next hour talking about the apartment. Skylar was grateful Julia had helped Anita and Jeff decorate their home last year. She had an amazing memory for the details of their apartment.

Chapter Thirty-Three

Houston, Texas

Skylar had no trouble finding her way around the apartment after having talked with Julia. It was a lovely place, and if she weren't a rancher at heart, she could picture herself living in this warm, welcoming place.

"Jordan, make yourself at home. I'm going to change into something more comfortable, and then I'll call the man with the picture."

"Nice place," he called out to her.

"Thank you, I like it."

A few minutes later Skylar returned to the living room dressed in black slacks and a teal, silk blouse. Jordan had taken her at her word in making himself at home, slipping off his shoes and stretching out on the couch. Breathing deeply, she prayed this would be over soon. Jordan expected to spend the evening with her which wasn't going to happen. She didn't like the uncertainty of undercover work. Her nerves weren't cut out for it.

Skylar was in the kitchen making sandwiches and coffee when the doorbell rang. She walked to the door. Through the peephole, she saw Carlos standing there in a dark-blue business suit. Turning to Jordan, she said, "It's him." She waited until Jordan shoved his feet back into his shoes and stood before she opened the door.

"Hello, Carlos, please come in."

Without speaking, Carlos entered the room. He scanned his surroundings and then glared at Jordan. "Is this the one interested in the merchandise?"

Skylar touched his arm. "Carlos, it's okay. He can be trusted."

Carlos looked skeptical. "Did you check him out?"

Glancing over at Jordan, Skylar could see the

puzzled look on his face. "Jordan, it's all right. You're not the first client I've introduced to Carlos and his friend." She turned her attention back to Carlos. "Did you bring the picture?"

Carlos reached into his inside coat pocket and pulled out the picture. He extended it to her. Taking it, she handed it to Jordan. The young man looked down at the photograph.

"Does it meet your expectations?" she asked.

Jordan scoured the picture of the Ming vase.

"This is a picture of a nice looking vase, but how can I be sure it's not just a picture of a vase you can buy anywhere?"

Carlos snatched the picture from Jordan's hand and started for the door.

"Carlos, wait," Skylar called. Looking at Jordan over her shoulder, she added. "Are you interested or not?" She maneuvered to stand in front of him. "Look, my reputation is on the line with these people. I told them you were serious about buying this vase."

Jordan's chuckle was a little shaky. "Look, all I meant, was I can't tell from a picture if I want to buy the merchandise. Something this expensive I want to see."

Carlos stared at Jordan. "Miss Hall told you what you need to do to see the product."

Skylar held her breath. *Will he take the bait?* Then he moved. She breathed.

Jordan's briefcase sat in a chair by the door. He pulled out an envelope and handed it to Carlos. Carlos took the envelope from him and looked inside.

"You don't mind if I count it, do you?"

"Of course not, but I assure you, it's all there."

Some uncertainty was beginning to show in Jordan's voice.

It only took Carlos a few seconds to thumb through the money. He looked at Skylar. "You will hear from me in a few hours. The Man wants to close the deal this evening, if possible. He has pressing business out of town."

"We will be right here." Skylar followed Carlos to the door. When Carlos turned to look at her, she mouthed, "Please hurry."

Carlos gave her a nod and then walked down the hall to the elevator.

****

Clayton paced the length of the hotel suite he occupied in downtown Houston. "Now is everyone clear on what we are going to do. I have to press Matthews hard enough to make him access the money as soon as possible and get him away from Skylar."

Redigo and Carlos nodded.

"Clayton, we didn't have to change my name, but don't you think we better call Redigo something else, just in case Jordan heard Redigo's name mentioned in connection with Skylar?"

"Just refer to me as the Indian. That way I'll sound tougher," Redigo laughed.

"We want you to sound tough all right," Clayton said. "I think Indian will work, and I think I can remember that."

Carlos walked to the phone and dialed Skylar's cell phone number.

After a short conversation, he turned to Clayton and Redigo. "Everything is all set. They should be here in about fifteen minutes."

Almost to the second fifteen minutes later, a knock sounded on the hotel door. Clayton nodded and walked into the bedroom, closing the door.

****

Both Redigo and Carlos took deep breaths. Redigo stationed himself in front of the bedroom door as Carlos crossed the room and opened the door allowing Skylar and Jordan to enter.

Carlos closed the door and stood in front of Jordan. "I have to check you for a weapon."

"You have to what?"

"Jordan, it's all right," Skylar said. "They just want to make sure you're not carrying a gun."

Before Jordan could protest further, Carlos began to pat him down. "He's clean."

"Now may I please see the vase," Jordan said in a demanding tone.

Carlos nodded at Redigo who knocked on the bedroom door.

"Enter," Clayton called.

Redigo walked into the room, and in a few moments, walked back through the door. Clayton followed him, carrying a small wooden crate.

****

Clayton put the crate on the coffee table and then smiled at Skylar. "Hello again, Miss Hall. It's good to see you."

"It's nice to see you, Mr. Stockwell." She extended her hand toward Clayton. He lifted it to his lips and kissed it.

Skylar smiled and then turned to Jordan. "Mr. Stockwell, this is Jordan Matthews. He's very interested in that lovely Ming vase."

Clayton grasped Jordan's hand and shook it. "Please, Mr. Matthews, make yourself comfortable on the couch." After Jordan sat down, Clayton took the chair across from the coffee table. Skylar perched on the arm of the couch beside Matthews.

"Mr. Matthews, I did a little checking on you, and from what I can tell, you are not really in a financial situation to afford my little trinket here."

"What do you mean—you checked me out?"

"I don't do business with just anyone. In my line of work, I can't take that chance."

Jordan leaned forward, and Redigo stepped up to stand closer to the young man. Jordan looked up to see the glowering man towering above him. He blanched. Clayton hid a grin. Jordan leaned back on the couch and took a ragged breath. "Well, Mr. Stockwell, all my funds aren't where just anyone who checks on me can find them. A man has to keep some things away from the watchful eyes of Uncle Sam."

Clayton laughed. "A man after my own heart. I'm all for not giving the government more than you have to."

Jordan nodded toward the wooden crate on the table. "Now, may I look at the merchandise?"

Clayton looked up at Redigo and nodded. He lifted the lid off the box and stepped back. Clayton reached over and removed the vase. He admired it for a few moments before handing it across the table to Jordan.

Clayton smiled. "This is one of the few Objects de' Art I've had possession of lately that I thought about keeping myself."

Jordan examined the vase. His eyes widened. "This definitely appears to be fourteenth century. How much?"

Clayton leaned back in his chair and placed the ankle of his left leg on his right knee. "A million dollars."

A twitch in Jordan's left eye gave him away. He was anxious. They had him hooked. He examined the vase again.

"You know there is a slight flaw here on the bottom rim...that...lowers the value considerably."

Clayton smiled. "You have a good eye, but...a million is considerably less than its actual value."

Still eyeing the vase Jordan countered. "That may be true, but you can't put this on the auction block." Another pause and then he said, "I'll give you two hundred and fifty thousand."

Clayton laughed out loud. "Mr. Matthews, I think this will conclude our business. I do have another client interested in this item. I only agreed to show it to you because Miss Hall requested it."

"Now, Uncle..."

Skylar's eyes rounded in alarm. Clayton was glad she sat where Matthews couldn't see her face.

Jordan looked spooked. Clayton covered her slip. "From the look on Mr. Matthews' face, you must not have mentioned to him that you're my niece."

Skylar looked at Matthews and rested her hand on his shoulder. Clayton had to give her credit; she had courage and pluck.

"I'm sorry, Jordan, I do my best to keep Uncle Jim's cover." She paused and looked from Jordan to Clayton and then back to Jordan. "But for you, I thought I might be able to help you negotiate. How about it Uncle Jim, surely you can lower the price a little?"

Clayton pursed his lips and laced his fingers together across his stomach. "Well for you, Elise, I guess I could accept three quarters of a million."

Skylar looked at their mark.

"What about it, Jordan; is seven hundred and fifty thousand good for you?"

Jordan shook his head. Skylar took over again as their go-between.

"Now, Uncle Jim, I know you could take half a million and still make a nice profit on this vase."

Clayton stood to his feet while shaking his head. "Elise, why don't I just give the thing away?"

Skylar laughed. "If I thought you would just give it away, I would have asked for it myself." She stood to her feet and walked to stand in front of Clayton. Placing her hand on his arm, she spoke. "Uncle Jim, do this for me." She glanced over her shoulder at Jordan and then looked back to Clayton. "This man is a real 'art lover'. Give him a break; let him have it for half a million."

Clayton ran his hand through his hair and paced for a few steps. When he sat back down, he asked, "Elise, why is it so important to you for this young man to get this vase?"

Skylar sank back down beside Jordan. "I don't know. I just saw his little collection, and I know he would truly like to have this one. You could easily sell this to a big collector, but sometimes it's good to help a small collector become a big one."

"I'm not exactly into doing charity work," Clayton stated.

Jordan found his voice. "Elise, thank you for your help, but I think I can handle it from here." Placing the vase back in the box, Jordan looked at Clayton. "Mr. Stockwell, I would love to add this vase to my collection, and I can give you a half million dollars for it. However, if you have a better offer than that, I guess you'd better take it." Jordan stood to his feet and started for the door.

"Wait just a minute, Mr. Matthews," Clayton stood to his feet again. "This seems to mean a lot to my niece, so I'll let you have this little vase for the low, *low* price of half a million dollars. She is my only sister's only child, so she means a lot to me."

A broad smile covered Jordan's face. He extended his hand to Clayton. "Thank you, Mr. Stockwell."

Clayton shook hands with the young man. "Now, let's close the deal, shall we?"

"I'll have your money on Monday," Jordan said.

"Monday?" Clayton shook his head. "That won't do. I'm leaving Houston tomorrow afternoon." Clayton turned to Carlos, "Carlos, call the other interested party. I guess

Mr. Matthews won't get to add our vase to his collection."

Carlos stepped to the phone and began to punch in numbers.

"Wait," Jordan looked at Skylar and then at Clayton. "I told you my money was not easily accessible."

"Mr. Matthews, even if your money is out of the country, you can have it here in a few hours, this is the computer age you know."

"But doing it all under the table takes a little longer," the young man stammered.

Clayton smiled and placed his hand on Jordan's shoulder. "This isn't under the table; it's all above board. I'm selling you my interest in a small oriental business."

"It will still be tomorrow before I can access my funds."

"We can do it this evening, if you really want this vase. My banker will meet us anytime I ask."

Jordan hesitated, so Skylar spoke up. "Jordan, just think...you could go to sleep tonight owning this great Ming vase."

Finally Jordan agreed, and Carlos made a phone call to the banker, a banker whose name happened to be Douglas. Ralph Douglas. FBI Special Agent Ralph Douglas.

A short while after the phone call, Clayton, Carlos, Redigo and Jordan exited a white limousine in front of Austin Savings and Loan. A man waited at the door to let them in. Clayton concentrated to control his breathing. Only moments more and the job would be done. This was the most dangerous time for the sting. One misstep, one wrong word, and Matthews might panic and back out of the deal.

Once inside the president's office, Jordan accessed his Swiss bank account by computer and transferred the funds to an account supposedly owned by Jim Stockwell. Once the transfer was accomplished, Agent Douglas stepped forward and snapped a pair of handcuffs on a confused Jordan Matthews, placing him under arrest. Then Douglas led a sputtering Matthews away. Clayton sighed and clapped Carlos on the shoulder. He pulled out his cell phone and punched in Skylar's number. Her phone rang once.

"It's over. We got him." Clayton heard her sob.
****

Adam answered the phone in his New York hotel room. As soon as he hung up, he turned to Julia. "Matthews has been arrested." She threw her arms around him and sobbed.

"How long before Brett gets out of jail?"

"I don't know," he said, wiping her tears away with his handkerchief. "They have to tie tonight's money to the money from Jacobs Industries. My guess is that as soon as Matthews is given the opportunity he will start talking and try to blame this on Victoria, who I know has to be involved."

"Skylar would tell us that now is a good time to pray," Julia said.

Adam sighed. "I'm not sure I know how to pray."

Julia took her husband's hand. "One thing I have learned from the short time I've known Skylar is that you can talk to God just like you talk to a friend."

The two bowed their heads and began to silently petition God on behalf of their son.

Chapter Thirty-Four

Skylar rented a room in the hotel where Clayton was staying. She spent a few restless hours trying to sleep. One minute she would dream about the wonderful reunion with Duke, and then in the next dream, she would see everything blow up in their faces. When she awoke, she asked God for forgiveness for any and all the wrongs she had done. She tried to justify her actions by telling herself that if it saved an innocent man it would be worth it. She was thankful she served a forgiving God. She had a strong urge to talk to Clayton. She pulled on a worn pair of jeans and soft, white T-shirt before walking the short distance down the hall to the older man's suite.

Clayton opened the door. "Skylar, what are you doing up and about already today?"

Skylar stepped into the room. "I see you're dressed, too. I guess I'm not the only one who couldn't sleep."

"Guilty. I won't be able to rest until this is all over and Duke's home where he belongs," he admitted. "You look like you have something bothering you."

Skylar walked over and looked out the window. "What if Douglas can't tie the money Jordan accessed back to Jacobs Industries?"

Duke's uncle joined her at the window.

"Don't worry. Jordan's the type to tell all once arrested. He'll be scared out of his wits, so he'll do whatever it takes to shorten his time when he realizes he won't get off scot-free."

Skylar looked up into Clayton's eyes. "Do you think Victoria Jacobs is involved?"

"I suspect she is."

"Clayton, do you think Duke knows about Jordan and Victoria's affair?"

Clayton looked down into the young woman's eyes. "Skylar, he has several things to talk over with you, and you need to hear them from him. Let him tell you in his own time. He was having a tough time dealing with some of his memories but is doing better." Clayton smiled. "Douglas told me yesterday that he had talked to Brett just before he came to Houston. A young minister came by to see Brett, and it did him a world of good. Just hang in there. I believe you two are meant to be together."

****

New York City

Duke was surprised to see Special Agent Douglas as he was ushered into the office of the Chief of Police.

"What's going on?"

The chief stood and walked around his desk. "You have been done a serious injustice, and I want to apologize."

In confusion, Duke turned to Agent Douglas for some kind of explanation.

Douglas smiled at Duke. "Brett, I want to apologize for the FBI. The charges have been dropped and you're a free man. We caught Jordan Matthews and got a full confession out of him and his accomplice."

Duke could feel his knees begin to buckle under him, so he dropped down in the chair closest to him. "I'm free? I don't have to go back to that cell?"

"No. That's why they had you put your own clothes on before you were brought over here. The officer collected your few belongings and brought them along also. The chief has all the paperwork. You're free to go."

Duke processed what Douglas had told him. *Accomplice?*

"Jordan had an accomplice?"

"Victoria Jacobs. But you already knew that, too, didn't you?"

Duke nodded. Pity for his boss filled him. "I...couldn't...I didn't want Larry to find out about his daughter."

"Speaking of parents, your mother and father are waiting outside."

Duke looked up at the agent. "They're here?"

"Yes. Just outside," Douglas answered before opening the door and allowing an anxious set of parents to enter the room.

Duke hugged his mother and turned to shake hands with his father. His father drew him close and pulled him into a bear hug of his own. The last time Duke remembered such a show of affection from his father he had been ten years old. Joy flooded through him and years of pain melted away. After being released by his father, Duke stood in front of his mother, looking beyond her into the empty hallway.

She cupped his face in her hands.

"Skylar's waiting at Clayton's ranch. After you told her not to come see you in jail anymore, she didn't know if you'd want her here." She smiled at him. "But she's waiting for you, son. She loves you, you know."

****

Duke adjusted his seatbelt for the hundredth time. *Will this plane ever land?* He had spent a short time with his parents after being released the day before, but sent them ahead so he could close down his life in New York. After all these years, his father had finally told him to live his own life and had given him his blessing on whatever he decided to do. He smiled as he looked down at the new Wranglers and boots he was wearing. His mother apparently had a pretty good idea of what his future might hold.

The cheerful mood he was in was marred only by the fact Victoria had been arrested. He remembered his brief visit with Lawrence before he left New York. Jacobs assured him everything was going to work out. The FBI had recovered most of the money, and now with Jordan out of the company and Brett's name cleared, he was sure he could get his clients back. Larry was hopeful Victoria would get off with at least a suspended sentence.

"Don't worry, son. We'll weather this storm, too. I only wish you weren't leaving. You sure you won't think about it a while? You could take as much time as you need to rest and visit with your family. The job will wait for you."

Larry had looked at him with such wistfulness that, for a brief second, his affection for the older man had caused him to waver. He had wanted to make everything all right for Lawrence Jacobs, but that wouldn't be what he knew was right for his own life. He had lived the way other people wanted him to for a lot of years. Now he had an obligation to live his life the way God wanted him to. The trick was going to be to understand how to know that.

"Larry..."

The older man had clapped him on the shoulder. "It's okay, Brett. I know you have to leave. Just promise me you'll keep in touch."

He had given Larry a big hug. "I promise."

He stared out the window. The wings of the jet cut through the patches of white clouds outside. A smile played on his lips. He was headed home. Back to where he really belonged. The airplane couldn't fly fast enough.

****

Uvalde, Texas

Duke ran up the steps of his uncle's colonial-style ranch house. The woman he loved was inside that house, and he had so much to tell her he could hardly wait. He wasn't sure his feet had ever hit the porch when the front door burst open, and he saw his Uncle Clayton's smiling face.

Pulling Duke into his arms, Clayton said, "Son, it is sure good to have you back where you belong."

Before he could respond, his brother and sister, along with Rosa, Carlos and Redigo, surrounded him, but he kept searching for the one face he had waited weeks to see. The crowd finally stepped back and let him enter the big living room. It was then that he caught sight of her. He would never forget this picture. Skylar stood in the middle of the great room dressed in a soft yellow sundress with her hair pulled up in a ponytail and tied with a yellow ribbon. He was sure his heart stopped for a moment when she smiled at him.

She hadn't rushed to the door with everyone else but remained in the middle of the room as if frozen in time and place.

He walked over and stood in front of her. "You look beautiful."

Skylar looked into his eyes. "You look pretty terrific yourself."

Stretching out his arms, he pulled her into his warm

embrace.

"It's so good to have you back," Skylar whispered in his ear.

Before he could reply, Jeff interrupted their moment. "Well, big brother, how does it feel to be a free man?"

"It feels wonderful." Duke turned to face the others in the room but held Skylar in his arms.

Duke choked back the tears. "I want to thank all of you for your support and mostly for believing in me."

"They did a lot more than just believe in you," his sister Krissy said.

Duke looked at his younger sister. "And what do you mean by that, little sister?"

Adam began the explanation of the great sting with Clayton and Redigo adding their interpretation from time to time.

Duke laughed. "So now I have an uncle who is a dealer in stolen art?"

"Not stolen, son, just borrowed." Clayton laughed.

At that point, Rosa called them to dinner.

When they were all seated around the table, Duke began to speak. "I can't believe you all risked so much for me, but I'm grateful I have a family and friends who love me that much. Now if you don't mind I'd like for us to join hands, and I'd like to say thanks to the best friend I have ever had for putting each one of you in my life."

He took Skylar's hand on one side and his mother's on the other and began to give thanks to the Good Lord for his freedom, his family and his friends. He ended his prayer by saying, "Now, Lord, give me the words and strength to do whatever it takes to ensure the future I believe You have in store for me." As he said amen, he gave Skylar's hand a squeeze.

As the others headed toward the living room after dinner, he grabbed Skylar's hand and pulled her toward the back door. With the door closed behind them, he looked down at her and whispered, "Finally. I've been wanting to be alone with you ever since I got here."

"Same here," she said as she moved closer to him.

Instead of drawing her into his arms, he took her hand and escorted her down the steps and across the lawn. His Aunt Norma had planted a beautiful rose garden years ago, and Uncle Clayton had seen to it that it had been kept up in her memory. They seated themselves on a small bench by the birdbath.

Skylar looked around her. "It's beautiful out here."

"Aunt Norma loved roses, especially yellow ones." He turned to look at her. "You look like the yellow rose of Texas tonight."

Skylar looked down at the ground. "I'm glad you can't see me really well right now; you're making me blush."

"On you, it would look beautiful." Duke squeezed Skylar's hand. "Listen, Skylar, I have some things I have to tell you."

He began to confess everything. He started with the fact he had never really loved Victoria and just asked her to marry him to make Larry happy. He didn't leave anything out. When he finished, Skylar looked up at him. Her expression was serious but there were no traces of tears. He waited.

"Duke, I'm glad you told me all that, but it doesn't really matter. All of that was before you met me or came to know Jesus as your Savior."

"It doesn't matter to you that I've been with another woman? I mean since you've saved yourself and all?"

"When you became a Christian, God made you clean again. You're brand new just like it says in II Corinthians 5:17. 'If you're in Christ, you are a new creation. The old man is gone and you have become new.' You're a new person, Duke."

Looking into Skylar's big, blue eyes, he slid off the bench and got down on one knee in front of her. "Skylar McCrea, will you marry me?"

There wasn't any hesitation from her.

She flung her arms around his neck and shouted, "Yes! Yes, I'll marry you."

He kissed her soundly. "You do realize it was Brett Carlisle who asked you to marry him, not Duke Green, don't you?"

Skylar smiled. "I look forward to being Mrs. Brett Carlisle." She held his face in her hands. "But you won't mind if I still call you Duke, will you?"

"You can call me anything you like as long as you call me with love," he whispered before kissing her once again.

A short time later, Duke entered the living room with one arm around Skylar's shoulder and her hand in his other one. "Attention everyone, I have an announcement to make." Duke looked down into Skylar's loving eyes. "Miss Skylar McCrea has just consented to become my wife."

The atmosphere in the room turned into pandemonium as everyone hugged them and gave them congratulations. When they finally had another moment alone, Duke looked into the face of the woman he loved and spoke words meant only for her ears.

"First I'm nobody, and then I'm Duke Green. Then I'm ten other people I can't even remember, and then I'm Brett Carlisle again. But now, most of all, I'm the man in love with you."

Epilogue

The courtroom grew hushed as two young men walked through a side door. Preceding them, a slightly balding man in a three-piece suit settled his briefcase on top of a desk and motioned for the two youths and their fathers to take a seat. Seated in the gallery were only a few people.

The prosecutor and his assistant took their places, and in only moments, a black-robed judge passed through a door to the left of his bench. The bailiff asked for everyone to rise. He announced that court was in session and all those present settled back in their seats.

Looking at the defendants, the judge paused and then spoke. "Because of special circumstances in this case, I have decided to make this a bit informal. The defendants have admitted their guilt and waived their right to a trial. I'll pass sentence on them. Since the prosecutor has agreed, we will proceed. Mr. Wilson, you may begin."

The young prosecutor stood and quickly laid out the facts of the case. He was immediately followed by the defense attorney who pled guilty for both of the young men, asking only for the mercy of the court due to their youth and previously clean records. He reminded the court the defendants had come forward and turned themselves in.

Leaning back in his chair, the judge listened intently, his fingers tented under his chin. The defendants looked as scared as any he'd ever seen. The background he'd read on them did indeed show they had never been in trouble before. Affidavits from upstanding citizens, including the boys' minister, let him know the two boys were basically good kids. They had turned in all the money they'd removed from the victim's wallet. It seemed, that after taking it, their consciences hadn't let them spend any of it. When the defense rested, the judge leaned forward.

"The defendants have decided to throw themselves on the mercy of the court, and I am prepared to pass sentence on this case. Normally, the sentence would be based solely on the facts of the case, but this is an unusual case. The victim has petitioned to speak on the record before this court, and I would like to hear his statement before I pronounce sentence. Would you step forward and take the witness stand, sir?

****

Giving Skylar's hand a squeeze, Duke rose and headed for the front of the court and stood with his hand on the Bible the bailiff held before him and promised to tell the complete truth. Settling into the straight-backed chair, he waited for his instructions.

"Go ahead, Mr. Carlisle, tell the court what you would like for us to know."

Looking first at the two scared boys, and then to the men who were obviously their fathers, and lastly to the little group of supporters sitting with Skylar, he smiled, singling the love of his life out. Then he turned his attention to the judge.

"Your Honor, everything that has been stated here today is true. I was hit by a car and injured badly. I guess the defendants deserve a severe sentence because I could have died that night." Pausing, he asked the judge, "Do you mind if I speak directly to them, Your Honor?"

"Just maintain control of yourself, Mr. Carlisle."

"Thank you, Your Honor." He stood and walked to stand in front of the boys. "Joe and Tom, what you did that night was very wrong. I could have died."

Joe spoke up with a squeaky voice, "But, Mr. Carlisle, we thought we had already killed you. Tom and me didn't know what to do! The only thing we could think of was to get away...fast, right, Tom?"

"Y...yes, sir. Neither Joe or me have been able to sleep very well since we had the accident. We both keep having these awful nightmares. I'm really sorry, sir," Tom finished quietly.

"Well, boys, I know how it feels to be in the middle of a situation you don't know how to get out of, so I can understand a little of what you have been going through.

In a way, I'm glad all this happened. If it had not been for the accident, I might not have ever met my wife nor turned my life over to Jesus—two things I am most heartily grateful for and will be for the rest of my life."

Duke continued to look into the boys' faces. "As the Bible teaches us, we must forgive those who do us wrong, so I forgive you. I understand the two of you attend church with your parents."

The boys nodded their heads in agreement with his latest statement.

"I feel that, because you two have finally confessed, the judge should be lenient with you. I hope he will consider my feelings when he sentences you. Personally, I think the only way you two are going to end the nightmares you have been having is to do a little talking to God before you sleep. It might not hurt that from now on you two sit in the front pew in church and really listen to what your minister is saying. It makes a world of difference. Trust me, I know."

Duke started to walk away and then paused to look back at the boys. "And, by the way, trusting God with your burdens can help you in a lot of ways. Your life will be much richer when you turn it over to Him. You might also want to remember that alcohol and driving never mix. The next time you two decide to party, you might want to choose a soft drink instead of beer. You'll feel a whole lot better when you wake up the next morning."

Turning to the judge, Duke said, "Your Honor, everyone deserves a second chance, especially two young boys. Based on what I've learned about them, I believe their fathers have and will continue to issue rather substantial punishment. I also think they have learned a lesson that will stick with them for a very long time. I guess that's all I have to say."

The judge cleared his throat. "Thank you, Mr. Carlisle. Gentlemen, if you would rise."

The two teenage defendants did as they were told. A few minutes later they all but collapsed back into their seats. Neither looked as though they could believe what his decision had been. They began to cry.

Duke's mother kissed him and took her husband's hand in hers as she started up the aisle. Duke and Skylar followed but were stopped by a quiet voice.

"Mr. Carlisle?"

Duke turned and saw the father of one of the boys standing behind him. "Yes, Mr. Turner?"

"Thank you for what you said. If you hadn't spoken to the judge, I don't think he would have let them off with community service."

Duke smiled. "You're welcome, Mr. Turner. I meant what I said. I'd hate to see two young lives destroyed for one mistake. I trust you will see to it that Joe carries through with his public service hours?"

"Yes, sir, he sure will. His buddy will be there along side him. I know God will bless you for your generosity."

Seeing his new bride smiling up at him and reflecting back on his newfound faith caused a smile to spread across Duke's face before he extended his hand.

"Oh, God has already blessed me, Mr. Turner. He has blessed me well."

A word about the author...

Kasandra Elaine is the writing team of Kassy Paris and Elaine Bonner. The writing partners have been friends since they were fifteen years of age. The pair met when Elaine's father moved to Kassy's community to pastor the Methodist church that just happened to be across the street from Kassy's home. Kassy and Elaine began their writing efforts as a team, when they wrote a church Christmas play those many years ago. Elaine lives in north Texas where she works as a registered nurse. She enjoys spending time with her grandchildren, working in her local church, writing, traveling and reading. In the past, Elaine has combined her profession with her love of travel and worked as a traveling nurse in order to give the writing pair the opportunity to visit other parts of the United States. Kassy lives in east Texas and recently retired from teaching fourth grade. Kassy's interests include going to church, reading, writing, and quilting – much to Elaine's chagrin when she has to haul around Kassy's stash of fabric and her sewing machine.

Printed in the United States
130929LV00001B/214-237/P